MW00460491

The
Demanding
River

C H E R Y L   J .   C O R R I V E A U

Fulton Books, Inc.
Meadville, PA

Published by Fulton Books 2020

ISBN 978-1-64654-680-0 (paperback)
ISBN 978-1-64654-681-7 (digital)

Printed in the United States of America

To:

Bill "Doc" Phillips—a supreme Master licensed captain, a superb marine certified mechanic, and foremost my lifeline.

And

Carolyn, one of my dearest friends, and mentor, who encouraged and motivated me to write about my adventures in owning a boat dealership.

Chapter 1

Bahamas Vacation

Jordan stood at the helm of her 26-foot cruiser, *Charisma,* watching the even rhythmic roll of the five-foot seas, thoughts of work pushed aside by the dire situation at hand. The boat climbed each wave as if they were on a slow-motion roller coaster. She could barely make out the other four boats traveling with them through the wind-blown spray. At this rate, it would take five hours to reach Indian Cay.

The one-night storm in West Palm Beach had delayed their crossing. Her patience had grown thin after days of playing cards, fast-food restaurants, and the other ten people traveling with them complaining about the weather. The tropical depression that had dumped thirty inches of rain in twelve hours was a long way from the rain showers the weatherman had predicted. The fact that she had already lost five days of her two-week vacation—two days traveling from the St. Johns River to West Palm Beach and the three days waiting for the seas to calm enough to cross—had only elevated her stress level.

Linda tapped her on the shoulder and pointed to the GPS. "We're entering the Bermuda Triangle.

Jordan nodded. "I see."

A rogue wave tumbled into the port side of their bow, making the boat do a 360-degree turn. The eight-foot wave drowned out the engine, drenched Linda, and washed her to the port gunnel. Jordan yelled, "Are you all right?"

"Yeah." Linda grabbed a towel from inside the cabin and sat down on the captain's bench next to her. "Where did that come from?"

"I don't know. I didn't see it until it hit the bow."

One of the captains behind them radioed, "Jordan, are you guys okay?"

"Yes, Linda got soaked, and I'm trying to get the engine restarted."

On the fourth try, the engine came back to life.

Thirty minutes later, Jordan glanced at the instrument panel. "Linda look, this is weird. The GPS screen had been black, and now it has switched back to blue and green and the compass has corrected itself."

The water around them had become calm and turned to a breath-taking teal color as they left the Bermuda Triangle. The crystal-clear water looked like they could reach down and touch the bottom even though they were in thirty feet of water.

Jordan gave Linda the helm and moved to the back of the boat. She lay across the cushions feeling the cool, salty breeze whisper across her skin in the Caribbean sun. This was the stress-free vacation she had waited for to clear her mind from her conflicts with her new CEO, Phillip Stover. She still couldn't believe he fired the auditor and added auditing to her responsibilities without a pay increase.

A couple of hours later, she watched the sun creep through the coconut palms casting long shadows over the customs docks at West End, Bahamas. When all five boats had docked, Jordan reminded the others, "Don't forget that according to Bahamian law, only the boat captain can disembark until the boat is cleared."

They were the only boats moored, but it took the customs office two hours to approve their entrance paperwork. Jordan remembered they were on island time, which meant everyone took their own sweet time to do anything.

After clearing customs, the women congregated on the dock. Jordan stepped off her boat. "What are y'all talking about?"

The youngest woman in the group swept her long hair back into a ponytail then tossed her head. "Is there anything to do here?"

Jordan pointed east. "We can walk into town. There's a straw market, restaurants, and music."

The men stayed on the dock drinking beer while the six women strolled into town. Jordan came to a halt when they reached the top of the hill. No steel drums or bands were playing, and the large fountain in the town square was crumbled and scattered. A few poles and part of a thatched roof remained where the straw market once stood. They continued to walk slowly down the hill.

One woman grabbed another woman's hand and whispered. "Do you think ghost sounds will bellow from these empty buildings?"

The Jack Tar Hotel and Casino had closed and so had all the restaurants. The only thing that looked familiar to Jordan was all the flora of the confederate roses and the hibiscus bushes.

Jordan was baffled. "I wonder what happened to all the people. How can a town just go away?"

The woman with the ponytail shrugged. "I guess we won't have dinner in town tonight."

On the way back to the boat, Jordan couldn't get the last conversation out of her head with Phillip. He had agreed with her irate clients before he had heard her side. She could still hear his screaming voice before the phone fell silent. The empty town made her evaluate her conflict at work. If she and Phillip couldn't agree, her life could become like this empty town.

The women pulled together a smorgasbord dinner from their boats while the men brought ice chests onto the dock to be used as tables along with folding beach chairs. The talk of the evening was how Bud, one of the captains, missed seeing the huge cargo tanker that had crossed in front of them. His compass and GPS had sent him far west.

Jordan touched Bud on his shoulder. "You know weird things happen in the Bermuda Triangle. Mine was off course, too."

An hour later, everyone agreed they had had a long day and tomorrow would probably be similar, but they didn't retire to their boats until all the clouds had stolen the stars.

Jordan poured herself a glass of pinot noir and propped her feet in a beach chair on the back of her boat. She lazily rested her head back and closed her eyes. She listened to the gentle waves splash against the side of the boat, remembering the butterflies in her stomach the first day she walked into the real estate office. The atmosphere was free compared to the schedule she had when she taught high school. Here she had felt like an uncaged bird. She didn't mind the irregular hours, working evenings and weekends or even presenting sale offers and having contracts signed at ten o'clock at night. She thrived on the challenge of working with people and each situation being different. She had learned about the residential markets, and the commercial markets and, how to work with investors. Compared to now those were simple days. Her father had preferred her to teach school. He felt she was protected in that environment. He did let her know he didn't want her in the business world. He considered that world was for men, a job for her brother if death hadn't snatched him at birth. She opened her eyes, smiled, and swirled the wine around in her glass. She could still hear her father's words as if he were sitting next to her, "You're going to have to be stronger than ever before. You're going to find out how cruel this old world can be."

Then the image of the abandoned town jumped back into her mind. Somehow, she and Phillip had to come to a cooperative agreement.

Chapter 2

Ten-Foot Waves

The thunder sounded like bowling balls over their heads all night, and the lightning gave one continuous finale fireworks show. The morning sun was smothered by the black ominous clouds and the storm still raged. The rain came down in sheets so heavy that Jordan couldn't see the boats tied next to them. By noon the lightning had stopped, and the rain was falling straight down instead of sideways, but the thunder was still rattling the sky in the far distance. The marine forecast gave warnings of ten-foot waves at Indian Cay Inlet. The hot, heavy humid air was causing personalities to flare. Two of the captains didn't want to leave West End until the seas calmed, then they wanted to head southwest to the casinos in Freeport. The other two captains, Bud and Travis, convinced Jordan to go with them.

After lunch, the rain had disappeared. Bud called over to Jordan and Travis, "Let's head out."

When they headed into the inlet, Jordan knew immediately, she had made the wrong decision. All she could see was a wall of water racing towards her as high as a twelve-story building. Instantly, Jordan realized that West End and Indian Cay were the same. She and Linda were committed. There was no way they could turn around without the waves pounding the side of their boat and capsizing them. She imagined her body bouncing across the ocean floor along with her past forty years racing before her like a streak of lightning. Her father and stepmother were staying with Matt, her son. She could see their faces as the police gave them the news of her death.

She radioed Bud and Travis, "We're in trouble."

Travis replied, "Don't panic. Get in behind my wake and stay as close to me as you can. My boat's wide and my wake will reduce the impact on your boat."

Climbing each large wave, Jordan's boat came completely out of the water, then hit like it was landing on a road of bricks. The hull creaked and moaned as if it was going to split wide open.

Bud, being the maverick with a short fuse, was already half-way out of the inlet. His boat bounced, rolled, and tipped as if he was going to capsize with each wave. Both Jordan and Linda were white-knuckled from their death grips—Linda from holding on to her seat and Jordan gripping the steering wheel. Linda sat speechless.

When they reached the quiet waters, Jordan hugged Linda. "There were only eight waves, but it felt like we came through fifty."

Travis radioed Jordan, "I looked back, and your boat was completely out of the water except for the prop."

Jordan screeched. "I assure you that's not going to happen again. From now on, I'm going to know where I am and where I'm going before I start."

Linda slid behind the helm while Jordan went below to check the condition of the cabin. It looked like a tornado had blown through. The cabinet doors were open and canned goods and plates were lying on the floor. One set of galley cabinet doors was off its hinges. The dinette table had bounced out of its bracket and was lying upside down between the galley and the berth.

Jordan looked out the glass porthole, while she stowed everything back in its place. The transparent crystal blue-green waters, the sugar-sand beaches and, the many lush green uninhabited islands gave her the sense of being lost in the pages of a travel magazine advertising paradise.

She joined Linda on the captain's bench. "I bet you're sorry you volunteered to come with me."

"I did it because I knew you and Nick had planned this trip with your friends last year. Then when Nick died, I knew you wouldn't come. You needed this trip."

Jordan gave a broad smile. "We both needed it. You haven't done anything but work since your divorce. Over the years, the island trips have always been a haven to leave my troubles behind, but so far this trip hasn't been stress-free."

Linda patted her hand and grinned. "It will be."

An hour later Jordan radioed Travis and Bud, "My gas gauge is on empty. Linda and I have checked the charts, but we didn't see a marina that sold gas."

"Not every marina in the Bahamas sells gas. Let me check our charts. I have extra gas tanks on board if we need them. We won't leave you stranded." Travis laughed.

They pulled into Hope Town Marina. Bud gently slapped Jordan on the shoulder. "It's a good thing Nick left you a lot of money. You can afford nine dollars a gallon."

Jordan punched Bud back in the arm. "You can too, or you wouldn't be here. Welcome to the islands."

Jordan gazed out over the blue-green water. "Where are Travis and Sherry?"

Bud radioed, "Where are you guys?"

"We stopped to watch a school of porpoises play."

Bud, being Bud, snapped, "Get your butt in gear. Jordan's all fueled and ready to go."

Travis and Sherry were pulling into the marina when Bud yelled, "Travis look behind you! Smoke is coming from your engine hatches!"

Travis did a U-turn, shut the ignition off, then opened the hatches. Flames shot twenty feet into the air. He hit the automatic fire extinguisher button, slammed the hatches shut, and yelled, "Sherry, jump overboard now!"

Everyone knew that when someone yelled to do something on a boat, don't ask questions just do it as fast as you can. Bud pulled Sherry and Travis out of the water onto his boat. Jordan rafted her boat next to Bud's to let Bud's wife, Lucy, and Sherry board her boat while Travis and Bud checked out his engines.

Travis looked at Bud. "When I opened the hatches, the air must have caused a spark to ignite from the hot engines. The closed hatches snuffed the flame immediately. I was lucky to stop an explosion and not have any damage."

A couple of hours later, Jordan radioed, "Those deserted islands look like a perfect place to anchor for the night."

Everyone brought their beach chairs to the water's edge and watched the day turn to dusk. The teal water reflected the orange and pink glows from the sun. The seagulls screeched their last calls before becoming silent for the night. The vast darkness drifted in, and the stars sprayed the sky like snowflakes.

Jordan sat on the back of her boat reflecting over the day's events. She had enough boating experience to know that weather, mechanical issues, and any other unforeseen things could happen on the water. She took another sip of wine thinking that her job description would have never changed or that she would have to decide to stay or leave a job she loved.

Chapter 3

Scott Williams

The big yellow ball rose to welcome another day. The men loaded all their fishing gear onto Travis's boat and motored away to find lobsters, fish, and anything else in the edible seafood category. Jordan passed a full pot of boiled eggs over to one of the other boats, then she stepped from the gunnel of her boat to the other boat, not noticing that one of the rafting lines had come untied. She screamed when the two boats started to separate. Linda reached for her hand, but it was too late. Jordan was in split mode and into the water between the two boats. The surprised look on everyone's face disappeared when they heard Jordan's laughter over the splashing waves when she surfaced. The dinner conversation that night was about Jordan's acrobatic debut.

The next morning, halfway to Walker's Cay, Jordan radioed, "Did y'all see the red coral reef and all the tropical fish we just passed over?"

Bud yelled, "No! Walker's Cay can wait! Let's turn around and go back to the reef.

After everyone had their boats anchored, Jordan announced. "Don't touch the red coral. It's fire coral, and it lives up to its name if you touch it, it burns like a hot poker."

They all laughed, and in unison yelled, "We know!"

While the others were swimming on one side of the reef, Jordan, Bud, and Sherry swam to the other side. Jordan was ready to surface when a shudder rocked her shoulders. She turned and saw a big gray-and-white shark swim past her. A chill ran over her entire body. Her heart was in her mouth. Gasping for breath, she grabbed Bud around his neck, making him fight to keep his head above water.

It took Bud a few minutes before he could get her arms unleashed from his neck. "Calm down. You're fine. The shark's gone." He finished his conversation laughing. "You know they only attack if they're hungry and with all these fish, you would be the last choice."

Jordan was still gasping for breath when she changed into a pair of shorts and a tee-shirt. "I swear I'm never going into the ocean again."

Linda burst into laughter. "You love the water too much, that's not going to happen."

Their last night in the Bahamas was spent at Walker's Cay. Linda was sleeping like a baby. In the quietness of the night, Jordan found herself restless. Slowly and quietly, she placed her feet on the floor, pulled a flashlight off the helm, and hopped onto the soft wet sand. She walked along the shore by the light of the full moon, feeling the gentle wind flow through her hair. She listened to the song of the sea lap against the sand. The seagrasses whispered dancing in the salty breeze. She swept the flashlight beam back and forth to avoid stepping on the crabs that ran sideways over the sand. Two hours later, she had walked in a full circle around the island and was back at her boat. She stared across the moon-lit water, taking in the beauty of it all, closed her eyes, and took a deep breath. Then a thought bounced into her head. If she could convince Phillip to pay her one-quarter of the auditor's salary, she would be happy. In the morning, she would be headed home, back to the office where her future would be determined by Phillip's response to her suggestion. She closed her eyes letting the rhythm of the lapping waves lull her to sleep.

The Atlantic Ocean waves were like sheets of glass allowing them to cross into West Palm Beach in forty-five minutes. The return was vastly different from their five-hour roller-coaster crossing the previous week.

Jordan smiled at the customs officer. "We have nothing to declare on the boat or on us except lots of salt. You should see our boat. It's covered with thick rock salt pebbles."

The customs officer smiled and nodded. "You're all clear. Next."

After everyone cleared customs, Bud announced, "Lucy and I have decided to run the intercoastal until dark. We can be home tomorrow."

Travis turned to Sherry. "We can make it to our marina in Daytona before night if we run outside the intercoastal in the Atlantic."

Jordan turned towards Linda. "I'm not in a hurry. We'll run the intercoastal until around 4:00 p.m."

Jordan was crossing the Jupiter Inlet when Linda stood and stretched. "Jordan, I'm ready to stop. Jupiter Inlet Marina looks like a good place to dock for the night."

"We're two and a half days from home. Are you sure you want to stop this early?"

Jordan woke to overcast skies. After she had poured her second cup of coffee, Linda entered the galley yawning. "Good morning, it's going to be a long run today to St. Augustine. Let's take a short walk before we start."

Linda nodded taking a sip of coffee.

They strolled down the oyster shell road where Jordan spied William's Boat Sales. She stopped and stared at the boatyard full of the same manufacturer's boats as hers. Most of Jordan's and Nick's boat adventurers had been one-week, overnight, or day trips. She knew if she was still going to take boating trips with her friends, her 26-foot boat was too small.

Jordan fell in love with the 36-foot flybridge cruiser with the twin engines.

To diffuse Jordan's enthusiasm, Linda pulled on her arm. "We need to go."

Jordan continued to concentrate on her conversation with Mr. Williams. "I'll be back in touch with you in a couple of days."

On their way back to the dock, Linda waved toward Jordan's boat. "You know if you want another boat, you're going to have to sell this one first. Think, Jordan. Do you really need a bigger boat?"

The last two nights when they docked in the marinas, anyone that walked by Jordan's boat and inquired about the manufacturer, she tried to sell them her boat. Fifty miles from home, she sat on the back cushions with her mind flipping back and forth between the struggle she still had to face at her office and the new boat's accessories price list. The trip had helped clear her head, but she still had to get the audit responsibility settled with Phillip. She dreaded going back to work to do audits. The more she thought, the more she wasn't sure she wanted to stay with her job even if Phillip did accept her proposal.

Chapter 4

Scott Meets Sam

Monday morning, Jordan woke up tired, like it had been the end of a long work week, and it hadn't even begun. At 5:30 p.m., she heaved a long sigh before calling Scott Williams to tell him she had changed her mind about buying the new boat. When he answered, he didn't wait for her to say why she called. Instead, he jumped to his own agenda.

"You're an incredible saleswoman. You sold five boats going up the intercoastal. All I had to do was fill out the bills of sale." He was almost screaming through the phone. "I want you to come to work for me!"

In her attempts to sell her boat, she had unknowingly persuaded people to purchase boats from him. "Scott, I tried teaching school and selling real estate on weekends and holidays, and that didn't work. My buyers didn't want to wait until I finished school in the afternoon or wait until the weekend or until I had another free day to show them property. I do know living in Central Florida and trying to sell boats in Jupiter from a catalog isn't going to work. Any item this big and expensive has to be personally seen and touched."

"I want—

She cut him off. "I am at a crossroad with my job in Orlando but selling boats from here is not going to happen." Her voice was adamant.

It was as if he wasn't listening to her. *What's wrong with these men? Phillip wouldn't listen, and now Scott isn't listening.*

"All right, if you won't come to work for me, then I want to buy a marina on the St. Johns River. You're in real estate and you know the river well."

"I do know the river, and I know there isn't a marina for sale."

After a late-night dinner, she called Linda. "I decided you were right. I don't need a new boat."

"I'm glad. You made the right decision, but I know you, something else is going on. You wouldn't give up on buying the boat that quickly."

The next morning, Jordan left word for Sam Powell to call her. He owned Marina 415 on the St. Johns River.

"Jordan, I'm sorry it has taken me a couple of days to return your call. My dragline business has kept me working from sun-up to sun-down."

"Sam, I know you're busy. I remember meeting you several times at dawn for you to give me estimates for my buyers to clean out clogged canals. The reason I'm calling is that I have someone interested in your marina for a boat dealership."

He cleared his throat. "The property isn't for sale. I acquired it in exchange for a debt. I tried to sell it for years without any success. I put up the seawall and now buyers are contacting me constantly. I've decided to finish the marina and operate it myself. However, I would like to have a boat dealership on the property."

Monday afternoon, Scott and Sam arranged a meeting and requested Jordan to be present. She never gave a thought about their personalities clashing or that the meeting would end in a disaster with them fighting like bulldogs. Scott wanted to pay minimal rent, and Sam wanted him to pay rent plus a percentage of his sales. The negotiating distance between them was were oceans apart. Jordan had done many business negotiations, but not like this one. These two were behaving like two military men arrogantly staring each other down. She tried to make a miraculously cooperative agreement between them, but without any success.

Tuesday morning, Scott called, "Jordan, "I've been thinking. Will you operate the boat dealership for me? You can get along with Sam, and this would be a solution for me, you, and Sam. You would be free from your Orlando job and Sam would have a dealership on his property, and I would have a boat business on the St. Johns River."

A few hours later, Sam called, "Jordan, you know boats and the river. I'd love for you to open a boat dealership."

She couldn't believe both men wanted her to open a boat business. How was she going to convince these two she knew nothing about running a boat dealership? She cycled through every possible version she could think of to be in the boat business. This hadn't been a choice or an option she had ever imagined. It would be like being alone in a foreign country and not being able to speak or understand the language. This idea to her was insane. Ridiculous! Doomed to fail. Still, she wondered—could she do it?

Six months later, Jordan's fears regarding the regional office had come to pass. The required monthly franchise fees weren't being paid by some brokers, and she was spending more time and effort working as a collection agent than doing her services job. Every day she struggled to keep her brain in gear. Exhaustion had become her norm.

She decided to make an appointment with Alan, her attorney.

"Jordan, I've known you a long time. I know you'll be a success because of the way you have conducted your real estate business. Your ethics are strong, and with your personality, you won't fail. If you accept the boat dealership position from either Scott or Sam, you'd be nothing more than an employee, and they could eliminate you at any time. If you're going to do this, do it for yourself, not for someone else."

The day after she met with Alan, Scott's ID showed on her phone. "Jordan, I want to take you to the manufacturer's dealer meeting in Oshkosh, Wisconsin. It's the week following the Fourth of July. You need to see the full boat line and meet the manufacturer owners. All your expenses will be paid."

"I'll think about it. You'll have my answer tomorrow."

At dinner, she reached across the table and touched Matt's arm "I have something to tell you. Scott Williams wants me to go to the annual boat dealers meeting. He wants me to open a boat dealership for him at Sam's marina. I told him no. Then Sam asked me to do the same. That set my mind in motion."

"Wow! That's awesome, Mom. I know you're not happy with your job. I never thought about you operating a boat dealership.

"It would be fun. I would be my own boss. I'll get your grandparents to come and stay with you the week I go to Oshkosh."

She tossed and turned, and her insides churned most of the night. She thought hard if she wanted to venture into the unknown and consider a boat dealership or stay in her comfort zone and be miserable in the franchise office. What did she have to lose at this point? Nothing ventured, nothing gained. The next morning, she made an airline reservation.

Chapter 5

Dealer Meeting

Jordan watched the clouds float by most of the flight to Wisconsin. *What are you doing on a plane, going to a place you've never been? Spending a week with people you don't know or have only met one time. You have no idea what to do with a boat dealership. All you know is that you own a boat. How could you have talked yourself into something you know nothing about?* She decided for the next hour and a half, she was going to stop thinking about boats and enjoy her first-class flight. She laid her head against the window wondering about her future.

The United Airlines baggage claim attendant promised Jordan her luggage would be delivered to the Oshkosh Lake Resort Hotel by 9:00 p.m. Here she was in a strange place, meeting people for the first time and stuck in her traveling clothes—high-heeled sandals and a multi-colored striped sundress with a white bolero jacket.

She searched the crowded hotel lobby for Scott. She was surprised to see so many boat dealers from all over the United States. Most of them were Scott's age and had his husky build and white hair. Where was Scott? His flight was earlier than hers. Why was his cell phone going to voicemail?

Jordan checked at the front desk for messages. The hotel clerk nodded. "Mr. Williams left word for you to meet him here in the lobby at 5:30 p.m."

There was no reason to go to her room without her luggage. She found a big over-stuffed pillow chair in the lobby to wait out the hour for Scott. People passed by, smiled, and spoke. She felt alone among all the strangers.

Scott entered the lobby and greeted her with a slightly bewildered gaze, "Hello, how are you?"

"Fine." She shrugged off his questioning look. "I know I don't meet the invitation's casual boating clothes. I was going to change when I arrived, but the airlines lost my luggage."

The evening's activities included a welcome dinner and cocktails aboard a 100-foot yacht moored on Lake Winnebago. She and Scott made pleasant chitchat as they crossed the hotel lawn to the dock. Then she asked, "Tell me how you got into the boat business?"

"I didn't have a choice. My father opened a marina and started a boat business when my brother and I were in grammar school. After high school graduation, we went to work for him. My brother still operates the business in New York. My wife and I wanted warm winters, so we moved to Florida. Boats are all I've ever known."

All the manufacturers' company officers and their wives greeted the dealers at the top of the gangplank. Scott Williams's name was called. He was handed a name badge with his dealership name. Jordan Harris's name was called. Her high heels click-clacked as she walked up the gangplank. Her name badge read prospective dealer.

The first person she met was Irene, the vice president's wife dressed in navy blue slacks and a white silk shirt with her blond hair smoothly fastened into a twist. Irene gave off a business-like yet relaxed impression. Her smile put Jordan at ease.

Irene's smile turned into a frown. "You need to be careful tonight. Jordan, your shoes aren't boat friendly."

Jordan explained about her lost luggage.

"Wait here. I'll be right back."

She returned with a pair of Gucci sandals. "I know these won't fit. They're a size nine but they'll be safer than your heels."

"I'm a size five. Right now, anything will fit, thank you."

She changed into the sandals. They were better than the heels, even though they gave her feet the appearance she was wearing clown shoes. She explored all the decks, including the buffet, while Scott socialized with the other dealers.

People nodded as they passed by, but no one stopped to engage her in a conversation. She wandered through the mid-deck, which reminded her of a large furniture store. Sofas and lounge chairs were placed everywhere. The focal point of the room was the turn-of-the-century bar. She ordered a blueberry lemon cosmopolitan from a bartender who resembled a thin penguin, then she made her way to the top deck and sat down behind the helm for a moment. She thought this wasn't her world. Why was she here?

Scott's voice made her jump, "Well, just the lady I'm looking for. The officers are starting to give their long-winded welcoming speeches."

She gave Scott a quick-spreading smile and followed him to the furniture deck, where they found two round back barrel chairs and settled into them for the speeches. She ordered another cosmopolitan when the waiter passed by. Scott explained the events for the next four days. She was glad when all the speeches turned out to be short. The mood was set to be festive and fun, and the drinks and food flowed freely to entice the dealers to order as many boats as their floor plans would allow.

At the end of the evening, Scott walked her back to her hotel room.

"Is there anything I can do for you?" he asked with a big smile.

She unlocked her door, gave a quick glance around her room, and said, "My luggage was supposed to be here. Can I borrow a T-shirt to sleep in? I went to buy one in the hotel gift shop, but all they had were snacks, drinks, and trinkets."

Early the next morning, Jordan walked along the dock, observing the marina glistening in the sunrise. The boats appeared to be lounging lazily on the lake. In a place like this, life seemed peaceful and without complications. Still, things weren't quite as harmonious as they seemed. She still couldn't shake the troubling sensation with her job and Phillip.

Scott waved and motioned her to his table when she was in the breakfast buffet line. She smiled and shook hands with the other dealers at Scott's table. "I'm surprised the manufacturer gives everyone free rein to drive next year's models. I never thought I would be driving boats or that I would be treated as a dealer."

Scott laughed. "Oh, but we intend to make you a dealer!" The other dealers laughed too.

All morning she climbed in and out of the boats that were staged on the lawn and test drove the ones in the water. Before lunch was served, Scott asked. "Are you okay? I know this is a lot to take in all at one time."

"I feel like I'm in a dream. I have pinched myself several times to make sure I'm awake. I didn't know what to expect. I guess I thought it was going to be like a convention."

After lunch, speeches were given by Floor Plan Services (FPS), Boat Dealers Insurance of America, and several engine manufacturers. Each company pitching what they could do for the dealers.

Midafternoon, the hotel manager approached Jordan. "Ms. Harris, your luggage has been taken to your room. Is there anything else I can do for you?"

She gave him a slight smile. "No, thank you."

An envelope was attached to her suitcase from United with a $200 check and an apology note for her luggage being left on the tarmac at the Orlando Airport. She showered again and redressed. How refreshing it felt to be out of the clothes she had worn for two days, and tonight she wouldn't have to do lingerie laundry in her bathroom sink. She hurried to meet Scott and Chuck Hart, the finance representative for FPS.

After learning about her background, Chuck's voice was curt. "Jordan, you're telling me you've never run a boat dealership, you've never had a floor plan, and you want us to provide you with a million-dollar credit line."

She sat straight up and looked him squarely in his eyes. "That's right. I'm a businesswoman. I've run a successful real estate office with forty associates. I own a photography flying company. I was a school principal and a teacher for twenty years. I have a Florida real estate broker's license and a Florida real estate instructor's license. I own a boat and have owned several in the past years with significant boating experience. I'm also in Outstanding Young Women of America."

She thought her accolades were impressive, and she was proud of her accomplishments. Chuck didn't seem to be impressed. Maybe what she had accomplished in her life's work so far wasn't worth a million dollars in credit. Chuck became aloof and cold. She had the feeling he was purposely trying to drive the point that she knew nothing about operating a boat dealership. At that moment, her self-confidence was the only thing she had going for her. She never expected to be confronted like this. She was on trial for something, and she didn't know for what. She closed her eyes, took in a deep breath, and let it out slowly, wishing this meeting was over.

Chuck saw the disillusion on her face. "Education doesn't equal experience."

Scott cut in, "I'll co-sign with her."

She heard the insistence in Scott's voice. In her head, she also heard Alan's cautioning words, "Do it for yourself."

She turned to Chuck, "Can I have a few minutes alone with Scott?"

She looked Scott in the eye. "I'm not sure I want you to co-sign. I know the manufacturer is asking for a million-dollar floor plan. Starting out I'm not going to take on that many boats. I know I only have to pay monthly interest on the boats that are at my dealership, but I have to watch my overhead."

Scott patted the back of her hand. "We have two more days here. Let's wait and see what happens. Don't get discouraged yet."

Scott hurried to their dinner table with a big smile. "I talked to Tom Eddy, the factory president, this afternoon, and he and the company officers agreed for me to co-sign on your floor plan."

He sat quietly, waiting for her answer. He was like a child waiting for praise on an accomplishment. She told herself she needed to consider all her potential options before she committed to Scott. The most important thing was, did she want to be in the boat business?

A strange flutter made her body shake. "Scott, I'm not prepared to talk about business right now. Give me some more time. Let's meet after breakfast tomorrow and we'll finish this conversation."

She excused herself from the table to escape to her room.

Sleep wasn't in her forecast. She walked along the dock and wandered through the staged boats on the hotel lawn. The sky was black with no moon only a few far-away stars. She went back over the day with Chuck and how she had felt humiliated. She sat on a bench and watched a raccoon raid a garbage can and then wander off into the darkness. She kept wrestling in her mind how to confront Scott with her decision. She decided the truth was the only way. She returned to her room feeling a little relieved.

At breakfast, she greeted Scott with a more relaxed attitude than she had last night. "Good morning Scott. I need to explain my actions yesterday. I met with my attorney a few weeks back, and he said if I was going into the boat business, I needed to do it for myself and not for or with someone else. I appreciate your offer, but this is all moving too fast. I need to decide if I even want to open a boat dealership."

He gave her a slight smile. "We're still friends and something may come from this in the future. I'm not going to give up on you. In the meantime, we'll stay in touch."

With that settled, she relaxed.

All the dealers, including Scott, had ordered their boats for a spring delivery. When lunch reached the dessert stage, all the officers gave their appreciation speeches to all the dealers.

Tom called out to her and Scott in the hotel lobby before they left. "I'm sorry you didn't get the floor plan without Scott. Jordan, don't give up."

On the way to the airport, she surprised herself that she was disappointed that she hadn't qualified on her own merits to be approved for a floor plan. The meetings, speeches, and personal insights accomplished at least one thing—she recognized her priorities and put her mind back home where it belonged.

Chapter 6

Resignation

T he smell of freshly brewed coffee brought Matt strolling into the kitchen rubbing his hand back and forth through his hair. "Sorry I didn't get to see you last night. I fell asleep early."

"I know. It was a long week for both of us."

"Are you a boat dealer now, Mom?" Jordan heard the excitement in his voice.

"No. The floor plan company wouldn't approve me."

"I'm sorry. See you tonight." After a quick peck on her cheek, he was out the door and off to school.

Monday morning Jordan's frustration of returning to work was added with her company car having a flat tire. The repairman her office sent, checked the tire, and the other three tires, then he informed her the steel threads were visible, and she needed four new tires. He called for a tow truck to pick up the car.

Phillip was waiting for her when she rushed into his office at 11:00 a.m. Before she could say anything, he said, "We aren't investing any more money into company cars. Everyone is going to be paid mileage for using their personal vehicle."

She threw her head back, turned, and marched out of his office. She stood at her office window taking in the Orlando skyline as her emotions ricocheted throughout her body. She thought no matter what she said Phillip wasn't going to be flexible.

That afternoon, Tom called from Wisconsin, "Jordan, the board has talked over your situation, and we decided we want our boats to have exposure in the Orlando area. We're willing to back you with FPS for the floor plan, but we want you to partner with Scott to take advantage of his expertise. Think it over. We'd like an answer by Wednesday, if possible."

Her excitement showed in her high-pitched reply, "I'll consider the offer. I'll have an answer for you no later than Wednesday."

The conversation was short and to the point. She hung up the phone and stared out the window wondering where her life might be headed.

She hit the five o'clock afternoon stop-and-go traffic on I-4. The hour drive home gave her time to think about all that had transpired over the last few days. The more she thought about the dealership the more her desire grew. Chills ran up and down her spine and the steering wheel was moist under her hands.

The minute she arrived home, she pulled Matt to the sofa. After telling him about the call from Tom, she said, "What do you think? It will be my own business. I know at the start the hours are going to be long, but I want your blessing."

"Mom, it's a big step. Just make sure you're not in a fantasy world after being wined, dined, and drawn in with big money and boats. I know Wisconsin was fun, and they painted a rosy picture. I've heard you say many times the grass may not be greener on the other side. I know you're strong, I saw what you went through with Dad's illness and his death. I know you are not happy at work, but I don't want you to take on more than you can handle. I remember the first time you saw the St. Johns River, and Dad saying your face lit up like a kid coming down the stairs on Christmas morning. I also remember Dad telling you before you do anything think long and hard before you jump."

Jordan smiled and gave her son a quick hug. "I know and thank you for reminding me. For a high school senior, you're pretty smart."

She could see the uncertainty playing across Matt's face—his eyes narrowed at her, his brow slightly furrowed. She knew he supported her in everything, but she could tell this leap worried him, which wasn't surprising because it scared her too.

"Matt, you know your dad had a dispassionate view on life and generally observed life from a safe distance. He was in total control of every aspect of his world. I'm the total opposite and have always been an entrepreneur, but I promise I won't let anything happen to us."

Jordan decided she was ready to take this adventure. She also knew the journey wasn't going to be easy. She was stubborn and confident enough to survive in this man's business world. She would jump in, sink or swim, and prove to herself she had the talent and the ingenuity to be successful.

Jordan met Sam on Saturday morning at his marina. She let out a long sigh. "Sam, we've been at this for several hours. I think we have enough for a rough draft lease. I'll give this to my attorney Monday morning."

Sam smiled. "I agree. It's going to be great having you here."

Monday morning, she told Alan what had transpired from the real estate franchise office to the dealer meeting in Wisconsin to her meeting with Sam.

"Jordan, after our last meeting I'm not surprised about your decision. I'll draw up a five-year lease with five-year options to renew. Remember, Sam can ask for anything he wants, but I am your attorney and I'm protecting you. I'm may not give Sam everything he asked for."

"What about Scott?"

"The situation with Scott is a different issue. You need to have your own corporation with a DBA (doing business as) with Scott Williams Boats, Inc. That way Scott won't have any control over your corporation. By the way, have you thought about a corporation name?"

"Yes, St. Johns River Yachts, Inc."

"I'll check with the Division of Corporations in Tallahassee to see if the name is available. I'll have the papers ready for you and Sam to sign next week."

Tuesday morning, Jordan called Tom giving him her decision. At noon Scott called Jordan. "Tom called me. Congratulations! Tom will ship the boats to me. I'll make them customer-ready for you to deliver. Then I'll transport them to you."

By the tone in Scott's voice, she knew he was pleased with her news. She had owned enough new boats to know that they had to be rigged and made water ready. She also knew there would be freight and delivery fees.

"How much will the rigging and transport fees add to the price of the boats?"

"The rigging cost doesn't matter. It would be the same if I rig them or if you do. I'll call Tom to get him to adjust the cost of the transport fees from me to you. He should be willing to do that and remember I'm a phone call away.

Friday morning, Jordan looked beyond her window at the Orlando skyline. She had thought she was going to be in this office for years. Now she knew she could plan her life, but she couldn't control it. Tapping her pen on her desk, she gave one last thought to if she really did want to walk down the hall to Phillip's office. If she took the walk, there would be no turning back. If she stayed, nothing would change, she would be doing a job she hated, and she didn't know what changes Phillip would make next. Owning her own business was an adventure into the unknown, but she would be in control. She boxed up her office—with her head high, her shoulders straight and pulled back, her lips pressed tightly together, she put her resignation letter on Phillip's desk.

He squinted his eyes, and his voice was cold. "Is there anything I can say to change your mind?"

"No, we don't see eye to eye on my job description, and you aren't willing to give an inch. It's time for me to move in a different direction."

"You don't understand business and bottom lines. If you leave, the door here is closed."

"I've made my decision, Phillip."

She walked to the parking lot without glancing back. Freedom surged through her with no regrets. It had been a good five years with the regional office. Now it was time to spread her wings.

Reality set in the day after she submitted her resignation. She faced the obvious truth—she'd quit her job and committed herself to run a boat dealership. Now she had to follow through.

Chapter 7

St. Johns River Yachts, Inc.

S am, her landlord, had a temporary small two-room building set on concrete blocks. His marina office consisted of a large old oak desk with a worn dark brown high-back leather chair behind it, which left very little space for the army-green steel file cabinet. A black gooseneck lamp sat next to the phone. A desk calendar occupied half of the desktop. A small wooden table and chair sat in front of the desk. The bathroom divided his office from the empty room on the other side, which was going to be her office. As she observed her surroundings, it hit her—this was what her office was going to be like until he could build her a permanent building.

Sam had added St. Johns River Yachts, Inc. name to his Marina 415 signage at no charge. It appeared to her he was willing to do anything he could do to help make her successful.

After lunch, she pulled into the local Chevy dealer and asked for George, the salesman, whom she'd known for years.

"Hi George, I'm opening a boat dealership. I need a vehicle that can pull large boats."

"I have a Suburban with a 454-horsepower engine with less than three hundred miles on the odometer. I sold it to an old farmer. After ten days he decided it was too big for him. It will pull up to a 32-foot boat and I'll make the price right for you."

The morning of October 5, she unlocked her temporary office door. She stood straight and stiff, faced the river, and felt an adrenaline rush as she announced out loud that St. Johns River Yachts, Inc. was officially open. No one heard her.

The St. Johns River winds, twists, and curves up through the middle of Florida. Its 310 miles make it the longest river in Florida. It flows south to north from Lake Okeechobee to Jacksonville. Many freshwater springs feed into the river, providing boaters with swimming areas and overnight stays. For many years, Jordan, Nick, and Matt boated the navigable 160 miles from Sanford to Jacksonville. St. Johns River Yachts was in the middle of all the boating activity.

With Jordan on-site, Sam became inspired. He finished the boat slips and the fuel dock and opened his marina. By the end of the second week, Tom had sent her a 25-foot boat with a 200-horsepower engine, that looked like an ocean fishing boat and a 24-foot boat with a 350-horsepower engine with thru-hull exhaust, which reminded her of a racing boat. The two boats didn't look like they belonged on the river.

She pondered all afternoon over the boats, then she decided to call Scott. "How am I going to sell these boats?"

"I was surprised when I saw them too. You are right, they aren't river boats. If you can't sell them, I'll have them transferred from your floor plan to mine."

She was at the marina every morning at six to wash both boats. Even if she didn't have customers, she wanted them to be in showroom condition. Tuesday morning, after she put her cleaning supplies away, she propped her feet up on the old-weathered desk that Sam had given her and took a sip of Dr. Pepper. A few seconds later, she heard a loud crash in Sam's office.

She quickly reached for the phone. "Sam, I'm glad I caught you. Is there anyone in your office? I heard a loud noise over there. Is there anything you want me to do?"

"No, there's nothing you can do!" His voice boomed. "I'll be there shortly. Stay where you are!"

When Sam opened his office door, Duke, his one-year-old golden retriever, launched himself past her and Sam before they could blink. A battle broke loose, the fox squirrel ran for its life, zig-zagging like a soldier under fire. He finally scampered to safety atop a pile of old boxed business records. Duke hit the stacked boxes with maximum force, almost reaching the squirrel before gravity took over. The tower of boxes sagged, teetered, and then tumbled to the floor. Yelping, Duke fell backward in what seemed like slow motion with all four feet running in the air. The fox squirrel, still running at lightning speed, clawed its way over the dog and out the door. Jordan pulled her head out of the doorway just as the fox squirrel ran across her foot, down the steps, and up a tree.

Jordan could not see Sam. "Are you all right?"

"Yes."

She waited for Sam to say more, but there was only silence. After a few seconds, she called out. "I'm here by myself! What's going on in there?"

"I don't want to frighten you."

"I'm more frightened not knowing."

Duke came through the door and laid on the front step as if he were having a normal day. Sam followed Duke with a frown on his face. "My son, Frank, is a land surveyor. He found a blue-indigo snake in the swamp. He asked me if I would keep him until the zoo came to pick it up. The squirrel must have run in the office when Frank came by this morning to check on the snake. The snake and squirrel thrashing around in the aquarium caused it to fall off the table."

"Where's the snake now?"

"I put him in a gunny-sack until Frank can get here this afternoon."

"Let me see him." She squealed. Her eyes widened. "It's beautiful. Look how unique its bright indigo blue and glossy black skin mesh together from its head to the tail. I've never seen a snake so magnificent or eloquent. Not even in a zoo. Is it poisonous?"

"No, Frank did some research about them. They are only in South Alabama, South Mississippi, and Florida."

"It doesn't seem fair to keep the snake in the sack all day. Is there anywhere else we can put him?"

"I don't have anything to keep him in. The aquarium is shattered."

"He's not poisonous. He can stay loose in the bathroom until Frank gets here."

"Are you sure about that?"

"He doesn't bite humans, and he's probably afraid of me. We'll be fine for the rest of the day."

She felt sorry for the snake when Sam released him. The snake's nose was bloody from rubbing against the burlap sack, It slowly slithered out and moved around the bathroom baseboard flicking its tongue, then it curled up in a corner to sleep.

The rest of her day seemed boring after the way her morning had started. She did have a few customers even though she hadn't advertised yet. Boaters stopped to inquire about the marina and her boats. She hadn't expected to see anyone during her first month.

Sam's son arrived around midafternoon and apologized for his snake startling her.

She laughed. "Well, you missed the show with Duke and the fox squirrel this morning. The squirrel started it all when he jumped into the snake's cage, then Duke didn't help matters."

Frank smiled. "I'm sure I'll hear all about it tonight from my dad."

After the squirrel and snake incident, the next two weeks were quiet. She cleaned her boats, fished, and finished reading two novels. The second month, a few boating industry salesmen had stopped to introduce themselves along with two engine manufacturers' salesmen.

Jordan was finding out the river was like a small gossipy town. Nothing went on without everyone knowing everything, and word had traveled fast about a new boat dealership opening on the St. Johns River with a woman proprietor.

With Sam's thirty boat slips rented, boat owners were asking her for oil changes and tune-ups. In all her planning, she never thought about the service end, and she certainly wasn't planning on becoming a boat mechanic. She and Scott never talked about boat repairs. How could she have overlooked the need for a mechanic?

She called Quinn, her boat mechanic.

"Quinn, did you know I opened my own boat dealership?"

"Yes, the river has loose tongues."

"I'm finding that out. Listen, I need someone to work part-time. Can you help me?"

"Since you're across the river from my marina, sure. I'll come over in the evenings when I finish here. I'll drop off some work orders tomorrow. You can fill them out and I'll do the rest."

Boaters came in wanting engine work done, new electronics installed, boat bottoms painted, propellers repaired, and any other various jobs that needed to be done on their boats.

Jordan asked Sam for advice. "People are coming in and want me to put their boats on consignment. Where do I park them?"

"I'll rope off a section in the parking lot for those boats." It wasn't long before half the space that Sam roped off was filled with used boats for sale.

The river was demanding more and more of her time, energy, and resources that she hadn't anticipated. Quinn complained about her taking in so many boat repair orders. It was becoming evident that the river did need another marina and boat dealership. Some days she questioned if it should be her.

Chapter 8

First Boat Delivery

Friday morning, Jordan hurried to greet a man who was walking around one of her consignment boats.

"Hi. I'm Jordan. Can I help you?"

"Hello. I'm Jim Knight. I was inspecting your boats. I want a 26-foot used cabin cruiser with a 10-foot-wide beam."

"I don't have a boat here with a 10-foot beam." She pointed to the end of the row. "The boat down there is a 26-footer and 8 feet wide. If you can wait a few minutes, let me check on something. I'll be right back."

She called Casey. He only sold used boats at the marina across the river. She returned to Jim with a big smile. "I found a boat. Will you go with me across the river? Casey said he has what you want."

"I was just over there, and I couldn't get anyone to talk to me. That's when I saw your boats over here. I'll go over with you, but I didn't see anything I liked."

"Sometimes some of the for-sale boats are still in their slips or under cover."

Casey sent Jordan and Jim down to the covered boat slips. An hour later, Jim had gone through everything on a boat he liked. "Would you deliver the boat to New Smyrna Beach?"

"Sure. When do you want it delivered?"

The morning Jordan was to deliver the boat, she called Sam in a fluster, "I've never driven a boat and trailer. The marina across the river is going to lend me one of their trailers."

"I'll come help you."

Sam hitched the trailer to her Suburban, "You said you'd never pulled a boat before, right?"

She nodded. "We keep our boat in the water. Nick always pulled it when we needed to."

He handed her the keys. "Don't drive over forty-five miles per hour and remember when you turn, swing wide."

"You're not going with me?"

"No, you'll be fine. Just remember to swing wide when turning corners."

She pulled onto the highway remembering to swing wide. When she made the turn, she understood why. If she turned too sharp, the trailer could jackknife, or she would be on the curb or off the road.

She tried to keep her head clear of all thoughts and concentrate on the road and the next forty miles in front of her to New Smyrna Beach. Suddenly, the boat started to sway and fishtail, she looked at the speed odometer—fifty miles per hour. Without panicking or using the brakes, she allowed the Suburban and trailer to slow on their own. From then on, she kept glancing at the speed odometer every few minutes to make sure she wasn't driving over forty-five miles per hour. Soon she found herself relaxing into the scenery. Weather-beaten live oaks with hanging curtains of Spanish moss-lined the roadway on the north side. The south side was lined with massive sand dunes full of sea oats. She smiled watching the herons fluttering and playing between the dunes. The road was covered with wind-swept sand, waiting for the DOT sweepers to brush the sand off the highway.

Jim was waiting at the New Smyrna Beach county boat ramp when she arrived. She launched the boat without any problems, shook his hand, and thanked him.

"You're not leaving yet. I need you to drive the boat to my house."

All her boats had been single engines. She never thought about having to drive twin-engine boats. Reality hit her. She hadn't thought about a lot of things until they happened. She resolved to keep her cool so Jim wouldn't know how nervous she was. Jim boarded the boat and sent his wife, Mary, home.

Slowly, she backed the boat away from the ramp. She played with the throttles to see which way the boat turned and what the reaction time was to make the turns.

On the way to Jim's house, she tried to get Jim to drive. "I'll show you how to operate the throttles and maneuver the boat."

"You're doing fine." He said.

Jordan pointed out to sea. "John, the inlet is beautiful today. I love the Atlantic on days like today with its deep blue ocean waves topped off with the white caps." John sat quietly.

The wind was catching the salt spray separating it from the waves. She had lost herself in watching the waves and the endless sky until a V of pelicans flew over interrupting the setting.

Jim touched Jordan on her shoulder. "There's the marina entrance. I want to top off the gas tank." He pointed to the left. "My house is the second one."

Her hands started trembling. Pressing one hand over her stomach, she gulped in a breath, let it out, and took in another big gulp. *You're having a panic attack. Stop it right now. Calm down.* The wind started to blow stronger as she pulled into the narrow entrance of the marina towards the fuel dock. She put the throttles into neutral to check which way the wind would blow the boat. Once the boat was close to the dock, she put one engine in neutral and the other in reverse. She backed the stern towards the dock then she let the wind push the bow against the dock. She gave a big sigh as she let her hands drop from the steering wheel.

The boys on the dock secured the boat. When the tank was fueled, she put one engine in forward to let the bow swing away from the dock. The boys pushed the stern out. She disturbed a flock of floating seagulls when she moved the boat forward back into the river. Their screeches echoed through the air.

"Jim, you can drive."

"No."

She couldn't figure out why he would buy a boat and not want to drive it.

Jim waved to Mary standing by the boat lift. All Jordan had to do was center the boat in the lift. On her first try, she squared the boat.

"Jim, is there anything else you need?"

Jim shook Jordan's hand. "No, we are fine. Thank you. I'll take you back to the county ramp."

Jordan was pleased with herself. She knew Jim never suspected it had been her first time driving a twin-engine boat. She climbed into her Suburban as the sun was slowly moving towards the water. When she turned onto the highway, the dunes were casting long shadows over the road. She turned the radio up to block out the thoughts of her stressful day. It was almost dark when she pulled into her dealership. She was surprised to find Sam waiting for her. She gave him a play-by-play detail of the boat delivery, including Jim not wanting to drive the boat.

Sam was beaming and gave her a quick hug. "I knew there wasn't anything you couldn't do. Now, what are you going to do next?"

She was excited to tell Matt about her day. When she arrived home, she saw the fear in Matt's eyes. "Mom, where have you been? Your cell kept going to voicemail. I was worried that you might have been in an accident."

"Matt, I'm sorry. I towed a 26-foot boat to New Smyrna Beach. The new owner wouldn't drive it, so I had to drive a twin-engine boat to his house. I didn't think to call."

"Mom, you scared me."

She tried to block Matt's fear from her mind while she prepared dinner. Her strength had been tested today, and she had survived.

Chapter 9

Catfish Fishing

Over her morning coffee, doubts invaded her mind after her conversation with Matt last night. She was mentally betwixt and between about what she should do. Her boat dealership was in the beginning stage, and it was going to require lots of attention, effort, and energy. She hated the thought of giving it up, but she had to put Matt first. She needed him to feel secure.

There were days when no one entered her dealership. She could feel in her bones that one day the long hours and her dedicated work would produce a steady, strong business. The river was calming to her, with the alligators croaking and the frogs trying to croak louder. Fishermen gently cast their lines floating down the river, and the seagulls, herons, egrets, and ospreys soared watching for food. The view from her small window to the peaceful river was quite different from that of her skyscraper office. She was a little surprised that she hadn't missed the tall buildings, the hustle of the people, and the noise of the city. She did miss some of her co-workers and lunch with her friends. The two worlds were far different, but every day on the river were days in paradise.

Sam's marina was the only inhabited property amid all the swampland and woods on the east side of the river. Sam came by the marina every afternoon to check on her even though he called her throughout the day, and he knew that Scott called her every couple of hours too.

On Wednesday afternoon, Sam came to check on her. His green-gray eyes danced as he surveyed her boats. "You should be proud of what you've accomplished in the last few months."

Jordan lit up under his admiration and looked at him with honest appreciation. His easy-going manner was comforting, and he enforced her confidence that she had made the right decision. She grinned. "I am proud."

"You have an inner strength that I've never seen in a woman," he added. "You've made me become a better person. I work harder now. I don't know when I would've finished the docks. It's all because of you."

She grabbed her fishing pole and asked. "Would you like to go fishing?"

Sitting at the end of the dock fishing and talking was one of their favorite past times. Their conversations were always about the marina and her dealership, and they gave each other helpful suggestions. She told Sam what the marina boaters liked or disliked or what they wanted or needed from him, and she asked advice about different situations that rose during her day. She searched for reassurance more than anything else.

The following week, late one afternoon, after a long boring day, she gathered her fishing gear and walked to the end of the last dock. After she had caught a bucket full of brim and catfish, she went back to her office to store her fishing gear. Sam drove up to the office when she opened the door.

"I'm sorry I'm so late. It's been a very busy day. When you didn't answer your phone, I got worried."

"I'm fine. I know you have other businesses to manage. It's been a slow day." She laughed. "I heard the fish calling."

He drove to the end of the marina to turn around. She bent over her fish bucket with a wet cloth to cover the fish for her trip home. The cloth startled one of the catfish, when it jumped, one of the fin barbs went through her left hand into the soft tissue between her thumb and index finger. Sam saw her go airborne. By the time he reached her, she was holding the fish tight with her right hand to keep it from thrashing about. He steadied her arm. She gasped when she saw the concern in his eyes. It was the first time, she had noticed how striking he looked with his black hair and gray temples. His sun-weathered skin showed he was definitely an outdoorsman.

He held her hand. "The barbs are open. There's no way to pull the fin back through the way it entered."

She tossed her head toward the door. "Get a pair of pliers from my toolbox and break off the barb."

He squinted his eyes. "I know you're a strong and determined woman, but do you know how bad that's going to hurt?"

"It can't hurt much worse than it does right now. I can't go home with a fish stuck in my hand."

They both laughed at the image.

She held the fish as tightly as she could. Once Sam broke the barb, the fish was free.

"I'll clean and freeze the fish for you. You need to go to the emergency room and get a tetanus shot."

She called Matt. Her voice was matter of fact. "I'll be home in an hour. I'll tell you why when I get home."

Matt approached her as she entered the kitchen. "Mom, why are you so late?"

"I had to go get a tetanus shot." Then she explained why. "The tetanus shot hurt worse than the fish barb."

"Mom, are sure you want to be in the boat business?"

"The boat business had nothing to do with me fishing. You know I've fished for years. I called you because I was going to be later than usual. Give me some time, I will make this easier on both of us."

Matt shook his head and headed to his bedroom.

Chapter 10

Quinn Quit

H er hand was still sore a week after the fish incident. She remembered when she was a child her father had put pine rosin on cuts to draw out the soreness. Tuesday morning, on her way to work, she bought a tube of pine tar from the compound pharmacist and covered her wound like her father would have done.

The next afternoon, Quinn smiled, "You're closing your hand."

"Yes, the pain and soreness is gone."

The long shadows had disappeared reminding Jordan what a long day it had been. She went to find Quinn. "Are you ready to leave?"

His eyes were dull and tired. His grizzly, brown-and-gray beard was brushed with oil and grease, and his red corduroy cap was sitting sideways on his head.

"Jordan, you have too much work. My wife is mad that I'm never home, and I'm exhausted night and day." He scuffed his shoe across the shell gravel. "I'm sorry. I can't handle my day job and work here every night until nine. You're going to have to find another mechanic."

Jordan frowned, "Do you know anyone?"

"No, I don't. I'll ask around. I won't leave until you can find someone."

Her stomach turned inside out and tightened in knots. How was she going to find another good mechanic? She had been through many bad ones with her boat until she found Quinn. A bad mechanic could break her before she ever got established. This was another challenge she had to face.

At the dinner table, she pushed her food around with her fork.

"Mom, what's wrong?"

"Quinn quit tonight. I don't know how or where to find a top-notch mechanic."

"Well, I know you, you'll find someone." He rose from the table, walked into the den, and turned on the TV.

She was suspended in a faraway distant place, even with Matt in the next room, she was alone in her own house.

The week after her conversation with Quinn, a sales rep, drove into the marina.

"Hi, I'm John Cook. I work for Marine Parts House in Ft. Lauderdale. We sell after-market marine parts and products, engines, and anything and everything that has to do with boats. Let me tell you about my company."

She listened to his fifteen-minute sales pitch then forced a smile. "Thank you for stopping by, but I don't need anything now. When I do, I'll let you know."

Before John left, a boater walked into her office. "Jordan, my boat needs an oil change. Can you have it done this week?"

"Yes." She smiled and handed him the clipboard. "I need you to sign the work order."

John sat and watched her lively spirit and her energy as she talked to the boater. After the man left, John handed her his card. "You're in my territory. I'll stop by twice a month."

Jordan walked outside with him, he turned and gave her a wry smile, which formed a dimple on the left side of his mouth.

Two days after John left, a houseboat owner docked in the marina stopped her on the dock. "Jordan, do you know anyone who can replace engines?"

She grinned from ear to ear. "Yes, let me go get his card."

She handed the boat owner John's card. After he left, she called John. "I think a boater might call you to replace his engines."

John chuckled. "Thank you for the call."

The next morning when she arrived at work, John was on the dock talking to the boat owner.

John followed her into her office. "I've set a date to install two new engines for the houseboat owner. Jordan, you need to fill out an account application with Marine Parts House. I quoted the owner the price for running the work order through St. Johns River Yachts, Inc."

John watched her write five work orders for oil changes while he waited for her to fill out his paperwork. "I can't believe you're running this busy business by yourself. Who is your mechanic?"

"That's a sore subject right now. My mechanic turned in his notice last week."

Even though Quinn had told her he would stay until she found someone, he wasn't showing up for work.

John's lopsided smile appeared again. "I'm a boat mechanic. I can come back Saturday to do the work orders if you want me to."

"Let me think about it. I'll call you Thursday and let you know."

Jordan knew she couldn't operate her business without a mechanic, but she couldn't take a chance on anyone who walked in and said they were a mechanic.

When John left, she called every rep she had met. Her factory engine rep said, "John's one of the best. He's the number two certified marine mechanic in the State of Florida."

All the other marine salesmen that knew John gave him a triple-A rating and told her he was the best they had known. She called Scott explaining the mechanic situation and John.

"I never expected you to be this busy, but I knew the St. Johns River would be profitable. I'll inquire about John. If everything is as you say, you should hire him."

John was at the dealership early Saturday morning to work until noon. All day long boaters came in and out with mechanical problems. At 6:00 p.m. there were still unfinished work orders. The river and its demands seemed to have dictated their day.

She locked the door and asked, "John, where do you live?"

"About ten miles from here. Marine Parts House had an opening in this area, my wife didn't like Ft. Lauderdale. I have the same number of clients here, but I travel more miles."

She smiled. "I watched you today. You're a good mechanic. Would you be interested in working here full time?"

"I don't think so, but I don't mind helping you when I can. I'm going to install the new engines in the boat next week when I take my two-week vacation."

"That sounds familiar. I took a two-week vacation then quit my corporate job to open this dealership. If you know a good mechanic you could recommend, please let me know."

Early Monday morning, John started his vacation with Sam helping him unload the engines from his truck. It took him three days to uninstall and install the engines. At the end of the day on Wednesday, he plopped down in the chair across from her desk. "Jordan, can we talk?"

"Sure. What about?"

"I've watched you write work orders every day knowing you don't have a mechanic. What are you going to do?"

"I told everyone that being new, I was backlogged. If they didn't mind waiting, I would get to their boat when I could. They said they understood. Why do you ask? Are you reconsidering my offer?"

He ran his hand through his wavy chestnut hair. "No, but I will work the rest of my vacation to help you clear out some of these work orders."

John was average height and in his mid-thirties. His appearance showed that he belonged on the seas, with his brown manicured beard and his keen denim-blue eyes. His grin was the kind that could draw you in if you didn't watch yourself, and his laugh was soft and came from deep within his chest. She hadn't anticipated hiring an employee this soon. She had known Quinn for years, hiring John was different. This was another giant leap.

John worked the next five days from eight in the morning to six in the evening and sometimes later. Jordan's days had become longer greeting the sunrise every morning and staying until John left at night. Word had spread she had a full-time mechanic, and now the work orders were really piling up. Jordan observed John being a perfectionist. Boats never returned with the same problem. He didn't want customers to wait more than a day for their boat unless he had to order parts or there was a major problem. Jordan had become his dependable mechanic's helper. She test-drove the boats while he checked hoses and oil connections for leaks. She was willing to help him with anything he needed.

Saturday afternoon around sunset, Jordan asked John to join her on the back of the 25-foot fishing boat. She smiled and handed him a beer. She struggled to untwist the cap off her wine cooler, after several tries, he took the bottle from her hand. When their hands touched, she felt the warmth of his skin. For the first time since she opened her dealership, she didn't feel alone.

"I can't thank you enough for what you have done these last two weeks. I wish I could change your mind about working here."

He peered out over the water then slowly turned his head back to her. "My wife is pregnant. I need the company insurance. I will have to admit being this close to home has been great. I will miss the river and your energy next week. I still can't believe you're here every day by yourself. If I get some free afternoons, I'll come and help you."

She watched the back of his truck pull onto Highway 415 wishing he would be back tomorrow.

Chapter 11

Hiring John

Three weeks after John left, Jordan hurried down to the canal when she saw a man paddle his boat to the dock.

"Hi, I'm Jordan. Can I help you?"

"Yes, I need a mechanic."

"I'm sorry. I don't have a mechanic here today."

The man climbed back in his boat and turned the ignition key. *Boom!* Ten-foot flames shot into the air. Jordan ran and grabbed two fire extinguishers from her office.

After the fire was snuffed, she asked, "Is there anyone I can call for you?"

He gave a slight chuckle and smiled. "Yes, a good mechanic."

She grinned. "Let me see what I can do about that. Your boat will be safe here. If you want to sign a work order, I'll call you with an estimate."

He signed the work order then called a friend to come and pick him up. She speed dialed John.

"I need your help. A boat caught on fire at the dock."

"Are you hurt?"

"No, the owner and I are fine. Can you help me out?" She held her breath waiting for his answer.

"I'm in Daytona Beach today. I'll come by before I go home tonight."

John checked the boat and gave Jordan an estimate for the repairs.

He grinned. "I told my wife how busy you are. She wants me home now that the baby's born. She asked me if you had an opening."

Jordan lightly punched his shoulder and laughed. "Two against one. Think I can talk you into working here now? What did you have, a boy or a girl?"

"Boy." His white teeth showed when he smiled.

"I love boys. I have a son."

He lowered his head and kept his eyes focused on the ground. "You do need a full-time mechanic. I know a lot of people on the river from Sanford to Jacksonville that will bring their boats to me for service." He rubbed his forehead and scuffed his feet across the sand. "I'll turn my resignation into Marine Parts House tomorrow and finish out the week there. I'll be here Saturday morning at eight."

Her smile covered her entire face. "You're hired."

Saturday morning, John came into the office to pick up an oil filter off the desk. "This is my son Matt. He's hanging out with me today."

"Hi, buddy. Do you want to be in here with your Mom all day or would you like to be my helper?"

She chuckled to herself as she watched Matt and John walk down the dock.

At 9:00 p.m., she was still working with potential buyers. Matt slouched down in a chair in her office. "Mom, I understand now why you come home so late. I can't believe people come after dark and want you to show them boats with a flashlight. Don't they know you close at five o'clock?"

"I promise the hours will get better, but right now I can't afford to lose a potential sale."

Jordan put the palm of her hand under her chin then propped her elbow on the desk. "Matt, I'm sorry. I didn't know the river and the boats would demand so much. It's been a long day. Let's go home. Tomorrow is Sunday, we can spend the whole day together."

Monday morning John pulled his truck next to her office and used it as his service department.

"Jordan, I know you have little space here, but I do need some items stocked like cans of oil, oil filters and, belts, so I don't have to keep running back and forth to the parts store, other parts we can order when we need them. I can get overnight shipping from the Marine Parts House."

"I will do whatever you ask. This is all new to me. Just let me know what you need." She saw the twinkle in his eyes.

"Well, for one thing, you'll need to open an account at the local parts store. That way I can get small parts immediately if I need to."

The week flew by. She had written enough work orders to keep John busy for three weeks. She had become a full-time mechanic's helper. He taught her how to paint boat bottoms and drive the fork-lift, which gave him more time to do the mechanical jobs. Her five-foot small frame allowed her to crawl into cramped spaces that he couldn't reach. She could stand inside the spoiler arches and pull electronic wires through as he fed them to her.

Late Friday afternoon, she climbed out of a boat, he steadied her arm with his hand then slid it slowly down to hold her hand. "You're a quick study, which makes my work go faster and easier. From what I've seen, I think you can conquer any obstacle."

She wanted to hug him but refrained. There was a natural, easy working relationship between them. It didn't take her long to get used to him being there and working together made her day go by faster when she didn't have prospective buyers. She liked his confidence and his decision-making. She knew there wasn't anything he didn't know about engines or boats. Their time together at the end of the day became a habit to recap the day's work.

One evening, she smiled at him. "I have a question. The first day you were here, you gave me a wry smile when you left. Why that smile?"

His little chuckle warmed the air even more between them. "I know how demanding the river is, and you were going to need help. I also knew the houseboat needed two engines when it was in another marina. I knew if I talked to the owner, I could sell him the engines."

She knew now she could not run the dealership without John. They had become a team. He helped her with buyers when she was flooded with customers, and he never left at night until she was finished with her day. There were many nights they both showed boats by flashlight.

Chapter 12

Jordan's Loss

Jordan was washing a consignment boat when John found her. "I've been searching for you everywhere. Tom, from the boat factory, is on the phone."

She swung her legs over the stern. He held her hand as she jumped off the trailer to the ground and ran to her office.

Out of breath, she tried to talk. "Hel-hello."

"Jordan, this is Tom. Are you all right?"

"Yes, I was cleaning a seat on the back of a boat. I forgot to take the phone with me. What can I do for you?"

"I'm supplying boats to the Ft. Lauderdale Boat Show in October and to the Miami Boat Show in February. Will you work with Scott and one of my west coast Florida dealers in the Ft. Lauderdale show?"

She almost squealed. She lowered her voice to stay in control. "Yes! Yes! I'd love to do that!"

Tom replied, "I thought you'd say yes. I'll see you in one month in Ft. Lauderdale." She could hear his smile in his voice.

Opening day at the Ft. Lauderdale Boat Show was a perfect fall day—no clouds, bright and sunny, and no humidity. Jordan's permanent smile reflected her excitement. She was part of the show this year rather than being a spectator, like in previous years. She couldn't believe one year after she opened St. Johns River Yachts that she would be selling boats at the Ft. Lauderdale Boat Show.

Scott paced back and forth as he said to her and the west coast dealer, "The buyer's address will determine which dealer sold the boat and the one that pays the commission to the salesman. That way, everyone can work with any buyer, and we won't have to worry about our territories"

Jordan laughed. "I'd love to pay a salesman a commission. What happens to the boats that don't sell?"

Scott winked. "Tom offers us big incentives to take the boats back to our dealerships. He doesn't want them back in Wisconsin."

The announcement came over the loudspeaker, "It's twelve o'clock. The show is officially open. We welcome the US Marine Band playing Stars and Stripes." Thousands of red, white, and blue balloons flew across the sky like a flock of birds. The humming of voices grew louder as people made their way through the gates and to the boat docks. Jordan's chest pounded feeling all the excitement in the air.

An hour after the show opened, a salesman from the west coast dealership, slipped and fell on the bow of a boat. Scott hurried to him when he saw him lying face-down. Jordan heard the thump and called 911. The paramedics popped his dislocated shoulder back in place before taking him by ambulance to the hospital for x-rays. In sympathy, Jordan could feel an ache in her arm knowing there was nothing she could do for his excruciating pain.

Scott reminded everyone, "Take your time. Don't hurry on the boats."

The daily show hours were from 10:00 a.m. to 10:00 p.m. Jordan was exhausted at the end of every day. Her days started at 9:00 a.m. and ended at 11:00 p.m. There had been no time for meals until after the show closed every day. She was glad the week was over.

The last night at dinner, Scott put his hand on Jordan's shoulder. "Well, Jordan, how did you like working the week-long show? Will you be ready for the two-week Miami show in February, or have you had enough?"

"I'm glad for two things. I get to pay a salesman a commission, and I have twelve weeks between shows. I'll be ready. I hope we don't lose a salesman again."

Scott nodded. "There are always unexpected events. The west coast dealer won't be at the Miami show. I'm going to bring extra salesmen to make sure we're covered. I'm glad you're not backing away."

A week after the Ft. Lauderdale show, Jordan evaluated her life. Matt was right she had leaped into the boat business without giving a full evaluation of what the dealership would demand of her. She was still determined to make her business a success, although she hadn't calculated the long hours and the weight of stress that bored down on her.

Jordan used her slow months from November to February to set an advertising budget and attend all chamber of commerce meetings within a fifty-mile radius of her dealership. She attended all local bank open houses and realtor picnics to advertise her company and her boats. She was overjoyed when the Rotary Club and the Jaycees asked her to be their guest speaker at their monthly meeting.

The second week in February, the Miami Boat Show was under-way. Midmorning, Jordan heard her name called over the PA system to come to the show office. When she arrived, a secretary handed her a number and a phone. A nurse at Sacred Heart Hospital in Pensacola answered.

"Ms. Harris, your father is in emergency surgery."

"Why? Is he going to be all right?"

"I'm sorry, I don't have any other information."

When she hung up the phone, the excitement of the show had been replaced with shock. Her knees went weak, and her eyes filled with tears. Her heart raced when she told Scott she had to leave. She called Matt, then called a neighbor to make arrangements for Matt to stay with them. She checked out of the hotel on her way to the airport.

The hour flight from Miami to Pensacola gave her mind time to conjecture all kinds of scenarios as to what might have happened to her father. When she arrived at the hospital her stepmother was sitting in the intensive care waiting room.

"Your father is stable. His colon burst during his routine colonoscopy exam."

She stood at the foot of her father's bed. "Jordan, Jor." His weak voice trailed away.

She moved to his side and forced her tears back, giving him a light kiss on his forehead. She pulled a chair to his bedside and rested her head next to him in silence. The thirty-minute visiting hour seemed like five minutes. It would be another two hours before she could see him again.

She called Matt from the intensive care waiting room, giving him an update on his grandfather. "Daddy looks all ashen and weak. I don't know what's going to happen. I'll know more when I talk to the doctor this afternoon."

"Mom, I can drive up."

"No, not right now. I'll talk to you tonight."

After two days in the intensive care unit, her father was moved to a private room. On the third day, Jordan met with the hospital chief of staff. "I've tried to meet with the gastroenterologist. He has ignored my calls and he's not making his hospital rounds."

Later that afternoon, Jordan became even more furious when the doctor's office nurse showed up to talk to her.

The next morning, the chief of staff came to her father's room. "How are you doing?"

The crow's feet around her eyes were deep, and her body needed rest. She lowered her head to her chest. The doctor put his hand on her shoulder.

"The colostomy surgeon is going to meet with you later today. Jordan, people don't realize how dangerous colonoscopy procedures are for people over seventy. It's not unusual for colons to burst with this exam. It is uncommon for a person to have a colostomy. Your father's problem now is infection. We are in a wait-and-see hold position."

Jordan was speechless. The surgeon squeezed her hand for a second then turned and left the room.

After a week with her father, she was back at the Miami show to move two boats back to her dealership. She was loading the last boat onto her trailer when she received a call from the surgeon.

"Jordan, your father is back in intensive care. You need to come immediately."

"I'll be there as soon as I can."

She ran to Scott with tears in her eyes. "Will you take one of my boats back to your dealership? I'll send John to pick it up later."

She called John. "I'm dropping off the Suburban and a boat at the dealership tonight. Then I'm heading to Pensacola. Daddy is worse."

"Jordan, I'm sorry." She could hear the sympathy in his voice. "Don't worry about the dealership. I'll take care of everything. Just go do what you need to do."

Emotion welled up in her throat. Her body was stiff, her eyes burned. She had been on the road five hours when she parked the Suburban at her dealership. It was 10:00 p.m. and she still had another eight hours ahead of her. She was used to being in control, but this situation she couldn't control. Helpless and scared, all she could do was pray that her father would still be alive when she arrived in Pensacola.

Matt had packed their bags and brought funeral clothes for her when he picked her up at the dealership. She tried to sleep on the back seat, but even in her exhausted state, she was wide awake. She had missed most of the Miami show and the excitement of the opening day had been replaced by the death angel. She called the nurses' station every hour to check on her father's condition. When she stepped off the elevator at 6:00 a.m., a surgical team rushed past her with her father.

She ran alongside the gurney. A nurse said, "Glad you're back, Ms. Harris. We're taking him back to surgery. We can't stop. The doctor will speak with you later."

Ten minutes had passed when the surgeon emerged from the operating room doors. "Your father died before we could start the surgery. We couldn't cool his fever, and all his organs were beginning to shut down. All of his doctors will meet with you in the conference room in an hour."

She, Matt, and her stepmother met with the physicians—nephrologist, cardiologist, and pulmonologist, but not with the gastroenterologist. The doctors told them the infection was too widespread, and there was nothing that could have been done. She had steeled herself for his death, but she was overcome with grief.

The death certificate listed heart failure as the cause when it should have been peritonitis.

The funeral was held three days later. Her father was placed next to her mother in the Bayview Memorial Gardens cemetery.

During the long trip home, there was little conversation between her and Matt. Jordan's thoughts of being an only child hit hard. Her father had been her strength and she, his. She had saved him years ago when his tractor slid down a hill on their farm after a heavy rainstorm. The mudslide and his tractor stopped in the soft creek bed with him pinned underneath. She only had to dig around the tractor a little to set him free. She saved him then; now she was helpless. They had been each other's rock for the long five years when her mother was dying of cancer. She tried to comfort him the best she could with his loss of thirty-six years. Jordan did know how much he loved her, and he expected nothing less of her than to succeed in life. She had so many memories with her father, but there would be no future ones. A phone call from John interrupted her thoughts.

Chapter 13

Daytona Boat Show

"Jordan, I know you've paid the entry fees for the Daytona Beach Boat Show. If you still want to do the show, I can start setting it up."

Life had been a blur with her father's death and the funeral. Hearing John's voice brought her back into focus. He was a comfort that warmed her from inside out, and she had come to rely on his strength more and more.

"What do you want to do? I hate putting all the responsibility of setting the show up on you. I know your work orders are heavy."

"The fees are paid. I think you should be in the show."

She and Matt arrived in Daytona Beach at 9:00 p.m., John was still setting up boats. When he saw her, he smiled that smile, the one that's reserved for close friends. She swallowed hard to force back the tears when the crew gave their condolences. John reached for her hand. She wanted more than to hold his hand. She laid her head against his chest. He folded his arms around her, and she wanted time to stand still. John didn't say anything sympathy-wise. His touch said it all. She knew at that moment he had become her constant in life, and no matter what happened, he would be there for her.

She backed away and gazed out over the boats. "John, where's the 25-foot fishing boat? You know if that boat doesn't sell over here on the ocean, I'm never going to sell it."

"Don't get excited. I left a place for it. I'm bringing it over in the morning."

It was 1:30 a.m. when her tired body crawled between her sheets and collapsed.

Jordan spent the entire week running back and forth from Lemon Bluff to Daytona Beach. Her body was running on adrenaline and caffeine. If she could get through this boat show and get her boats back to the dealership, she could finally take a much-needed break. John had gone way beyond his job description, and she knew he was just as exhausted as she was.

On the last day of the show, she heard someone whisper in her ear behind her. "Hi, Jordan."

She jumped and turned around to see one of her investment buyers from her real estate days. "Hi, Rick, what brings you to the show? Are you looking for a new boat?"

"No. I heard you were here and wanted to say hi and tell you how surprised I am that you're in the boat business. I guess this means I've lost my real estate agent."

"It seems I've surprised a lot of people. Don't worry, you'll find another good agent."

He backed away not taking his eyes off her. She called out, "If you need a boat come and see me."

She watched him walk away and felt an empty pang in the pit of her stomach. It was clients like him that made her miss the real estate business. The boat business was her life now; there was no looking back. Sam came to the show, and so did many of her friends. Jordan hadn't seen the Bahamas crew since their trip. Everyone gave her their support and reassurance that she had made the right decision.

The show manager made his rounds to thank all the dealers for participating. "Jordan, if it hadn't been for your big boats, we would've never convinced the county council to let us have the boat show in the coliseum. Your boats brought in record crowds. We all owe you. Thank you."

Jordan shook his hand and smiled. With all that had happened, she had forgotten how she had to fight with the county council to allow the boat show to be held indoors.

Jordan awoke to Monday's sunrise, excitement and exhaustion bubbled to the surface as soon as she opened her eyes. As much as she wanted to, she couldn't stay in bed. She had made two late trips last night pulling boats from the show. One more trip to Daytona Beach today, and she would have all her boats back at her dealership.

Fifteen miles outside Daytona, she saw smoke boiling from under the hood of the pick-up truck. In her tired state, she screamed out loud, "No! This can't be happening now!"

While waiting for John to come to her rescue on I-4, a big rig trucker pulled over in front of her. "Can I help?"

"I don't know what happened. It started running hot, and before I could pull to the shoulder, smoke came boiling from under the hood."

The truck driver raised the hood; instantly flames flared into the air. She knew enough not to open the hood before the engine cooled. There were many reasons why this would happen, but the main one was there could be a fuel hose leak.

The driver raised one shoulder in a shrug and backed away, then almost running in a fast trot he yelled, "I'm sorry, you're on your own! There's nothing I can do!"

John parked the Suburban behind her. He gawked at the black char under the hood. "What happened?"

She told him how the flames started. His voice was loud. "The trucker should have known better than to open a hood on a boiling engine."

Jordan glanced at him. "I understand now why my father always said anything can happen on the road and the road can eat your profit."

"That's true. I try to keep all your vehicles serviced so this doesn't happen. I'll come back tomorrow with help and get the truck. Let's go get that last boat."

On the way back, John reached over and patted the back of her hand. His touch reminded her how lucky she was that he found her.

She felt the butterflies in her stomach and wondered if he felt a flutter too. His smile and blue eyes drew her to him and kept her there moments longer than was necessary. She wanted to lay her head on his shoulder, but if either of them moved the spell would be broken. She stared at him as if he had hypnotized her. A car honked as it whizzed past. She flinched, breaking the spell.

She sat quietly for a long time thinking how different her business would have been if John hadn't come into her life. She realized at that moment; she could fall in love with him.

Chapter 14

Fishing Boat Sold

M onday afternoon, Sam came into Jordan's office with the final plans on her six-thousand-square-foot sales and service building. The first thing she studied was the electrical outlets. Every place she had worked never had enough outlets. She convinced Sam to add two more outlets in her office and the service bays and five more in the showroom, then she made extra sure John didn't need anything else in the service area.

On her last review of the plans, she noticed the blueprint had a shower. "Sam why is there a shower in the bathroom. I don't think we need one."

He smiled. "Jordan, you have used my office shower several times. I thought you would want one here."

Sam and John both ganged up on her about the shower.

She laughed. "Okay, you two win. I give up. I can't fight the both of you. A shower it is."

Sam pointed to the plans. "I'll build a ramp and viewing dock on the outside of the building and extend the roof. Your boats can be backed to the dock and be undercover. Your buyers can walk the dock for easy access into the boats. You can put 24 to 30-footers undercover. What do you think?"

"Oh, I like that idea."

After a few minor changes, she signed the plans for the construction to begin.

Six months later, Sam, John, and Jordan stood in the middle of the ship's store showroom. The empty room looked massive. She turned and did a 360-degree visual. John picked up on her quietness.

"Is something wrong?"

"Wrong? No, just big." She answered as if she was distracted.

Sam assured her it wasn't too big. "It will shrink when you get it stocked with merchandise."

It was great to be out of the one-room building that had served as her sales office, parts department, and service shop the past two years. She felt a sense of permanence now instead of feeling like a transient. Her new office was big enough to add a small desk for John. There were times he needed privacy to talk to reps, manufacturers, and customers.

Now it was time to increase her staff. She hired a boat salesman from another dealership.

John pointed to the service bays. "I want to hire Randy. He's a good mechanic. He has worked at several marinas on the river but has never found the right one. He will work well here."

Jordan ordered work uniforms for John and Randy, and on the shirt's left pocket, she added the St. Johns River Yacht, Inc. logo and their first name. She found a salvage business with new store shelving for the ship's store, parts room, and the service bay area. She gave John full reign to order and stock the parts department.

Jordan stood eyeing the service bays. "John, the industrial air compressor has been delivered, and the walls are lined with workbenches and vices. Do you need anything else?"

"No, you have given me everything I asked for." He smiled and gave her a quick hug.

Jordan filled her boutique corner in the ship's store with nautical clothing and jewelry from the merchandising marts in Miami and Atlanta. She bought matching anchor necklaces for her and John. The only difference—John's anchor was larger and heavier than hers. John stocked the boating supply section with merchandise from his old company in Ft. Lauderdale. A month later, she stood and eyeballed everything in stock, making sure she could supply everyone with what they wanted or would need for their boat.

After the 25-foot fishing boat didn't sell at the Daytona show that the factory had forced on her, she thought her odds of ever selling it had become nil. Maybe she should call in Scott's promise to take the boat.

Tuesday morning, Tom's voice was like that of an excited child. "I'm calling to let you know that Stuart Clark called the factory about a 25-foot fishing boat. He lives not too far from you. I informed him you had the boat there. You should be hearing from him shortly."

"Thanks, Tom, for letting me know. Do you have a phone number for him?"

"No, I told him to come see you."

That afternoon, Jordan saw a man and woman walking around the consignment boats. "Hi, I'm Jordan." She smiled and offered her hand.

"Hi, I'm Stuart, and this is my wife, Karen. I came to see the 25-foot fishing boat. The factory said you had the boat here that I was inquiring about. I live over in Lake County. I didn't know you were here or that I'd find this boat so close to me."

She pointed to the front of the building. "The boat is over there."

He walked around the boat, touching, and patting it like he would a baby. "I just sold an older model of this boat. I've been fishing with manufacturers for years. I forgot to ask the factory what their incentives were."

She smiled. "I'll find out. I'll be right back."

Stuart's demeanor showed he was used to having his way. He had a never-ending grin that made Jordan suspect it was his way of trying to control people. She wished John was here, but he doing some warranty work on one of her customer's boats in another marina.

She hated being blindsided by not having information that Tom or Scott should've told her. She was familiar with boats and engine manufacturers paying for fishing tournament entry fees and giving their boat owners various logo products like hats, shirts, floating key fobs, and any other factory logo items to advertise their boats in tournaments. Why hadn't they told her an incentive was included with this boat?

She called Scott and then Tom. Both were away from their desks. She hoped one of them would return her call before Stuart left. A sigh of relief came over her when she heard John's voice in the service bay. She knew John could keep Stuart interested in the boat until she could talk to Scott or Tom. She also knew John could talk him into signing a bill of sale. Before she went back to Stuart, she decided to wait by the phone for five more minutes. Thankfully, Tom called before her five minutes expired.

"I'll email you the paperwork and explain how to fill out the papers for the entry fees, and the other rebates. You won't need my signature, just yours."

Jordan replayed to Stuart the conversation with Tom. "The factory will pay all your fishing tournament entry fees and the gas."

Karen nudged Stuart in the side. Jordan could tell by the twinkle in Stuart's eyes he was pleased with the factory incentives. Jordan left John with Stuart to decide what electronics Stuart wanted to have installed. It was exacting work for John with Stuart's daily afternoon visits. Stuart reminded Jordan of an impatient child, asking incessant questions, and expecting immediate answers and results. There wasn't an inch of the helm or the overhead hardtop that wasn't covered with electronics.

Jordan eavesdropped on Stuart praising John's work on the day he came to pick up the boat. "John, I'm impressed with your knowledge and workmanship. I can't believe how you hid most of the wires. You did a great professional job, far better than other mechanics that have worked on my boats before."

Jordan walked through the service bay door. "Hi, Stuart."

Stuart shook Jordan's hand. "I was telling John how great he's been to work with. I want to show my appreciation by doing something special for all of you. How about a Louisiana boil?"

"Stuart, that's not necessary. We were just doing our job."

"I want to do this, and I won't take no for an answer."

Jordan walked over to the marina office. "Sam, I sold the fishing boat to a construction contractor in Leesburg. He does fish fry's for his crews several times a year. He wants to do a Louisiana boil here. He's inviting everyone in the marina and their families."

Sam had some lumber left from the construction of her sales and service building. Friday afternoon, he took several 2 x 4's and covered them with plywood to make one long table. Saturday morning, Jordan covered the plywood with heavy brown paper before Stuart came to start cooking at 3:00 p.m. When the potatoes, corn, and crawfish were done, he drained the liquid and scattered the food on the paper tabletop. The steam rose, mingling all the aromas together, which drew everyone to the tables. There was enough food to feed an army.

Tim, a Volusia County deputy, drove into the marina to make his nightly security check. With so many leftovers, Jordan insisted he eat and invite other deputies to join him. It wasn't long before half of the police force had their plates full.

John charged into Jordan's office. "What are you doing in here? I've been looking for you everywhere."

"I've been writing sales contracts. I sold two boats to Stuart's friends. They had rather buy boats than eat." She laughed.

"You need to eat. The party's in full swing."

She stood up, and everything went dark. John grabbed a flashlight off his desk. Sam and Stuart walked in to check the fuse box.

Sam guided Jordan to the door. "What were you doing?"

"Working. What's going on?"

"The parking lot security lights flickered then died, leaving everyone in the dark."

The moon showed its face from behind a cloud, giving everyone a dim light. Sam and Stuart tried the fuse breaker box without any luck. Cell phone lights and flashlights finished the evening, or the party would have gone on until dawn.

Most of the town's-people had told Jordan she couldn't be friends with her customers. She proved them wrong. She had become good friends with Jim Knight in New Smyrna Beach and now with Stuart. This was how she was going to build her business and be successful.

Two months after the new building was finished, John came into her office. "Jordan, can we hire a parts person? With all the work we have, it takes Randy and me too long to run into the parts room, look up the part, and add it to the work order. If we had a parts person we could continue working. I know an excellent guy, and he's unhappy at the marina where he is now."

Will was divorced, and a happy-go-lucky person. He had the brightest strawberry-orange hair she had ever seen. She didn't know why he wasn't nicknamed "Red". John was right, he did know boat parts like the back of his hand.

When she and John offered Will the job, he didn't blink or bat an eye before answering. "Yes, I have wanted to work with John before I ever met him. His reputation is known up and down the river that he's the best mechanic on the St. Johns."

For now, she was fully staffed. She might be flying by the seat of her pants, but she knew how to surround herself with smart people, ones who could make her appear professional—John the best mechanic and Will the most knowledgeable in boat parts. She may have started knowing nothing about a boat business, but she knew in time she would be as accomplished as anyone else in this business, if not better. Somedays, she mentally thanked her old CEO for being a jerk, or she wouldn't be here. Phillip had been wrong about her. She did understand business and bottom lines. There were no two days alike, nor did they always run smooth. Still no matter what, she was glad she had made this decision. She was accused of being a tough businesswoman. She owned the business, and it was her right to run her ship as she pleased.

As if to test her resolve, her salesman confronted her immediately after his first sale, demanding his commission for the consignment boat he had sold.

"You signed the dealership agreement. Did you read the company's policy manual?"

"Yes." His tone was cold along with his stare. Then he turned and walked away.

An hour later, she saw him reading the policy manual, which stated that checks would be distributed to salesmen after the buyers check cleared the bank.

At the end of the day, in a gruff voice, the salesman announced, "I won't be back tomorrow."

She watched him drive away without an explanation. It was obvious to her that he had never read the policy manual. From then on, she would treat each salesman like a student and have them sign a statement saying they had read and understood the company policies.

It was one of those days. After the conflict with her salesman, Will called her to the parts department. "We have had two duplicate orders sent on this part. This is the second time it's happened. I sent the first duplicate back. Now they're telling me I can't return another duplicate on the same part."

"Have you talked to John about this?"

"Not yet."

John poked his head in the parts room. "Jordan, some woman is on the phone. She's crying, and I can't understand a word she is saying."

"I'll talk to her. You and Will need to straighten out this duplicate order mess."

Chapter 15

Father's Farm

Through the crying, Jordan recognized her stepmother's voice. "Calm down, Lynette, take a deep breath. I can't understand what you're saying."

Her stepmother kept taking breaths and releasing long sighs. Jordan still couldn't understand her. "I'll call you back in twenty minutes."

Lynnette seemed to have regained control over her emotions when Jordan called her back.

"I've been trying to clean out the farmhouse of all your father's things. It's too overwhelming, and I don't know what to do with all the farm equipment. Plus, the Cadillac dealership called about some parts your father had ordered. I need you here." Her sobs started again.

Jordan tried to reassure her. "Relax, I'll come take care of it. Everything will be fine."

When she hung up the phone, she folded her arms on top of the desk then buried her face in them. She had accomplished a degree of success in her business and felt a personal pride in her family life, but when she thought about her father, she felt like her world had crumbled around her. Her confidence was at an all-time low. She wasn't Superwoman. She was having doubts about everything. Why did she think she could run a boat business, and be a mother? Now she had promised to go take care of her father's estate.

John stuck his head in her office door. "What's going on?"

She gave him a short version of the conversation with her stepmother.

"I'll keep the dealership running. You go and do what needs to be done."

The next morning, she left at sunrise and was in Alabama by 2:00 p.m. She surveyed the barn and the storage shed. She called the Cadillac parts department to find out what part her father had ordered.

At the breakfast table, Jordan reached for Lynette's hand and gave her a reassuring smile. "After breakfast, you need to pack for a few days and go stay with your daughter in Pensacola. It'll be easier for both of us. I can clean out the buildings, call a few neighbors and the used tractor company in town and try to liquidate as much of the equipment as possible."

Jordan walked outside to call John. "What should I do about the Cadillac? It's in excellent condition, just old."

"Try to sell it. It's going to cost more than it's worth to keep it running."

Not long after their conversation, Matt called. "Mom, what are you going to do with Granddaddy's car?"

"I'm going to try and sell it. It's going to constantly have mechanical problems."

"I know, but I want it. He promised me I could have it after high school graduation. The car has sentimental value to me. John can keep it running."

"Matt, you're at the University of Florida and you have a car. You don't need the Cadillac." At the end of her long day, she called John to tell him about the Cadillac and the five-hundred-dollar tail-light her father had ordered.

"Do the taillights work at all?"

"I don't know. I haven't checked the lights or cranked the car."

"If the taillight works even with just a little bit of light, tell the Cadillac parts department you don't want it. They'll send it back to the factory."

"John, here's the sixty-four-thousand-dollar question. Matt wants the Cadillac. I will fly you to Pensacola, pick you up at the airport, and bring you to Evergreen. I need someone I can trust to make sure the car can make the drive down south.

John didn't hesitate. "Get me an afternoon flight tomorrow. I'll get Randy set for three days."

The next morning, her stepmother tried to talk through her uncontrollable tears. It was good she was going to stay with her daughter in Pensacola. After the three of them had lunch, Jordan shopped at the airport mall, while she anxiously waited for John's plane to land.

On the way back to the farm, Jordan chatted non-stop. "I sold two tractors, and a retired construction worker bought the D-9 tractor and the road grader. He is coming the day after tomorrow to pick them up."

She turned off the gravel road onto the red clay farm road. John's eyes widened when she pulled into the driveway. "I can't believe how much you've accomplished in two days and how much equipment is still here."

"This farm was my Daddy's hobby and his life on the weekends. If he needed any kind of equipment to do what he wanted, he went and bought it. The house across the street is where he grew up. I spent my summers and weekends here with my grandmother and sometimes with one of my cousins, JD—short for Jeremiah David. Of all our eighteen first cousins, he and one other cousin are closest to my age. As I look around at the equipment, the fields, and the ponds, it brings back so many memories. One I will never forget was the morning JD went fishing. He didn't like the fact that Grandmother told him he had to take me with him. After three hours, JD hadn't caught any fish and said we could go back to the house. Grandmother met us on the front porch to find out why I was yelling and punching JD. I told her he put his hands on my shoulders and pushed me down on an old-rusted paint can and told me not to move until he said so or he would belt me. He said he wasn't catching any fish because I was talking too much. I was so mad I kicked the can when I stood up, and a big water moccasin side winded its way to the pond. I remember saying to Grandmother, 'JD made me sit on top of that moccasin for two hours.' She laughed. I guess it was funny, but at that time, I didn't think so."

"How old were you?"

"Eleven. Oh, and Grandmother told JD my talking didn't have anything to do with him not catching fish. She and Daddy always stood up for me. That's why Daddy bought the D-9 and dragline to keep the first pond clean and to build a second pond. At the time, if the second pond had been built, we could've each had our own pond to fish in. Every time Daddy came here, he worked on the two ponds, made roads and paths through the woods. He only farmed ten acres out of the two hundred after the government quit paying him not to grow peanuts, corn, soybeans, and cotton. He was successful here and in everything he did. Even though he isn't here now, I feel I still have to prove myself to him. That's why my boat dealership can't fail. Being here this week has made me realize how much I miss him and how much grief and raw pain I still feel."

She wiped the moisture from her eyes with a shaky hand.

John put his arms around her and drew her next to him, then whispered, "I'm here."

She wanted to lean into him, but instead, she pushed away. "You go on into the house. I'm going to water the peonies."

After twelve years, her father and Lynette had kept her mother's flower bed, by the back door, filled with gladiolas and peonies. After watering the flowers, she had gained her composure and took John on a tour of the house, stopping at her old bedroom.

"You can sleep here. I think you'll be comfortable. I'm sleeping in my father's room."

The next morning after breakfast, John checked out the Cadillac. Midmorning, he approached her in the barn. "The car should make the trip to Central Florida without any problems. I don't want to leave you here by yourself. Anything can happen cleaning out these old buildings. I don't want you to get snake bit, especially after I moved an old straw basket in the shed and one hissed at me yesterday. If I stay and help, it'll cut your time in half here. We can travel south together. If you send me back today, I couldn't stand not knowing if you were all right or not." He planted his feet firmly on the ground and waited for her to answer.

Chapter 16

Jordan's Strength Renewed

Jordan took John into town the next afternoon. When they came around the high curve on the bridge that overlooked the town, his voice sounded like an excited child's. "Look, the railroad tracks divide the town in half." He pointed to the people walking on the sidewalk. "No one looks like they are in a hurry. Country life is moving at a snail's pace. It's a step back in time nothing like the years when I lived in Tampa and Ft. Lauderdale."

She smiled. "I never gave it a thought, but you're right. It's always been this way. When I was growing up Evergreen didn't have a traffic light now they have two. The Piggly Wiggly and the A & P grocery stores are across the street from one another. The bank and post office are side by side. There is one barber shop, a beauty parlor, and two mercantile stores: one on either side of the tracks. The First Methodist Church is on the east side of the tracks and the First Baptist Church is on the west. With a population of 2500 people everyone calls each other by their first name. The Greyhound bus and the Blue Bird school bus factory keeps all the people around the small towns employed. The window manufacturer here supplies Gibson Houseboats with all their windows. The Coneuch Sausage Company is also here that employs a lot of people. I'll stop by their store on the way home. It's the best sausage you will ever eat."

They passed several churches on their way back to the farm. John pointed to the grave sites. "I can't believe all the churches have their own cemeteries. I've only seen that in pictures."

73

"That's my mother's family plot over there next to the Olive Baptist Church."

"Really? Would you like to stop?"

"You don't want to walk through my family's headstones. You'd be bored."

His eyes danced. "It's part of you. That's not boring."

"John, are you flirting with me?"

"Maybe?"

They walked past the brick columns and rusted wrought-iron fence. Some of the headstones were broken; dirt and leaves covered a lot of the grave slabs. Jordan was a little shocked at the neglect. The old oaks had scattered thousands of acorns everywhere. Roots spread from the trunks and protruded above the ground like small knotty stumps. She walked to the back of the cemetery and up a hill.

"This is my mother's twin sister, and those are her two brothers' headstones. That's my brother's headstone." They followed a red clay rutted pathway to the other side of the cemetery. "This is where my grandparents, aunts, and uncles on my mother's mother's side are."

John lowered his head and kicked the red clay with the toe of his shoe. "I was raised by my stepmother. I don't know anything about my mother or father's family. I'm not even sure where their graves are."

John's words hit her like a ton of bricks. Her strength had come from her family roots and her ancestry. This is what made her strong and willing to fight for what she wanted. John didn't have any connection or knowledge of his family. Sadness welled inside her.

He opened the car door for her.

She pointed left. "About a mile down the road, my father's family is buried in the Pentecostal church cemetery."

"I see the love in your eyes when you talk about your family, the town, and the memories of your childhood. I wished I had known my family like you did."

Again, she felt a loss and emptiness for him.

The afternoon sun stretched long shadows across the yards on the way back to the farmhouse. This time of day, the elderly sat in their rocking chairs on the front porch waving as people drove by on their way home from work. She could see them straining their necks to see who was driving the unfamiliar car.

She stopped at Mr. Linsley's country store and bought a smoked ham for dinner. She collected sweet potatoes from the straw in the barn, cooked a package of butter beans from the freezer, made cornbread, and pulled enough pears from the tree next to the well to make a pear pie.

John watched her set the food on the table. "How do you do this? You make cooking appear effortless."

"That's because it is. I've been cooking since I was nine. I learned on my grandmother's wood-burning stove across the road. Would you like anything else to eat?"

"No. It was delicious, but I can't eat another bite."

John slid his arms around her waist and pulled her against him when she put the last dish in the cupboard. "I've been trying to keep my hands off you all day."

He slowly turned her around to face him. He lowered his head and placed his hand on the back of her neck. He gently guided her lips to his. His soft kiss evaporated when untamed passion overcame them. She leaned into his pull and toward something she wanted. She had imagined his kiss more times than she wanted to admit. She let him know by her response that the attraction wasn't one-sided. She slowly pushed him away. He stared at her with more serious eyes than she had ever seen before. She wanted to lead him to her bedroom, but she turned away, refusing to let her feelings take over her head.

"John, we can't. You're married. I won't give into my attraction for you."

He took two steps back. "I didn't tell you that Lisa and I are getting a divorce. She's moved out."

She stepped forward, nodded, and smiled. He kissed her again as time seemed to melt into space. They walked into the living room and sat on the sofa, never letting go of each other's arms.

It was Jordan who spoke first; her voice was low and soft. "I wonder how different it would have been if we had known what we know now if we would have married them. Nick hated talking about his feelings, and what lay beneath he wasn't willing to share. I think to him it showed weakness."

"If I met Lisa today, I wouldn't marry her. All she was interested in was a marriage that looked good. I hate to make her sound so shallow, but all she wants to do is teach school. She cares for our son and the two dogs more than me. We're a million miles apart even when we're together."

"John, I had no idea. How long ago did this happen?"

"When Billy turned four. I'm staying in the house until it sells."

Jordan's inner strength surged. She stood, leaned over, and gave him a final good-night kiss on his cheek. "It's late. I'll see you in the morning."

He didn't move. His eyes followed her until she closed her bedroom door.

The next morning, the sun rose fast, reflecting its gleaming rays off the pond. She was dressed in paint-stained jeans and a long-sleeved plaid shirt with the hem knotted at her waist. She grabbed a wide-brimmed straw hat off the back-porch hook and headed to the shed. She was taking the last basket from the shed when John wandered down the porch steps.

"Good morning, sleepy-head!" she yelled. "I thought maybe you were going to sleep all day!" Then she laughed. "This is the last day. Can't let the grass grow under our feet. I left the coffee pot on."

After lunch, she slumped down in an old, worn-out black, white, and brown cowhide chair. Her hair was matted like a bird's nest, her face was smudged with dirt, and her blue jeans were brown with grime.

"You're a mess," he teased. "You look like a rag doll that's been thrown away."

"Well, you aren't dressed like you're going to a fancy ball." They both laughed, keenly aware of the passion from last night's kiss.

At five that afternoon, she stood on the front porch and surveyed the fields and ponds, then turned to John with a smile. "I'm done for now." She gazed up the red clay road. "All the equipment has been picked up except that one tractor. The neighbor who bought it will come for it at the end of the week. The only thing left in the shed is a stack of garden tools, which I'm leaving. The barn is a lost cause for now. It's full of large rusty file cabinets from my father's business, broken tractor parts, rusty heavy equipment tools, and anything else that was tossed in there over the past fifty years. I'll tackle the barn in another trip."

"Jordan, I understand now. This land is where your strength comes from. If you want something, nothing stands in your way. Someday, I hope I can give you added strength. I want you to feel about me the way I feel about you."

She put the last dinner dish in the cabinet, turned and headed to her room. "John, it's late. We have a long travel day tomorrow. I'll see you in the morning." She hesitated at the door, then she took two steps forward and closed the door behind her.

At dawn, the neighbor's rooster woke her, crowing. She dressed, knocked on John's door, then started the coffee pot. She'd barely touched makeup to her face and her hair lay softly on her shoulders. John sat two cups of coffee on the table. When she sat down, he reached across the table and gently put her hand in his. An electric shock rushed through her. Her heart flipped over, and the wall around it cracked.

He ran the palm of his hand along her cheek. "Sometimes the things that matter most involve the greatest risk."

She thought for a few seconds, then brought herself back to reality.

"I've taken so many risks. Right now, this isn't a risk I'm ready to take."

They finished their coffee in silence. She wasn't ready to engage in another lengthy discussion that wasn't going to go anywhere. They had said all they could at this point in their lives.

She gathered her purse and motioned him to the door. "Let's go through the drive-through and get a steak biscuit and keep going. We should be at the dealership by four if we don't have any problems. I'll follow you in case something happens to the car."

It had been an unusually quiet morning between them. John didn't say anything, only followed her out the door.

Each time they stopped at rest stops and for lunch, John checked under the car's hood. It surprised her the car made the trip without any problems.

The car was faring far better than her heart.

Chapter 17

Lake X

The long drive back to Lemon Bluff gave Jordan time to evaluate her relationship with John. She had regained her vigor while on the farm. Matt was her first priority, and the dealership was second. She couldn't and wouldn't commit to going forward in an emotional involvement. The farm was gone, and now the river was her strength and her peaceful place.

The morning after she and John returned from Alabama, Jordan took a long walk down the dock. It was clear to her this is where she belonged. John met her on the dock. "Some man is calling from Atlanta." She hurried back to her office, leaving John on the dock.

She yelled back to John. "I don't know anyone in Atlanta."

"Hello, this is Jordan."

"You probably don't remember me. I'm Les Turner. I talked to you briefly at the Daytona Beach Boat Show about a 26-foot used boat you were selling on consignment. I found a boat here in Atlanta like the one you described, but they want a lot more money than what you quoted me. I want your honest opinion on the boat you have, that the cabin and engine are in good condition."

"For a used boat, it's in exceptional condition and the price is right. If this is the boat you want, it's a good purchase."

"My business won't allow me to come back to Florida at this time. I'll buy the boat on your word if you deliver it to Lake Lanier."

She chuckled to herself, hung up the phone, and ran to find John. "We're going to Atlanta."

John rolled his eyes. "That's strange, I've never known anyone to buy a used boat sight unseen. Are you sure you want to sell the boat this way?"

"I see no reason not to. He's wiring me the money before we leave. You need to make sure the boat is checked out from bow to stern." She turned to Randy. "I'm going to do the sea trial with John today."

Les wired the money. John still didn't think it was a good idea for her to deliver the boat to Atlanta sight unseen.

When they rounded the last bend coming down the mountain to the marina, Jordan yelled. John! Look! Lake Lanier is almost dry."

Les arrived shortly after them. His surprised look told Jordan he had not been to Lake Lanier. He stood by his car staring wide-eyed at Jordan. "Where's the water?"

Jordan pursed her lips. "You're going to have to do something with the boat."

"I don't know what to do."

She held her scream inside. "Go find the marina manager." He stood frozen.

She brushed past him in haste to find the manager. "I need help. The buyer is clueless about what to do. I need to get back to Florida."

The marina manager pointed to Les. "He never contacted me about slip rental or dry stack storage." He explained the reason the lake was dry. "The Corp of Engineers drained the lake in anticipation of spring rain flooding, but the rains didn't come this spring. I'll go find a trailer to put his boat on."

The marina mechanic used the forklift to lift the boat off her trailer onto a marina trailer. Les stood with a blank stare, not saying a word.

On the way home, Jordan shook her head. "I can't believe Les didn't make any preparations with the marina to have his boat delivered." She closed her eyes and rested her head on the back of the seat. "I bet he'll run it aground the first time he takes it out."

John cracked a half-smile. "He never asked me one thing about the boat or how to operate anything on it. Did you see the expression on his face when he looked at the lake? I bet he sells it and never puts it in the water."

She turned her thoughts back to the river. "John, I never expected the business would demand so much from me. I have fishermen wanting bass boats, retired people asking for pontoon boats and houseboats, families wanting cabin cruisers, and young people looking for bow riders. If I want to stay competitive and accommodate everyone's boating needs, I need to increase my boat lines. What do you think?"

"Jordan, you know the St. Johns River is the large-mouth bass capital of the world and you know how many fishermen come to the river. If you are going to increase your inventory, I'd start with the bass boats. I'll call Dennis tomorrow, he's our largest outboard rep, and inquire about his bass boats."

Late the next afternoon, Jordan heard heavy footsteps in the showroom. Dennis greeted her with his big wide smile. "Good afternoon, Jordan."

"Hi, Dennis. I didn't expect to see you today."

"John inquired about our bass boat line yesterday. How can I help you?"

"I'm going to take on a bass boat line, but I know very little about them. I've had experience with many fishermen wanting us to increase the maximum horsepower so they can get to their fishing holes first. They don't care if we break the law and push the maximum horsepower past the boat rating. Of course, John has refused. He and I have agreed we aren't going to be sued for that kind of liability."

"I told John yesterday we have our own bass boat line. Since you're one of our dealers, you're already approved for a floor plan. We know we have competition, but we'd love for you to take a hard look at our line. I'll arrange for you and John to go to our test site on Lake X in Kissimmee. You can test-drive different bass boats with different horsepower engines. That'll help you make your decision."

The day she and John arrived at Lake X, they were assigned a performance test-driver. Jordan sat in the viewing stands, watched, and made a list of questions to ask. She wasn't interested in testing the boats and engines; that was John's job. After the test-driver made several trial runs, he changed seats with John. During lunch, the three of them discussed the horsepowers, and how the boats performed. In the middle of their conversation, red lights started flashing and sirens sounded from all directions. Everyone in the lunchroom jumped up and ran outside.

Their driver stared at her and John. "This isn't good. That sound means there has been an accident. The red lights alert the workers that are in the soundproof booths."

By the time, the three of them were outside, the paramedics and ambulances had arrived. Forty-five minutes later, divers found the test boat driver's body.

John pulled her close to him. "Are you sure you want to see this?"

She pressed his taut muscles with her hands. He intertwined one of her hands with his fingers. Warmth and life—a connection happened that was soul-deep in one moment.

As the paramedics lifted the body into the ambulance, the driver's left arm fell to the ground. Blood splattered the concrete and the paramedics' shoes. She gasped.

John's fingers sank into her hair as he pulled her head into his chest, then whispered, "Take some deep breaths."

"I wasn't expecting to see a mangled body."

Nausea overtook her. She broke away and ran to the restroom.

She surprised herself. She had seen many farm animals slaughtered and never got queasy. Maybe it was because this was a human being.

When she returned, she asked her assigned driver, "Does this happen often?"

"We are a test facility, and we all know the risks. We crash, walk away or we may get hurt, but death is rare."

Reality set in. An accident could happen at any time, and life could be gone like a vapor, like her father. Shock hit her hard. She shook all over when she thought that this could've been John. She didn't know how she would survive if something happened to him.

That evening she called Matt just to hear his voice. She was surprised at his response when she told him about her day. "Mom, do you need another boat line, especially bass boats?"

"Your father always observed life from a safe distance. He always watched the game but never played it. I'm not trying to take on every boat line, but the river has more fishermen than weekend boaters. Matt, I can stand on my own two feet, and I do know when and where to draw the line."

"Mom, I was trying to make sure that you had considered all the angles."

She was aware, she had snapped at him. "I know, honey. Thanks for trying to keep me in check."

Jordan had stopped her everyday ties with Scott in Jupiter. Since John was working full time all her boats were being transported directly from the factory to her. She had missed the camaraderie with Scott.

All ten bass boats that Jordan ordered arrived on the same day. Instead of the two a week that she and Dennis had agreed on.

John stared at the boats being unloaded. He shook his head and turned to Jordan. "I'm going to need another mechanic to keep up with your expansion. Even though the boats come in with engines on them, we still have a lot of prep work."

"That's your decision. Do you know someone?"

"No, but I'll find someone who will work well with Randy and me."

The bass fishermen's arrogance was different from her other clientele. They treated her without respect and talked down to her. John wasn't always available to talk to them, and she could tell by the tone in their voice that they hated having to deal with a female, but she always kept her cool.

Despite having ten new bass boats on the sales floor, a retired engineer from Ocala requested a special-order boat. She used every sales tactic she could think of to sell him one of the boats she had in stock. Clint insisted on his 19-foot bass boat have gold metal fleck in the fiberglass, tan carpet, and maximum horsepower. She couldn't visualize this being a fishing boat.

After Clint's boat arrived, he kept it docked at Marina 415. He asked John to crank the boat every day when he wasn't there. Jordan encouraged John to charge for his service, and whatever agreement he and Clint came to would be between the two of them. Clint kept his distance from her, only acknowledging her when it couldn't be avoided. Four months later, Clint's wife started coming to the boat with him. Some days she would go out in the boat, or she would sit in the car and knit. After a while, she and Jordan became friends. Jordan invited her to sit in her office and knit while Clint fished. Over time Clint's personality changed from high and mighty to somewhat down to earth. In his own way, he tried to be friends with Jordan.

One day, Clint barged into her office, then hesitated. "Oh, sorry, I didn't know you were busy."

"Wait, Clint, I want you to meet my son, Matt. He's home on college break."

Clint took a couple more steps and shook Matt's hand. "Matt, I'm going fishing, if you don't have anything else to do, why don't you come with me?"

When they returned, Jordan could hear Matt and Clint laughing walking up the dock as if they were long-lost buddies. Clint handed Matt a set of keys. "You can use the boat anytime you want."

Matt shuffled his feet. "Thanks, but no. I fish with my friends."

"You can take anyone you want."

When Matt's friends saw the fishing boat, one of them said, "Wow, I can't believe he gave you the keys to this boat."

Every time Clint came to the river, he made sure to say hello to Jordan and asked if Matt was home. Another friendship had developed between Jordan and one of her customers. Throughout the year Clint sent her prospective buyers.

Matt spent more time at the marina when he was home. "I don't think you're against me taking on the bass boats now."

"You know I like to fish."

"I know you didn't like going out in our boat when I went fishing after school. I remember when I was teaching you did your homework while I fished."

"Mom, I'm older now. That was when I was in elementary school."

She watched him walk down the dock to Clint's boat with his two fishing rods on his shoulder and swinging his tackle box.

Chapter 18

Business Expansion

B etween the river people and the sales rep's grapevines, word had traveled quickly about Jordan's new bass boats. She was overwhelmed with invitations to attend every boat manufacturer's dealer meeting in the country.

She did her research on the boats she liked and the ones that would be right for her customers and the river. She decided on one pontoon boat line and one houseboat line. She had to make sure her profit would justify the increase in her floor plan.

She took her financial statements to the two dealer meetings prepared to fill out floor plan applications. She wasn't expecting both manufacturers to use Floor Plan Services, which meant she was already approved.

Now with her three additional boat lines—bass boats, pontoon boats, and houseboats—Trey, her marine electronics salesman was in her dealership every week. He had sold John electronics for years, and he had supplied her with all the electronics for Stuart's 25-foot fishing boat. John ordered depth finders and GPS trackers every time a bass boat sold. Word had spread that John was at St. Johns River Yachts, which led to Jordan's dealership being crowded constantly with salesmen. There were days when her showroom looked like a marine industry salesmen convention. She wasn't sure if it was because she was a successful woman in a male-dominated business or if it was John. Maybe it was a combination of both.

Her spring and summer months were her busiest, and with her expansion, her working days were longer. The boat shows accounted for the largest portion of her annual sales, and with four boat lines, this meant more boat shows. She participated in every local weekend show in the spring and fall including the Ft. Lauderdale show in October and the Miami show in February.

She was overwhelmed by the 150 applications from the Orlando Sentinel classified ads where she had advertised for salesmen, a parts person, and a full-time secretary. Did that many people want to work around boats, or were jobs that scarce?

"John, here are the applications for the parts position. You and Will need to go through them and let me know who you want to interview. Just keep in mind we are a small company. We work in close quarters."

She permitted John and Will to hire a part's woman who had been a parts manager at a boat dealership in South Florida. Jordan hired three salespeople—a retired F-16 Air Force fighter pilot in his early forties, a retired corporate industrial salesman in his sixties, and a woman who had worked in real estate sales. The secretary she hired had been a CEO's assistant. She also hired a husband-and-wife cleaning team which she should have hired long ago instead of spending her mornings or nights cleaning boats.

The new boats were delivered from the factory with a protective plastic covering over the beds and a white chalky fiberglass residue covered the inside of the boats. The shrink-wrap on the outside had to be removed along with the road grime. The heavy foot traffic at the boat shows demanded the cleaning crew be on site all day.

Jordan's spring shows included Orlando, Palm Coast, Ocala, Daytona Beach, and St. Augustine. Before each show, Jordan met with her salespeople. She smiled. "Lady and gentlemen, here are your detailed plans, goals, and a notebook with our new, used, and consignment boats, current finance rates, sales contracts, business cards, and brochures."

Being an opportunist, she wasn't going to let a sale slip away from her or her salesmen because they didn't have all their tools.

She tried to outwit the other dealers by advertising her show prices the week before the shows. She wanted to encourage prospective buyers to come to her dealership before they could shop her boats against the other dealers at the show. She was lucky to be able to pull the sale off for two years before the other dealers followed her lead and started advertising their show prices before the boat shows started.

Her days were whirl spun, hauling boats every Tuesday and Wednesday to a boat show for set-up then transported them back to her dealership on Sunday nights and Monday mornings.

One Monday morning, coming from the Daytona Beach Boat Show, she thought it would be easier to make the bank deposit when she came through town rather than going to the dealership, unload the boat and trailer, and then trek back to town to the bank. When the tellers saw the boat in the drive-through lane, one let out a scream and another one covered her mouth, and her eyes widened as if they were going to pop. The bank manager ran into the parking lot waving his hands and yelled, "Stop! You can't pull a boat through the drive-through lane."

Jordan stuck her head out the window and yelled back, "I just did!"

To her, a 22-foot boat was small. She was too tired to have to deal with something that had already happened. As she pulled away, she laughed thinking about the fear she felt the first time she pulled the 26-foot boat to New Smyrna Beach.

Chapter 19

Boat Stolen

J ordan was still trying everything she knew how to sell the red-looking race boat that the factory had sent her on the first order. Local newspaper ads, *Boat Trader* ads, and advertising in the boating magazines had all failed. The only news media she hadn't tapped was a TV commercial shoot.

She waited on the dock while John put the boat in the water. John saw her eyes dance when he tied the boat to the dock. "Give me your hand. Let's run it up the river."

The boat was fast and stable, and the loud thru-hull exhaust could be heard echoing through the trees. She loved that sound and the wind in her face. She inhaled a deep breath, closed her eyes, and smelled the freshness of the river.

When she turned her attention back to the water, she screamed, "John! Watch out for the orange-and-white buoys!"

He jerked the steering wheel to the right, barely missing all six of them.

The buoys mark where the fishermen toss their crab traps and warn the boaters to stay clear. John had repaired many outdrives and props because boaters had run over the traps.

She tapped John on the shoulder. "Look over there." She pointed to the canoers and kayakers paddling close to the bank. Her high-pitched voice sounded like a child. "I haven't seen the river this busy in ages."

"It's because you haven't been on the river in a long time."

Canoeing and kayaking clubs were popular on the river. River trips could be booked at the state park ranger's office. The canoe club members paddled down the river every Saturday morning, weather permitting. The long-run started at Hontoon State Park with the short-run starting at Blue Springs. Both starting places ended at Highbanks Marina for lunch. A canoe club member met the canoers with his canoe rack pickup truck at Highbanks to take the canoers back to their starting places.

She propped her feet on the dash, tilted her head back, and felt how the river made all her senses come alive. "John, look at all the wildlife that's out this morning. The monkeys are sitting and swinging in the trees watching the kayakers." She pointed over towards the shore. "There's an alligator swimming. He's got to be at least thirteen-to-fifteen feet long, and another one is over there sunning on a log."

"You sound as if you've never seen the river before."

"I've been so busy with the boats I forgot how much I loved seeing all the wildlife."

Continuing farther down the river, she saw a herd of cows standing in the water cooling their tummies while swatting flies with their tails, and wild hogs were rooting for grubs on the bank. The ospreys gave daring stares, from their huge, scruffy nests atop the channel markers, to all wildlife and boaters below. Seagulls floated, watching for food while large blue herons and white egrets stood still at the water's edge waiting for their dinner to swim close to their feet.

"John, I wasn't aware how much I'd missed being on the water until now."

"You're on it every day."

"You know what I meant." She laughed and lightly punched his bicep. "I'm not on the river taking in the sights and sounds."

He winked. "Then I have to see that you are."

After the commercial shoot, she pointed to the boat. "John, let's leave the boat in the slip. It looks good with the water reflecting off the hull, maybe it will attract a buyer."

Everyone in the marina had become like family. They always made sure to say hello to Jordan when they came to their boats and always let her know where they were going and how long they'd be gone. Jordan always checked their boats every morning to make sure they were floating and weren't making any unusual sounds.

The morning after the commercial shoot, she ran back to the service bay yelling, "John! The boat's gone! The red boat's gone!"

The deputy handed Jordan the finished report with a frown. "I don't think you're going to recover your boat. The people on the river know what boats run the river. I'll spot check with them and maybe someone has seen something."

She could attest to the river people knowing everything on the river.

She called Scott, asking for advice. "Call your insurance company. There is a good possibility the boat will be recovered. My experience has been when a boat is stolen on the water, it's usually found. A boat stolen on a trailer isn't."

Midafternoon the deputy sauntered into her office, plopped himself into the chair across from her desk then removed his cap. "People heard a boat running the river around three o'clock a.m. The thru-hull exhaust vibrating through the trees woke up almost everyone. Now that I have this information, it gives us a starting point. We should be able to find the boat unless the thieves put it on a trailer somewhere."

Four days later, Jordan heard the deputy talking to John in the service bay. "Bring two tow ropes and come with me. My boat is docked in the end slip."

Jordan paced up and down the dock for an hour before she heard John yell. "Meet us in the canal!" She ran to help John tie the boat to the dock.

"The boat was stuck in some fallen trees along the riverbank. It seems that when the boat ran out of gas, the thieves abandoned it. The boat is in good condition other than just a few minor scratches. I can buff those out." He smiled and squeezed her hand.

Later that afternoon, John locked the boat in one of the service bays. Jordan ran her hand down the side of the boat and thought whatever possessed her to think she could run a boat dealership. She only thought about selling boats, not the many other responsibilities that went along with operating a full boat dealership.

Chapter 20

Miami

The stolen boat had made the headlines in the *Daytona Beach News Journal* and the *Orlando Sentinel* newspaper. She thought it was curiosity that brought more people into her dealership although she did have a few viable buyers from the article.

One man came into her dealership with a scowl on his face. He snapped, "I want to hear the engine on the boat that's for sale in the canal."

"I have a contract with sellers that prevent me from cranking sellers' boats without a written offer. Otherwise, I would be cranking boats all day using the owners' gas."

"I'm not going through all the paperwork to find out I don't like the boat." His voice was harsh and indignant.

She didn't want to lose a sale for an owner over not turning the ignition key. She cranked the boat. His voice was still harsh along with a sinister glare. "I just wanted to see if you knew how to crank a boat."

He stepped off the boat and went to his car. She watched his red taillights disappear on Highway 415. After the obnoxious man left, she walked down the dock to find the man that had been patiently waiting for her help.

"Sir, I'm Jordan. What can I do for you?"

"Hi, I'm Wyatt from Daytona. Sorry to hear about your stolen boat."

She nodded, "I'm glad it ended well." Then she smiled at him.

"I want a 50-foot trawler with diesel engines."

"Why did you come to me? The boat you're looking for is a saltwater boat, not one you'd find here on the river."

"All the local boating world is impressed with you and your boats. They say you're honest and trustworthy. I watched you for several years at the Daytona Boat Show. You're making an honorable reputation for yourself, young lady. I trust you can find me a boat."

She wondered if he was sincere or if he was being a male chauvinist like the man that had just left. She had encountered that male personality many times. Men had been sarcastic, flirty, and some had asked for dates while others asked frivolous questions that even a child could have answered. She decided to give this buyer the benefit of the doubt about buying a trawler.

She replied, "Give me a couple of days and I'll see what I can find. It's probably not going to be in this area."

"I trust you. Wherever you find the boat, I will go. I assure you I'm not wasting your time."

She knew there were lots of trawlers in the Jupiter area. "Scott, I have a buyer that wants a trawler. Do you have one or know of any for sale?"

"Jordan, search in the *Boat Trader* magazine. If you don't find one, call me back and I will try to find one."

She found a trawler with all the specifications the buyer had described. She called the owner to find out if his boat was still for sale.

"My boat is moored on the Miami River. Bring me the buyer, and I'll sea trial it with him. If he buys it, I'll pay you a commission." Jorge sounded very professional, giving her confidence that she could trust him.

The morning after her conversation with Jorge, Jordan picked up Wyatt in Daytona Beach at 7:00 a.m. They were to meet Jorge at his boat at noon. She exited off I-95 one exit before the Orange Bowl. She knew immediately she had exited too soon. She would go around the block and return to I-95.

"Wyatt, why are blue lights flashing behind me? I didn't do anything wrong."

She pulled off the pavement. The police car stopped beside her. The officer motioned for her to roll down her window. "You're in the wrong neighborhood. Don't get out of your car. Follow me until I stop. I can't emphasize enough do not stop until I stop." His voice was strong and stern.

She rolled up her window and followed the officer. "Wyatt, was that gunshots?"

In a soft voice, Wyatt answered. "Sounded like it."

Three blocks later, the policeman flashed his blue lights again. He motioned for a big front-end loader to move off the road. Jordan and the policeman zig-zagged around the torn-up pavement. Two blocks farther, the policeman made a left turn. Her heart was beating faster than the music on the radio.

"Wyatt, where is he taking us?" I don't think I-95 is this way." Wyatt didn't answer. He continued to sit frozen.

The policeman made one more turn to the right and stopped at the bottom of the I-95 ramp. He walked back to her car. "Miss, you were in the wrong neighborhood. There are shootings here every night and day. I needed to get you out of there as quickly as possible. You're okay now."

She didn't understand. This was Florida, her state, she thought she was safe anywhere during the day. She took a deep breath. "I'm going to Waterside Marina on the Miami River. The moment I exited I knew it was wrong."

He waved her on. "Take the next exit. You'll be fine."

Wyatt glanced at her out of the corner of his eye. "I've never seen anyone be so calm with shots being fired."

She smiled, "You don't know me."

After the sea trial, Wyatt signed the contract with Jorge. He smiled and shook Jordan's hand. "I had faith in you. I knew you would find me the right boat."

Wyatt stayed with the boat until his friend could fly down from Daytona to Miami to help him sail the boat back to Daytona Beach.

On the way home, Jordan decided she wasn't going to tell John about taking the wrong exit. He would never let her go anywhere again without him.

Chapter 21

Houseboat Repossession

Jordan's phone rang at 2:00 a.m. the morning after she returned from Miami. A man from Floor Plan Services was requesting her to meet him at Marina 415. Jordan didn't call John. Instead, she called Sam to meet her.

Floor Plan Services was repossessing River Johns Houseboat Rentals from another marina for six months of delinquent mortgage payments. The owner had been dodging the FPS repo person for four months. The rep was known for being a bloodhound, and the owner never expected him to be at his house at 1:00 a.m. with the sheriff. Jordan's dealership was three miles up the river, and since she was FPS's customer, he wanted her to store the houseboats.

The rep from FPS reminded her of the Harvey Specter character on the television series *Suits*. He had been drinking coffee all night and was bouncing off the ground and the sky. He had fifteen men with him ready to deliver fifty-five 36-foot houseboats by water to Marina 415.

Jordan and Sam tied as many boats as they could in the canal. She and "Harvey" started moving boats to help speed up the process, while Sam became the traffic director telling everyone where to dock the boats. They rafted the remaining boats together side by side behind the boat slips on the river.

She called John at 5:00 a.m. to give him the short version of the night's repo boats. She was retrieving more ropes from the service bay area when she heard gravel crunch behind her.

She turned. "Oh, John, I'm glad you're here. Sorry to call you so early." She stood still and eyed him up and down. "Hey, I like those tight jeans." She gave him a wink. "Not your usual uniform though. Why are you not wearing your khaki shorts?" Her smile was automatic.

"Wasn't sure what I was going to be involved in. Randy is going to handle the service customers today."

Sam forklifted the boats from the canal to the ground behind the service bays. John moved the boats off the river to the canal. Jordan crawled through each boat with a pad and pencil to see what needed to be done to get them ready to sell. In one of the boats, a spider-web caught her face, when she pulled the fine silk away, she ran into another one. She looked like she was swatting air when John walked in.

"What are you doing?"

"Spider-webs."

He picked the rest of the silk from her hair. He pulled her next to him. "You're a mess, but beautiful." His chest moved under her cheek. Her tired body collapsed against him. He gently released her when Randy called his name.

Midafternoon, she moved the last boat from the river to the canal for Sam to haul it out. She pressed her fingertips to the sudden throb between her eyebrows. It was 2:00 p.m., she was tired and hungry. She had been on her feet since 2:00 a.m.

Jordan stepped off the boat, her foot slipped on the muddy bank. She grabbed the boat railing with one hand but not quick enough to keep her feet out of the water. She closed her eyes trying to concentrate on holding onto the railing. Sam saw her dangling off the side of the boat. He hurried towards her but couldn't rescue her before she slipped waist-deep in the water.

"Thank you for pulling me out. That's what happens when you hurry and get careless."

"No, that's what happens when you're tired and hungry. Let's go to lunch."

"I have to shower first." Again, she was glad Sam had insisted on a shower in the bathroom.

After lunch, she saw Rick, her investor friend, walking down the dock. She ran to meet him. "What are you doing here? I haven't seen you since the Daytona Beach show. Don't tell me you want to buy a houseboat?"

"No, just curious. The buzz in town piqued my curiosity, I came to see what was going on. Plus, it gave me an excuse to be with you."

She ran her hand through her hair. "You wouldn't have wanted to see me earlier all covered in river mud."

He smiled. "You would look good in anything, even river mud."

John walked by and scowled.

"What's his problem?"

"Nothing. Sam and I have been here since 2:00 a.m., and John has been here since five. We're all tired."

They walked across the marina to the houseboats. "How's Theresa?"

He frowned. "You didn't hear? Theresa and I divorced."

"Rick, I'm sorry. That must have been hard to deal with." She gave him a slight smile. "Are you sure you're not interested in buying a houseboat?"

"No, I haven't had time to come out until now."

She pointed to the houseboats. "Look around. Let me know if you need anything. I've got to get back to work."

He gave her a wink. "Maybe we can have lunch one day."

She glanced back at him. "Maybe."

She knew what was what. Rick was one of the most prominent businessmen in town, and he just didn't come to see what was going on. He was divorced and wanted something. She didn't have time to analyze the whole situation now, but he was looking in the wrong place if he thought it was her.

"Harvey" lumbered into Jordan's office. "Thank you for letting me bring the boats here. I need you to sign the paperwork stating St. Johns River Yachts has the right to sell the boats for compensation.

Sam has already signed his papers for the boats to be placed on his property."

She signed and handed the paper back to him. "It's been nice meeting you. I hope your next job is better."

"Me too, but all my days aren't like this one."

The river was buzzing about the multitude of houseboats at St. Johns River Yachts. People came from a hundred miles away thinking the repossessed boats were going to be sold like a fire sale. FPS had given her their bottom line and the leeway to negotiate between her price and theirs.

Some buyers were buying the boats "as is." Others wanted new outboards and others wanted to make the boats look like new by refurbishing the entire inside. John ordered outboard engines by the dozen. Two engines per boat on fifty-five boats was a lot, even taking into consideration that not every buyer wanted to replace the engines. Jordan and John made sure the buyers knew which waters they were boating in and how to flush the lower units with fresh water to remove any salt residue. John didn't want the engines back in for repair work due to neglect and corrosion.

Jordan watched the sea of people moving in and out of the boats like ants. On one side of the marina, two men were in a heated confrontation over one boat.

"John, this is insanity. We need to organize the hull numbers, the rental company's numbers, engine numbers, and work order numbers into one. All the boats look alike, and all these different numbers are driving me crazy. Tape the work order number in the same place on each boat and on the engine cowling. People are going to have to wait until we get organized. We're not going to run ourselves into the ground trying to please everyone at the same time."

After seven weeks of dealing with customers and houseboats, the marina grounds were empty, and the chaos had subsided. It was good to be back to what seemed normal. At least she thought it was normal until a buyer came in on Friday morning raging at John because his houseboat had sunk.

"You signed the contract that the boat was being sold as-is and that it was a repo. There were no warranties with these boats and the boat was floating when it left here."

He yelled. "I'll sue!"

John placed his hands firmly on the counter. "Go ahead. We have your signed contract."

Jordan came out of her office. John quickly motioned her to back away. After the man left, John joined her in her office. "You have been through enough with these boats. And I wasn't going to let you be bullied by an irate buyer."

She laughed. "Thank you, but I could have handled him."

He squinted his eyes "I know. The point is you shouldn't have had to. I'm here." Then he smiled.

She would think long and hard before she agreed to take on another major repo. She never had a dull moment dealing with people, and each problem and adventure made her more confident and stronger both in her work and herself.

Chapter 22

Blue Springs

Midday, two days after all the madness with the repo boats, John gently tugged on Jordan's arm. "Come with me and don't ask any questions."

"What are you doing?"

"You'll see. I said don't ask questions."

He led her down the dock. "We're going on the river."

She backed away. "No, I don't have time."

"We're making time after having to deal with all those houseboats."

John stepped into his bass boat then reached for her hand. Reluctantly, she stepped in.

"Where are we going?"

"Shhhhhhhh."

Jordan sat quietly taking in all the beauty of the river that she loved so much. Lily pads with their white blooms swayed in the lazy current at the water's edge of the big green manicured lawns that belonged to the mansions above the river. The trees along the shoreline bent their limbs to let their leaves touch the water as if they were taking a drink. The river always gave the first glimpse of fall and the first buds of spring. Around each crooked turn, boaters waved to one another while some stopped on the banks for picnics and others stopped to play at the water's edge. On the weekends, the river was a great getaway for people to leave their everyday grind behind and for those that worked in the concrete and asphalt jungle Monday through Friday. Now she knew what John was doing, he was making this day her getaway break. She glanced at him, gave him a big smile, and patted his shoulder. He returned an even bigger familiar smile that warmed her heart.

"You're beautiful with the river glistening in the background and the breeze blowing through your hair. The sun is casting amber highlights around you."

He pulled his boat onto the beach at Blue Springs State Park.

"What are we doing here?"

"You'll see. It's lunchtime. We're allowed a lunch break, right?"

He brought the cooler from the back of the boat up the hill to a flat shady area. She followed close behind until they reached a picnic table.

Jordan stopped to take in all the familiar surroundings. "When Matt was little, we came here all the time to swim in the springs, picnic, and watch the manatees."

"You said the other day you missed being on the river. We work here. We can enjoy it too, and *casual* relationships are about enjoying the moment."

She caught how he emphasized casual. "Have you been here any-time from November to March? The manatees come to the springs for warmth. I love swimming here in the winter months when the air temperature is colder than seventy-two degrees and the springs feel like bathwater. Years ago, people could swim with the big gray sea cows before the environmentalists banned swimmers when the manatees were present. I loved to watch the docile mammals nibble on the vegetation along the edge of the water. There's also a wooded four-and-half-mile Pine Island Trail that winds around the springs and through the woods."

John handed her a sandwich and a drink from the cooler. "Now, are you going to yell at me?"

"No, this is very nice. I won't balk. Thank you, but you know we can't stay long. Next trip we'll take the Pine Island Trail."

He lowered his head and reached for her hand. "Jordan, you know I'm in love with you."

She gazed out over the river. She didn't allow herself any eye contact with him. "John. I can't give you anything in return. St. John's River Yachts consumes me."

"Jordan, I watch you every day handle situations that most men would run from."

"Now the truth comes out. You're not in love with me. You're in love with my stamina. It's time to head back." She winked and smiled.

On the way back to the marina, John passed a fuel barge. The barges run from the storage tanks in Jacksonville south to the power plant in Sanford every five days.

Jokingly, Jordan said, "I hope the bridge tender is awake today."

She leaned over and gave John a light kiss on his cheek. "Thank you for lunch."

He gave her hand a light squeeze. "You deserved it."

They had been back at the marina thirty minutes when Jordan heard the barge captain blow his horn for the bridge to open. Ten minutes after the first sound of the horn, the barge captain was blowing the horn constantly. She ran to get John, they collided coming through the service bay door. He grabbed her to keep her from falling.

"John, the bridge tender isn't opening the bridge."

"I know, he must be asleep. I'm going to get my boat. Maybe I can get to him in time."

She saw John get out of his boat at the bridge. There was no way the tender had time to open the bridge now.

Barges need a mile to come to a complete stop, and the barge was already around the bend with less than a mile to the bridge. This would be the second time a barge had been lodged under the bridge since she opened her business.

The captain tried to stop the barge by ramming the right side of the barge into the bank before the bridge. John woke the bridge tender as the tug's wheelhouse came to rest against the bridge. Jordan knew the bridge could be closed for days while the Corp of Engineers removed the lodged barge and the DOT crews inspected the bridge for any structural damage.

Jordan met John down at the canal. "The bridge tender explained to the sheriff and the DOT superintendent that he had pulled a double shift. DOT didn't fire him. When his replacement arrives, he will be dismissed for the day."

"I feel for the tender, but the captain and people traveling across the bridge could have been hurt."

She thought about how many accidents there had been with the barges over the years with the boaters and water-skiers not paying attention coming around the bends in the river. Several water-skiers had been killed whiplashing around a blind curve and encountering a barge trying to maneuver a tight twist in the river. No one thinks about the calm, unsuspecting river being dangerous.

Chapter 23

John's Broken Foot

It was after five o'clock when Jordan heard an excruciating scream. She ran to the service bay. John was lying on the floor.

Randy rushed past her. "I need to get ice."

"What happened?" He kept running.

She knelt next to John. His eyes blinked and started to roll upward under his thick, dark lashes.

Jordan yelled, "John, stay with me!"

She rolled up the sleeves of her white shirt and wiped his eyes with her shirttail. She raised his head to her lap.

Randy handed her a cold wet cloth. "I've called 911."

John opened his eyes. She stared at him through her haze of tears. "John, what happened?"

"I jumped off the swim platform. I guess I landed wrong. My foot hurts the worst. I don't know if I've broken my leg, my ankle, or my foot. I hurt all over."

She couldn't fathom his pain. She tried to keep him still until the ambulance arrived.

"Randy, will you lock up for the night?"

On the way to the hospital, Jordan called Lisa, John's ex-wife. After a three-hour surgery, the surgeon said to Jordan and Lisa, "I don't know how well his foot will heal. The x-rays showed the ankle was broken where it joins the foot, and the impact crushed the bone on top of the foot. I have put steel bolts and pins in his ankle. I'm going to keep him sedated tonight. He will be in pain a few days, and he's going to be in a cast for ten weeks."

Lisa turned to Jordan. "Thanks for calling me. He's still living in our house. I'll come and stay with him."

Jordan took Lisa's hand. "If you or he needs anything at all, call me."

Early the next morning, Jordan was at the hospital. She gasped a deep breath and steeled herself before she pushed his door open. His eyes were closed. She quietly pulled a chair next to his bed. His face was hard and wrinkled, and his eyes were encased with dark circles. His deep frown lines showed his pain, frustration, and tiredness.

John moaned and opened his eyes. She took a wet cloth and softly rubbed his face. He frowned. "I have jumped off swim platforms hundreds of times and never gave a thought about getting hurt. I'm sorry. I shouldn't have done this to you."

"You haven't done anything to me. You're the one hurt."

She wanted to crawl up next to him, hold him close, and reassure him everything was going to be all right. Instead, she laid a hand on his warm arm. She could feel life beneath her fingers through his stillness.

"This was a freak accident. You're going to be fine."

She wished she really did believe that.

"Now is not the time for you to think about work. I can hire someone temporarily to help Randy."

"No, I can direct Randy from home by phone."

The ajar door opened with authority. The doctor kept his eyes on John's chart. "Good morning. You've had a very bad break. It's going to take at least three months to heal. I don't think your foot and ankle will ever be the same. You can't go back to work until your foot has completely healed." He looked up from the chart and gave John a slight smile. "I'm letting you go home today. The discharge nurse will be in shortly."

They both stared at the back of his white coat as he retreated into the hallway.

She laid her head on his chest and held him tight for a few minutes. He patted and stroked her hair. When she raised her head, she saw his tear-streaked cheeks.

"I'm mad with myself for allowing this to happen."

She tried to calm him, but this was his battle, and he was going to have to fight it on his own.

She couldn't stop her flow of tears in the elevator. She was helpless. On the way to the marina, she knew he was in pain, and blamed himself.

Two weeks later, John and Lisa walked into her office.

"What are you doing here?"

"I can't sit at home."

"You can't do anything here on crutches but sit and bark orders." Then she gave him a wink.

"It makes me feel better to bark."

All three of them laughed and the tension eased, but she knew she had lost the battle.

"I didn't know I was going to be out for three months, so, I called Jib to come this weekend. You can meet him and make a decision about hiring him."

"Do you think we need him?"

"Randy's good, but Jib works like I do. He's fast and accurate and can assess a problem as quickly as I can."

"This is your decision. You know the service department is yours."

John was methodical. She had always been drawn to his honesty and the way he could calm an irate customer. Especially when the customer came in with a dead battery and then came back with a bent prop and accused the service department. She was fascinated by how John could listen to an engine and make a correct diagnosis. His work never came back for the same problem.

"I'm curious, tell me about Jib. If he is as good as you, then how can he leave his job and come here?"

"He owes me. He's going through a divorce, and he wants to get out of Ft. Lauderdale for a while. We worked together for years. We used to race changing engine oil. He would be faster some days and I would be faster others. If you tallied all the oil changes we did, we were probably even. You know the engine rep told you I was the number two marine mechanic in the state, well Jib is number one. I've already talked to him. He's going to stay with me."

Jib, a large husky man, with a full, plump face, arrived two days later. His hazel eyes had a piercing gaze, his voice was mellow, and his handshake was strong. He had narrow eyes and a sharp, pointed nose that matched his pointed chin. She wasn't sure she would've hired him if he had applied for the mechanic's job. She surmised from their conversation he was arrogant and pompous, and his attitude was cocky. He gave her the impression it was his way or no way. She wasn't sure she trusted him to be reliable, but John trusted him, and she would never intentionally disappoint John.

Jordan and John walked Jib through the service bays. John and Jib joked and carried on like long-lost brothers. She found out Jib was the one who introduced John to Lisa and was his best man at their wedding.

After a tour around the marina, Jordan confronted him. "Jib, do you think you could work for me? I don't interfere with the service work, but I do run the business. If you think you can work for me, you have the job until John returns full time."

"Yes, and by the time John returns, I'll be ready to go back to Ft. Lauderdale."

She saw the light in John's eyes and knew he was pleased.

John occasionally came in during the three months to work a few half days. Randy looked relieved that he didn't have to carry the full responsibility of the service area. Randy and Jib worked well together. On the days' John came in Jordan could hear them laughing and goading each other. She almost wished she could keep Jib.

After John's cast was removed, he walked with a cane, and his ankle and foot were still swollen. His foot wouldn't have any flexibility even after the swelling went down. For the time being, she was his mechanic's helper again.

Chapter 24

Captain's Death

J ordan walked into the parts room at 7:30 a.m. Tuesday morning,
Will pointed to the phone. "The oldest boat manufacturer in the
United States is still calling you. Are you going to take on their
boat line?"

"I don't know. I don't want more boats on my floor plan. I keep
delaying meeting with him. Tell him I'll call him back later."

She returned David's call around mid-morning and agreed to
meet with him at 8:00 a.m. the next morning.

"Hi, David, good to see you." She greeted him with indifference
as she unlocked the showroom door. "You're here early. Did you have
a pleasant drive up from Sarasota?"

"Yes, I came over late yesterday and toured your boats. Just want
you to know our boat line won't conflict with the boats you already
carry if that's your hesitation for not taking our boats."

She smiled. "I'm flattered that you have offered me this opportunity. My hesitation is that I'm not sure I want to take on another
line."

"You know our fishing boats are open console and range from
20 to 36 feet, our runabouts are 18 to 22 feet, and our luxury yachts
are 40 feet to 60 feet. We'll give you six months free floor plan with
FPS."

"Yes, I know all that. We discussed all of it on the phone yesterday, and it does sound like a good offer. Give me a few days to think about it."

He turned around when he opened his car door. "Don't think too hard or wait too long. There are other dealers close by that are begging for our boats, but you are the only dealer on the water."

After David left, she called her friend in Jupiter, "Scott, I don't know that I want more boats."

"I know you can sell them." She heard his enthusiasm. "The boat name is well known. They almost sell themselves. I wish I could get them, but they already have a dealer close to me. You're a good negotiator. Since they came to you, I'd put the pressure on them for a better deal."

Two days later, David was back at her dealership. He sighed heavily. "Jordan, you drive a hard bargain. I'll give you free freight and a year's free floor plan if that will make you take my boats."

Her eyes danced when she told John about her conversation with David. "I couldn't help myself, I ordered one of every center console fishing boat from 20 to 26 feet and a 39-foot open back deck fishing boat with a fighting chair. The best one is the 42-foot luxury yacht. The 42 and 39 footers have Caterpillar diesel engines."

John grinned. "You know, I've been to Caterpillar school. I'm certified in diesel engines."

She wrinkled her forehead. "No, I didn't know. Why did you leave that off your resume?"

"I didn't think it mattered. There are not many diesel engines on the river."

She felt at that moment, there wasn't anything he couldn't do. A warm jolt ran from her toes to the top of her head. Every time she was around him, she learned about another piece of his life. He was like a complex puzzle.

The new boat line stretched her territory from Orlando to Atlanta. The news traveled up the river grapevine faster than lightning.

A new marina owner in Daytona Beach heard about Jordan's new boats. "I know you're expanding your boat line to yachts. I need some large boats in my slips. I'll give you slip rent for half price if you help me."

"Why should I move some of my boats to your marina when I have free slip rent here?"

"I'm a new marina, and I need the exposure of new and bigger boats to attract boat owners with large boats. You know, supply and demand. If the boat owners think the marina is filling up, they'll rent my slips."

"If you want me there, you'll have to negotiate harder. I'll have more expense with boats over there. My mechanic and cleaning crew will have to go over at least once a week to check out the boats."

"I heard you were tough, but I want you here. I'll give you free slip rent with the understanding you have to keep your boats here until I can rent the slips."

"I'll keep the boats there until I sell them."

She agreed to put the 39-foot fishing boat and the 42-foot motor yacht in his marina. She knew there wasn't a market for those boats on the St. Johns River.

Zeke, a certified boat captain, and owner of a 42-foot motor yacht, that was docked in front of her office, heard she had ordered the exact same boat as his and she was going to dock it in Daytona Beach.

"Jordan, I'll bring the boat from North Carolina to Daytona for you. You can show my boat to any potential buyer. It will be a lot easier than you traveling back and forth to Daytona.

"Zeke, I negotiated free freight with the factory. I'll let them know you are willing to deliver the boat."

The week after Zeke returned with her boat from North Carolina, he spent the entire day cleaning his boat inside and out. He even polished the stainless-steel railing. He bought boat soap, wax, and other cleaning supplies in Jordan's ship's store. He took breaks with the mechanics and had lunch with her and John. He told them about the boat and the trip down the intercoastal waterway.

At the close of her day, she walked down to Zeke's boat. "I'm leaving for the night. Is there anything you need before I go?"

"No, I'm fine. I'm not going to be here much longer. I have a few things left to do, then I am going home."

Zeke's wife called Jordan around 9:00 p.m. "Did you see Zeke today?"

"Yes, I saw him right before I left at six. He was on the bow of his boat getting ready to leave."

"He's not home, and he's not answering his phone."

Jordan glanced at the time. Zeke lived two counties away; he should have been home hours ago. "I'll go to the marina and check on him."

His cleaning supplies were on the deck of the boat where she had last seen him. "Zeke! Zeke! Where are you?"

No answer. She stepped on board. "Zeke!" She walked around the boat. There was no sign of him anywhere. The darkness and the quietness gave her an eerie feeling. She rubbed away the goosebumps that crawled over her skin. She jumped when the cabin door smacked shut. She heard a horrified gasp in the silence. It took her a moment before she realized that she'd made the sound and it was the wind that had slammed the cabin door.

"Hello! Zeke, are you here?"

Still no reply.

The mooring lines pulled tautly and then relaxed, giving the boat a creaking and groaning sound. The wind had shifted to the southeast making the waves change direction. Now the water was slapping against the hull of the boat, making a loud flat echoing sound.

A deputy responding to the 911 call from Zeke's wife parked in front of his boat.

Jordan waved her to the dock. "I've looked everywhere for him."

The deputy covered the same steps in her search that Jordan had made. "Have you looked in the water?"

Jordan whispered. "I couldn't see anything."

Not only was the water dark from the pitch-black night and no moon, but the water looked even darker from the tannic acid produced by all the tree leaves along the riverbank. Even with the deputy's flashlight, they couldn't see past the shimmering reflections off the water. She and the deputy were standing on the swim platform discussing all the possibilities of what might have happened to Zeke when they heard a splash in the water. The deputy screamed, then Jordan screamed.

"What was that?" The flashlight in the deputy's hand shook.

"A bullfrog jumped off the swim platform."

She knew the deputy was as frightened as she was. They concluded that Zeke must be in the water. A head-to-toe shiver ran over Jordan's body. At that moment, there was a sense of foreboding they both shared.

"Do you know anything about the river?

The deputy whispered. "No."

"It's infested with alligators and snakes. If he fell in, he's probably on the bottom."

The deputy looked over the side of the boat into the water. "I had the same thoughts but, I didn't want to say anything."

After an hour of futile searching, the deputy called the sheriff's dive team. They assessed the situation and decided they had to wait until daylight to search the water.

Jordan arrived at the dealership at 7:00 a.m. to see Zeke's body shape lying on the dock under a white sheet. The dive team was standing with their thumbs and fingers braced in their in their-rolled-down wetsuits waiting for the coroner.

The master diver's lips were pursed in a way that deepened the dimple in his chin. "We found him between his boat and the dock. He has a cut on his forehead. We think he slipped off the dock or the swim platform and hit his head. The mud is so soft on the river bottom he had sunk in up to his waist. He couldn't have gotten free, even if he was conscious."

The muscles in her neck tightened. She couldn't believe it had only been thirteen hours earlier that they were laughing and talking with one another. Now, this healthy man lay lifeless on the dock, his life had gone cold and no longer existed. Jordan stood quietly, then felt her warm tears fall onto her shirt.

Chapter 25

Wisconsin Dealer Meeting

Wednesday afternoon, Jordan and John attended Zeke's funeral. It was hard for her to see Zeke's boat everyday docked outside her office window, but life on the river kept its own rhythm and flow.

Jordan's new boat lines and extended territory forced her to enter every boat show from Jacksonville south to Melbourne on the east coast, Ocala to Lakeland in the middle of the state, and Tampa on the west coast.

John had helped her sketch out the floor plan layouts, where each boat would be placed in her space to give the buyers' optimum viewing. John and Randy made and ordered ramps and stairs for easy access into all the boats. The warm weather and summer vacations had brought her sales to a record high.

Her overhead was $25,000 a month before she could show a profit. That figure included payroll, floor plan, insurance, rent, taxes, utilities, truck payments, and any parts she needed to restock. The majority of her profit had to go back into the business to cover any unknown slippery slope in the future. So far, she had been able to cover her expenses, although in the back of her mind there was always the fear of running short during the slow months.

She had procured a line of credit at the local bank as a back-up plan, which she had never used. She wouldn't have to use it this year either with her summer this profitable. This gave her enough in reserve to carry her through March. Scott had borrowed money from her several times to get him through his slow months. She didn't understand why he came up short. He had been in the business a lot longer than she, and he should've been prepared for his slow periods.

She had been back to Wisconsin to the manufacturer's dealer meeting every year, and it always surprised her how everyone had remembered her first year there with her missing luggage fiasco. She had ordered a couple of boats earlier that were underpowered. She wasn't going to make that mistake again. This time John went with her to run the boats and get the feel of the hulls and engines together. From the airport to the hotel, John was in awe at all the cheese shops. He was acting like a little boy wanting candy. She promised him they would buy Wisconsin cheese to take back to Florida.

After lunch, Tom congratulated her. "Jordan, you've worked hard and smart and have a proven track record. I've talked to FPS and we feel you can stand on your own. I'm not co-signing on your floor plan any longer."

"Thank you for the compliment." She shook his hand hard.

Scott placed his hand on her shoulder. "I knew you would be a success."

The good-byes after the meeting extended longer than she had planned. On the way to the airport, she made John take a detour to her favorite cheese shop.

"We don't have time. We're going to miss our flight."

"I promised you cheese and we're buying cheese."

She flew through the cheese shop, throwing aged, soft, hard, and flavored cheeses into the basket, while John did taste tests. He dropped her off at the front of the terminal before he returned the rental car. She ran as fast as she could to the boarding gate.

The attendant had called for the last boarding. "You have to board now. If you don't, I am going to close the door."

"My partner is on his way."

The attendant exerted her authority. "You get on now or you'll have to take another flight."

John arrived when she was removing her hand from the closed door, but she refused to let them board.

"I told you we shouldn't have stopped for cheese."

"The cheese subject is closed. You've done so much for me, and you never ask for anything in return. The least I could do was buy you some cheese."

"If I hadn't asked about the cheese, we would've made the flight. It was my fault, not yours."

"We made a joint decision. We can fly home tomorrow."

The next day, back at the dealership, she placed a cheese tray with all the cheese selections in front of her employees and laughed. "If you don't like the cheese, you better not say a word."

They had no idea what she meant, but John did. When she added the cost of the changed flight tickets and two hotel rooms, it was some of the most expensive cheeses she had ever eaten.

Chapter 26

Cozumel

The last week in August, Jim Knight, whom she had sold the 26-foot boat to in New Smyrna Beach, called. "Mary and I would like to talk to you. Do you have time in the morning?" His voice sounded weak and tired.

"Sure, how about ten, and then I'll take you and Mary to lunch."

Jordan still didn't understand why people had told her when she started her business that friendships didn't belong in business. They were wrong. Her passion for her business and her honesty had proven customers could be her friends.

Tuesday morning, Mary sat quietly while Jim told her about his lung cancer and surviving with one lung. "As you know, I never drove the boat. I don't have the strength. I was thinking I could handle a smaller boat."

Now it all made sense why he didn't drive the boat the day she delivered it to his house and why he called her occasionally on Sundays to come and spend the day with them on the boat.

"Well, I have a 24-foot, 8-foot beam, single engine with almost the same amenities as your 26."

John sea trialed the boat with Jim. Jordan and Mary walked to the end of the dock to see if Jim could pull it into the slip. Mary turned to Jordan. "I think Jim can handle this one."

Jim and Mary signed the bill of sale. Jordan stood and pointed to the door. "Are you ready for lunch?"

After the waiter took their order, Jim reached for Mary's hand. "I can't thank you enough for all you've done for us. Whenever we called and asked you to come and spend Sundays with us so we could go out in the boat, you always came. We were also glad when Matt came with you. I learned after I retired how unpredictable life could be. We want to do something special for you and Matt. Will you let us take you to Cozumel?"

Jim smiled when he saw the surprised expression on her face. "I'll ask Matt if he wants to go and let you know. I can't go until October when my sales slow down. Would that work for y'all?"

Jim and Mary smiled at each other. "October will be fine with us."

John followed Jim and Mary home with the new boat, then brought the 26-footer back for consignment.

On October 15th, Jim, Mary, Jordan, and Matt flew to Cozumel. The company that had hired Matt the month before graduation had downsized. Jobs were scarce, and Jordan thought the Cozumel trip would help Matt's view on life.

The four of them entered the hotel lobby. The thatched roof and open beams let gentle tropical breezes blow through, eliminating air-conditioning. Colorful parrots talked and squawked on their uncaged swings that hung from the ceiling beams. Laughter echoed from the large kidney-shaped swimming pool across from the lobby check-in desk. The three young women that sat on the bar stools in the pool were being splashed by their male companions.

After Mary and Jordan checked in, they waited on the bright flowered sofas for Jim and Matt to bring their drinks.

Their suites had a large balcony with a swing hammock that overlooked the Gulf of Mexico. Jordan spent an hour watching and listening to the waves lapping along the shoreline making a symphony of their own. Her thoughts of how she arrived at this place in her life brought happy memories and how the river had given her peace.

At 6:00 p.m., she and Matt met Mary and John in the lobby. John announced, "I want authentic Mexican food."

Mary glanced down the street. "I didn't know all the restaurants and shops were within walking distance of our hotel. There are so many people out this time of night."

The streets were bustling with small children, teenagers, and shoppers. The shops were closed every day from two to four for siesta time then stayed open until midnight. After dinner, they joined in the hustle and bustle with the other shoppers.

Unfortunately, Matt felt ill. He went back to the hotel. The next morning Matt still was down with Montezuma's revenge. "I don't know how I got this."

"I'm not sure," Jordan replied. "It may have been the melted ice in the drinks."

Matt was down for the count. Mary and Jordan spent the day shopping, and Jim spent the day in a hammock under a palm tree on the beach.

Jordan and Mary stood at the fudge shop window to watch a confectioner pour hot fudge on a large marble slab.

Mary was intrigued. "Let's go in for some samples."

They both agreed that the chocolates at Kakao Chocolates Darnarsicheli shop were the second-best to the chocolates in St. Kitts.

The kite shop next to the fudge shop was filled with elaborate kites, a favorite to both locals and tourists. Behind the kite shop, she and Mary watched the afternoon sky filled with the multicolored kites in all shapes and sizes imaginable. Children, as well as adults, were running up and down the beach with the colorful kites, seeing who could make them fly the highest in the gulf breezes over the high waves.

Jordan and Mary ordered a glass of wine from the wine tasting bar next to the kite shop. They took a seat on the back patio overlooking the gulf. They sat in silence watching the waves scatter seashells along the shoreline and the white sea foam washed over them like they were small pebbles. The fall breezes pushed lazy puffy white clouds across the horizon, making a background for all the colorful kites that rose and dipped with the wind. Mary and Jordan sat for over an hour letting the peace of it all settled over them.

They continued their walk down the main street. They passed a Diamonds International shop, Jordan pointed to the display window. "Did you know DI will give you a bracelet if you ask for their free charm? I don't have one from Cozumel. I have charms from every place I've been where there's a DI shop. I have a monkey from St. Kitts, a cruise ship from Nassau, a conch shell from St. Thomas, and a clock tower from Disney World, to name a few. Look the Cozumel charm is a sombrero."

Jordan heard the shrill in Mary's voice. "Can I get one?"

The sales clerk handed Mary a bracelet and secured a sombrero charm. After the DI shop, they returned to the hotel.

The third day, Jim rented an open four-wheel jeep. All four of them climbed in to explore the island. A couple of miles out of town they were in the desert. Everything was barren. It reminded Jordan of a planet from outer space. The flat ground was covered in lava rock and black sand with only a few cacti growing here and there. After thirty minutes of driving around in no man's land, the jeep died. Jim banged his fist on the steering wheel.

"We're out of gas."

Jordan laughed. "You're kidding."

Matt looked behind them. "I hear music."

The music became louder and louder. A carload of locals pulled up beside them in an old red Cadillac with the vinyl top in shreds. Jordan moved close to Matt and grabbed his hand.

Several of them talked all at one time in Spanish. One man got out of the car, opened the trunk, and took out a rusted gas can. His English was broken, but his smile was big. After he had put gas in the jeep, Jim handed him twenty dollars, but he refused.

Jim stopped the jeep on the top of the next high hill. They were out of the desert and back on their side of the island. As far as they could see there were lush mountains, small towns in the valleys, and the brown beaches were full of sunbathers.

After returning to civilization, Jordan reflected on the episode, wondering how one island could look like two different planets. "Why couldn't we have run out of gas on this side of the island? Not much scares me, but when the carload of locals pulled up beside us in that old Cadillac, I was scared. I just knew we were going to be robbed or killed in the middle of nowhere and no one would know. We could've been there for days before anyone found us."

Matt stared at his mom. "I've never heard you talk this way. You must've been scared."

Jim chimed in, "I was glad one of them could speak English, or we might still be there."

"The only other time that I can remember being this scared was when I took a wrong exit in Miami. I ended up in a neighborhood hearing what I thought were gunshots. I was lucky that a policeman saw me and led me back to I-95."

Matt's eyes widened. "You never told me you got lost in Miami."

Jordan laughed. "It was better you didn't know at the time."

Then Jim laughed. "I'm just glad they had an old gas can with some gas in it."

"I thought boating around in the Bahamas on empty trying to find a marina that had gas was bad." Jordan tapped Jim on the shoulder. "At least I was able to pull into the Hope Town dock on fumes. However, it was nothing like being there in no man's land."

Between the planet from outer space and the tropical paradise side, there was a hole-in-the-wall roadside taco restaurant. Half the fluorescent lights were out, and the ground was visible under the slatted wood floor. There was a small counter to place an order in front of the kitchen. Behind the structure, a few wooden tables were placed under palm trees.

Jordan scrunched her face. "Do you think it's wise to eat tacos here?"

"Sure, where is your sense of adventure?" Jim replied.

She glanced at Matt. "Not an adventure. I just don't want to get Zuma's Revenge."

Surprisingly, Matt wasn't against stopping. They all ordered tacos.

When the food arrived, Matt bit into his taco and grinned. "I wouldn't have thought a roadside trailer would have the best tacos I have ever eaten."

Jim added additional hot sauce to his tacos. Even after coaching everyone to try the hot sauce, he had no takers. Late afternoon, Jim and Matt dropped Mary and Jordan off at the hotel before they returned the jeep.

"You two need to ask for a refund since the gas gauge is broken," Mary shouted.

When Jim and Matt returned, Jordan and Mary were sitting on the bar stools in the pool drinking Bloody Mary's.

Mary hollered to them, "Go get your swim trunks on, and come join us!"

After several hours at the pool bar, Jim asked for a menu. "I'm hungry."

Mary chimed in. "I want Italian."

Jim leaned against Mary's shoulder. "That's not a good choice. We need to eat Mexican in Mexico." Jim looked over the menu. "I want a fine dining restaurant with white tablecloths."

Matt had met some girls at the pool and elected not to go to dinner. The concierge recommended La Cocay restaurant to Jim and made a reservation for the three of them at seven-thirty.

The surf-and-turf dinners were excellent with a Mediterranean cuisine. The red flowers on the almond trees hung over their table and votive candles were placed in the center of the white tablecloth giving them an ambiance of a formal affair, even though they were seated on the patio.

On their last day, they met on the crowded beach around mid-morning. Children were collecting seashells close to the water's edge, while teenagers played volleyball and sunbathers caught the morning rays. The warm blue-green gulf water enticed Jordan and Mary to sit and let the soft waves rush over their legs while the tropical fish nibbled at their toes. Matt spent the day on the beach with one of the girls he had met the night before. Jordan watched Matt and the girl swim and sit at the gulf's edge as it softly doused the beach and them. Jim was restless. He was everywhere, in and out of the water and the pool and taking naps. During dinner, they all agreed the beach had been the best place to spend their last day.

Jordan gave Jim and Mary a hug. "Thank you for everything."

Laughing, Jim gave Matt a light punch in his stomach. "Good luck, buddy. Go find that job of your dreams."

They said their good-byes at the Orlando Airport.

Chapter 27

Break-In

Sheriffs' cars were parked everywhere when Jordan turned left into Marina 415. She had no idea why they were there, but this wasn't how she wanted to start her week returning from Cozumel.

She parked her car at the service bay. "John, what's going on?"

"I arrived early and found all the outboard engines missing from the open fishing boats, bass boats, and four lower units are gone from the consignment boats. I called the sheriff's department."

The sheriff stared at the ground and kicked the gravel. "There's been a lot of outboards stolen from all the boat dealerships and marinas in the area. We know there's a theft ring operating in Central Florida sending the engines to the Bahamas. We haven't been able to catch them. I'm sorry, but you aren't going to get the engines back. I'll give you a copy of my theft report for you to file with your insurance claim."

The sheriff walked around her dealership like he was inspecting everything, including the marina. He turned to Jordan. "I'd like to dock my boat here. I have a 36-foot houseboat on Lake Harris. The marina there doesn't have a mechanic."

"Sam owns the marina. He's in his office. You need to go over and sign a dockage contract with him."

The sheriff returned to Jordan's office. "I'm having my boat transported over in a couple of days. I want John to do an engine tune-up and give the entire boat an annual inspection."

Jordan gave John the sheriff's work order and left the two of them to finish their conversation.

The way her morning had started, it was midafternoon before Jordan had a chance to give John the sombrero that he had asked for. "Why do you look so surprised?"

"I didn't think you would remember or that it would be too big to carry on the plane."

She winked. "I'd do anything for you."

She saw Sam leaving for the day, she yelled. "Stop!" Sam backed his truck up close to her. "I brought you a Mexican blanket. I thought you might need it this winter when you were on your dragline."

He reached for the blanket and smiled. "Thank you. It is something that I can definitely use."

As usual, everyone on the river knew in a day that the Lake County sheriff's boat was docked on the St. Johns River. The sheriff sat on the stern of his boat every weekend watching the boaters. Even though he wasn't in uniform, it was good to have his presence known. If nothing else, the boaters adhered to the no-wake zone.

After a month, the insurance company had settled all the outboard claims. All the consignment engines had been covered under the owner's insurance policies. John found some used lower units in good condition and installed them for the owners who didn't want to buy new units.

A couple of weeks after the engine theft occurred, a bright yellow VW beetle drove through the marina at fifty miles per hour. Jordan jumped from her desk, ran out the side door, and down the dock to the canal. When the driver reached the dead end, he turned around, doing a semi-wheelie, raced behind the marina office through the service bay area, and out onto Highway 415.

"John, that was strange. Why would a carload of teenagers speed through the marina?"

He shrugged his shoulders. "I don't know. Kids being kids."

Monday morning, Julia, the cleaning lady, ran into Jordan's office. Gasping for breath between each word, she finally blurted out, "All the radios and speakers have been stolen."

It took Jordan a few minutes to understand that all the Bose units had been taken out of all the new boats. John knew immediately the thieves weren't professionals by the way the wires were yanked and stripped.

A squad from the sheriff's department dressed in black crime unit uniforms arrived and dusted all the boats for fingerprints, made tire track molds, and lifted shoe prints. They looked like FBI agents investigating a murder scene.

Jordan said to the sheriff. "A bright yellow VW full of teenagers drove through the marina last week. The only thing I could make out on the tag was Volusia County."

The sheriff took off his cap and rubbed his head. "This was an amateur job. It sounds like the teenagers stole the equipment. I can and will find them."

Two weeks later, the sheriff strolled into Jordan's office. "I found the teenagers. They're four seniors at Pierson High School. They installed all nine speakers and two of the radios in the VW."

She laughed. "Wow, that must be some sound system in that small car. Pierson is thirty miles away. I'm surprised I didn't hear the music blasting all the way to here."

The sheriff strutted his chest. "I walked in the classroom and arrested them. One of the teens asked me how I found them. I told him his bright yellow VW was the only one registered in Volusia County. The tire molds at the marina matched the VW tires, and he was wearing the same tennis shoes that he wore that night." He laughed. "I told them they should've tossed the shoes. The parents have agreed to pay for all new equipment and to discipline their sons. Do you want to press charges?"

"I won't press charges under the condition that they do twenty hours of community service to underprivileged children. Maybe they will understand how lucky they are."

The sheriff scratched his head. "No one knows why the boys decided to steal. They've never been in trouble before, and they have nice homes and their parents have good jobs."

The next week, Jordan read in the newspaper the boys were doing volunteer work at a rescue animal shelter for the rest of the school year.

Jordan helped John and Randy install the stereos and speakers. It was reminiscent of years ago when she was John's helper standing inside the spoilers pulling the electrical wires thru the arches.

The first week of summer vacation, the boys and their parents came to her dealership. One of the boys was the spokesman for the group. "We're sorry. We have no explanation why we did it." Jordan smiled and accepted their apology.

Chapter 28

Drug Run

The September sun woke Jordan bright and early. She tried to go back to sleep but that was a lost cause. She dressed quickly then headed to Wal-Mart to shop for cleaning supplies while waiting for the bank to open to make a deposit. When she entered the service bay, John waved at her. "Is your cell phone off? Scott's been calling here every five minutes."

"That's one of the reasons I am so late. I had to go back home to get my phone."

She hurried to her office to return his call. "Hi, Scott, what's going on?"

"I need your help at the Ft. Lauderdale show. I'm putting four boats in the water this year instead of two. I don't have enough salesmen to cover all six boats. After the show, I'm driving the boats to my second location in Port Salerno. I need your help at the show and then help get them to the marina. I also need John to come on the last day of the show and drive one of the boats."

"I will help you at the show, and if Randy can handle the workload for a couple of days, I know John will."

The show coordinator always tried to get the boats that were traveling the farthest out of the show first. Scott's departure time was scheduled for 9:00 a.m. It was now 3:00 p.m. and his first boat was pulling away from the dock.

John grumbled, "I wouldn't have had to get up at the crack of dawn to fly down if I had known we weren't leaving the show until now."

"It's going to be a long day for all of us." Jordan gave him a pat on the back. "I don't know what happened that has made us start so late."

Scott lined everyone in single file along the shoreline in the intercoastal waterway. His 33-footer was the lead boat with one of his salesmen in a 20-footer behind him. Jordan was in the middle driving a 24-foot boat, and John was bringing up the rear in a 30-footer. The other two boats were being trailered back to Jupiter.

All the bridges open on demand when a boat approaches, but in rush hour times, the bridges open every half hour. They had missed the on-demand time. At the first bridge, they had to wait five minutes. They arrived at the second bridge after it closed. Scott was the only boat that couldn't go under the bridge. He had insisted all the boats stay together. They floundered and idled in circles for thirty minutes, keeping their boats out of the channel to allow the boats that could travel under the bridge to pass.

Jordan pulled next to John. "This is the most disorganized departure I've ever seen. I don't know why Scott didn't talk to the show coordinator."

John listened to her complaining. He had learned over the years it was better to listen and let her have her say than to try and placate her.

The bridge opened, allowing the boats to start in single file up the intercoastal again. Night fell as they arrived at the West Palm Beach inlet along with a soft slow rain. Jordan stopped in the inlet to put up the eisenglass covers to keep her and the inside of the boat dry. John pulled alongside her to help.

"I'm fine. It's only going to take me a few minutes. You need to keep up with the rest of the boats since we don't know where we're going. I'll keep you in my sight and catch up to you."

She saw him glancing back at her while he kept the other boats in his sight. Jordan was running at full speed trying to see John. The rain was now being propelled by the wind. Out of nowhere, blue lights surrounded her from all directions. She watched John disappear into the darkness. He was too far ahead to hear her horn over the roar of his engine. She tried her cell phone, but it was dead. Scott and John had the hand-held radios. New boats like the one she was driving weren't equipped with electronics until they were sold.

The marine sheriff called out to her, "I'm coming aboard."

"No, you're not!" she yelled.

She didn't care if he was the sheriff. She was alone. She wasn't going to let any strange man board her boat even if he was the police. As the captain, it was her right to say who could and could not come aboard.

The sheriff pulled his boat next to hers. She yelled to him. "Why did you stop me?"

"I'm going to search your boat for drugs."

"I'm coming out of the Ft. Lauderdale Boat Show to the Port Salerno Marina. I don't have any drugs on-board."

"Then I'll follow you to the marina."

"You've made me lose the boats I was traveling with. I don't know where the marina is. I need to follow you."

"You're stalling. You go first."

He was arrogant. She wasn't going to argue with him any longer, even though she didn't know where she was going. She pushed the throttle forward.

The rain was pounding the eisenglass harder, and the darkness seemed blacker. She couldn't see anything in front of her. The next thing she knew, she was in the middle of about fifty anchored sailboats. The sheriff pulled beside her again.

"I'm coming aboard!"

"No! I told you I didn't know where I was going. My dealership is on the St. Johns River. I'm not from around here."

His temper flared, and he gritted his teeth. "You're stalling!"

"I told you I don't know where I'm going!"

He pulled around her, she pulled in behind him, and another sheriff's boat pulled in behind her. When she pulled up to the dock, Scott and John were waving flashlights.

"Where have you been?" She heard the concern in John's voice.

She jumped off the boat and whispered to Scott. "Go call the local sheriff now."

The marine sheriff climbed off his boat and onto the one she was driving.

She turned to John. "He's looking for drugs. He doesn't believe I was coming from the boat show."

Scott returned and went straight to the marine sheriff. "These boats are new. We just came out of the Ft. Lauderdale Boat Show. You're not going to find any drugs."

The marine sheriff searched thoroughly and found nothing. He called the other deputy over. "Go get my knife."

Jordan stepped next to him. "What do you need a knife for? I told you I don't have any drugs aboard."

"I'm slashing the seats. That's where your drugs are."

"If you cut these seats, the sheriff's department is going to pay for the damage."

The local sheriff arrived, yelling to the marine sheriff as he ran down the dock. He pulled the marine officer to the side. After their conversation, the marine sheriff boarded his boat and left without saying a word.

Jordan turned to the local sheriff. "What's going on? He wouldn't listen to a word I said. Why was he so angry with me?"

"It was rumored there was a big drug bust going down tonight, and he missed the boat or boats that were involved. He took his frustration out on you."

She reached for John's hand. "That's the last time I get on a boat with a dead cell phone."

He pulled her towards him, rested his cheek on the top of her head, and gave her a slight hug.

Chapter 29

Christmas Boat Parade

The time flew by from November to December. The river towns were getting ready for their Christmas boat parade committee meetings. Jacksonville and DeLand were the two largest parades with Sanford, Astor, and Palatka parades being smaller; no matter how big or small the parade, they were all exciting and beautiful.

Jordan smiled as she read the invitation:

You are invited to the DeLand Christmas Boat Parade committee meeting on the first Tuesday in November at 7:00 p.m. at the Lake Beresford Yacht Club.

"John, what do you think about St. Johns River Yachts being in the Christmas boat parade?

"Sure, if you want to. What boat would you use?"

"The 36-foot houseboat. It's wide and has lots of room to move around on the front and back decks. It has a generator, twin engines, and a flybridge."

He nodded. "Good, that would've been my choice too."

She followed him into the service bay. "What's involved mechanically?"

He leaned against his workbench. "Nothing, except a routine engine check. What you add to the boat determines what I need to do. You need to let me know how many strings of lights you want, and if you're going to have any animations, and how many. The boat generator may not have enough voltage depending on what you do. I can add a portable generator if I need to."

Jordan called her staff together. "Would you like to be in the Christmas boat parade? Your families can ride on the boat. It will be long hours designing and decorating the boat. We can't get everything done during our working hours."

They all answered with a roaring, "Yes!"

She smiled. "Great, we're going to use the 36-foot houseboat. We need to decide on a theme and what you want on the boat."

Tuesday night, Jordan attended the boat committee meeting. They had already petitioned the county and city councils for boat parade permits. Jordan paid her entry fee, which covered advertising costs, dinner before the parade, and prizes for first, second, and third-place winners. After the committee president was elected, he asked for volunteers; a treasurer, to collect the entry fees and make sure all entries were paid by the deadline; an advertising person; and a person to oversee the dinner. After the chairmen had agreed with their selections, they asked for volunteers to work on their committees. Jordan didn't volunteer for any committees. The man who had been Santa Claus for the last five years volunteered to be Santa again. The president announced that the sheriff's department had set the parade date for December 12, and the starting time was 6:00 p.m. A deadline date was set for entries.

The president walked Jordan to her car. "What model and footage boat are you entering?"

"I'm decorating a 36-foot houseboat with a flybridge."

"That's a perfect boat for Santa. Can he ride on your boat?"

Jordan grinned. "Sure."

"That means your boat will be last. The *Grand Island* boat will be the lead boat."

Jordan's salesmen called a meeting with her. "We have a theme *Children Visiting Santa*. Santa will sit in a big red chair on the flybridge with our children dressed as elves. On the back of the fly-bridge, a big live Christmas tree will be fully decorated with lights and ornaments. On the front and back decks, animated reindeer will stand in cotton looking like they are in the snow. We want the entire boat to be outlined in Christmas lights, including the bow rails."

John grinned. "I can do everything y'all have proposed."

Jordan went to Home Depot and purchased six reindeer, twelve large rolls of cotton, twenty-five big boxes of large Christmas lights, and a gallon of white paint. She and John met with Randy and the other mechanics and explained what they needed to do. She stood the reindeer on the deck of the boat to check the height and visuals from a hundred yards away. The gunnels were too high, allowing her to see only the chest of the reindeer and above. The cleaning crew volunteered to build a platform to raise the reindeer.

The mechanics secured the platform to the boat around the front and back decks.

Jordan clasped her hand in John's and pulled him to the stern. "If there's an engine problem, how are you going to open the hatch?"

"We're going to hinge the platform for the back deck to operate like a hatch." His smug smile conveyed, that, as always, he knew what he was doing.

She gave him a wink and a smile. "Just checking."

The day before the boat parade, Matt helped John secure the big red Santa chair in six places and tied the Christmas tree to the railings using hundred-pound weight fishing line.

She, her staff, and everyone who worked at the marina including Sam had strung lights everywhere on the boat. She filled different-sized boxes with rocks and wrapped them in Christmas paper, then placed them under the tree. John nailed the feet of the reindeer to the wood platform and stapled cotton to the plywood. He ran a three-socket extension cord to the reindeer to give them electricity to move their heads and tails back and forth. Randy anchored a medium-size lighted Christmas tree among the reindeer and John placed two large spotlights to shine on them. The cleaning crew cut two 8 x 3 pieces of plywood which Jordan painted white. The cleaning crew,

Sam, and Matt spelled out "Merry Christmas" in lights. Sam secured the boards to each side of the boat.

The afternoon of the parade, Jordan gathered all the children together. "Y'all have to wear life jackets under your elf's costumes."

One child stuck out her tongue. "I don't want to."

The others chimed in, "Me neither." The parents agreed with Jordan and made sure all the children wore life jackets.

John, the captain, announced three hours before the parade, "All aboard!"

A jolt of anticipation zinged through Jordan. St. Johns River Yachts boat was perfect, and there had to be no mechanical failures.

There was a magical festive mood when they arrived at the yacht club. Everyone was in high spirits, and the Christmas dinner added to the festive night with the desserts giving the children an extra sugar high. Santa Claus sat in his big red chair with all the squealing children swarming around him. They all wanted to sit on his lap at the same time.

After dinner, the first-place ribbon went to a pontoon boat decorated as Cinderella's castle with Tinkerbell strung on a monofilament line from the anchor light on top down to the bow rail. St. Johns River Yachts was in second place, and the *Grand Island* came in third.

The boats left the yacht club in Lake Beresford and traveled south to where the lake flowed into the St. Johns River. The parade was underway, with the sheriff's deputies stationed in their boats along the parade route. The reflection from all the lights bounced off the water, giving the appearance that the river was dancing in color. The third boat making the turn into the river kept going straight across the river then came to an abrupt stop in a clump of water hyacinths.

John saw the stranded boat and yelled, "What's wrong, Captain?"

"When I started to turn, I had no steering. The boat kept going straight."

"Your steering cable broke. There's nothing that can be done about it now."

John nudged his boat next to theirs. Jordan and Matt helped everyone off the stranded boat.

She stood next to John at the helm. "At least they get to ride in the parade."

Homeowners and their friends and town people were camped along the riverbank, clapping, and setting off fireworks as the boats floated by. A lit roman candle exploded sideways instead of up and landed in a manger scene igniting, the pine straw on the boat in front of them.

The captain yelled, "Everyone, get off now!" At that point, he quickly rammed the boat into the shoreline.

Some of the riders reached shore with wet costumes and feet. The spectators on the bank sprinted to retrieve water hoses from the houses close by. When the fireboat arrived on the scene there were only smoking embers. Police boats sped ahead announcing over their loudspeakers, "No fireworks!"

The boats traveled north for six miles past the second channel marker after the Crows Bluff curve. The *Grand Island* had to keep going north until the river was wide enough for them to turn around. After the parade, the boats that weren't docked at the yacht club stopped at their marinas or in their boat slips behind their houses.

When John reached the stranded boat, the men tied the two boats together. John tied the towed boat to the dock in the canal. Then he tied their Christmas boat to the fuel dock until morning. Sam and some of the marina boat owners clapped when everyone exited the boat.

Sam hugged Jordan then announced to everyone that cider and cookies were ready in the marina office for the children. He pointed to an ice chest towards the ship's store. All the men headed south.

Jordan moved away from the cider table and peered over at John. He moved next to her. She gave him a quick hug. "Thank you." He put his arm around her and steered her to the doorway under the mistletoe. He kissed her softly and whispered, "Merry Christmas."

Chapter 30

Ice Storm

The second week in December, her boat sales had quieted. Families shopped for Christmas gifts in the ship's store, but not for boats.

Jordan was working in her office when Maggie, her secretary, entered, but her normal jovial expression was replaced with deep concern. "Jim Knight is on his way to see you."

Jordan frowned. "Did he say why? He always makes an appointment."

"No, just that he was on his way."

She wondered what was wrong. She had only talked to Mary once since they returned from Cozumel.

A few hours later, Jim strode into her office. "Hi, Jordan, I'm glad you're here."

"Hi, Jim. Is anything wrong?"

"I wanted you to know my mother died, and Mary and I have moved into her house in Leesburg. I've sold my house on the river in New Smyrna Beach. The buyer that was going to buy the 24-foot cruiser changed his mind. I want to put the 24-footer on consignment. The house in Leesburg is on Lake Harris, so my children and grandchildren want a pontoon boat. I know nothing about pontoons."

"How many people are going to be on the boat at one time, and how do you plan to use the boat?"

"Probably, ten people max, if they all come at one time. The older ones want to water-ski."

"Jim, if it was just you and Mary using the boat, I would recommend a 24-footer with a 50-horsepower engine because of your limited ability. Since there are so many of you and some want to water-ski you need a 26-footer with 125 horsepower. You can handle the pontoon boat if you and Mary want to take it out on the lake by yourselves, but don't run it wide open. The pontoon boat's hull is much easier to handle than the cruiser's hull."

Jim liked her suggestions and purchased a 26-foot pontoon boat. After Jim left, Jordan registered the boat at the courthouse. The next morning, she gave John all the paperwork to give to Jim when he delivered the pontoon boat to Lake Harris.

On December 23, the weatherman predicted rain, sleet, and a hard freeze for Central Florida for the next two nights. Jordan posted a sign on the ship's store front door. "Closed December 24th and 25th."

"John, it's going to be a bad night. What do we need to do to protect the boats?"

"The sleet is already falling. I've drained all the water out of the lower engine units and pulled the drain plugs on the boats that are on the trailers. You can check the boats in the water to make sure all their bilge pumps are turned on."

Early Christmas Eve morning, Jordan went to check on the boats, after the night's hard freeze. The strong winds almost blew her off the iced-over docks. The boats had weathered the nights' ice storm. The dark gray skies made the river look darker than normal, and the entire marina had a spooky feel. The tin roof creaked and whistled when the wind shifted directions. This was the first time in a long time she had been in the building by herself and never on a day like this. Eeriness crept throughout her showroom when she turned off the lights. She was almost to the front door when the service bay door opened. She screamed and jumped.

Her hands were shaking. "John, you scared me. What are you doing here?"

"I could say the same to you. You should be home with Matt."

"I came to check on the boats." The phone rang, making her jump again.

John reached for the receiver. "Who would be calling now?"

She shrugged her shoulders. "I don't know. I thought everyone knew we were closed."

"Hello. Jim, calm down. I'll be there in thirty minutes."

John placed the receiver back in its cradle. "Jim's battery is dead. He can't turn on his bilge pump. I'm going to Lake Harris."

"We're going. You aren't driving by yourself over there in these icy conditions."

On the way, Jordan remembered the weather being like this a couple of times growing up. She laughed and touched John's hand. "Florida is supposed to be the warm state." When she and John arrived at Jim's house, the sleet was blowing horizontally.

She and John met Jim at his boat. The wind had gained strength making Jordan shiver harder.

John shivered. "This cold air is going under my leather jacket and through my three layers of clothes. My ribs feel cold, and the icy air is burning my lungs. The twenty-degree weather conditions seem to be worse here than at the marina. The ice on Jim's dock is over an inch thick."

John put his hand on her shoulders and turned her around. "Jordan, you don't need to be out here. Go into the house."

She took one step, and her feet went flying into the air. John and Jim helped her up and made sure she wasn't hurt. John gave her his smile that always put a knot in the pit of her stomach. He wrapped his arms around her and she buried her face in his coat to shield against the sleet and the howling wind. John went back to the boat and brought the bilge pump into the house.

"The pump is frozen. I need to submerge it in hot water. It won't take but a few minutes to thaw."

She followed him out to the porch. His face was ashen, and he was shivering from head to toe. "You don't need to be out here."

"I don't want to get warm and then have to go back to the boat. I'm better off staying cold."

"Well, all I need is for you to get sick."

He looked at her laughing. "I'll be fine, Mother Hen."

A few minutes later, he had the pump working and hooked back up to the battery.

Jordan turned to Jim. "Is there anything else we can do for you?"

"No, I can't think of anything. You've done more than enough to come and help me on a day like this. He gave Jordan a hug and shook John's hand. Merry Christmas!"

When they arrived at the bridge, many blue lights were flashing everywhere. John yelled to a deputy. "What's going on?"

The deputy turned his fur collar up against his neck. "DOT has closed the bridge due to the icy conditions. You need to turn around."

John pointed to the marina. "We are going over there."

"I'm sorry. I can't let you cross."

John said. "This means we have to drive an hour north to avoid crossing any bridges and then back south to the marina."

The deputy shook his head up and down. "Sorry, I do understand."

The last curve before turning into the marina, a fox crossed the road in front of them. John slammed on the brakes, forcing the Suburban into a skid. The road disappeared when the lights hit the patches of black ice. Jordan gripped the dashboard and John leaned into the steering wheel, turning it to a hard right into the marina driveway. John pumped the brakes several times but the vehicle continued to slide. When the tires hit the gravel, the Suburban came to an abrupt stop.

Jordan stared at John. Her face was pale. "That was sheer ice."

They sat speechless with their eyes locked on one another. A strange familiar sensation traveled through her, something unpredictable and dangerous. John's facial expression showed her he was as stunned as she. He pulled her close to him. She felt a bond that defied words. Their eyes met again, then he put his lips to hers. The kiss was short but passionate.

She smiled and whispered, "Merry Christmas." Time froze. She pulled her wits back together. "We could've been in the ditch."

His eyes were teary. "I don't know what I would do if I let you get hurt."

"It's not about me. It's about us."

The attraction between them grew stronger. He kissed her again, not letting her go this time.

He stroked her hair. "I know you have to go."

"I do. You have no idea how many times I've wished it was us. Come home with me."

"I don't want to intrude on you and Matt. One more Christmas kiss."

The kiss lasted longer than the other two. She didn't want the moment to end.

Chapter 31

Boat Deliveries

Christmas and the ice storm were over. The temperature was back in the high sixties. Jordan had sold a houseboat to a buyer in Pensacola. All the quotes she received from the boat transport companies were astronomical. She needed to find another way, if possible. She called the transport department at the factory.

"Shawn, this is Jordan at St. Johns River Yachts. Tell me the most economical way to transport a houseboat to Pensacola."

"Jordan, it's going to be easier for you to place an order for a new boat with all the buyer's specifications. We'll transport it from here to Pensacola. You'll need to find a marina there that will let an outside mechanic work on an owner's boat. Many marinas that employ a mechanic won't let another mechanic work in their marina. They won't even let a boat owner do major work on their own boat."

After her phone call with Shawn, she found a marina that would allow John to work on the boat. She gave the marina owner the date the houseboat would arrive.

John saw her bite her lower lip when they drove through the collapsed chain link gates.

"What's wrong?"

"I wasn't expecting the marina to be this small and dirty. Trash and boat parts are lying everywhere."

"I should've warned you. This is common when marinas allow people to work on their own boats. There's no supervision, and no one is responsible for clean up."

She jumped out of the Suburban to watch the factory transport pull through the gate. She held her breath watching the boat barely miss the overhead electrical lines. The buyer pulled in behind the transport. Before Jordan let the boat be unloaded, she, John, and the buyer checked to make sure everything that was ordered on the boat was correct.

She paced back and forth waiting for Shawn to answer. "The flybridge is damaged."

"Hold on, Jordan, I'll be right back." She continued to pace until he returned. "You'll have a new one delivered in four days."

"John's going to have to stay extra days. Who's going to pay for the added expense?"

"I'll pick up John's extra hours, food, and lodging."

She knew that both of them couldn't be away from the dealership that long.

Jordan found the buyer in the marina office. "Will you sign the paperwork before the boat is launched? I need to get back to Lemon Bluff. John will stay until the boat is finished to your satisfaction."

"That's fine. Will you register the boat and give me full possession?"

"Yes, and I promise you'll be happy."

She went to the Escambia County courthouse and filled out all the paperwork.

She handed the buyer the registration. "John will make sure you will be satisfied with the boat before he leaves." She shook his hand and left him with one of her big smiles.

John reached for her hand. "Are you sure you want to leave for home this late in the day? It will be after midnight before you get there."

"I'll be fine. Remember, I grew up here. I've traveled from Pensacola to Lemon Bluff many times over the years."

This was the first time she had been back to Pensacola since her father's death. She took a quick detour by the cemetery. She stood gazing at her mother's and father's graves and thought about Nick's ashes lying next to them. She had kept herself busy, never letting time stand still to think about them. She confirmed in her mind that she had done the right thing owning the boat dealership. Her father would be proud of what she had accomplished.

On her way home, she pondered the houseboat sale and was glad she had thought to call Shawn. Having the factory deliver the boat to Pensacola was much easier than her trying to get it transported. She wished she could have sold one of her stock boats to reduce her floor plan, but the sale would help pay part of her floor plan next month.

An hour later, her phone rang. It was unusual for one of her salesmen to call her while she was away. "Hi, Luke. What's going on?"

"Jordan, when will you be home? I have a husband and wife that want to buy the 30-foot cruiser with the 10-foot beam. They want to meet you before they sign the bill of sale."

"I'll be there in the morning at eight, so whatever time is good for them is fine with me. I'll see you then."

She was at work at seven. The couple showed up at eight—a tall man with big chocolate eyes and his petite blond wife."

"I'm Keith, this is my wife, Sara. We're visiting Sara's sister in Orange City for a week."

She shook Sara and Keith's hand. "I'm Jordan. What can I do for you?"

"We've been looking for a boat for several months. The 30-foot cabin cruiser is exactly what we want. We'd like to use the boat while we're here, but then we need you to deliver it to our dock in Columbia, South Carolina."

"Sure, we can do that. When do you want it delivered?"

"We'll be leaving here next week."

"How about the week after you get home? Randy will go through the boat with you now. I'll keep it in the last slip. You and Sara can use it anytime while you're here. My head mechanic and service manager, John, is delivering a boat in Pensacola now. When John gets back, he and I will trailer your boat to South Carolina."

"That's great. Sara and I would like to take you to dinner tonight to thank you."

"Keith, that's not necessary."

"We insist."

At dinner, Jordan found out—they had no children, Keith was an emergency room doctor, and by Sara's conversation, she was one of the town's socialites.

After a pleasant evening, Keith shook Jordan's hand, and Sara gave Jordan a slight hug. "We come to Sara's sister's house twice a year. Let's have dinner next year. We'd love to meet Matt."

Jordan smiled to herself on the way home, she had become friends with another customer.

John stayed in Pensacola another five days, rigging the boat to be seaworthy and making sure the buyer was knowledgeable and comfortable with his new boat. When John arrived at work Saturday morning, Jordan met him at the service bay door.

"You're not going to believe this. We're going to South Carolina to deliver a boat."

Keith and Sara came in that afternoon to say their good-byes. She introduced John and gave Sara a light hug. "We'll see you week after next. Drive safely."

In preparation for their trip, Jordan researched wide load regulations in Georgia and South Carolina. She knew she didn't need a wide load permit in Florida. The DOT in Atlanta told her she didn't need a permit if the Manufacture's Statement of Origin (MSO) from the factory stated the boat's width was ten feet or less.

Monday morning, John did a final check through the boat. "We're good to go."

"John, I thought we would be on the road before now. This will put us at Keith's house around ten tonight, and that's if we don't have any problems."

They had been on the road an hour when Jordan reached for John's hand. "I'm sorry you haven't been home. I feel guilty. You came to work with me to stop traveling, and it seems I've kept you on the road ever since you started. I never expected you to have to run from Pensacola to South Carolina or even to Atlanta, Ft. Lauderdale, and Miami as well as Evergreen. I know I've asked a lot."

"It's fine. You know I like being with you, and I would never expect you to turn down a sale or be on the road by yourself."

The guilty pang didn't go away. She never expected to be this busy or to be delivering boats all over the country. Sixty miles into Georgia they passed the first weight station. Shortly, blue lights flashed behind them.

A short obese DOT female officer walked to Jordan's side of the Suburban. "You didn't pull into the scales."

"I called DOT in Atlanta. They said if the boat was ten feet wide or less, I didn't need to stop. Here's the MSO."

"You have to talk to the deputy sheriff. You need to follow me."

She pulled around them and drove more than twelve miles. When they passed the second exit, Jordan became alarmed. "John, where is she taking us?"

"She said to the scales."

They exited off on the third exit onto a rough, dusty dirt road. "John, where is she going? This isn't good, and the boat is going to be covered in red dust."

"I know, but I can't outrun her. We'll just have to follow her."

Eighteen miles down the dusty clay road, John followed her into the scales lot.

A deputy approached her yelling in a deep raspy voice. "You bypassed the scales!"

She showed him the MSO. "I talked to the DOT in Atlanta. The boat is ten feet wide."

He scowled. "Your information was wrong."

"The DOT in Atlanta should know their own highway laws." She quipped.

She saw the daggers in his eyes. "Don't get smart with me, lady."

He took a string with a weight on it and tied it to the bow rail, letting it drop to the ground.

"This is over ten feet."

"That's not the hull of the boat. The bow rails stick farther out than the hull."

He gritted his teeth. "The bow rail is going over the highway, and it's over ten feet wide. The fine is a hundred-seventy-five-dollars in cash paid to me now. If you continue to argue with me, the fine will go higher. You need to go back to Truck Stops of America and get the correct paperwork, wide load signs, and flares. The boat stays here."

He was a short, overweight, unshaven gruff deputy who reminded her of Boss Hogg in the *Dukes of Hazzard* TV series. She was in the middle of nowhere, in the middle of the night, and he would only take cash. She was uneasy about the whole situation, and she knew she was being ramrodded.

John unhooked the trailer from the Suburban. She gave him a frown. "You stay with the boat."

"No, I am going with you. I don't want you on the back roads and in a truck stop alone."

"What if the boat is gone when we get back?"

"It will be fine." She heard the concern in his voice.

"John, the truck stop is forty-five miles back in Brunswick. We're going to lose two and half hours running back and forth on I-95."

"I know, but there's nothing we can do about it. Just try to stay calm."

She told the store manager what had happened at the scales. He shook his head and rolled his eyes. She read into his reaction that this wasn't the first time this had happened. At the checkout counter, her company credit card rose to three hundred and fifty dollars for permits and supplies. When they returned to the scales lot, John put the wide load sign on the back of the trailer and across the front of the grill on the Suburban.

The deputy sneered. "Have a safe trip."

Jordan threw her head back against the seat and closed her eyes. "He just pocketed hundred and seventy-five dollars."

"No, he split it with the DOT woman."

She called Keith. "I'm sorry. We've lost two hours. We'll be there around midnight."

Keith was standing in the front yard with a flashlight when she and John arrived. He shook John's hand. "We're going to the public boat ramp. Sara and Jordan will follow us."

She and John were exhausted. Jordan sighed. "Keith, it's after midnight. Let's wait until morning."

"It won't take long. It's not that far."

Sara and Jordan followed John and Keith to the public ramp. Jordan drove the Suburban and trailer back to Keith's house while John and Keith ran the boat to the dock behind his house.

Sara handed Jordan a cup of tea. "I gave up years ago trying to change Keith's off-time schedule. He says it's a reminder of his residency days."

Sara gave Jordan the guest room upstairs and John the guest room downstairs. At breakfast, John's eyes were droopy, and the lines in his face were deeper than usual. "Keith was on the boat all night going through everything. I went to bed at three."

Jordan peered across the table. "Keith, you haven't been to bed?"

"No. I run on very little sleep. After so many years of being an emergency room doctor, it doesn't bother me anymore."

After breakfast, the four of them ran the boat on Lake Carolina. John made sure Keith was satisfied with the boat. "Keith, do you have any questions before we leave?"

"No, thank you. Everything is good."

She and John were back on the road at 11:00 a.m. headed to Florida.

Jordan opened her eyes. "Where are we?"

"You've been napping. We're still six hours from home."

She inhaled a deep breath and let it out slowly.

"Jordan, I know we have a great friendship, by now you have to know I want more. As I watched you sleep, my mind went into overload. You have a quality that I've never met in any woman. You're intelligent, independent, charming, and affectionate all rolled into one, and you have the capability to do anything you set your mind to. You're the most interesting person I know. There's never a dull moment with you, and you aren't afraid of anything. I never want to be away from you."

"I know we have a bond. I still go over in my mind the first day you came to the marina. I knew there was a connection that day. I've given a lot of thought about us. If we ask for more than we have now, or try to take it, we'll only hurt each other in the end. I'd love to throw caution to the wind but I have to think about Matt. We have to be grateful for our friendship."

They sat quietly with unspoken words hanging thick in the air between them.

Chapter 32

John Quit

After the trips to Pensacola and South Carolina, Jordan hadn't had time to get organized or get caught up on her everyday duties. She was buried in paperwork at her desk.

Mid-day, Matt called from the University of Florida, "Mom, I was changing my oil, and I locked my keys in the car with the engine running."

"Hold on, I'll go get John."

"Hey buddy, you're in a bind." John chuckled.

"John, it's not funny. The car is full of gas."

"I know, I was just messing with ya. Stick a screwdriver in the carburetor and choke down the engine."

Jordan listened to their banter and smiled. She had chastised herself ever since she started the dealership for never having enough time for Matt.

John handed the phone back to Jordan. "Matt, I'll be in Gainesville in an hour and a half with a spare set of keys. It never occurred to me that you should've had a spare set."

A couple of weeks later, Matt called asking to talk to John.

"Why do you need, John?"

"Something's wrong with my car."

When Matt and John's conversation ended, John told her he was going to Gainesville.

"Why?"

"I need to fix Matt's car." John didn't give her any details. He turned and headed out the door.

Jordan waited at the dealership until John returned. "What's going on with Matt's car?"

He shrugged. "It's fixed. How was your day?"

She knew Matt was up to something and John was covering for him. The summer after Matt graduated from high school, John removed the first gear from the Camaro's automatic transmission. She never understood why they wanted to make an automatic transmission shift. After that, the car always seemed to have problems. John tinkered with it every weekend when Matt came home.

After lunch on Thursday, John told her he was going to Gainesville.

"What's wrong with Matt's car?"

John avoided her question and scooted out of her office. The phone calls kept coming from Matt to John.

After the second phone call in one week, she met John at his truck. In a matter-of-fact tone, she said. "We are going to Gainesville."

John kept the conversation to Gainesville at a minimum. When they arrived at Matt's apartment, she made the two of them sit on the sofa. "One of you or both of you are going to explain what is going on with this car. I want the truth now." She gave Matt her most serious glare.

Matt knew he had to answer her question. In a soft voice, he said, "The pushrods are bent and need to be replaced."

"How did the pushrods get bent, Matt?" Her voice was strong and stern.

Sheepishly, Matt lowered his head. "I've been drag racing."

She tried to stay calm but her stomach tightened. She could feel all the oxygen being sucked from her lungs.

Matt continued, "The Gainesville Raceway has a separate road course from the Gatornationals drag strip. The road course was built for vehicle testing, driving schools, law enforcement training, high-performance driving, and amateur racing. I've been racing on the road course with my friends."

She was caught off guard. She couldn't believe Matt was racing. Her tears seeped down her cheeks into her lap.

"Never again, Matt," was all the words she could say.

"I thought if I told you, you wouldn't let me race but if I had told you, maybe you wouldn't be so mad now."

"Matt, I'm not mad. I'm hurt that you thought you couldn't tell me."

"Mom, you're fearless, strong, and an entrepreneur. You can take on the world. I never thought you would be this unnerved."

Jordan saw John's jaw drop. His reaction was the same as Matt's.

She fought with everything inside her to stay quiet on the way home. She'd never been good at playing the silent game, but she wanted John to know how upset she was. John shifted forward in his seat saying nothing, then shifted back. She glanced over at him. He was sulking like a possum. She forced herself to put the brakes on her runaway thoughts, trying to put the day's events out of her mind. She knew Matt and John couldn't understand a mother's love. She couldn't live if anything happened to Matt.

Her relationship with John remained strained the week after Gainesville. She knew he wasn't going to apologize. Maybe in time things with her, with the two of them, would be back to normal. She knew he was hurt at her response. She didn't like either one of them working under these circumstances. He had kept his distance and only talked to her when necessary.

She didn't understand she had crossed an invisible line. It wasn't just Matt's racing. Couldn't he see how desperately she was trying to deal with their deception?

After two days, she couldn't take the tension anymore. She had held her silence long enough. She found John in a boat at the back of the work yard.

"You put Matt's life in danger. You aren't his father."

"I haven't done anything wrong. Matt asked me for more horsepower. You agreed. Y'all knew I had raced cars." He blinked and blinked again and stared at her. Then a serious mad frown covered his face. "You're being unreasonable. I don't want to argue with you."

"Then stop doing it."

John climbed out of the boat. Walked to his truck with his tool-box, gave her a glaring stare, and drove away.

Her mind went blank and tears filled her eyes as she stood there watching him turn onto Highway 415, not knowing if he would ever be back.

Chapter 33

Chicago

John had been gone four months. Randy had taken over the mechanics. He didn't have John's expertise despite his work habits having become somewhat like John's. She didn't scold Randy when he and the two mechanics had let the work orders fall behind. Randy, Chuck, and Peter all seemed to be as lost without John as she was.

Her heart couldn't take the distance that had developed between her, Matt, and John. She had called John asking him to come back many times, only to hear stubborn silence on the other end of the phone. He was gone, and she hadn't found a way to get him back.

Depression overtook her when she thought about him working at another marina. He didn't belong anywhere else but with her. Why did she continue to hope that she could will him back? People don't come into other people's lives by accident, and she had pushed him away.

She dwelled on the thoughts of John not being there. Her shoulders sank with misery until she could barely function some days. Her emotions rocked as she remembered the looks, he gave her when he thought she wasn't watching. How he had made her thoughts scatter to the edges of her mind of what life would be like if they were together. The smile he gave her said she was the most important person in the world. He drew her to him like no other person she had ever known. She remembered how his lips brushed her cheek sometimes when they were working closely in an engine hatch. Even now she could feel the electricity that flowed through her when he touched her hand, her cheek, or her arm. She could see the amusement on his face when he thought he had surprised her or caught her off guard. She missed his companionship. They had shared a few passionate kisses that were few and far between, and he always left her wanting more. He had never demanded anything from her. His protective side made sure nothing happened to her. He had let her know he was there for her no matter what. Her feelings surprised her when her body shivered. Was she the only one with these feelings, or did he have them too? Was there love there that she wasn't aware of or willing to admit? She would promise him anything to get him back. She needed a well-planned presentation to get him to listen to her.

The morning sun was a welcomed sight. Last night was one of the worst July thunderstorms Jordan had experienced in a long time. The lightning show had been bigger than any fireworks finale she had ever seen, and the deafening thunder had stolen her sleep.

She almost stopped on top of the bridge when she saw her row of boats lying on the ground like dominoes. They looked like they had been victims of a level-five earthquake. She drove close to the boats to assess the damage. The rain had been like a gully washer, pulling the sand from under the blocks that caused them to shift and break. A total of five boats ranging from 25 feet to 33 feet were lying on their sides.

She drove past Randy, who was driving the forklift from the back of the marina to the boats. Peter hurried to pull what equipment they were going to need to put the boats back on the blocks. Chuck didn't waste any time bringing new concrete blocks from the back of the service bays to replace the broken ones.

Sam drove up next to her. "I thought there might be a problem from the rain last night, but I never expected to see this. I'll go get the tractor and grade the ground flat."

John drove by the boats lying on the ground. Her heart skipped a beat or two. He bypassed her and never glanced at her. He went straight to Randy, said a few words, then replaced Randy on the forklift. Randy brought the Suburban and hydraulic trailer from the service bay to the boats. John picked each boat from the ground and placed it on the trailer. Peter, Randy, and Chuck placed blocks under the boat on the trailer. Randy lowered the trailer to reposition the boat on the blocks then removed the trailer. The process continued until all five boats were back on their blocks. Jordan was glad the lower units on the engines weren't damaged and the propellers weren't bent. She did need her fiberglass man to repair the scratches on the boat hulls. After all the boats were back in place, John drove away like he drove in never looking at her.

Jordan settled into seat 5-A of her flight to Chicago. She had thought earlier with the boat ordeal that she wouldn't make her flight. The International Women in Boating Organization had requested her to be the guest speaker for their annual meeting at the Chicago boat trade show (IMTEC). The non-profit organization was aimed at providing professional development services, support systems, and educational programs for marine industry women. This included women boat owners, women working for boat manufacturing companies, boat finance companies, boat dealerships, boat parts companies, and any woman whose work involved being in the boating industry.

She walked to the podium with her head held high and a big smile. She was surprised to see a hundred or more women in the audience. She thanked everyone for coming and relayed how she started her boat dealership in the male-dominated business world. She continued by saying, "Men and women have different viewpoints and different business ideas especially in the boating industry. You have to cover your bottom lines and one way to do this is to bond with your customers. Make them feel like they are your most important customer. You will be surprised how many of them will become repeat customers. You ladies have to become creative problem solvers and overcome the no's and can-nots. Every one of you should have the opportunity to achieve your full potential in any field you choose. There are still inequalities in the boating industry, just as in other businesses, and there are still barriers women face, one of them being the lack of female role models. There are more and more self-employed women starting their own businesses. As women in this business, we have to be sharper and keener. Status quo will never make you successful, and when you seek financial help, you should have all your financials and projections in presentation form. International Women in Boating is a support network, and we are here to help you. Use the resources that are available to you, but most of all believe in yourself. No matter how many times you think you can't push forward, remember anyone can quit. Your being here indicates to me that you are already not just anyone." At the end of her speech, she was astonished at the standing ovation.

She heard at the meeting that Louise, at Floor Plan Services had nominated her for the Darlene Briggs Woman of the Year Award. She was proud that someone else acknowledged her accomplishments.

The late Darlene Briggs of Wayzata, Minnesota, was admired for her tireless dedication to the marine industry. The Marine Retailers Association and *Boating Industry* magazine together presented the Darlene Briggs Woman of the Year Award to honor her memory, an award that was presented annually during the Marine Dealer Conference and Expo in Las Vegas to an outstanding woman actively involved in the marine industry. It recognized long and devoted service, untiring commitment, and the advancement of women in the boating industry.

She received the invitation for the Marine Dealer Conference and Expo to be held December 2nd through December 4th in Las Vegas. She still couldn't believe she had been nominated for Marine Woman of the Year even though she held the invitation in her hand.

Chapter 34

Las Vegas

The morning after she returned from Chicago, Jordan was surprised to see Sam, her landlord, sitting in her office. "To what do I owe this pleasure so early in the morning?"

"I wanted to tell you again what a great job you've done. I knew you could do it the first time I saw you pull that 26-foot boat out of the marina to New Smyrna Beach." He smiled. "I'm here for you to renew your lease."

"Thank you for the recognition of my hard work. I can't believe it's been five years. I had forgotten about the lease."

"Is there anything you want to change?"

"No, everything is working for me. What do you want to change?

"Everything's good. I just want you happy."

She called her attorney. "Alan, I need to renew my lease with Sam. Neither one of us have any changes."

"If you're satisfied, I'll change the dates and extend it for another five years. You can pick up the new lease in a couple of days."

The thoughts about what she had done and all that had happened in the previous five years overwhelmed her. She had amazed herself with her determination and strength. She pinched her arm to make sure she wasn't in a dream. The five years in business influenced her perspective that maybe she would be the "Marine Woman of the Year."

December 1st, Jordan put five dollars in a slot machine at the McCarran airport in Las Vegas. She laughed out loud when the machine spit out a hundred-dollar bill. This could be a good omen.

"Good afternoon, Ms. Harris. Welcome to the Mirage Hotel. Here is your packet. It explains all your activities and meeting times. There are no formal activities planned for tonight. Is there anything I can do for you?" The concierge smiled and pressed the bell for an attendant. She handed him the room key.

After dinner, Jordan walked down the strip to Stratosphere Tower. She could see for miles all the magnificent casino lights down the strip and downtown Vegas. The next morning at ten, she and the other finalists—from Wyoming, Texas, Virginia, and Minnesota met in a conference room with the public relations coordinator of *Boating Industry* magazine.

The next morning at nine, donuts, breakfast breads, and coffee was served in the conference room. All the finalist contestants were introduced to one another by their name, state, and company.

The *Boating Magazine* coordinator smiled and shook everyone's hand. "Ladies, tonight at dinner, you will be presented as finalist for the Marine Woman of the Year award. Each of you need to prepare a short speech about how and why you chose to be in the boat business. Tomorrow night at the awards banquet the winner will be announced."

After the meeting, Jordan spent the rest of the day sightseeing the Hoover Dam and enjoyed a helicopter ride over part of the Grand Canyon. The next day she stayed around the heated pool with the other contestants. With John not being at the dealership, she worried about Randy. She had talked to him several times a day and he assured her everything was running smoothly. She was still uneasy leaving him in charge. A part of her was missing, like a mother who had left her baby behind.

She had a spa time at 3:00 p.m. and a hair appointment at 4:30 p.m., followed by a meeting with the makeup consultant.

She resisted. "I haven't worn makeup in five years. I found out quickly that the hot days and sweat didn't mix well with makeup at the marina."

Tobias ignored her and started applying makeup.

She held up her hand. "Tobias, that foundation is too dark."

"Trust me, Ms. Harris. With your dark hair and your hydrangea-blue eyes and the bright red lip gloss over the dark red lipstick, it will be perfect."

Jordan consoled herself. It was only one night. She would never see these people again. Tobias wasn't worth an energy confrontation.

Before she went to the convention hall, she took one last glance at herself in the floor-length mirror. She didn't like her hairstyle, but it was satisfactory. She did have to give Tobias credit for her perfectly applied make-up, which had made her sun wrinkles disappear, at least for tonight anyway. Her long white sequined gown with the white and silver appliqued vine and grape leaves that ran from her left shoulder down past her waistline and hugged her hips, made her look slimmer—if ninety-five pounds wasn't slim enough. She smiled at herself, opened her door, and stepped into the corridor.

The white sequin puff sleeves, and the side split that ran halfway up her right leg, and the two hundred thousand sequins that made her dress glisten, turned everyone's head when she walked into the banquet room.

The award finalists were called to the stage at eight. Last year's recipient gave the welcome speech then gave a little background on the nominated recipient. "This year's recipient is the sole owner of her boat dealership. She has fourteen staff members and six boat lines. She has a full-service dealership and has nearly two million dollars in annual sales revenues."

Jordan felt her knees trying to buckle. The next thing she heard was, "The winner of the Marine Woman of the Year is Jordan Harris, owner of St. Johns River Yachts, Incorporated in Central Florida."

Her hands were folded in front of her. She quickly pinched the top of her left hand to make sure she wasn't dreaming. The next few minutes were a blur as the bouquet of roses was presented to her along with a plaque naming her *Marine Woman of the Year*. Now she had to get through her speech without quivering or shaking in front of eight hundred people.

"The vision to start your own business is just as viable as pursuing any traditional profession. Financial pursuit is not the only goal. It's how we choose to pursue that goal. It's the lessons we learn and the people we influence and help along the way that gives me my drive, determination, and passion. To be successful, I had to take risks without panicking, and be confident and knowledgeable." She felt the lump form in her throat. She couldn't hold back the tears any longer. "Thank you for choosing me for this award."

This was her night. Next year she would be presenting this award to the next Woman of the Year.

Chapter 35

Contract Conflict

R ick, the wealthy divorced businessman, and her long-time investor friend had popped in and out of Jordan's office ever since the houseboat repo's, and now that he had moved his boat to Marina 415, he was in her office two to three times a week. Every time he came, he tried to persuade her to go to lunch with him, and every time she refused.

On Wednesday morning, she saw Rick park in front of her office window in a new red diesel truck. She greeted him at the showroom door and pointed to the truck. "When did you get that?

"Earlier this morning. I got it for you. You know I want to help now that John's not here."

"I don't need a diesel truck, Rick, and I don't need dual wheels."

"Do you have a boat that needs to be pulled out of the water? I want to show you what it'll do."

She carried her coffee cup with her down the dock to the boat where Randy had taken the Suburban. "Randy, are you at a stopping point to where we can pull the boat out of the water? Rick wants to show me what his diesel can do."

"That truck isn't going to pull big boats up this wet ramp."

"Well, let him try. If it doesn't, that will be the end of it."

Randy drove the boat onto the trailer and gave Rick the sign to pull forward. The wheels spun but the truck didn't budge. After his third try, Jordan backed the Suburban down to the trailer. With her left foot on the brake and her right foot on the gas, the boat came out of the water effortlessly.

Rick stood there for a moment dumbfounded. "I really thought the diesel would be good for you."

She smiled. "Nothing beats my Suburban and it's 454."

Disappointment covered his face. Rick drove away to return the truck to the dealership. Rick trying to help reminded her how much she missed John.

It had been six months and John still wasn't answering his phone or returning her voicemails. She kept trying to find a way to get him back.

After lunch, Jordan's secretary, Maggie, was filing papers when a man buzzed past her desk. "Wait a minute. Where do you think you're going.?

"To see Jordan."

"Who are you? You don't just barge in on her."

Maggie had become very protective over Jordan. She screened her calls and wouldn't let anyone walk into her office without being announced. Maggie walked at a snail's pace to Jordan's office.

"Trace is here to see you."

Trace stuck his head from behind Maggie's back. "Hi, Jordan."

Trace was a longtime boating friend. She tolerated him, but she never liked his high-and-mighty attitude or his stubbornness.

"Hi, Trace. How are you?"

"Good, thank you. I came to ask you if you would haul my boat over to Clearwater. Patsy and I are taking a week's vacation to tour the islands around Tampa."

"Sure, let me gather your boat specs."

After surveying all the specs on his boat and her trailer. She bit her lower lip and pointed to the papers.

"Trace, your 33-foot boat at dry weight is at the maximum for my trailer. Bring your boat to the marina empty of fuel and water. I can't emphasize to you enough that your boat must be empty. You'll also need to sign a delivery contract."

"We're friends. Friends don't sign contracts."

"This is a business contract, not a friend contract. If you don't agree to my terms, I'm not hauling your boat."

He curled the corner of his mouth down. She would not have been surprised if he'd stuck his tongue out at her. Ever since she had known him, he had always bullied people to get his way.

"I'll sign the agreement, but it's under protest."

"You can protest all you want. This is a business agreement."

Her cleaning crew was also long-distance haulers. She contracted with them to haul Trace's boat to Clearwater. Halfway across the state, her driver called. "We just cleared the scales when the trailer broke. The boat is on its side in the road."

Jordan squealed. "What do you mean the trailer broke?"

"We made the U-turn back onto the highway from the scales. The fuel and water shifted to the left side of the boat. All the weight on one side broke the trailer and the boat fell on the road. The boat is over the maximum weight for the trailer."

"I'll call the boat transport company, and I'll call you right back."

"There's a big rig repair shop next to the scales. I can get the trailer repaired there."

She gave him her approval.

She wanted to scream at Trace but she kept her composure. "You didn't comply with the contract. The boat is full of fuel and water, my trailer is broken, and your boat is lying on the side of the road. You're going to have to pay for the trailer repair, the crew's wait time, and the big rig hauling."

Trace growled into the phone. "I'm calling my attorney. You can't charge me."

"Go ahead, call him. I'll call mine. Keep in mind I have your signature on a signed contract, which you violated."

Jordan called the marina manager in Clearwater, giving him instructions not to give the boat keys to Trace. She thought about driving to Tampa but decided to wait until in the morning.

She left Lemon Bluff early, to avoid the rush hour traffic on I-4. She breezed through Orlando and was at the Clearwater marina in an hour and a half. When Trace arrived, she handed him an envelope.

"Here's your bill for the trailer repair, boat replacement back onto the trailer, the night's lodging for the driver, and the driver's extra time."

"I'm not paying."

"Then you aren't getting your boat and I'll call the local sheriff. I have your signed contract and your violations."

Trace called his attorney. After a short conversation, he returned to her in silence and threw the check at her.

Trace told everyone at the yacht club and everyone else he knew that she had charged him for the extra expense and the repairs.

The next two weeks after the incident, Jordan received supportive calls from his friends. To her it was business, he didn't comply with the provisions in the contract.

Chapter 36

Jordan and John

J ohn had always protected her from irate customers. Jordan thought if John had been there, she wouldn't have had to deal with Trace. She missed him more than she ever thought possible. She wanted to stop time and turn back the clock. She knew John was as strong-willed as she, but she thought he would have missed her enough to have caved in by now. She had erected a wall between them that she didn't know how to scale. Somehow, she had to get John to meet with her. She knew he wouldn't come to the dealership or go to lunch. The county park across from the marina was neutral ground. She and John had been there many times when they didn't want ears overhearing them discussing business decisions. She left a message for him to meet her at the county park Friday at 3:00 p.m.

She waited in the park not knowing if he would meet her or not. Her stomach quivered, and she braced herself for an awkward reunion when his truck pulled up next to hers. He opened her passenger door and slid in slowly. His beard was scraggly, and the dark circles under his eyes showed tiredness. She waited for him to speak, but he sat in silence. She wanted to reach for his hand and feel his warmth. She refrained.

After several minutes, she couldn't stay quiet any longer. "The thing about mistakes is that someone has to forgive you for them. I was upset with Matt's racing. I lashed out, and you happened to be the closest person. I'm sorry I took it out on you. All I could think about was myself. I couldn't exist without Matt. The thought of him racing scared me to death. I need you to forgive me."

He listened, but his reaction told her nothing. Deep down she was in pain—wrenching, heartbreaking pain.

He continued to remain silent, showing no emotions.

Was he thinking about what she had said all this time, or was he being deliberate in making her wait? Was she all wrong about her thoughts? He didn't care. She was in a fantasy world of her own to think he would come back. Still unspoken words hung thick in the air between them. She couldn't say anything else. Her only choice now was to sit quietly and wait for him to answer.

After twenty minutes, in a dry soft voice, he spoke. "It's a long way back. You hurt me more than anyone has ever hurt me. My three divorces didn't hurt like this."

He shocked her. She didn't know he had been divorced three times. She thought Lisa had been his second wife. She didn't know him as well as she thought she did, but now wasn't the time to intrude into his personal life. She needed to get the issues between them resolved. She wanted his love, but she needed his friendship first. She had already apologized and tried to explain her side. She searched her brain to find the right trigger word to get him to agree to come back. She carefully chose her words not to make him bolt again.

"John, do you remember how I knew nothing about boats and how I tried your patience when you taught me to paint boat bottoms? You thought I would never learn how to keep the streaks out. The laughs we had over the 5200-silicone sealant caulk. Oh, how it loved me. No matter how careful I was when I sealed holes around installed wiring or the thru-hull holes in the bottoms after electronics were installed, it always seemed to jump from the tube and cover me. My clothing and body were like magnets to the thick, white, waterproof goop."

He nodded. "I remember one morning helping you off a boat and asked what was on your elbow. You touched your skin and answered, 'Dried 5200.' You said you didn't even know how long it had been there. It became a standing joke with you and the silicone in the service department."

She turned and faced him. He couldn't hold his poker face. She saw that familiar corner of his mouth curl. He stared at the flowing river and watched the seagulls bob up and down. After what seemed like five minutes to her, he reached over and pulled her towards him. He gave her a quick hug and a soft kiss on the cheek. He took her small hands and held both of them in his one.

"Love is one thing that matters in life. It makes everything else worthwhile. I didn't really understand love until I left you. I do miss us. It's a special love with you that I've never had with anyone else. I guess that's why it hurt so much."

His words felt warm and reassuring. She took in a long breath. She waited for her heart to settle to a slow beat. "John."

He raised his index finger to her lips. "Jordan, we make a good team. Everyone sees our connection to each other."

She laid her head against his chest. "I've always heard you hurt the ones you love. John, I never meant to hurt you. I promise I'll never hurt you again."

"I've missed so much with you that I can't get back. I was proud when I heard you were in Chicago speaking to the International Women in Boating group. I would have given anything to have been with you in Las Vegas. You deserved the Marine Woman of the Year award.

She rubbed her eyes. "I didn't know you knew any of that."

They started talking as though the last ten months hadn't existed. Suddenly, he seemed to be far away again. She was skeptical to say anything else, fearing the wrong words would come out of her mouth and she would lose what she had regained.

In slow motion, he pulled her closer, wrapping his arms around her shoulders. She felt his warm breath close to her ear and heard his labored breathing. He released his arms and held her face in his hands. He placed a gentle kiss on each cheek before placing his lips to hers. His kiss was full of emotion, love, and passion. It was a kiss like they had never shared before. She felt the fire ignite in the pit of her stomach.

Time stood still before he gently pulled away. Seconds ticked by while she waited for his next words.

"I'll come back."

A chill skidded down her spine, and her lips quivered. She wiped a tear from her cheek. "I couldn't live without Matt and I can't survive without you."

He cradled her in his arms. "I promise. I won't leave again."

"Thank you." She whispered and buried her face in his chest.

They had reached an understanding. Any hurdles that may have existed before would no longer exist.

Chapter 37

The County Park

The summer showers had passed. Jordan had finished her housework. She was tired of reading, and she abhorred television. She walked around the house restless and bored. She needed a diversion. She drove to the county park to watch the Sunday boaters load their boats after drinking spirits on the water all day.

Boats from small to large, always returned to the boat ramps at the same time, clogging the canal causing impatience and making tempers flare.

Late Sunday afternoon, Jordan arrived at the park to watch a sailboat, who was waiting for the bridge to open, add to the confusion. The sailboat bobbed silently in the middle of the river when the drunk boaters honked and gunned their engines for him to move out of their way. The bridge tender sounded the familiar horn to stop the cars behind the closed gates. She watched the center of the bridge rise while the sailboat positioned itself in the middle of the river, which made the boaters even more irate.

A man yelling at his wife made Jordan turn her attention to the boat ramp. She watched the man back his trailer down the boat ramp sideways. His wife yelled at him to turn right then left then right again. He jumped out of the truck and told her to back the trailer. People started yelling at them to get out of the way. Finally, one man offered to back the trailer down the ramp. She had thought about offering her help but that would have added more fuel to his fire with her being a female. They left, and everyone could still hear them yelling at one another when they pulled out of the park onto Highway 415. She had not laughed this hard in a long time.

One husband backed his trailer down the ramp, and his wife pulled the boat onto the trailer. When he pulled the boat up the ramp, the boat floated off across the canal. She stood on the bank with a puzzled look while her husband yelled obscene words at her for not hooking the boat to the trailer. Another boater coming into the canal pulled the floating boat back to the ramp.

This was what she needed. She hadn't had this much amusement in months. Now she knew what the expression *"Laughter is good for the soul"* meant.

She continued to watch another man back his boat into the water. He tied the boat to the dock then parked his car and trailer. When he cranked the engine, flames shot into the air. People ran everywhere grabbing their fire extinguishers. After the fire was contained, he floated his boat to the end of the canal. He set the anchor and tied the boat to the bank, then he walked to his car and drove away. No one knew who he was or why the boat caught fire.

The afternoon shadows had grown long. She had had enough hilarity for the afternoon. On her way out of the park, she drove past the last boat ramp. An elderly man had backed his boat and trailer into the water and had missed the ramp. His boat, trailer, and truck were in the water.

She stopped and rolled down her window. "Can I help? I own the dealership across the river."

"No, thanks. My son was behind me. He should be here any minute."

"This ramp is uneven and slants to the left. Most people don't use it."

"If you're trying to make me feel better, it isn't working. This is the third time I've backed my truck, trailer, and boat into the water here."

She couldn't help herself. She started laughing then he joined her with a bigger laugh.

The next morning on her way to work, she saw the man standing in his boat that had caught fire yesterday. She pulled close to the boat and yelled. "Hi! I'm Jordan, I own the boat dealership across the river. Would you like for me to send my mechanic over?"

"Yes, please." She saw relief cover his face.

John and Randy towed the boat over to the marina dock. John checked out the engine and told the owner it was going to be several days before his boat would be repaired.

Chapter 38

Boat on I-95

Jordan smiled watching John whistle while he worked. She had missed his presence in so many ways. To her, this sunny Monday morning was brighter than it had been in a long time.

Jordan ran from the service bay to answer the phone. She passed Will, who was waiting on a parts customer. It was too early for Maggie to be at work. She took a second to get her breath.

"Hello, St. Johns River Yachts."

"Jordan, this is Tom."

She laughed. "I didn't know manufacturers worked this early on a Monday morning."

"I work all the time." She heard his chuckle. "I wanted to know how that new boat line was working out for you? I didn't think you wanted any more boats. If you can take on another line, you can take more boats from me. I'll give you free freight if you'll take the 26 and 28-foot boats after the Ft. Lauderdale show in October."

Jordan considered his offer and made a quick decision. "My new line doesn't conflict with your boats. I'll take the boats after the show."

October was the start of the service departments slowing period. "John, Tom has asked me to take two boats after the Ft. Lauderdale show. I will bring one boat back and Scott will loan me a truck and trailer to bring the other one here. The factory will fly you to Ft. Lauderdale after the show. Would you be willing to do that?"

"Sure, you know I'd do anything you asked."

After the show, John said. "Jordan, the 26-foot boat is hitched behind the Suburban. You need to leave now. I won't be far behind you."

Thirty minutes after she left the show staging area, she called John. "Where are you? I need help." Her voice was loud and high-pitched.

"Don't panic. Tell me what's wrong."

"I'm on the shoulder of I-95 north of the Coconut Creek exit. The boat is half on and off the trailer."

John arrived with a puzzled look. "What on earth happened? Why are you parked behind the boat?"

"Whoever hooked the tongue of the trailer to the Suburban didn't secure it. I was driving in the right lane moving with the traffic at 50 miles per hour when suddenly the boat and trailer passed me in the left lane. Sparks were flying everywhere from the tongue scraping the pavement. Cars were honking, gawking, and slowing down. No one would let me move into the left lane. I knew I needed to get beside the boat to nudge it off the road." She sighed and continued. "Someone finally let me in the left lane. I bumped the boat with the right front fender of the Suburban to get the boat to the right shoulder. When the tongue hit the dirt, the trailer abruptly stopped. The impact shifted the boat sideways on the trailer. Everyone started slowing down to gape, traffic became bumper to bumper, and no one would let me back onto the interstate. Eventually, someone let me in, but I had to go to the next exit and come back around. That's how I ended up behind the boat."

John stood in silence observing her. He lightly rubbed her cheek with the back of his hand. She turned away. He wrapped his arms around her. His chest pressed against her back, his chin rested on her head, and his breath stirred her hair. Momentarily, her body was enveloped by his. The massive fear and panic attack she had earlier lifted. She slowly turned to face him.

He arched a single brow upward, then smiled.

She became lost in his deep blue eyes, thinking everything is all right now that John is here.

Her brain jumped back in gear. "Do we need to call a tow truck?"

"No. I know lots of people that will come and help us. Remember, I worked in this area for years."

Six men arrived. Under John's direction, they used a leverage jack and put the tongue of the trailer back onto the Suburban. Three men on port and three on starboard sides of the boat pulled and pushed until the boat was back on the slats.

John gave her a quick hug. "From now on, I'm going to double-check your trailer hitches. I'm not going to let you out of my sight. I will be behind you the rest of the way home."

She looked in the rear-view mirror. Her mind retraced what had happened when she saw the boat pass her. In a split second, so many thoughts raced through her mind at lightning speed. She surprised herself that she could think so quickly to get the boat off the road. She couldn't believe there hadn't been an accident. There were so many horrendous possibilities like—a ten-car pile-up or the boat flipping in the middle of the interstate or people being hurt or killed, including her.

Chapter 39

Matt's Wedding

The first Saturday in September, Matt came to tell everyone good-bye. All the employees toasted Matt with beers and congratulated him on his marriage in two weeks. John jokingly gave his condolences, which made everyone laugh.

Matt was the timeshare sales director at Disney World. He had met his wife-to-be, Suzanne, when he had her transferred into his department to be a supervisor. She was a Virginia Tech graduate and a beautiful Richmond southern lady. She had more poise and charm than all the whole South.

The 1800's Western bar on the second floor of Sam Miller's in downtown Richmond was a step back in time. Jordan had chosen the bar as the venue for the rehearsal dinner. The wedding party, close friends, fraternity brothers, and sorority sisters all gathered and partied in the rustic bar until dawn.

Jordan, the mother of the groom, was the first one to light the unity candle. The wax on the wick was so thick, she couldn't get the candle to light. She held her breath. Lighting a candle couldn't be this difficult. She could run a multi-million-dollar business, how could she not light a simple little candle? Finally, the wick sparked. The bride's mother took as long to light her candle, which made the candle lighting look like it was staged for two minutes.

Suzanne's silk crepe lily-white gown flowed elegantly with each graceful step she took down the aisle of the Southminister Presbyterian

Church. The toes of her white pointed stilettos were covered with white beads and rhinestones, matching her cathedral-length white lace veil. At the end of the ceremony, Matt and Suzanne's candle lit immediately, signifying uniting them as one.

During the ceremony, Jordan became lost in her thoughts of how her life had changed—her husband's death, almost losing John, and now Matt would have his own family. The organ pipes bellowed out the wedding march, bringing her back to the present.

Jordan stood at the reception door taking in the start of Matt's and Suzanne's life together. The three four-foot-high vases filled with river rocks held the tall willows straight at the entrance to the ballroom at the Downtown Club. Through the windows, the sun cast reflections of rainbows across the floor from the St. James River. The branches of five wrought iron trees were filled with votives candles and glittering white ornaments that cast a mellow light around the room. Gold and magenta tablecloths matched the organza bridesmaids' dresses along with different-sized votive candles ranging in height from small, medium, and tall in the center of the table. Magenta chrysanthemum petals were scattered among the candles for the centerpieces. All the colors were Suzanne's favorites.

Jordan had her phone on vibrate during the ceremony. When it buzzed now, she noticed she had five missed calls from Randy. She made her way to a private area outside the ballroom.

"Randy, I'm at Matt's reception. What's wrong?"

"John has had a heart attack."

The shock triggered a series of questions. "When? Where is he now? Is he going to be all right?

"Early this morning, I think. The hospital called asking for you. He's still at the hospital."

"I'll try to get a flight out tonight."

Jordan searched through the crowd to find Matt. Her friends from high school and college who were now living in the Richmond area tried to stop her and carry on a conversation. She had talked to them earlier to catch up on life, families, and careers. Now wasn't the time for chit-chat. She needed to find Matt.

By the time she found Matt, she had changed her mind about telling him about John's heart attack. He was going on his honeymoon. He didn't need to have to worry about her or John.

Matt and Suzanne were saying their good-byes to everyone. She gave them both a quick hug. "Have fun in Barbados. I'll see you in two weeks."

She caught the last night's flight out of Richmond to Orlando. When she arrived home, it was too late to try to find out about John's condition.

The next morning, she called John's house at seven to make sure he wasn't home. She rushed into John's hospital room as he was signing the last page of the release papers.

She made an effort to smile which was a little more than a grimace. "How are you?"

"I'm fine. The doctor kept me overnight for observation. The attack was mild. I don't know if I'll have any restrictions or not."

"Is there anything I can do for you?"

"Yes, get me out of here." It was the first smile she had seen from him since she walked into his room.

The nurse returned. "Mr. Cook, the only restriction on the doctor's orders is one cup of coffee a day. The orderly is on his way to take you to the front door."

"Let's go to work. I feel fine. Randy shouldn't have called you."

"He said the hospital called asking for me. I didn't know how serious the attack was. Randy did the right thing. I do think you should go home."

"How was the wedding? They are hitched now, right?

She smiled. "Yes, and on their honeymoon. You do need to rest today. Randy can take care of the service department for one more day."

"I'm fine. I'll stay a couple of hours then you can take me home."

Jordan didn't know which one of them was more stubborn, him or her.

He reached for her hand. "I'm here for you. Nothing is going to happen to me. You can count on that."

He had become her rock and anchor. She closed her eyes for a moment to get her bearings. She couldn't go through losing John. She held his hand and wondered why did it always seem to take a tragedy to mend feelings and emotions.

In the weeks to come, John was like a puppy on her heels. He made sure she didn't need or want anything and was sufficient in everything. She was glad he was there for her, but she had come to the actualization that she needed a working relationship and nothing more. She had let herself become reliant on him and let her feelings for him overpower her. She reminded herself that life gave no certainties. She had to suppress her feelings. She'd been strong her whole life. She needed to pull her inner strength together and not rely on anyone.

Chapter 40

St. Simons Island Trip

The last week in March, Nate and Lydia, one of her long-time boating friends, pulled their boat, the *"Grand Island"*, up to the marina's fuel dock. Jordan finished mooring a boat before she could greet them.

Lydia came out of Jordan's office. "I've been searching for you everywhere!" She hugged Jordan. "We've missed seeing you at the yacht club!"

Jordan gave Lydia a hug back. "I've been busy here."

"I'm sure you have. That's why we want you to go with our old boating group to St. Simons Island in two weeks. We all think you need a break. We have five houseboats going and twenty people if you go."

"I don't think I can leave the business for a week." She ran her hand across her forehead. "I would like to see everyone again."

She shifted from foot to foot and gazed out over the river. She wanted to go but felt guilty leaving the burden of the business on John. It had been six months since his heart attack. His health was good, and his heart tests were normal. "Let me see what I can do. I'll let you know tomorrow."

When she told John about the trip, he insisted that she should go.

Two weeks later, everyone met on the yacht club dock. The morning forecast had predicted no rain, but they had their doubts observing the black sky and the thunder rumbling in the distance.

Nate raised his beer mug. "A toast to no rain."

Jordan frowned. "A toast at eight o'clock in the morning?"

Everyone yelled, "Yes!"

Jordan knew then this was going to be a drinking trip. She wasn't a drinker. She squinted her eyes and turned to Lydia. "Can I have a sip of your screwdriver?"

Jordan took in a deep breath when she saw Rick standing in the crowd. She went to Lydia's boat and fixed her own screwdriver. She braced herself for the encounter on the dock.

"Rick, I didn't know you knew my friends."

"You know the boating world is small."

She took another sip of her screwdriver. "Which boat are you on?"

"I'm with Jack and Georgia."

An hour later, the captains checked their boats for the last time before they headed up the river. Jordan didn't think about there being an odd number. Lydia had told her she would make twenty, but it didn't register they had nineteen without her. If Lydia didn't plan this connection, then who did? Jordan felt she had been sideswiped.

The rain clouds had disappeared. "A toast to the sun and to all the River Rats!" hollered a heavy-set man with his glass raised to the sky. A dozen people raised their glasses and shared the toast.

Jordan had forgotten years ago that all her houseboat friends had called themselves the River Rats. Jordan and her late husband had met the houseboat group one Sunday afternoon when their engine had stalled coming back from Silver Glen Springs. Ever since then, she and Nick had become part of the group. Every weekend they would meet at the yacht club or raft their boats together in a cove on the river, or at one of the springs and sometimes they would raft their boats together behind one of their houses on the river. It was funny to think of themselves as river rats. At this point in their lives, they all had big homes, big boats, big cars, sports cars, and money. It's almost a depressing thought to wake up one day and you're older and those good times are now few and far between. Jordan scanned the crowd; it was hard to believe it had been five years since she had seen any of them.

Halfway to Jacksonville, they stopped at the crab-packing house for crab claws.

Lydia announced. "We have our appetizers and snacks for tonight."

Moving on up the river, the women planned their menus and each boat cooked an assigned dish. They passed the tugboat factory where the "*Grand Island*" was built.

The "*Grand Island*" was a houseboat placed on a tugboat hull. It is 60 feet long with a 14-foot beam. The tugboat's owner built the boat for himself. When his wife died, he sold the boat to Nate and Lydia. They documented the boat as the *Grand Island*. The gangway deck has a large salon area with three sofas and six-barrel back lounge chairs and a galley. Eight barstools surrounded the beer taps bar. The lounge area, bar area, and galley are one big open room that can accommodate thirty people. Going forward past the galley, the hallway dead-ends at the master stateroom with a tub and walk-in shower. On either side of the hallway are two staterooms. The top deck has an enclosed wheelhouse with a stateroom. A covered screen deck is located behind the wheelhouse. It is filled with lounge chairs and named the lido deck. It's the party deck and can accommodate fifty or more people. The washer and dryer are in the engine room along with two 800-horsepower Caterpillar diesel engines, a 600-gallon freshwater tank, and two 500-gallon diesel fuel tanks.

They docked for the night at the Jacksonville City Marina. All their meals were served on the lido deck. After dinner, Rick sat down next to Jordan. She twitched and turned in her chair. She had known Rick in business, but she didn't want to be deliberately thrown together into a social situation. She had refused Rick's help when he tried to give her a diesel truck, and she had intentionally ignored all his flirtations. She didn't want to be rude so she talked to him briefly then excused herself and joined the other women.

The next morning, the women were preparing breakfast together in the galley on the *Grand Island*. Nate walked to the back of his boat and yelled, "Everyone, come look!" The dockmaster heard Nate's yell.

Nate watched the short stocky dockmaster waddled down the dock. "Why is there a car in the river behind my boat?"

The dockmaster pointed to the boat ramp. "During the night, the car missed the bridge and came down the boat ramp. I helped the man out of the car around two this morning. The tow truck is on the way. People miss the bridge all the time especially during rainstorms."

Jordan peered into the dark water below. "With that many people thinking the boat ramp was the highway, why doesn't the DOT put a sign on the highway with an arrow pointing right to the boat ramp and an arrow pointing straight up for the bridge?"

The dockmaster scratched his head. "I've asked DOT several times for a sign, but it hasn't happened."

Nate pulled his boat forward, then in reverse enough to swing the bow into the river. He nodded towards the dock. "No telling how long we would have had to wait for the car to be towed. I'm glad I had enough room to maneuver out into the river."

Midafternoon, all their boats were docked at the Fernandina Beach City Docks. "Nate yelled. "Everyone to the Palace Saloon!"

The *Grand Island* group seated themselves in several booths. Rick rushed to sit next to Jordan. Everyone ordered chicken wings and draft beers.

"Hi, everybody. My name is Joe. I'm the bartender. I'll keep your mugs full."

Jordan motioned for Joe to come to her booth. "How old is this saloon?"

Joe's face lit up. "It's the oldest building in Florida and was turned into a bar in 1903 and in 1905, it was the first bar to serve Coca-Cola." His eyes danced. "The owner was friends with Adolphus Bush, the owner of Anheuser-Bush. Mr. Bush helped him design the wide mahogany and brass bar over there." Joe was about to tell them more when another group called for Joe to come over to their table.

Jordan peered around the room. All the flickering gas lamps cast a reflection off the embossed tin ceiling to the high-gloss polished bar. She turned her eyes across the inlaid mosaic floors, to the hand-carved mahogany undraped female fixtures that stood on pedestals around all the walls in the saloon. Jordan couldn't imagine the cost of the large hand-painted murals that covered the walls.

Joe returned with another round of beers. "Is there anything else I can get for anyone?" He turned his head. "That 40-foot bar is going to be filled shortly. Every afternoon at five, the saloon is packed with the rich and famous and the local bureaucrats enjoying the happy-hour booze. During the day most of our customers are boaters like yourselves and sea captains who stop in for a few stiff ones."

Nate pulled out his wallet. "I think we are good for now, Joe."

After a party night at the saloon, the next morning all the boat captains topped off their fuel tanks. Nate yelled, "Everyone to the saloon for one last beer!"

Rick shuffled his feet before he followed them. Half-way up the hill, the men stopped to look at an old tugboat. Jordan watched Rick from the lido deck glance back at her.

Jordan sat down next to Lydia. "I can't believe they would go drinking at eight in the morning."

Lydia stood. "If the men are going to have a beer, we can go for a Bloody Mary. Let's catch up to them."

They pushed open the swinging saloon door. A drunk sitting at the bar turned around. "Been wait'n all night for y'all. Where ya been?" They all laughed. Two of the men went and sat on either side of him with their beers.

Nate stood and motioned to everyone. "We've been here an hour. We need to head up the river." The drunk looked like he was tied to the barstool. His body was comatose and his forehead rested on the bar. He was unaware he was being left alone to sleep it off.

Jordan raised her hand to push the saloon's swinging doors open. Two policemen rushed through almost knocking her down. They grabbed the drunk from the barstool. His speech was slurred, and his face showed he was confused.

One policeman grabbed the man's shirt collar and pushed him toward the door. Joe yelled from behind the bar, "What's going on! He's not disturbing anyone!"

The other policeman pointed to the street. "There was a murder last night. Someone saw a man run in here."

Joe came from behind the bar. "I think you have the wrong man. He's been here at the bar all night."

Nate grabbed Lydia's arm and Rick grabbed Jordan around her waist. They hurried out of the bar with the rest of the crew following.

Outside Nate motioned everyone back to the boats. "We don't need to get involved in a local situation. Let Joe and the policemen figure it out. We need to head to St. Simons."

Rick laughed. "Send Jordan back in. She would straighten all of them out."

They all laughed. There was truth in that statement, and they all knew it.

The Cumberland River and the St. Johns River merging with the Atlantic Ocean always made the Cumberland Inlet rough and tricky to cross. One of the boats was pushed sideways crossing from the St. Johns River into the intercoastal waterway north to the Cumberland River. The captain tried to keep his boat steered into the waves until two other captains could toss him lines to stabilize his boat. The captain kept one engine in full throttle and the other one in reverse while two other boats pulled his bow back on course, solving what could've ended in a capsizing disaster.

At 4:00 p.m. they docked at Emmaline Hessie's Restaurant and Marina on St. Simons Island. The women were hungry and brought snacks to the lido deck, while the men went swimming in the marina pool. After dinner, the captains decided which boat would host the gin game and what boat would host the poker game. The ones that didn't want to play cards could socialize on the lido deck until bedtime.

The next night, when they arrived at Emmaline's for dinner, the group moaned and complained when they passed the winding sea of people waiting in line for dinner.

Jordan pushed her way up to Nate. "Wait here, I'll be right back." She bypassed the line and went directly to the hostess stand.

"The boat party of twenty has arrived."

The hostess ran her finger down the sign-in sheet. Not finding a reservation for the group, she became flustered then asked, "Do you have a reservation?"

Jordan answered with her biggest smile. "You don't think I'd bring twenty people for dinner without a reservation, do you?"

"Wait here one minute, please."

Through the open door, Jordan saw the manager and wait staff running to put tables together.

Ten minutes later, Jordan said to Nate. "Get the group and follow me."

They passed the line of people, passed the hostess stand, and were greeted inside by the manager, who personally seated them.

Everyone wanted to know how Jordan pulled off their fast seating. After dinner, she told them the conversation with the hostess.

Nate announced to everyone, "Only Jordan would do something like that."

Early the next morning, part of the group climbed to the top of the St. Simon's Lighthouse while others went shopping. The third morning, everyone was untying their boats getting ready to head south. Georgia was trying to untangle an anchor line when she dropped the anchor on her foot. Jordan ran down the dock to get Judy.

Judy hurried with her nurse's bag and bandages. She touched Georgia's foot. "Georgia, you can't rotate your foot. It's already swelling and turning color. You may have broken it. You need to go to the emergency room."

Georgia refused. Judy bandaged a sock tightly around her foot. All the ladies became Georgia's personal servants to make sure she kept her foot elevated.

Heading south it was decided to stop for the night at the Holiday Inn transient dock in Palatka. Lydia and Jordan were ready to cast the bow line to the dockhand when a speed boat gunned his engine close to them causing a big wake. Nate was fighting the current and the wake but couldn't stop the boat from ramming the dock. The force sent Jordan over the bow headfirst into the dock. Seconds later the right side of her head was swelling, and her scalp was turning black.

Judy put an ice pack on her head. "Jordan, you have a concussion. You need to go to the hospital."

"They can't do anything for me. They'll take scans, tell me it's a concussion, and nothing will be done. I'll see my doctor tomorrow when we get home. The only good thing about this is that it didn't happen at the beginning of the trip."

They ordered pizza delivery for dinner, and the gin and poker games were on for the last night.

The river narrowed as they headed south to Lake George and the boat traffic became heavy. Two cabin cruisers and three bow riders passed them, throwing a large wake into their port side bow. The *Grand Island* never rocked, but with five boats passing at full speed, Lydia and Jordan held on to the galley cabinet doors to keep them closed. A trawler pulled in behind Nate to avoid some of the wakes.

Nate radioed, "Captain of the trawler, are you good?

The captain laughed and responded, "I am now."

"Stay behind me until the waters calm."

Back at the yacht club, everyone said their good-byes and agreed it was one of their best fun trips.

Rick reached for Jordan's hand, pulling her next to him. "I'm sorry you didn't know I was going on the trip. I wasn't going to go until they told me you were coming. Then I changed my mind."

"Rick, it was a fun trip and I know you tried to be with me every chance you could, but we are not a couple." He released her hand and walked away. This time he didn't stop to look back.

The next morning when John heard about her concussion, he insisted that she see a doctor. She finally convinced him there was nothing that could be done except to wait on time. She didn't tell him about her severe headaches and dizziness. His protective side was showing again. He insisted that she do nothing except sit at her desk.

Midafternoon, she walked to the end of the dock to see what boat or boats the mechanics were working on. She leaned over to pick up a wrench that someone had dropped. The next thing she knew she was face-down on the ground. For a minute, she was in freeze-frame mode then she felt John pulling her up.

She brushed away her dark-brown auburn curls that covered her eyes. "I'm fine. I was just picking up a wrench."

"You're so stubborn. This is why I wanted you to stay in your office."

She went to her office for the rest of the day, just to stay out of John's sight.

Chapter 41

Bad Cashier's Check

The second day Jordan was back from her St. Simon's Island trip, she heard a familiar voice in the showroom. "Hi, Scott, this is a surprise, I didn't know you were coming. What are you doing here?"

He smiled and eyed the showroom. "I wanted to see you. I haven't been here since you moved into this building. I also came up to see the 36-foot cruiser, if you haven't sold it."

She pointed down the dock. "No. It's in the slip."

"I have a buyer. I'll buy it for $270,000. That will give you a $25,000 profit and takes it off your floor plan."

"That sounds good. Who's your buyer?"

"I don't know. The buyer is sending it to Taiwan."

"Scott, that doesn't make sense. Some of the best boats are built in Taiwan and sent to the US. Why would someone there want to buy a boat here?"

"I don't know. All I'm interested in is selling the boat." His tone turned harsh and sharp. He backed away creating space between them.

"Scott, what's going on? Something doesn't sound right."

"I'm buying the boat from you. That's all you need to know."

She needed the boat off her floor plan. She made the transaction knowing the feeling in her bones told her something was wrong.

Three days after she deposited the $270,000 check, the bank president came into her office.

She extended her hand. "Well, Walter, this is a surprise. To what do I owe the honor?"

Walter sat in the chair in front of her desk and placed his left ankle on his right knee. "Jordan, the cashier's check you deposited has been canceled."

She frowned. "I don't understand. Cashier's checks can't be canceled."

Walter sighed. "A cashier's check means the money is in the bank when the check was written. It can be canceled by the person who issues it. Scott Williams canceled the check. There's nothing the bank or you can do. I didn't want to tell you this over the phone."

She had requested the Manufacturer's Statement of Origin (MSO) from Floor Plan Services to be sent to Scott since he had paid her for the boat. It hit her like a ton of bricks—she didn't have the money to pay the boat off her floor plan. In a panic, she called Scott, not surprised that he didn't answer. The trouble she was in now was only going to escalate into a nightmare. At this moment, she couldn't think of any miraculous possibilities. If FPS knew she was out of trust, they would take all her boats. She felt the panic of being thrust into a turbulent sea.

John walked into her office. She didn't turn around. She kept watching the river's flow.

"What's wrong?"

"How can you tell something's wrong?" she whispered. He had always been able to read her like a book.

"You never keep your back to me."

She turned towards him with a tear-streaked face.

He walked over to her. She stood and fell into his arms, finding some comfort in his embrace, and told him about the canceled check.

"Don't overreact."

She pushed away from him. "I've got to find Scott."

She left Lemon Bluff that afternoon for Jupiter. When she arrived at Scott's business everything was locked. Her anger flared with tidal force. Why had he done this to her? She let out a scream. Scott had left her no choice at this point except to call the factory.

Her voice was shaky. "Tom, Scott sold my 36-foot boat, and FPS sent him the MSO. I'm in Jupiter and Scott is nowhere to be found. I've called everyone I know, but no one has seen him in days."

"Did he pay you for the boat?"

"He gave me a cashier's check."

Her voice sounded calmer than she felt. She didn't lie. She didn't tell him Scott had canceled the check. "Scott said the buyer was sending the boat to Taiwan. I don't understand why."

"Let me see what I can do."

She gripped the steering wheel and headed north to her dealership. She told herself that no matter what, she could resolve the situation.

Chapter 42

Miami Boat Show

It had been three months, and she still hadn't found Scott or heard from Tom. She had called FPS to make sure that Scott had documented the boat. Which he had. She knew she was in deep trouble.

Jordan was reading a flyer from the Miami boat show organization when Tom called. "Jordan, I'm sending a new engine rep to see you. When he arrives, I want a conference call with the three of us. I'm putting one of his engines in our boats. I'm going to showcase the boat in the Miami water show."

"I was reading about the show's expansion. I was also wondering; did you ever find Scott?"

"No, it's like you said. He has disappeared."

"Have a good day. Call me when the engine rep gets to your dealership."

Jordan finished reading the information on the Miami show. They were having two shows, one in the convention center and an in-water show on Watson Island.

When the new engine rep arrived, Jordan asked John to join them in her office. "Tom said you had a new engine."

"It's a new prop concept, twin propellers. Tom has ordered twin propellers on one of his 28-foot boats. We want you to demo the boat to potential buyers at the Miami in-water show. We'll give you the boat after the show if it doesn't sell. It won't be on your floor plan.

This is our incentive to introduce the twin propellers to the Orlando market."

She made the conference call to Tom. "Jordan, what do you think about running the boat at the Miami show? An attractive woman running the boat might bring in more buyers." She heard the playfulness in his voice.

"Let me remind you I'm thirty-nine years old and I don't look like one of the eighteen to twenty-two olds sprawled out on the bow of a boat at these shows."

All of them laughed.

After the phone call and the rep had gone, Jordan thought about what might be involved with the boat being in the water. If she was going to be demonstrating the boat, it would be in her best interest to apply for a captain's license. She wasn't going to take a chance on getting into any trouble with the Miami deputies, marine patrol, or the coast guard. If someone at the in-water show asked her to move boats around or offered to pay her for driving a boat, she would need the license.

The man in the coast guard office asked, "Which license are you applying for? There are two main captain's licenses—the operator, known as a six-pack, and a master. The six-pack is for uninspected vessels up to 100 gross tons and up to 100 miles offshore."

"I'm going to be at the Miami In-Water Show."

"The six-pack license is the one you need. The coast guard doesn't give the license course. You'll need to go to a Maritime Professional Training (MPT) class that's approved by the coast guard. We only issue the license."

She took two weeks of evening classes and two Saturday classes with a final exam given on the second Saturday. After passing the course, she had to have the following documentation: proof of her sea time experience, which was 360 boating days including ninety days offshore, evidence of ownership of her boat and permanent residency, a physical exam and drug test, certification in a first aid course and CPR, and the certificate from the MPT class showing successful program completion. She had met all the requirements.

At the show, the big offshore racing boats were docked next to her. All day long the roar of the thru-hull exhaust boats made it hard for her to talk to potential buyers.

A condo resident, who lived above where the boats were docked, asked if he could board her boat. "I've been watching you for three days, and your boat has been test-driven more than any other boat in the water. Would you give me a test run?"

When they returned to the dock, the resident signed the bill of sale. Jordan explained, "You can't take possession of the boat until after the show. I'll have my mechanic go through the boat with you."

She was excited about the sale and even more excited not to have to take the boat back to her dealership. She flew John to Miami to make sure the boat was customer-ready and to give the buyer a course in operating the boat.

John spoke to the race boat drivers docked next to her when he stepped on the dock. He turned to Jordan. "Have you ever ridden in a race boat?"

"No." Then she gave him a quizzical look.

"Well, I'm going to make it happen. I'll be right back."

John knew several of the drivers. She had almost forgotten this was his territory before moving to the middle of the state.

The next morning before the show opened, the race boat driver gave her a quick lesson in racing engines. "The Mercury Racing Engine 1550 has an advanced control system. It allows the driver to switch from leisure mode to racing mode. The leisure key fob changes the engine to 1350 horsepower and runs on 91-octane gas. The key fob changes the engine to 1550 horsepower and runs on 112 AKI race fuel."

The spotter of the Fountain boat gave her a crash course about her job. There were three people positions in the boat, a driver, a throttle person, and a spotter. There were no seats. All three people stood strapped in a padded half circle.

The driver explained, "Speeding over the water at 140 miles per hour, one person can't see or control everything at once, and a slight rogue wave or wind shift can flip the boat. The driver handles the steering wheel, the throttle person is under the direction of the driver and knows when to speed up or slow down, and the spotter tells the driver which way to steer or what obstacles might be coming towards them."

She wasn't familiar with Biscayne Bay which made the throttle position the best place for her.

The driver's voice was stern. "You do what I tell you and when I tell you. Don't hesitate. Here are your goggles and headset. You can hear both of us talking. The important thing to remember is everyone does their job. He smiled and patted her shoulder. "Are you ready?"

Jordan nodded. "Yes."

Her mouth was dry, and her heart was beating so hard her chest hurt. The driver gave her his first command. "Slowly push both throttles forward."

When they had cleared all the docks, the spotter announced, "All clear."

The driver responded, "Quickly push both throttles forward all the way."

The boat was on a full plane in seconds. Nothing was in the water except a small section of the stern. The spotter was constantly on the look-out, and the driver had both hands tightly gripped on the steering wheel. The bay was smooth like glass, giving them the sensation that they were flying across the water. Occasionally, the driver and spotter would talk. Jordan stood frozen in place.

The driver said, "Jordan, you can smile and relax. Enjoy the ride."

"I'm afraid I'm going to make a mistake."

"You're doing what I tell you. Everything is fine, except you're too tense. Relax and have fun."

The driver and spotter started talking about dinner plans. Jordan relaxed a little, although she never let her guard down. She liked the feeling of working as a team. The driver started turning the boat in figure eights, making the boat go air-borne over its own wakes. It was fun, fast, and furious.

On the way back to the dock, the driver switched the leisure fob on and slowed the boat down to 50 miles per hour. After 140 miles per hour, 50 was snail speed. The driver docked next to her boat and told John she was a great throttle person and a quick study.

The owners of one of the racing teams had been watching Jordan all week. They overheard what the driver said about her. One of the racing chiefs wandered over to Jordan.

"Hi, I'm George." He shook Jordan's hand. "The crew chief for that black race boat over there." He pointed down the dock.

She laughed. "You mean the one I docked next to."

He nodded. "I've watched you all week. I'd like to invite you to our booth at the World Class Championship offshore race week. It's always held the second week in November in Key West. I'll send you an invitation." He walked away then turned and looked back at her. "I'll see you in Key West in November."

"Thank you. That sounds like fun." She answered in a high pitch squeal.

She lightly pinched her arm. She couldn't believe she had been invited to the offshore race week.

Jordan waved to John. "I'm going over to the convention center and check on Tom."

When she entered the convention hall, people were yelling and clapping. The noise was almost deafening.

She climbed into the back of the boat and sat next to Tom. "What's going on?"

He smiled and pointed to the left. "Some celebrity is over on a boat."

"Oh, that cost the manufacturer a pretty penny. It's been a fun show. Thank you. By the way, have you found Scott?"

He frowned. "No, and he's still not answering his phone."

Whoever the celebrity was, his appearance time was over and the crowd was dispersing. She told Tom she had sold the twin prop boat and about her race boat adventure.

She stood up to leave and turned around to see Brad Pitt climbing aboard her boat. She held her composure and professionalism. "Welcome, Mr. Pitt." He gave her a big smile, shook her hand, and nodded. He turned and walked into the cabin. She and Tom stayed on the back of the boat. He walked out, gave her another big wide smile, and said, "Nice boat." She stared at the back of his flowered Tommy Bahama shirt until all she could see were the backs of his security guards. Celebrities were at the Ft. Lauderdale and Miami boat shows every year. This was the first time she had a celebrity walk onto one of her boats. To her they were working people doing a job—their job just happens to be the movies. She was going to enjoy the expressions on her friends' faces when she told them she shook Brad Pitt's hand.

She took the last shuttle back to Watson Island to finish the paperwork with the buyer of the 28-foot boat. John had sea-trialed the boat earlier with the buyer. She and John buttoned up the boat, when she stepped off the boat, she shook the buyer's hand, handed him the keys, and smiled. "Enjoy your boat and be safe."

She turned to John. "I feel like I've been rushing around for two weeks. Can we take our time driving home?"

"What do you know about Ft. Lauderdale?"

"Nothing really, except what I've seen around the convention center."

"We'll be in Ft. Lauderdale in about thirty minutes. Would you like to have an early dinner?"

"Sure."

"The Sea Watch restaurant isn't too far off I-95 on A1A in Lauderdale By The Sea. It's a great restaurant on the ocean."

He slipped his hand against the small of her back and guided her up the front steps. A pair of brass doors, that looked like they could've come from the dining room off an old luxury liner, greeted them. Potted bougainvilleas lined the steps, and the scent of freshly baked bread filled the air. The weathered wood walls gave the restaurant a feel of being old and rustic. The outswing casement windows let in the fall ocean air. The dining rooms were decorated with old sea captain's memorabilia.

They watched the roaring rhythm of the waves and two wind-surfers tack back and forth on the choppy surf. The strong wind let the screeching seagulls ride the wind currents effortlessly.

John asked the waiter, "Is Sergio cooking tonight?"

"As a matter of fact, he is, sir."

"Tell him Doc John is here."

In a few minutes, there were hugs and back-slapping as if they were long-lost brothers.

John looked at Jordan. "He wouldn't let anyone work on his race boat but me. He called me The Doctor."

The Sea Watch was everything John had said. The food was great, the atmosphere, and the setting couldn't have been better. This was the downtime she needed after the long Miami show. This place, this food, this company.

Chapter 43

Photo Shoot

Jordan was settling into summer after all the boat shows had ended. Bill, the president of one of her manufacturers, asked her to do a catalog photoshoot for his boat line on the St. Johns River.

"Jordan, you're the only one of my dealers that has next year's models in stock. All my catalog shots from previous years have been on lakes. The St. Johns River shots would give us a new and different look."

"Bill, I sold the 26-footer to a young attorney with two children."

"Do you think you could get him to use his boat and his family for the shoot? We'll pay him for the day."

She called Greg and gave him the manufacture's phone number and Bill's name. Greg and his family agreed to Bill's terms, and they set a date for the shoot.

The film crew arrived with staging people, photographers, and a coordinator. The staging person's job gave all the boat's interiors a lived-in look, except for Greg's boat. She set the table with a meal, made the beds, and set out books and toys in the salon area.

The first day's shoot with Greg's family took the whole day. Pictures were taken with him driving the boat with his family, and the boat beached on a sandy clearing on the bank with the children playing at the water's edge. The sunlit clouds that drifted across the blue sky cast different shadows and light reflections making the shots appear they were shot at different times in the day.

Jordan stayed with the children on the sandy bank while Greg and his wife did a couple's shoot. The children were running and playing at the water's edge when one of them let out a loud screech. Jordan jumped up in a panic, thinking one of them was hurt.

Both of the children screamed at the same time, "Monkeys, there in that tree. Look!" They pointed to a large oak nestled among some pine trees. "See! See! There they are! Three of them!"

They watched the monkeys swing from tree to tree before disappearing into the dark shaded woods.

Jordan said. "Did you know years ago Tarzan movies were filmed on location in Silver Springs near Ocala? When the film company finished their work, they left the monkeys behind. Over the years the monkeys had baby monkeys, and now they're in the trees all along the river."

When their parents returned, the children ran to them. "We saw monkeys. Three of them were swinging in the trees."

Their mother smiled and patted them on their heads. "I don't think so, but it's fun to play make-believe."

She turned to Jordan. "Sometimes they have great imaginations."

Jordan laughed. "No, they are telling the truth. We do have monkeys."

The mother gasped. "I had no idea! I wish I'd seen them."

Greg smiled and reached for his wife's hand then turned to face Jordan. "It was a fun getaway day. I never expected to be paid to have fun on my boat. We're going to put the money in a college fund for the children."

Jordan shook Greg's hand. "Thank you for giving your time today. I'm glad you had fun."

Over the next three days, Jordan and sometimes John were on locations with the boats. The 20-foot boat was shot at sunrise. The photographer grinned. "I've been doing this for a long time. I use the sunrise for a sunset a lot of times because the morning light is brighter. I can filter the shot to give it a sunset effect."

They did an early morning shoot with fog rising from the water that gave the 28-foot boat an eerie cast. At high noon, they anchored the boat off the bank in front of a grove of palm trees. Photoshoots were taken when the shadows grew long as the sun sank into the trees, which gave the appearance that the boat was anchored for the night. A blue heron was caught in one shot as he clumsily launched himself from a fallen log to the bow of a boat.

When the catalog was distributed, the manufacturer told Jordan it was one of their best shoots.

The last Wednesday in July, one of Jordan's dealership friends in Daytona Beach called her. "Jordan, I've taken on a new boat line. The manufacturer wouldn't let me have the boats I wanted unless I bought one 32-foot cruiser with a flybridge. I know nothing about your size boats. Can you come help me this weekend with my in-house boat show?"

Jordan was surprised at Taylor's request. "You know manufacturers have done that to me several times. As many small runabout and fishing boats that you order, I'm surprised they made you take a 32-footer. Send me the specs."

Two days later, Jordan called Taylor. "Your 32-foot boat doesn't have a generator. I can tell you now, this is going to be a tough sell without a generator on that size boat."

"I didn't order a generator because it added too much cost to the boat."

"Taylor, if you're going to sell big boats, you're going to have additional costs. You'll recover the extra expense in the sale."

Taylor's boat line was less expensive than hers, which wasn't a conflict with her lines. The more she listened to Taylor, the more she felt sorry for him, he didn't know how to sell the higher-priced boats.

"I'll come Saturday and Sunday afternoon."

"If you sell the boat, I'll give you half of my profit. I only bought this boat so I could get the rest of the line." Jordan could hear the relief in Taylor's voice.

"Taylor, I don't want half. Just pay me a salesman commission if I sell it."

When Jordan walked into his showroom, it was filled with small fishing boats, nothing looked professional, including his salesmen. They were dressed in cut-off jeans and T-shirts. She thought maybe she didn't know how to sell small boats. She did know her clientele wouldn't stay long in this atmosphere.

Taylor hurried across his booth space to greet her. "I'm glad you're here. I put the boat in front."

She walked over to the boat then through the maze of small boats. There was no way for people to see the inside of the 32-footer. She didn't want to come in and take over, but it was obvious to her he needed some pointers. Everything was cluttered and mismatched, like an unkept used car lot.

She couldn't hold back any longer. "Taylor, I don't want to be critical, but your staging restricts access to the most expensive boat you're trying to sell."

"I put the big boat here to draw attention to it."

She pointed to the boat. "The size alone draws attention. Give your big boat a straight path and angle your smaller boats on the sides. I'm curious. Have you sold any boats yesterday or this morning?"

Taylor looked away from her. "No."

"Do you have any steps or a way for your buyers to get into the big boat?"

"No. I was letting them walk around and look. I gave them a catalog so they could see the inside if they were interested."

"Taylor, that's not going to work. They need to physically see the inside. I'm going to call John and have him bring over some stairs."

John arrived with the steps and surveyed the surroundings. Jordan wasn't surprised when he approached her after seeing the setup. "Taylor's boats are laid out wrong. You need to tell him how to arrange them and tell him how the dress attire of his salesmen affects the buyers' perception."

"I'm only here the rest of today and tomorrow afternoon. Taylor has a different clientele than we do. If he takes it the wrong way, it's not worth making him mad or losing a friendship."

Jordan weighed what John had said. She approached Taylor. "Can I make some suggestions? The big boat is your draw to buyers. Move it to the center in the back of your booth. Place your small boats at an angle in front. That way buyers looking for the small boats can weave in and out of them easily. The buyers for the big boat have a direct path. What do you think?"

"I never thought about putting the big boat in the back. I wanted people to see it. I do need to sell it."

"It's big enough that buyers can see it." She turned to leave then turned back around. "Oh, and one more thing. I know your buyers are dressed casually, and this is a boat show, but your salesmen don't need to look like they've just come off a fishing boat. They need to be in nice shorts and short-sleeved collared polo shirts."

Taylor shook John's hand and smiled at Jordan. "In your short time in business, you've done more boat shows than I probably ever will. I trust your judgment. I'll get my crew to make the changes. Thank you."

At the end of the show, Jordan regretted she didn't have a buyer for his 32-foot boat.

Chapter 44

Firing and Hiring Mechanics

It was one of the hottest July mornings in years. John walked into Jordan's office wiping his brow. "We need to talk."

She put her paperwork to the side and folded her hands on top of her desk, expecting bad news, "What about?"

"Chuck. We need to fire him."

"Why? What did he do to make you so mad?"

"His work isn't satisfactory. He's doesn't pay attention to details, and he makes too many mistakes. Randy and I have been going behind him constantly to redo what he's done. I'm afraid we're going to miss something and it's going to come back on you and me. You know I don't like or want boats coming back because of problems not being resolved."

"I'm sure you've had conversations with Chuck about this."

"Yes, many times. He does things right, then nothing's right. It's an on-going merry-go-round, and this morning he's doing nothing right. It's like his brain is not in his head."

"Why am I hearing about this now?"

"Randy and I thought we could work with him and solve the problem. You and I don't want boats returning for the same issues that weren't properly fixed."

"I don't like firing anyone, especially a family man." She sat thinking it through, then took a deep breath. "Let him finish out the day, and the both of us will talk to him at five, then I'll give him his final paycheck."

The thought of firing him sat heavily in the core of her stomach all day. She did trust John's decision. At the end of the day, she steeled her nerves when John and Chuck entered her office. Chuck begged to keep his job and promised he would try harder. John went back over what he had told Chuck for the last couple of months. Chuck walked slowly out of her office in silence, never looking up.

When the meeting was over, she was in tears. "That was one of the hardest things I've ever had to do."

"I know, and if I could've done anything, I would've. I couldn't. I did try. Now, that's over I need a replacement. I want to hire Mark."

"Who's Mark?"

"He came in about a month ago wanting a job. You were gone to the bank. I had him fill out an application then I filed it away."

"Have you checked his references?"

"No, I was still hoping to save Chuck."

She scanned Mark's resume. "He's worked for several marinas in and around our area, and he's still employed at one. Why does he want to work here?"

"You know, we all move around."

Jordan wasn't convinced he was the right choice. "Check him out. We will go from there."

John followed up on Mark's references and discovered he was in his early fifties with good recommendations.

John interviewed Mark, then sent him to Jordan's office. Jordan eyed him up and down. He was thin and scrawny, his big horn-rimmed glasses made his face look smaller than it was, and his long gray sideburns didn't help.

After some trivial conversation, Jordan asked why he wanted to work for them.

Mark leaned forward in his chair. "All I've heard is good things about your operation, and I'd like to be part of it. I've also heard John is the best mechanic in the state."

Jordan smiled. "John is your boss, and he is the best."

At the end of Mark's first working day, he knocked on Jordan's door, "I wanted you to know this is one of the best mechanic shops I've ever worked in and John is one of the best bosses I have ever had. His knowledge is limitless. It's a pleasure to work in an atmosphere like this."

She laughed, "Glad you feel that way since I don't know what I'm doing."

He laughed. She knew he didn't know what she meant.

Thursday afternoon, John popped his head in her door. "Jordan, come with me. I have a problem with a new generator. I've been working on it for the last three days. Whatever is wrong with it, I don't think it can be fixed. I'm waiting on the factory tech to come and see if he can find the problem."

"I'm not familiar with generators, but isn't this unusual for a new generator?"

"Yes, especially one that I can't fix."

"Can't we replace it with a new one?"

"They won't replace it until the manufacturer's mechanic authorizes it."

The generator was part of John's limitless knowledge that Mark had referred to. She smiled to herself. Despite the generator problem, John was a true treasure, and she was glad Mark had recognized how special he was. She hoped all her mechanics took the time to learn from him.

The manufacturer's mechanic spent most of the morning with John. Time and time again the generator started then shut down. The Mercury tech concluded something inside wasn't put together right at the factory.

He said to Jordan and John, "This is what we refer to as a Friday afternoon five o'clock engine problem. I'll get the factory to ship you another one."

Two days later the customer was pleased with his new generator.

Chapter 45

Hogs

Jordan thought they were going to escape hurricane season this year. There had been several up the east and west coasts of Florida in June and July. The third week of August, Hurricane Charley had crossed from the east coast to the west coast of Florida, and then reversed itself and was coming from Tampa to Orlando.

Jordan, John, Randy, Peter, and Mark had moved as many small boats as they could into the service bay area. Sam had boarded and taped all the windows. John put extra fenders on the docks to absorb the impact of the waves against the boats.

The rain came down in horizontal sheets, and the wind speed increased. The ship's store letters were flying off the building, rising and dipping across the parking lot like flying kites. The trees were beginning to lose branches, and their leaves were sailing through the air like particles of dust.

The 2:00 p.m. weather forecast reported Charley wasn't losing strength coming up the middle of the state. Jordan ran into the service bay. "Everyone needs to go home now."

Four hours later, Hurricane Charley's eye was over Orlando. At midnight, the lightning and thunder was still flashing and roaring. She watched the sky cry out in desperation through the dark gray morning light. At 7:00 a.m. the storm had been downgraded to a tropical depression. The rain still pounded her roof and windows, and there was no sign that the sun's rays would poke through the dark sky. The wind howled and the torrential rain poured all day. The electricity came back on, but there was no change in the weather. The low depression was predicted to stay on top of them for two more days. On the third day, the sky was still murky, and the thunder rumbled in the distance. Jordan tried to make her way to the marina through roads that were still running like rivers. She weaved on and off the road, avoiding small waterfalls and downed trees. She turned off Highway 415 to find Sam waiting at the gate. A few minutes later John pulled in behind her.

Sam shook his head. "The river is out of its banks, and you can't see the dock bulkhead. I can't tell the marshland from the river, and wild hogs have taken over the marina looking for higher ground."

Some of the boats were sitting on top of the docks and the parking lot was under a blanket of black hogs. Jordan drove slowly over to the service bay door. Sam and John stood by her car.

She pointed towards the river. "Sam, what are we going to do with them?"

John did a 360 observation of all the surroundings and shrugged his shoulders. "Nothing we can do until the water goes down and they go back into the woods."

At that moment, Sam's golden retriever, Duke, leaped from the back of his truck barking and running around in circles trying to herd the hogs.

Jordan opened her car door and stepped out into the slick mud. Both feet went out from under her at the same time. She landed on her back in the churned-up mess of brown. Her hair, clothes, and body were covered in mud. Duke ran over and began licking her face. Sam pulled Duke away, and John helped her up.

Jordan went to her bathroom to shower. "John."

No answer.

She screamed louder, "John!"

She thought he and Sam were still outside, so she screamed louder. "John!"

On her third yell, John called from the other side of the bathroom door. "What?"

"The shower water is nothing more than a trickle. I'm going to be in here for hours."

"Hold on, I'll check."

She waited and waited for him to return. "What took you so long? It's still trickling."

"The pressure is heavier above ground than below due to the flooding. That trickle is all you're going to get."

It took her over an hour in the shower, and she still felt like mud was clinging to her body.

The hog catcher Sam had called arrived two days later. "Everyone has hogs. There are too many to haul away, and all the land around the river is flooded. You're going to have to wait until the water recedes and the hogs go back into the woods."

The next day the river had receded enough for part of the parking lot to appear. A few hogs had started to retreat into the marshy woods, but the marina grounds still looked like a black moving mass. The hog catcher came with monster wire cages filled with corn and grain. He set the traps where he could find a few pockets of dry ground. It wasn't long before the cages were full of hungry squealing hogs. After three days of hauling hungry hogs away, the hog population was under control. Jordan was still seeing several blue indigo snakes and lots of water moccasins swimming to find dry ground. The entire river wildlife was displaced.

Meanwhile, the service department was the busiest it had been in months. The river was still out of its banks, causing boaters to hit submerged logs and sandbars, tearing holes in their hulls and destroying outdrives and props.

Jordan went down to the canal checking on the boats that were still tied to the submerged docks. She had radioed Randy to come re-tie and reposition a couple of boats. She heard the roar of engines and she knew by the sound the boats were traveling too fast on the curvy swollen river.

"Randy, did you hear those engines?"

"No, I was down in an engine hatch."

She ran to find John. She kept listening to hear if the boats were headed south. She was almost to the service bay when two boats sped around the curve. One boat was too close to the bank and hit a submerged log. The boat came to an abrupt stop, throwing the driver over the steering wheel into the woods. The other boat crossed the stopped boat's wake. When the driver swerved to miss the boat, he lost control and went airborne. When the boat landed back on the water, the driver flew over the bow into the river.

Jordan called 911 while John ran to get his boat to help. She stood motionless on the dock with the feeling that time was standing still waiting to see if the drivers were all right, hurt, or dead. The Florida Fish and Game warden had heard the boats too and were in pursuit of them, but he arrived after their crash.

Jordan watched John reach for the driver in the water. When she saw John's face, she knew immediately there was nothing he could do for him. The game warden pulled the other driver out of the woods to the bank. The look on his face was the same as John's.

The game warden said to Jordan and John, "The Florida Fish and Wildlife Conservation Commission investigates all river accidents. They will need to determine whether the boats were racing or engaged in horseplay."

The week after the accident, the game warden's report came back stating the boat that had crossed the other boat's wake sideswiped the boat, causing the boat to flip sideways onto the bank. It was ruled an accident and not a deliberate hit. The cause was recorded that the drivers were engaged in horseplay. The two drivers didn't know each other.

Two days after Jordan received the report, the wife of the driver, who went airborne into the water, came to see Jordan. She knew from the reports filed that Jordan was a witness to the accident. She thought Jordan could tell her more than what was in the report.

Jordan smiled. "Did you ever ride in the boat with your husband?"

"Oh yes, many times."

"Then you know freaky accidents can happen in seconds. I know this isn't a comfort to you. However, this was one of those accidents."

"I don't have anyone else. I don't know what to do. You know about boating accidents. Do you think I need to get an attorney?"

"If you decide to retain an attorney, you should get a maritime specialist. I don't think this is a maritime case since it wasn't offshore, but maritime attorneys know the boating laws. They know the liabilities, who's at fault, and how it applies to damages. I'm sure the river comes under the recreational boating laws. You can ask him if he thinks you have any rights, and I would also ask him about the Wrongful Death Act."

Jordan knew about the Wrongful Death Act when her father died. She didn't have any rights because she wasn't the spouse, and she was over twenty-one and wasn't dependent on any compensation from her father.

Life stared her in the face again. She called Matt just to hear his voice, then she went to find John. She needed to feel his arms around her.

Chapter 46

Rick

The beautiful fall day turned to gloom when the bank president knocked on Jordan's office door. The frown on his face told her this was not going to be a good meeting.

"Hi, Walter."

"Jordan, I know you're in financial trouble, and I didn't want to tell you over the phone." He hesitated and rubbed his forehead. "A $5,000 check has bounced."

"I knew things were going to get worse, and the snowball is now screaming down the summit. Before Scott disappeared from Jupiter, I had bought a pontoon boat from a west coast dealer. Will you make me a loan to pay for the boat?"

"I'm sorry. Our friendship is separate from our business transactions. Under your circumstances, I can't."

"For years you tried to get me to take loans out with you. I didn't need your help then. I'm begging you now, and you're telling me no. I know this is a business deal, but it's not like you don't know me. You can make me a personal loan."

"You're right. This is business, and with your business situation right now the board would never approve your loan. I'm sorry."

She sat alone at her desk and pressed her fists against her temples. She tried to keep herself calm to think clearly. She had never mastered good decisions when under extreme pressure. She made a vow to herself that she would rally out of this financial mess.

Thoughts of her father jumped into her head. She desperately wished he was still alive so she could talk to him. He would know what to do. She was glad he had let her know she had met his expectations before he died. What would he think of her now? She wanted to change things, to alter the course of events, but wanting them badly enough wouldn't make it happen. She wanted to find a place where trouble couldn't touch her. She knew now what her father meant when he told her she would find out how cruel the business world could be.

She called the west coast dealer to inform him why his check had bounced. She knew he was part of the Mafia and wasn't sure how he would react.

Charles grunted. "I already know. Word is traveling fast about Scott. He passed a bad cashier's check on you."

"I promise I'll pay you. Please give me some time."

"You have enough to worry about right now. I'm not worried about you paying me."

She was relieved he gave her some time. How did he know about the cashier's check? She was afraid if anyone knew what had happened, her business would be in more trouble than it was now.

Six weeks later, the west coast dealer's attorney came to her dealership. She explained her situation to him knowing he already knew. He was pleasant and made no threats. She assured him she would pay for the boat. After he left, she wondered why he came. Was it to make sure she was still in business, or to form opinions of her or judge her when he didn't even know her?

The river town of Lemon Bluff was like the town of Mayberry. The locals loved to gossip and would keep it stirred up for weeks. Now that word had spread about the $270,000 bad check, this would keep them talking for years.

Businesses contacted Jordan offering their help. It was a small comfort to know the town wanted to help her. She didn't need comfort, she needed corrective results.

Rick, her prominent business friend, whom she hadn't seen since the St. Simon's trip called, "Jordan, can I see you around three this afternoon? I want to help you."

"Thanks, Rick. No one can help me."

"I'll see you at three." The tone in his voice was emphatic.

When he arrived, he offered her the full amount.

"Rick, I can't let you give me $270,000. I have no way to pay you back. Yes, it would solve my financial problems, but I'm not going to be indebted to any person for that amount of money."

"I'm not worried about the money. I'm concerned about you. I can't imagine what you're going through."

"Jordan, please let me help you."

"Rick. No! The issue is closed."

"Let me take you to dinner."

"Rick, I can't."

Why was he willing to make her these offers? Was he interested in her? After his divorce, he had flirted with her at the Daytona Boat Show, and he brought her a diesel truck, which didn't work pulling boats up the wet ramp. He had tried to get her to date him after the St. Simon's trip. He had let her know on many occasions what a great businessperson she was. It still didn't make sense to her why he would offer to give her $270,000.

Chapter 47

Floor Plan Services

On a crisp January morning, Jordan hurried down the dock to meet Brandt from Floor Plan Services.

"Hi, Brandt. Two times in one month. To what do I owe this pleasure?"

"You know how the river talks. Tell me about the 36-foot boat. Did Scott, in Jupiter, buy the boat from you?"

"Let's go inside where it's warm. I must say, you're straight to the point."

She closed her eyes and lowered her head to try to compose an explanation.

"I didn't lie to you. I didn't tell you the entire story. FPS sent the Manufacturer's Statement Origin to Scott. The boat is still here."

"We trusted you, and you signed the monthly floor plan sheets indicating everything was correct and there had been no change."

She tried to explain her side if there was a side, but he wouldn't listen. She was desperate and doing the best she could under the circumstances. He was treating her like it was her fault when it was Scott's.

Her panic mode had caused her to make a bad judgment call. Procrastination at the time seemed like a good idea. She had never been a woman who lived her life by should and could. What she did was done, and her stellar reputation would be damaged. She would take full responsibility for her actions, successes, and failures. Why couldn't they understand the complexity of the situation and her motives? After he left, she sat alone in her office staring at the river. Thinking how she was going to get out of this quagmire of a mess.

She called the factory president, Tom, and confessed the whole story.

"Jordan, there's nothing I can do to help," he responded. "You have violated federal finance laws and your written contract with FPS." The word *federal* rang loudly in her head. Was she a federal criminal? Would she be sentenced?

She tried to wipe the image of jail from her mind. The only way to manage her fear was to focus on the future. She felt alone, exhausted, and like a criminal. She wiped the hot tears away with the heel of her hand.

John came into her office with long, hurried strides, yelling, "Come with me!"

"What's going on?"

When she entered the service bays, two black escalades with black tinted windows came flying past the building spraying dust and gravel everywhere. She ran into the parking lot. The sound system boomed from both cars, tickling her throat and making her ears itch. The cars raced to the edge of the river, turned around, and came to a lurching stop a little past her, then reversed a few feet back so the driver's window was level with her. The sound system fell silent, and she could hear the hum of the engine. She peered at the tinted inky glass window, but only saw her face reflecting back at her. She tried to open the locked door. She banged on the window with her fist and tried the door again.

"I'm not going to play games with you. You're trying to intimidate me. I don't get intimidated!" she yelled.

She thought her heart was going to jump out of her chest. She whirled her feet around and went back into the service bay. The cars remained motionless, their engines still humming. The cars inched forward, stopped, inched forward again, and stopped again, then they pulled away almost soundlessly back onto the highway.

Her face had turned white. She knew who they were and who sent them. She pinched her eyelids tight and then tighter to hold back the tears. She still refused to be intimidated.

John held her tight against him. "You're going to be fine."

She didn't say a word. She pulled away from him and ran back to her office. She called the west coast dealer. Someone picked up the phone then placed it back in the cradle. She knew Charles wasn't going to talk to her. He had sent her a warning.

She had no choice now. She had to go see Rick.

"I want to do more than $5,000. You're by far the most amazing person I've ever met. I've been watching an independent woman build a successful business in a man's business world. I admired you the first day you opened your doors."

She wasn't aware that anyone had been watching her. She would think about that later. Right now, she knew her time had run out with the west coast dealer.

Rick wrote her a check for $10,000. "This is my gift to you."

"I can't take this as a gift. I'll pay you back and with interest."

"Now you have to go to dinner with me. Dinner and someone to talk to, nothing else."

He stood waiting for her answer. She was completely blindsided and said nothing.

He asked again. "Dinner?"

She was an emotional wreck but not stupid. She wasn't going to mix business with her personal life.

Why did he want to take her to dinner? Her chest tightened. She was thinking no when yes came out of her mouth. Was she curious, fascinated, flattered, or lonely? She didn't know, but she wasn't going to take the time to analyze it now.

She hurried to see Walter. He wired the $5,000 to the west coast dealer. She deposited the other $5,000 in her business account.

Chapter 48

Key West Racing

J ordan was standing at her office window staring at the tree-lined bank and the rivers' slow current, clutching the Key West racing invitation when John slipped his arms around her. "What are you looking at?"

"The racing invitation. I'm not going."

He turned her around, put his hands on her shoulders, and stared straight into her eyes. "You are going! I'm here. It's next month, our slow time. You can't miss this!" His voice was strong and adamant.

Two weeks later, Jordan was on her way to Key West. The US Navy had approved the Conch OffShore Race for the second weekend in November. She had bought a powerboat racing magazine to read on the plane. She learned from the article that Key West racing was known for having the meanest and most powerful racing boats. The race course layout showed the boats would run in a horseshoe pattern. Starting in the Gulf of Mexico race around the end of Key West, up the Atlantic side, and then back into the gulf. The article also stated that the waters were the roughest this time of year. Boats could be torn apart if the driver lost concentration for a second.

Upon landing, Jordan's flight circled over Key West. She could see boats of all sizes and descriptions covering every square foot of Key West's ground surface. The minute she stepped off the plane, she could feel the ground move under her feet from the thru-hull exhausts, motorcycles, and rumble cars. Race fans and race boating teams were everywhere. She made her way to the racing booth on the west side of Mallory Square.

George, the crew chief, gave her a quick hug. "It's good to see you again. You're going to be with me most of the week. Let me introduce you to the pit crews."

"Sounds like you were appointed to be my babysitter. You have so many people to be in charge of this week. I promise I'll stay out of your way. I'm pretty self-sufficient."

All morning George supervised the crew testing the boat in and out of the water. At 2:00 p.m. George pulled Jordan's arm. "We're going to walk down Duval Street. The best and the biggest hang-out places in Key West are the Pier House or Ocean Key House, that's where most of the drivers and crews stay. The Wyndham Casa Marina, on the gulf side, is the hang out for the pleasure boat owners. My Blue Heaven restaurant is known for the best lobster omelets and Louie's Backyard Bar is the place to be in the evenings. For now, we're all going to Sloppy Joe's Bar for a late lunch and drinks. You aren't going to sit in the booth all week. There's fun to be had in Key West."

They had ordered their food and drinks when she heard a voice over the mic. "Hi, I'm Jimmy Buffett. Don't mind me, I'm just going to play a bit."

"George, I can't believe he would walk on the band platform and start playing."

"Jordan, anything can happen in Key West."

Then the pit crew chimed in. "And it usually does."

After Sloppy Joe's, they walked over to the tie-down area. In the evenings, race fans could talk to the drivers and the crews and get a close view at the boats and engines. These race boats were different from the ones that were docked next to her at the Miami show. They had one driver with a canopy cockpit and an oxygen tank on board. She hung around the booth listening to all the chatter until bedtime.

Jordan grabbed George's arm. "Good morning. I'm as excited as a kid in a candy store."

"Good morning. The race is about to start." He pointed over to Mallory Square. "You can stand over there. That's the first turn. I'll be over in a few."

The roar of the boat engines and the helicopters flying overhead was deafening. She couldn't believe the sound could be heard from Key West to Marathon.

Joe Cannon won the race last year and was favored this year. The waters were extremely rough with the wind gusting up to 40 miles per hour. The drivers were trying to stay close together to avoid as much rough water as possible. On the first turn, Jordan saw Joe's head flop to one side.

George walked over to Jordan and tapped her on the shoulder. "He must have lost oxygen and passed out."

The boat made it to the next turn but didn't turn. The boat hit a rough wave and went airborne then rolled several times when it hit the water. The 52-foot V-bottom boat shattered into large and small pieces.

George pulled Jordan close to him. "Joe's dead. It was only last month that Joe's best friend was killed racing on the Lake of the Ozarks."

Jordan couldn't take her eyes off the water. Fiberglass and boat pieces fell into the gulf like rain. She stood still next to George with her hand over her mouth. After a few minutes, Jordan looked around to see the effects on the rest of the crew.

"George, no one seems to be upset. Did they expect him to crash?"

"We all know the risks, and the race must go on."

The boats stayed on course. The crews had time to remove the boat debris and Joe before the boats had to make the turn again.

Cutter Johns was in the lead going into Sunday's race. Cutter's engine went down early. His two-thousand-point lead still qualified him for the next race, which was The Nationals. Bud Manning won the Conch race.

George smiled and gave Jordan a slight hug. "I wish I could find a place for you on the crew."

She laughed. "That's just what you need—me on your crew."

She found goodbyes harder to say than she had expected. It was a week she would never forget, and the friendships she made that week would last a lifetime.

Jordan turned her phone on when she landed in Orlando. She had three messages from Linda. She hadn't seen her since their Bahamas trip. When she and Linda were in real estate together, they formed a partnership to market aerial photos. She and Linda still owned Photo Air.

Linda sounded miffed when she heard Jordan's voice. "Where have you been? I need you to fly with me."

"I was in Key West. What's going on?" Her voice rose to a panicked pitch. "I just listed Hog Island, and I can't find anyone to take pictures. You promised you would take my pictures if I couldn't find anyone."

"I will. When do you want to fly?"

"I was hoping today. Now it's too late. Can we go tomorrow?"

"Yes, I'll meet you at the airport at 9:00 a.m."

Hog Island was in the middle of the St. Johns River. She and Linda had flown over it many times when they listed large commercial and vacant land parcels along the river.

Jordan knew the island well. She had spent many weekends with the owners after they bought the island from the State of Florida. The island was overrun with wild hogs, which they relocated and then named the land Hog Island. They built an enormous log cabin that would sleep twelve and ran city water and electricity under the river from the mainland.

She and Linda rented a 152 Cessna. Jordan missed some things in the real estate business, and flying was one of them. She had forgotten how much fun and carefree her days were before the boat dealership, though there was nothing she loved more than her boats.

"Linda, to make this trip profitable today, why don't we take pictures of the mansions along the river and the two marinas close to Hog Island? You can develop them and market the pictures to the property owners. That will help offset some of the expenses today."

Jordan snapped as many pictures as daylight allowed. Late afternoon, Linda pointed to the east. "We can take a shortcut back to the airport if we fly over the federal bombing range in Lake George."

"Can we do that?"

"It's a restricted area, but I noticed earlier today they weren't bombing."

Jordan replied. "Sure, if we don't get in trouble."

They were in the middle of the bombing air space when two F-16 fighter jets flanked them on both sides. One of the pilots motioned them to veer left.

Jordan gasped. "Where did they come from?"

"We showed up on their radar. It didn't take them long to zero in on us being in federal air space."

When they were out of the restricted area, the pilots gave them a salute and peeled away.

Jordan rubbed her hands together. "This is the second time I've been in the bombing range area. Years ago, when Nick and I were coming back from Silver Glen Springs, a quick summer downpour came up while we were crossing Lake George. I couldn't see the bow of the boat, and there was no place to stop. The next thing I knew, I was in a lot of pilings with fifty-gallon drums attached to the top of them. It was like a maze, I kept weaving in and out of them trying to find my way back into the channel. The heavy rain turned to sprinkles, then I could see the channel markers again. I guess the rain kept us from being escorted out. Do you think we're in trouble for the jets finding us?"

"When we land, we may be arrested."

For the rest of the flight, Jordan was quiet. The shock had smacked Jordan hard along with a dose of perspective. Her mind raced with all kinds of possibilities. What would happen to her business if she were arrested? Could she be arrested for two different federal accounts—one for violating federal finance laws and now the federal invasion of air space? She had worked too hard to have it all disappear because of two stupid mistakes. Would she go to jail, and if so for how long? Would she serve double time on the accounts? John was going to be furious with her for not thinking.

Linda interrupted her thoughts and broke the tense silence. "Are you okay?"

"Yes, too bad we don't have a parachute. We could use one about now. If you didn't jump I would."

Linda laughed. Jordan could only force a half-smile.

The feds or the local sheriff wasn't there to greet them when they landed. A sigh of relief came over Jordan. They did agree never to fly in a restricted area again.

The entire experience had put Jordan on edge and made her rethink her priorities. "Linda, we need to think about what we want to do with Photo Air. Do we need to keep it? Maybe we should dissolve it. I don't have time to devote to it, nor do I need to fly any more for business."

"Let me think about it, and I'll let you know."

Jordan sighed. She hoped Linda would agree to end the endeavor. She needed one less thing to worry about.

Chapter 49

Lawsuit Served

The week after Linda and Jordan had flown, Jordan peeked out her office door to see who the deep, barking voice belonged to in her showroom. A burly sheriff was talking to Maggie. His mustache wiggled as he spoke. "Is there a Jordan Harris here?"

Maggie, being the protective secretary, answered, "Yes, what do you want?"

"This is a matter between Ms. Harris and me."

Jordan sucked in a deep breath and bit her bottom lip when she heard her name. She paced around her desk waiting for Maggie to come into her office.

"A deputy sheriff is asking for you."

"Did he say what he wanted?"

"No. He has papers in his hand."

"Well, he's not going to go away. Send him back."

The deputy filled her office door with his bulky frame. He had a gentle manner along with a pleasant face. "I'm sorry." Then he handed her the court papers.

She accepted the papers with a frown. "Thank you."

She scanned through the papers and stood gasping, dumbfounded, and her breathing became labored. FPS was suing her for one million dollars for violating her contract and breaking federal finance laws. She had thirty days to respond. This was the final blow in a series of disasters that already seemed endless with Scott.

Shock hit first and then nausea. She was being accused like she was a criminal. She closed her eyes and let the tears flow down her shirt. She wanted to find a place to hide where she could leave behind her obligations, her cares, and her duties. She felt like surrendering. Life had turned on a dime. Was it time to give up?

John walked by her office. "Hey, what's wrong?"

She was speechless and couldn't face him. Her throat tightened, and her tears began to flow again. The warmth of his arms gently folded around her and his familiar scent of musk cologne reassured her she was safe for a moment. He held her in silence while uncontrollable tears poured down her cheeks. Her life was shifting under her feet like an earthquake. No one could help her, and no one would understand the enormity of her situation.

She pulled away and wiped the tears from her face. "We need to get back to work."

John let his arms fall slowly to his side and walked back to the service bay.

Rick bounced through the side door next to her office with his big smile. "Good day or bad?"

"It's just a day." Her voice trembled. She hated the sound of weakness. Her throat was dry and she had a choking feeling like dry cotton was stuffed in her mouth.

She wasn't ready for anyone to know she was being sued and the charges that were involved.

"Hungry at all?"

"No Rick, I haven't thought about food."

He smiled. "Think about what you're hungry for. I've got to run down to my boat. I'll be back in ten minutes." He glanced back at her when he reached the door. "No strings. Just lunch. Nothing else. I promise." She watched him slide into his orange Boxster Porsche, acting like he was twenty years old again.

She was out of practice at gauging this kind of thing. She hadn't been anywhere near a pickup line in years. She didn't even know if it was one. Since John had been at the dealership, he had been her protector, watching her every move to make sure no one made any off-color gesture or made a pass at her. This time was different. She knew Rick, and it was lunch, but having lunch with him probably wasn't a good idea, especially in her present state of mind. She was vulnerable and unsure of herself, or her feelings, and her judgment.

True to his word, Rick was back in ten minutes. "Are you ready?"

Everything about him was perfect—his designer clothes, his short sandy-blond hair with not one hair out of place, and his clean-shaven face accented his round jawline. It all matched his charm and charisma. He appeared to be prepared for more than a simple lunch.

Did he know about the lawsuit? He had given her thousands of dollars. She was so involved in herself and what was happening to her business she never gave a thought about how much money he had. Her stomach had turned into a hardball. There were so many may-be's—maybe this wasn't a pickup attempt, maybe a mercy mission, maybe he knew she was in meltdown mode, maybe the lunch invitation was well-meaning, or maybe he wanted to offer her financial advice. She convinced herself to stop guessing and have a nice lunch with him.

He opened and closed the passenger door for her then slid in behind the steering wheel. "I thought Wally and Julie's would be a good place for lunch today."

Wally and Julie were husband-and-wife and owned the restaurant. The name didn't fit the upscale restaurant with the white table-cloths, crystal glasses, and fine china. All the judges, lawyers, real estate brokers, and bank presidents ate lunch there most days. Many business deals were conducted during the lunch hours. This was one of Jordan's favorite restaurants, but it was too far from the river for her to come for lunch. Rick had made the right choice for whatever he was up to.

The conversation was light and cordial speeding through town. She caught herself reaching for the door when she saw him coming to her side. He offered his hand to help her out of the low-lying seat. His blue eyes danced when he touched her hand. She could tell by his actions she was a person of interest to him and this had nothing to do with business. He leaned closer and stared at her in a way that held her against the seat. She was confused. He had given her money with no strings attached, and he had offered her a way out of the biggest financial mess of her life. Did he think by helping her financially that she would fall in love with him? She was baffled by his actions and her thoughts.

The chatter came to a halt when she and Rick entered the restaurant. It was as if everyone was surprised to see her, or was it they were surprised to see her with Rick? One by one they all acknowledged her in one way or another, whether by a soft-spoken hello, a nod, or a wave.

Rick chose a corner table at the back of the room. Before she could take a seat, Chase, a long-time friend, and judge walked over to say hello. They exchanged quick kisses on both cheeks.

Rick settled into the black velvet chair and studied her deeply. Whatever he was thinking he kept to himself. "I'm not trying to pry, but I got the impression when you were in my office the other day that you might have a little too much on your plate."

Another surprise from him. His gaze held hers and offered a host of hidden meanings. She decided to stop analyzing or to try to speculate what he might be thinking. He watched her eyes as if he could read her secrets as if he knew something was definitely wrong.

On impulse, he leaned over, lightly held her chin in his hand, and laid his soft lips lightly on hers. Her lips parted under his before she could think to block his kiss. Her pulse shivered, and her heart skipped a beat. A rush of warmth flooded through her. The kiss only lasted seconds, but it was easy, smooth, and skilled, and lasted longer than she wanted. He had caught her by surprise. His gaze had given her a warning, but she had ignored it and allowed herself the experience. When he drew back, she raised an eyebrow.

"And that was because?"

"You needed it." He gently took her hand in his.

He leaned forward again. This time she found the presence of mind to lay a hand on his chest. A hand that wanted to hold him in place rather than nudge him away. The kiss was unexpected and nice, but she wasn't going to allow one moment to dictate her feelings. She recoiled, shaken but determined to stay in control.

Rick grinned. "I think the appetizer was great. Would you like to order now?"

He uncorked the bottle to let it breathe, sniffed it with approval, and poured two glasses. She cradled her fluted crystal glass in her hand. He took a sip, never disconnecting his eyes from hers. She pushed her food around then put her fork back on her plate. She muted him in her mind. He wanted a woman who would be interested in him. She wasn't that woman.

He rubbed the back of her hand. "I wish you would tell me what's wrong. I'm sure I can help."

She knew he wanted to smooth the dark shadows away from her eyes and make her laugh again. Things would have to change drastically if he wanted to see more than darkness. Since all this started with Scott, deep lines of concern had overtaken her face.

She forced herself to smile through the fog that threatened to choke her. "Let's just have a nice lunch and leave the problems behind."

She could tell by the way he leaned forward, and the twitch on his lips that he wanted so much more. The last thing she needed was more complications in her life. A monetary lifeline was a great temptation. She wasn't going to destroy everything she had worked for the sake of solving her debt. She turned her attention to the dessert menu.

Chapter 50

Finding an Attorney

Lunch with Rick had been a distraction, but reality had set back in. Jordan made an appointment with her attorney. At 10:00 a.m. the next morning, she walked into Alan's office dressed to the nines. She needed all the self-confidence she could muster.

"Good morning, Jordan. Can I get you anything? Coffee or water."

"She forced a slight smile. "No, thank you."

She handed him the court papers and settled into a large high-back chair in front of his desk. Alan read the contents, rubbed his forehead, and placed his glasses on the desk. "This case is way out of my field. You need a high-profile law firm that has experience going up against big corporate guns. Let me see if I can find you someone that is experienced in fighting big corporations."

The calls Alan made seemed to alert every attorney in town about her situation.

A week later, her judge friend, Chase, called. "Jordan, I have several attorneys working on finding you the best law firm. I have called every reputable law firm from Jacksonville to Tampa. Floor Plan Services has every large law firm on retainer. All of us are working on this. We will find you, someone."

Two weeks later, Chase called her with an update. "Jordan, I've found a high-powered law firm in Daytona Beach that will take your case. Ryan Young is a criminal law litigation attorney with a winning track record for large settlements with corporations."

Jordan's late husband was an attorney. She had socialized with attorneys her whole married life, but this was different, she wasn't in a social setting this time. Butterflies fluttered in her stomach driving on I-4 to Daytona Beach to meet with Ryan Young.

Ryan shook Jordan's hand. "Hi, Ms. Harris. May I call you Jordan? I am Ryan."

She smiled. "Sure."

Ryan was in his mid-thirties, handsome and intelligent, and from his preliminary introduction, he had won many lawsuits for clients that had been sued by large corporations.

"Jordan, this lawsuit is going to take several years to litigate. I'm sure we can win this. Floor Plan Services filed the lawsuit in Tampa, which means I'll have to respond to the court orders and the court hearings in Tampa. I'll try to do as much as I can to keep travel times and your costs to a minimum."

He touched her arm sympathetically when she left his office, giving her a ray of hope.

The following week, Ryan picked her up at the dealership for their first court appearance at the Tampa courthouse. Ryan spent the two-hour trip preparing her on what to expect from the judge.

"Ryan, I still don't understand how Scott stopped the cashier's check."

"The legal term is kiting. It's a form of check fraud and it is a federal offense. He had the money. He used it for something else. You could bring a lawsuit charging him with kiting. In business law-suits—fraud, honest mistakes, and coincidences are the most com-mon reasons for lawsuits."

"This wasn't an honest mistake or a coincidence," she replied. "He knew what he was doing. I don't want two lawsuits going on at the same time."

She still found it hard to believe that Scott had intentionally done this to her. No one still had found Scott or could determine what happened or why.

Ryan shifted his position behind the steering wheel. "I was a CPA before getting my law degree, and now that I know Scott is guilty of kiting, I'm obligated by law to put out an arrest warrant for him. Scott sold the 36-foot boat to an Arab through Taiwan. The Arab changed his mind about buying the boat and wanted his money back. Scott had already spent the money, which is why he stopped the check. Did you know Scott filed for bankruptcy?"

She shook her head. "No. He's full of surprises. How do know about the Arab?"

Ryan looked at her with a big smile. "I have my sources."

"Why did FPS wait almost a year before serving me?"

"I can't answer that. Could be for many reasons. Maybe they were trying to find Scott."

The long oak bench she was sitting on outside the courtroom doors was becoming harder and harder. Her blouse felt damp underneath her suit. With each passing minute, she felt more and more like a criminal as lawyers, clerks, and others who passed by stared at her as if she had already been convicted. In her mind, she was here because of two people, Scott Williams and Phillip Stover. Scott because he sold her boat without paying her and she was being sued for his fraudulent action and if Phillip hadn't changed her corporate job description, she would've never been involved with Scott or a boat dealership.

The sound of the courtroom doors opened and jolted her back to the present. Ryan sat down beside her and chuckled. "I'm sure I made the right call having you wait out here. You wouldn't have sat quietly listening to all the accusations." He placed his hand on top of hers for a brief moment. "The judge ruled for the proceedings to go forward. I'm going to request the depositions be taken in my office. It's better for FPS to absorb the expense and have their attorney drive to Daytona Beach. It will also be more comfortable for you in my office than in theirs."

Monday morning, two weeks after she returned from Tampa, Jordan was on her way to Daytona Beach for her deposition with FPS. She had stayed awake all night reviewing over and over in her mind how Ryan had prepped her. FPS was going to take her deposition, and Ryan was going to take FPS's representative deposition.

Shortly after FPS's attorney started deposing her, she felt like a criminal sitting across from Brandt. Her skirt had twisted in her wringing hands under the table. Brandt's manner was professional. He looked comfortable as if he had done this many times before. He was pleasant to her, although he sat rigid. His personality was totally different from when he came to her dealership each month checking her boats.

The questions from FPS's attorney made her head spin. It was as if she were floating in darkness through endless hallways with no doors or windows and no way out. He was rapid-firing questions at her, not giving her time to think. A rising tide of nervousness mingled with guilt made her answers sound vague and incomplete. She felt drugged and dizzy. It was obvious she was extremely ill at ease. The questions weren't anything like Ryan had prepared her for. Fear rose inside her.

Ryan asked FPS's attorney for a recess to confer with his client.

"Jordan, what's wrong? I'm here to help you. All you need to do is answer the questions truthfully. Stay calm. I hope to heaven you aren't trying to protect Scott Williams in some way."

"No, I don't know how to answer the questions. I'm afraid I might say something that could incriminate me."

Her self-defense mechanism had shut down. Nerves shimmered in her stomach, making her nauseated, and perspiration beaded on her brow.

"I'm asking the questions next, and I prepped you well."

She had never been so out of control in her life. All she could think about was going to prison. She was used to being in a win-win situation, and she was in a non-win position now. The deposition couldn't have been worse for her, and it couldn't have gone better for FPS.

After FPS's attorney and Brandt left, Ryan paced back and forth. "You didn't help your case today. I'll do what I can. Brandt is sharp, smart, and knows his job. If we go to trial, FPS will be hard to beat. The odds aren't in your favor at this point."

When she reached her car, she inhaled an enormous breath of fresh air. On the way home, all she could think about was Ryan telling her she didn't help her case. This was only the beginning of what Ryan said was going to be a long haul. She never envisioned the predicament she was in now.

Friday morning, Ryan came to her dealership. "Jordan, the judge has set a preliminary court date for FPS and you. You don't have to go. I'll let you know the judge's ruling."

"No, I want to go. I couldn't stand waiting. I want to know what's happening when you know."

Ryan stepped before the judge's bench. "Judge, my client hasn't done anything wrong, and she is going to fight the lawsuit." The judge told both attorneys they would hear when the court date was set. On the way home, she tried Scott's number again. No answer. Then immediately, her phone rang back showing Scott's name. When she answered, there was nothing but silence. Was he going to tell her the truth or tell her more lies? Where was he? What was he doing? Why had he done this?

Maggie knocked on Jordan's door. "Tom is on line two."

"Tom, what can I do for you?"

"Jordan, this is an information call. Brandt has informed me that FPS is going to pick up all your boats. I tried to co-sign for your floor plan but FPS said that you couldn't be on any floor plan with them while there was an ongoing lawsuit. I'm going to take over your floor plan on my boats except for the 36-foot boat. That way you will still have your boats. Brandt didn't think this was a good decision on my part. He said you could do this again. Jordan, I trust that you didn't have anything to do with Scott's fraudulent acts."

"Tom, thank you for trusting me. I promise you I didn't know what Scott was doing."

Jordan stared into the mirror in the bathroom. All she could think about was she was being sued for Scott's fraudulent acts. Her despair morphed into a fit of feverish anger. She saw her face turn purple. Her rage sparkled in her bright blue eyes, making them as glassy as ice. She never hated anyone the way she hated Scott at that moment

Chapter 51

New Judge

Five months after the first court date with the Tampa judge, Ryan received a letter from the court informing him that Jordan's judge had a heart attack and another judge would be assigned to her case.

Monday morning, John saw her at her desk in a daze watching the river. "What are you doing?"

"Nothing." She cleared her throat. "Thinking. It's amazing what we do to our lives by the choices we choose."

John stood silent next to her; she could see the pain in his eyes. "I'm here for you, but you already know that. I can't stand to see you this depressed."

"I keep telling myself that strong women aren't born, they are made by the storms they walk through. I wonder if I will survive this storm."

The tears were brimming in his eyes. "I can't stand to see you like this." Then he walked out of her office.

Jordan thought about filing bankruptcy. She left a message on Ryan's voicemail. Ten minutes later her phone rang. "Ryan, if Scott could file bankruptcy and walk away free, why can't I?"

"You don't need to file bankruptcy. Bankruptcy only frees you from creditors, not from criminal lawsuits. Scott isn't free from kiting."

There was that word again—criminal. She had a hard time thinking she was one. Her world was being pressed in a vice, trying to destroy everything she'd accomplished. She wasn't going to give up, and she would fight to survive to the end.

Ten months later, Ryan went before the new judge telling him she was defending the lawsuit. The pressure kept building inside Jordan. She thought she couldn't take much more.

"Ryan, this is dragging on forever. Customers are few and far between, and I'm working out of my reserve account. Am I going to have to sell my inventory at auction? The idea of losing my business is unbearable to me."

"Remember, I told you when we started this was going to take years. It has only been twenty-two months."

"I didn't know it was going to be this draining or that my hopes and dreams were going to die. I never thought that I might lose everything. There are times when it is all I can do to get out of bed, drive to work, and face my employees and what customers I may have."

"We haven't lost yet. The new judge was a setback but don't give up."

She was traveling down a road of humiliation, guilt, and failure. There was no hope left in her body thinking this could be the death of St. Johns River Yachts. She was isolated and alone, even with people around her. She wept a lot throughout each day, feeling all the zeal and enthusiasm being zapped from her body. She slept very little and went days without eating. Her hours were short at the dealership, which put all the work on John. She condemned herself to death without actually dying. She contemplated jumping in the river with no intention of returning to shore. Despite her depression, she was still hoping for a loophole and wishing for an eleventh-hour miracle.

She knew John was doing everything he could to keep her off the ledge. She saw the pain in his hollow eyes every time he looked at her. She knew he would do anything for her, but there was nothing he could do. There was nothing anyone could do.

John stuck his head into her office. "The buyer for the 45-foot houseboat is here for his sea trial."

"I don't know why he has insisted that I go. Let me straighten my desk. I'll meet him at the boat."

The buyer was pleased with the sea trial. On the way back to her dealership, he said to John. "I don't know how to tie the boat to the riverbank to anchor overnight."

John turned the boat into a back-water slue away from the heavy boat traffic in the river. He scouted for a suitable bank to tie the bow to. The bright midday sun peeked through old tree branches, casting shimmering highlights on the rippling dark water.

John stood next to the buyer and pointed to the bank. "Pick a spot where there are no low bushes or trees. It's good if you can find a solid low log to tie to."

The buyer squinted. "It's hard to tell with the shimmering sunlight reflecting off the water."

"Yes, it is, and when you get to places where the sun gets blocked the shadows make it harder to see where the bank ends, and the water begins." John pointed to the bank. "Tie the bow to that low solid log. After you tie the bow then set your anchor in the water. Here's how you make knots to tie the boat from the bow cleats to the heavy tree branches."

The buyer leaned too far over the back of the boat to see the depth of the water, lost his balance, and fell head-first overboard. Jordan yelped. She and John helped him back onboard. He looked like he had been baptized with water pouring from his clothes. He pulled his wallet from his pocket and spread its contents on the dining table to dry.

He gave a slight smile. "I'm not hurt. I'm embarrassed."

The owner saw Jordan's grin and her biting her lower lip. He started to laugh. Jordan and John laughed. The three of them belly laughed for several minutes.

Jordan wiped her eyes. "I needed this laugh. It's been months since I've laughed this hard." She took the bottle of champagne and three plastic stemmed glasses from her bag. "I always give a bottle to every new owner who buys a boat over thirty feet. I think we need the champagne now."

The buyer gave a toast. The three of them sat on the back of the boat and polished off the bottle of champagne.

The owner was semi-dry now. "I've never had an experience like this before."

John chuckled. "Being a new boat owner, you're going to have many unusual and new experiences. The next spot you're on your own. You're going to pick the docking site, tie, and anchor the boat."

On the way to the next slue, they were still laughing.

Chapter 52

Green Turtle

Wednesday morning, Jordan's co-owner of Photo Air and longtime friend, Linda, bounced into her office. "I heard about your problems. I've got some free time. Why don't we go to the Bahamas? You need a break from all this legal stuff."

"I can't leave."

"Did the judge say anything about leaving the state or the country?"

"No."

"You need to get away and clear your head. Call and get us a house for two weeks. I'll fly us over."

This was the only bright thought that had swirled around in Jordan's head in two years. Why not? She wasn't any good to anyone here in her current state of mind. At the end of the day, she told John about Linda's suggestion.

John put her hand in his. "I think that's an excellent idea. You need to get out of here. We aren't that busy. I can handle everything."

She found Henry's business card from the last time she was in Green Turtle Cay. She stared at the card and played with it in her hand. She didn't know if Henry was still there, it was long before she had started St. Johns River Yachts.

She was surprised when he answered on the first ring. "Henry, this is Jordan Harris in Florida." They spent a few minutes catching up on the last few years, and then she asked. "Do you have a house I could rent now for two weeks?"

She thought she could hear him chuckle. "Yes, I do. Four-bedroom, two baths, and on the water, and I'll throw in a runabout boat."

"I don't need four bedrooms. It's my friend and me."

"I tell you what. I'll let you have it for the price of a two-bedroom."

"Thanks, I'll see you Monday."

Treasure Cay and Green Turtle Cay were two small islands separated by a three-hundred-foot canal. The landing strip was on Treasure Cay. Boats stayed on both sides of the canal for anyone to use going back and forth. There were no cars on Green Turtle only golf carts and bicycles. Henry had arranged for a boat to meet them on Treasure Cay and bring them to the dock at the house on the south end of Green Turtle.

Henry waved when he saw her coming up the cobblestone street. His smile was familiar and friendly. He welcomed her and Linda. "I came to unlock the door. Here is your key." Jordan gave a quick glance down at the skeleton key.

The screen door was swaying in the breeze. The windows were all open except for the four-bedroom windows on the second floor. Jordan could hear the air-conditioner and see the flutter of the white organdy curtains. The light blue shutters across the front of the house looked freshly painted, and the two blue Adirondack chairs on the porch matched the shutters. A rose-draped whitewashed picket fence gave the house a warm inviting welcome. It gave the appearance of peace and serenity, not at all like the sort of house that had time for people with problems.

Henry turned to leave. "The 19-foot runabout has a 60-horse-power motor. It's stripped-down, but it will get you everywhere you want to go. I'll make sure the boat stays full of gas. It's easier to run it up on the beach and tie it to a rock."

The locals passed by waved and smiled. The neighbors next door came to welcome them with information about grocery stores, shopping, and where the locals' partied. Everyone considered them being part of their island.

A middle-aged woman stopped by to tell them to go to Abaco Groceries, Ltd. "It's a big wholesale grocery warehouse in Marsh Harbour. That's where everyone on the east side of the Bahamas and Abacos buys groceries." She pointed east with her crooked index finger. "There's also a bakery at the top of the hill." Using the same bent finger, she pointed up the hill. "It's in a gray-haired woman's house. You have to go there no later than seven-thirty every morning or the hot bread will be sold out."

The next morning, Jordan walked up the steps to the open door of the bakery house. She knocked and waited. No one came to the door. She knocked again. On the third knock, a heavy-set woman came to the door.

"No one round here knocks. They's just come on in. You'd be the new lady down the street."

Jordan smiled. "Yes, I want to buy bread."

"You knows the breads made from bread fruit trees. We'd been making these breads for hundreds of years in all these Caribbean and West Indies islands."

"How do you make bread from a tree? Or is that a secret?"

"Nos secret. We's just peel the fruit, mash it, and use it like flour. It be's moist and only last a day."

The bumpy dark green fruits were the size of honeydew melons.

After the bakery visit, Jordan and Linda made a full-page grocery list. Early the next morning, they set out in the 19-foot runabout for Marsh Harbour. The nautical chart Jordan had was weathered, torn, and hard to read. She never thought about bringing the charts from her own boat or a compass. The man next door had given her directions, but out on the open water all the islands, sky, and water looked the same, making it hard to tell where they were.

Jordan's father had taught her how to navigate by the sun when she was five. If she got separated from him in the cornfields, he wanted her to be able to find her way back to the road. He said, "The sun rises in the east and sets in the west. If you are facing the morning sun, north is left and south is right."

The further south they went, the smaller the coral islands became. Now they were barely hovering above sea level. To the west, the big mountain islands ascended out of the sea like a tapestry of ridges into the clouds. The turquoise-blue water gently rolled onto the white sand. It was amazing how the palm trees could be so adaptable, growing in the lush terrain of the mountains and the barren sand on the beaches. The beauty was something she would never forget or ever get tired of seeing.

Jordan and Linda were laughing and talking when they were interrupted by the silence of the engine. Jordan tried everything she knew to make the engine start. She stood up to reach for the oars when she lost her balance, almost toppling overboard. She started spinning her arms to regain her balance. Jordan hadn't noticed the waves when the engine was running, but now that they were dead in the water, she realized how hard the waves were slapping against the boat. The oars were no match for the waves.

"How much further to Marsh Harbour?" Linda asked.

"I'm not sure. We should almost be there. Keep paddling. I don't want the current and wind to drift us in a different direction. Let's try to keep the boat going straight."

What seemed like an hour was only fifteen minutes when they saw a small boat coming toward them. A man and a young boy tossed them a rope and towed them a short distance around a small island. To their surprise, Marsh Harbour came into full view.

He pulled them to a small dock where one boat was half sunk and another one lay on its side. He pointed to the left. "You's find the mechanic's house four streets over. Just yell and he be's right out."

She and Linda ate lunch at an open-air bar then bought groceries while the weathered, white-haired man tightened the loose spark plug.

Jordan tried to pay him. He shook his head. "Everyone in these islands be's family."

She knew to look for loose wires and plugs. John wouldn't believe she had missed that. Just because she was on vacation didn't mean her brain should be. The thought of John made her realize how much she missed him.

After grocery shopping, she and Linda splurged on ice cream sundaes from a vendor's ice-cream stand. Two men were sitting at an outdoor wrought iron table playing checkers. Neither one of them seemed inclined to make a move. Two women were chatting in a store doorway across the street, but only one of them carried a shopping bag. It was fun to sit among the sea grape trees and observe the local culture. Lemon Bluff seemed so far away, and so did her troubles for the moment. Linda was right this trip was exactly what she needed.

They paused at a straw lean-to. Jordan asked, "How much?"

"Three dollars, ma'am," the young girl replied.

Jordan handed her a five-dollar bill.

"No, you keep that." Jordan patted the girl's hand when she tried to hand her two colorful Bahamian dollars.

"Thank you, ma'am." Her big smile showed her pearly white teeth.

Linda said, "I saw several straw hats in your room. Why didn't you bargain with her?"

"I know how long it takes them to gather the palm fronds, dry, and weave them into hats or whatever else they make from the fronds. Besides, I don't have a wide brim with woven red flowers."

Halfway back to Green Turtle, they heard, "Meow, meow."

Linda jumped. "What's that cat doing in the boat?"

"I don't know, but I'm not going to take him back. He's island-hopping now. He was probably a stray anyway. A lot of the islands are overrun with cats."

Linda petted him, then the tabby jumped on Jordan's lap and slept the rest of the way.

Linda laughed. "I suppose you are going to give him a name."

"Tabby's a good name. He'll be my vacation keepsake while we're here."

Chapter 53

Miss Emily's Blue Bee Bar

The shadows were long, and the sun was low when they beached the boat. Jordan had told Linda about Miss Emily's Blue Bee Bar and her world-famous Goom Bay Smash drink. After the long day, drinks at Miss Emily's were going to have to wait until another night.

At midnight, the thunder rolled, and the lightning scattered over the dark sky. A gust of wind blew the front door open. Jordan rushed to close the creaking screen door and then shut the solid wood door. Lightning slashed the sky again and the house shook.

Jordan walked from room to room to survey any damage. Linda followed her around in her furry slippers. "I think everything is good. There's a tree lying against the kitchen wall."

Linda shuffled into the kitchen. "Some storm."

Jordan and Linda sat in two rocking chairs in the kitchen and drank coffee until the wind died down. Tabby slept on the floor under Jordan's chair, as if nothing was happening.

The rain was still pounding the roof when the sky grew light.

Jordan had already made coffee when Linda meandered down the stairs. "What are we going to do about the tree?"

"I'm sure Henry will be by soon to check on us."

The landlord's crew came early to remove the tree. Another crew came to fix the damaged roof and eaves.

Jordan stared out the window. "Linda, the sea is still rough from the storm. We won't be fishing today, but we can hunt for conch shells along the water's edge. It would be a good day for conch chowder."

They headed to the beach and before long they found two large conch shells. An islander walked by. "You ladies knows how to fix them conch?"

Jordan shrugged her shoulders. "Not really."

He showed them how to cut the conch from the shell and pound the meat to make it tender for cooking. After dinner, they went to Miss Emily's for Goom Bay Smashes. Jordan and Linda entertained themselves with billiards and darts and kept urging the steel drum band to play until they refused to play any longer.

Miss Emily was eighty years old, thin, and frail. She was in the bar every night and had been for the past sixty-five years. The recipe for her concoction was several different kinds of rums, cream, and fruit juices. Miss Emily's was the only bar on Green Turtle. All the locals and people from other islands came to drink her world-famous Goom Bay Smashes.

It was after midnight when Jordan's eyes flew open. Confused for a moment, she couldn't decide if the noise she heard was in a dream or if the noise had awakened her. She lay still, taking slow shallow breaths listening for the noise again.

A soft moan echoed against the weathered walls and drifted its way up the stairs. Was Linda up? If not, was she hearing the same noise? The feeling in her bones told her it wasn't Linda. Jordan slowly crept to peer over the stair rail. A man in a dark plaid shirt was sitting in the shadows on the bottom step. Her heart pounded so hard; she was sure he could hear it. Linda had said she locked all the doors. Who would have come in? She peered out the window. The street was quiet. She moved closer to the landing, ready to bolt down the stairs and out the front door.

His head rolled sideways against the white peeling spindles, and long strands of sun-bleached braided hair lay on his shoulders. Who was this person? Where did he come from? Why was he in the house?

Jordan scurried down the stairs past him, flipped on the light, and ran out onto the front porch. Henry, the homeowner had arrived and yelled, "Skipper!" She gasped and jumped to the sidewalk.

Henry turned to see Jordan standing behind him. "I didn't mean to frighten you."

"Who is he? Why is he here?"

"This used to be Skipper's mama's house before I bought it. He lives with his cousins over yonder." He pointed over to the base of the mountain. "Sometimes when he has too many spirits, he comes here, like coming home, I guess. He's a good boy and harmless. I'll talk to him tomorrow when he sobers up."

Henry got Skipper up and out the door. Jordan let out a long sigh.

Linda appeared at the top of the stairs. "What's going on?"

Jordan waved her hand towards the stairs. "Nothing, I'll tell you in the morning. Go back to bed."

Jordan knew she wouldn't be able to sleep. She walked to the water's edge. The moon was a fat ball floating across the night sky. It shed its soft white light over the high choppy water. The cicadas were singing in their high monotonous tones, and an owl called out in tireless two-toned notes. She loved the peace and the stability she found here. She could live here and never give a thought about big city life. She knew John would love the island life, too.

Skipper came by midafternoon. Tabby wandered in and out between his ankles in a figure-eight loop. He picked up the cat, gave him a quick pat on the head, then released him. "Miss Jordan, I'm sorry I came into your house last night. I was kinda confused."

"It's okay, Skipper. I understand, but you did startle me. I accept your apology." She knew Henry had sent him over.

She and Linda sat on the front porch looking at the streets, which were nothing more than wide pathways with salt-weathered houses lining them. There was no roar of car engines or honking horns. The small, sleepy island was peacefully dozing in the sun, nothing seemed to matter, it was the sea and endless sky. The view from the porch went for miles, and the quietness expanded out into the soft lapping waves. The sounds of boat engines off in the distance gave way to light humming sounds. The sounds of the island were all around, with another cotton candy sunset. She could smell the white jasmine hedge along the fencerow at the back of the house. Scenes and smells like these were made to persuade her that her problems were smaller than she imagined.

The wind wrenched the door from Jordan's hand. She caught it in time to stop a thunderous slam against the wall. She flipped on the lights to chase away the shadows of the evening. The pale green walls gave a cast-like fog was throughout the room.

Linda yawned. "I'm going to my room."

Jordan grabbed a book from one of the shelves, but she couldn't get her brain to concentrate. She went to lock the door then wondered why she should bother. Was she the only one with a skeleton key, or did everyone on the island have them? What good was it going to do to lock the door? After all, Skipper had gotten in. She decided to lock it anyway.

She made her way to the kitchen and poured herself a glass of pinot noir. The floor groaned when she walked to the fridge. The streetlights outside flickered as the moon slipped below the rooftops. Through the open windows, she could hear the soothing night sounds of the crickets, the frogs, and the lapping water. She climbed the creaking stairs hearing the mice scampering in the walls. Back in her bedroom, she rocked slowly in the antique rocker, sipping her wine and watching the palm fronds sway in the shadows while Tabby slept on her bed. This place seemed to have a magical aura, a haven where problems didn't exist. People here understood the allure of the island.

The next week, she and Linda fished, and on a couple of days, Skipper joined them. It was as if she had been here all her life. She refused to think about what was happening at Lemon Bluff, although she wished John was here.

Time was short on the island now. She would soon be back to reality, not knowing what her future held.

Skipper came by the morning they left, picked up Tabby, and said his good-byes. They cleared customs in Ft. Pierce and were home in two hours after leaving what Jordan thought was a fantasy dream.

Chapter 54

E-15

The morning after returning from Green Turtle Cay, Jordan returned to the dealership not wanting to be there.

John greeted her with enthusiasm. "I'm glad you're back. I missed you. You look rested and happy. I can tell the two weeks were what you needed. Everything here has been fine."

She smiled and gave him a hug. "It was good to take my mind off the lawsuit. I missed you, and there were days I wished you were there with me."

He smiled coquettishly. "Let me bring you up to date." Jordan sat down behind her desk and John sat in the chair in front of her. "*Boating Industry* Magazine has been calling you. They want you to meet with them in New York."

"What about?"

"They wouldn't say. They've been persistent in trying to reach you. I did find out that Mr. Cohen is the president of the magazine. Here's his phone number."

Jordan sighed and stared at the number. She picked up the paperweight that Tom had given her at the first dealer's meeting with the company logo on it. It was hard to believe she had been on the river nine years. The last two years had been a challenge with the lawsuit, and she still didn't know how that was going to end. She had renewed her strength in the Bahamas and was ready to take on FPS to the end. She turned around in her chair and faced the river. What if the magazine wanted an article about her lawsuit? She wouldn't know unless she called. She reached for the phone and dialed the number.

"Mr. Cohen, this is Jordan Harris at St. Johns River Yachts. I understand you've been trying to contact me."

"Yes, I have. Thank you for returning my call. My committee wants to meet with you. We'll fly you to New York."

"What committee? What's this about?"

"I was hoping being president of *Boating Magazine* would make you come. I'm afraid if I tell you, you won't come."

"I can tell you don't know me. I can assure you I won't come if I don't know the reason. What's the meeting about and with whom?"

"We want you to speak to the International Women in Boating about fuel."

She cleared her throat. "Fuel? I don't know anything about fuel."

He continued. "The boating industry needs help with the EPA. We need a spokesperson for the women, and we think you're the best person."

"This sounds like an industry problem. I'll meet with your committee, but I won't make you any promises. Can you send me any information to bring me up to date?"

"Yes, I'll do that. I need you to be in New York City next Thursday. Your ticket will be waiting for you at the Delta ticket counter in Orlando."

She studied the material and information carefully and concluded this was way out of her field. She understood what the EPA was trying to do. This had been an ongoing battle with the marine industry ever since ethanol had been added to gasoline. She didn't know how she could help. She had been through the engine problems when gas went from leaded to unleaded, E-0, then to 10 percent ethanol, E-10, and now the EPA was trying to get 15 percent, ethanol, E-15 in the marine engines.

The committee included the president of the Chicago boat trade show, the presidents of *Boating Magazine* and *Boat Industry*, a congressional lobbyist, the presidents of Mercury Marine and Johnson Marine. At the meeting, Jordan was asked to speak to the women at the Chicago IMTEC annual meeting the following month. The committee explained they needed everyone to get behind their congressional representatives to stop the EPA from adding more ethanol to marine gas. They gave her all the reports and studies verifying what they wanted her to say to the women. Women would be there representing every state, and with their knowledge of the fuel problem, they could get the marinas and boaters in their area active in the efforts to stop the EPA. The *Boating Industry* committee would help the International Women in Boating organization push for a large turnout to their annual meeting.

Jordan asked, "Why me? The president of International Women in Boating should speak."

"You've spoken to this group before and being Marine Woman of the Year gives you the credibility and influence. You're a very interesting person, and you do inspire women."

Jordan shook her head. "I do know E-15 won't work in marine engines. We're having enough problems with E-10. If you think I can help, I'll do it."

The next month over 250 women attended the annual meeting. Jordan couldn't believe she was going to talk to this many women. She could feel her knees shake when she walked to the podium. Then she reminded herself that these women were like her, and the marine industry had asked for her help. Jordan started her speech by telling them how they could make a difference in their towns and state.

"The EPA is trying to use fewer fossil fuels and is moving towards renewable green alternatives. Using 15 percent of ethanol has been proved to be a dangerous risk to boater safety and boating performance. It damages the engine rods and causes the rod bearings to break into small pieces. Boater safety is compromised when the engine suddenly cuts off. Marine engines aren't normally used every day like car engines. They're infrequently used, and the interaction with water is impacted by the ethanol blends. The chemical properties in ethanol cause it to attract and absorb water. When ethanol gas sits for periods of time, the water separates from the gas. A marine engine won't run on a water-soaked ethanol solution that sinks to the bottom of the gas tank, which makes the solution highly corrosive. The results of ethanol in marine engines cause safety problems, significant engine damage, poor engine operation and performance, and difficulty starting the engine. Higher oxygen in E-15 causes the fuel to burn hotter, which raises temperatures, which in turn reduces the strength of metallic components in the engine. Congress can veto the EPA's proposal with enough protest from consumers and proof that the product is unsafe and harmful. You can make a difference in your towns and state. I'll give each of you a copy of my speech so that you can share it with your customers, friends, and congressmen."

The women gave Jordan a standing ovation and said they would oppose E-15. Some of the committee members she had met with in New York were in the audience. Mr. Cobb waited behind Jordan until she was free from talking to some of the women one on one.

He shook her hand. "Jordan, you did a great job in promoting awareness and support. The women could relate to you. Would you be open to being president of International Women in Boating?"

She smiled. "I'm flattered, and I appreciate the offer. I'm a sole proprietor. I can't afford the time away from my business. Ask me next year, if you still want me."

If the committee knew about her lawsuit, would they still want her? She had been humiliated enough. She wasn't going to take a chance on the lawsuit becoming public.

Chapter 55

Belize

John met Jordan at her arrival gate. "How was Chicago?"

She gave him a long hug. "It was good. There was a huge group of women there, and they listened to me." Her voice was light and airy. "They said they would do what they could. I think I did do some good. They made me feel better about myself." She grinned. "Maybe I'm not so bad." Then she smiled.

He gave her a quick hug. "Who is Ken Stoutman?"

"I don't know. Why?"

"He's been in the dealership several days while you were in Chicago. I tried to talk to him, but he will only talk to you."

"Well, I assure you that name isn't familiar to me at all." Laughing, she leaned into him. "Are you jealous?"

John parked at the service bay. Randy ran and opened Jordan's door. "He's here now asking for Ms. Harris."

She turned to John. "That should tell you he doesn't know me if he's asking for Ms. Harris."

She peered into the showroom through the service bay door. He was a medium-sized man with graying brown hair and nicely dressed. He looked more like a businessman than a boater.

She walked through the service door with confidence. "Mr. Stoutman, I am Jordan Harris. Please come to my office and tell me what I can do for you."

"I've read about you being the Marine Woman of the Year. I've researched you in the public records and talked with people in the marine business. You're a very impressive and outstanding businesswoman."

She frowned and narrowed her eyes. "Are you some kind of investigator?"

In her present situation, she didn't trust anyone. She didn't know who was going to come after her next.

"No, I own property and a banana plantation in Belize. I want to open a resort and for you to be my partner. Ms. Harris, I want you to supply pontoon boats for the rentals. I will split the rental fee with you fifty-fifty."

She stopped him at that point. "I'll sell you as many boats and engines as you want. I won't be responsible for the boats and engines once they leave my dealership. I'm not getting involved with the Mexican government or the possibility of the Mexican cartel."

He moved forward in his chair. "The boats can be hauled over the road from Texas down through Mexico."

She placed the palm of her hand flat on her desk. "That's all well and good for you. I'm not going to haul boats to Mexico."

He sat back in his chair. "I'll acquire all the necessary forms from the immigration office to enter Mexico, including a temporary vehicle import permit for your trailers and vehicles."

She stood and walked to the front of her desk. "Ken, you're not listening!" In a stern voice, she continued. "I'm not taking boats into Mexico. Thank you for coming in." She walked to the door. "Our conversation is over."

Ken continued to visit her dealership for the next several months with different businessmen, bankers, investors, and friends trying to persuade her to deliver the boats and engines and to be a part of his rental boat business. John wanted her to get a court order restricting him from the property.

She did some research to satisfy her curiosity and found that boats entering Mexico had to be certified to a marina and the marina had to inform the proper tax office. The next time Ken came to see her, she invited him into her office.

"Ken, please have a seat. I've done some investigating into Belize's businesses. "What's your status in Belize? Is the marina built? Is it open for business?"

He shook his head. "I'm trying to get investors. I've only cleared the ground."

Her voice was pleasant, but stern. "When you first came to me, you led me to believe your business was ready to open. You don't have any investors. You tried to get me to agree to do a partnership for the boats, then you'd tell the investors you already had the boats. You pitted everyone against each other. I want you to understand that my final answer is no. I'll sell you the boats and engines and rig them for rental use. I've told you before that's all I'm doing. I don't know who's helping you in Mexico, but it seems to me you're a long way from opening your resort."

"I was lining everything up getting ready for your boats to be delivered."

She stared at him without blinking. "I'm sorry. I'm not going to get involved with you or Mexico. You need to go find a partner that speaks Spanish. I do wish you luck."

Ken walked to her door hesitated then continued to his car.

Chapter 56

IRS

Two months after she had last seen Ken, Will placed the morning paper on Jordan's desk. He pointed to the obituary page. Her eyes widened as she read the name Kenneth Stoutman. At the end of his column were the words, "After a short illness, cancer was the cause of death." Jordan swiveled her chair around to watch the flow of the river. The river was her peace and her strength despite the fact it demanded so much from her.

After lunch, John sent Randy to get Jordan to help them launch a boat. On her way back to her office, Maggie, her secretary, approached her on the dock. "An IRS agent is waiting to see you." She handed Jordan his card.

Jordan slowed her pace. "What else is going to be thrown at me?"

When she walked into the showroom, she didn't see anyone. "Will, do you know where the gentleman went who was waiting to see me?"

"I think he walked outside."

She opened the door where her new boats were backed to the ramp. The man turned, faced her, then extended his hand. "Nice boats. I'm Larry Wilson, Ms. Harris. I'm from the IRS. I need to see your payroll records." His voice was emphatic and deep.

She gave him a quick once-over. He was tall with a round bulging middle. His chocolate eyes matched his short curly black hair.

His suit coat was unbuttoned and wrinkled as if he had slept in it. She turned, opened the door, and gestured for him to enter before her.

When inside the showroom, she asked him to follow her to her office. "I have no problem with you checking my records. I've paid all my payroll taxes."

She placed all the records on her conference table, then she offered him a cup of coffee. His eyes widened when he reached for the cup. She kept checking with him throughout the afternoon. He stood and his eyes always widened when she came in to have casual conversations with him. Her motive was to see why he was checking her payroll taxes.

At five o'clock, he asked her to take a seat. "Your records are well-kept. You were reported for not paying overtime."

Her voice was strong. "That isn't true. I've always paid over-time. Who reported me?"

"I can't say, but that person doesn't work here anymore."

She knew immediately that Chuck, the fired mechanic, had reported her.

Mr. Wilson smiled. "Ms. Harris, you owe thirty dollars to Charlotte Adams for overtime."

Jordan glared at him. "Charlotte hasn't worked here in five years. I have no idea where to find her. She was a boat cleaner I hired to help the regular cleaning crew during boat shows and to clean this building." Jordan laughed. "I remember she almost blew up the building the day she poured bleach and two other cleaning chemicals in the toilet bowl. We were lucky that she ran to get me before she flushed the toilet. When I approached the bathroom, smoke was boiling from under the door. My service manager said the toilet water had to be dipped out. He didn't know what would have happened if the toilet was flushed into the septic tank. If she had flushed the toilet, she might have blown us up." Then they laughed. "It wasn't funny at the time."

Mr. Wilson shuffled his papers. "Mail the check to her last known address. If the check is returned, you need to advertise in the newspaper under the personal ads, or personally go to her last known address and see if anyone knows where she can be found. In thirty days, if she hasn't contacted you, you don't have to do anything else."

When Mr. Wilson turned to leave, he extended his hand again to her. "I've never been treated so nicely doing an audit."

She smiled. "I know a little bit about auditing. I had nothing to hide, and you were doing your job."

After Mr. Wilson left, John peered into her office. "Is everything good?"

"I owe thirty dollars in overtime to Charlotte Adams. I have to try and find her."

He sat down behind his desk. "I know where she works. I can stop on my way home and give her the check."

To keep from showing how surprised she was, Jordan ran out of her office and down the dock. Why was John still in touch with Charlotte? How could he be seeing her when he spent so much time here? It wasn't any of her business, and she had no hold on him. How and why did he know where she lived? There had to be an explanation. She didn't have the nerve to ask, or maybe she was afraid of his answer.

Chapter 57

Jordan's Surgery

Jordan watched from her office window at the summer thunderstorm clouds rolling in. The sky turned black and the wind whipped and bent the trees. John gave a courtesy knock as he entered.

She folded her arms on top of her desk and gave John a slight smile. "I'm glad you're here. I have something to ask you?"

His eyes danced. "Shoot."

She stared at him. "We've always been honest with each other. Right?"

He frowned. "Yes, where is this going, Jordan?"

"You and Charlotte. How do you know where she's working?"

John chuckled. "Why are you stewing over Charlotte? After she left here, she contacted me for grocery money. You know she's a single mom. I gave her money, and then a week later she asked for more. I did some investigating and found out she was on drugs. I reported her to child services. She's out of rehab, clean, and she has her child back. I check on her occasionally."

She smiled. "Why didn't you tell me?"

"I didn't think about it. There wasn't anything to tell." He laughed. "Anything else on your mind?

She grinned. "No. Thanks for the honesty."

He laughed. "Before you attacked me, I came in to tell you Randy and I are going to do a test run on a boat before the rain starts."

Jordan turned to the window and looked at the sky. "Do you have to do that now? When did you tell the owner his boat would be ready?"

"This afternoon."

Jordan watched John and Randy walk down the dock to the boat from her side office window. She felt better now that she knew why John had seen Charlotte. She wished he hadn't given her money. Big-hearted John—that was another reason why she loved him.

She continued to watch the black clouds race across the sky. She hoped John and Randy would be back before the rain and lightning became too fierce. She watched them past a boat with an open engine hatch. She ran down the dock to close the hatch before the rain soaked the engine. Randy had left his big toolbox sitting on top of the manifold. She had to lift one end of the box and prop it on the deck, then push the other end onto the edge of the deck. It took her several times moving the toolbox a little at a time before she could close the hatches.

She sat on the floor in the main salon of the boat listening to the torrential rain until it let up enough for her to run back to her office. She ran through the parts room, stubbing her toe, and stumbled on the two engine manifold boxes that the UPS driver had left in the middle of the parts doorway. She had asked Will to move them two days ago. She pushed and pulled the heavy boxes along the floor until she could get them into the service bay area.

A month later, Jordan saw her GYN doctor down at his boat with John.

She waved to him. "Can you come into my office when you finish with John?"

He took a seat in front of her desk. She described the changes she had felt in her body.

He crossed his arms and smiled. "You're going to deny what I am going to tell you because you think you're indestructible. You've lifted things that were too heavy for you. You have a prolapsed uterus.

Your only option is surgery. If you choose to opt-out and keep lifting and straining, the condition is going to worsen."

She knew the manifolds, toolbox, and hatches were heavy. She didn't know lifting them would cause a prolapse. She made an appointment for the following week. He set the surgery date for the second Monday in July.

Monday afternoon when she woke from surgery, John was sitting by her bed. He gave her a quick kiss on her forehead and left.

Early Tuesday morning, John stuck his head in her doorway. "Hi, I wanted to see how you were doing this morning."

Before she could answer he was gone. That afternoon, she was surprised when most of the marina boaters came to see her.

Wednesday morning, John stuck his head in her door again. She motioned for him to come in. "What are you doing? You poke your head in the door and then leave."

"I wanted to check on you. I'll talk to you later."

She grabbed his arm. "John, thanks for coming and giving me the business updates. You don't have to rush off."

Thursday morning, John stood in her hospital doorway. "How are you today? Feeling any better?"

"Come in. The pain isn't so intense today."

He took one step into her room. "Have a better day today. I'll see you later."

"John, wait. What's wrong? The last two days you have rushed in and out."

"The truth is, I can't stand to see the IV lines attached to you. His voice was low and cracked. She saw his watery eyes. "This isn't you. You're too active to be lying in a hospital bed."

"Give me a little time. There were some complications in surgery. I will be fine. Please don't go." He surprised her and stayed an hour.

Thursday at noon, John brought her a chick-fil-a sandwich and informed her of what was happening at the dealership.

The nurse woke her early Friday morning when she came to check her bandage. She pulled back the sheet and with a cheery smile said. "You're going home today after the doctor sees you."

Jordan was packing her suitcase when a man walked by her door. He stopped, turned around, and stepped inside her room.

His face turned pale, and in a shrill tone asked. "What happened? Tell me what I can do?"

"Hi, Rick. How are you?"

"Fine, but I'm on this side of the door." He gave her a half-smile.

"I had surgery five days ago. I'm going home today."

"I didn't know you were here. Why didn't you let me know?"

"I'm fine. Honest. I'll see you next week at the marina."

The orderly was rolling Jordan to the elevator. She raised her hand. "Stop. Back up, please." It was her friend and Photo Air partner.

"Linda, what are you doing here? I've been two doors down for a week."

Linda's face was white and drawn, her body was thin and frail. Jordan approached her bedside and saw her tears.

Jordan asked the orderly to leave. "I'll call for you shortly."

"I have ovarian cancer. The doctors are sure it has metastasized. I'm refusing chemo treatments. I'm considering homeopathic herbs."

The news stunned Jordan. She could feel her own eyes start to burn.

"I was going to call you." Linda gave a slight smile. "I never dissolved Photo Air."

"I'll do it. Is there anything I can do for you?"

"No. I'm going home tomorrow and wait on time."

She sat next to Linda on the side of her bed. She held her hand until Linda drifted off to sleep. She sighed, leaned over, and lightly kissed her cheek. "Goodbye, my dear friend."

Jordan spotted Linda's husband in the waiting room. Steve's conversation stopped when Jordan sat down next to Pat.

"Can I do anything for the two of you?"

Steve kept his eyes focused on the floor. "No. I'm going to close my automotive shop, and Pat came home for her mother's surgery. She's going back to California to close her surf shop. She will come back and take care of her mother."

"Steve, I know what it's like to lose a spouse." She reached for Pat's hand. "I lost my mother when I was much younger than you.

It's going to be rough. I know, I've been there. Both of you will get through this."

Jordan's doctor gave her strict orders not to leave her house for six weeks. The fourth and fifth week she went to the dealership for a couple of hours a day. Her doctor had kept a close eye on her, not releasing her until after nine weeks. She wasn't sure why so long unless he knew she would be back doing something she shouldn't.

John was like a watchdog when Jordan returned to work. She had to admit she liked the attention. "I promise I won't pick up anything heavier than a cat. Stop hovering."

She caught him several times watching her out of the corner of his eye.

Chapter 58

Barbecue

It had been seven months since she had heard from Ryan. She was surprised when he walked into her office.

"Jordan, I just came back from Tampa for a hearing with the new judge. He told FPS's attorney they couldn't sue you for a million dollars when you were out of trust for $245,000., and the boat is still in your possession and your other floor plan boats are still on your property. He told him he had to get FPS to reduce the amount or he was going to rule this as a frivolous lawsuit."

Her body shuddered, and tears filled her eyes. "Ryan, that's great news. Thank you."

Ryan frowned. "Don't get excited yet. This is not over, but it is a step in our favor."

Maybe there was a glimpse of hope after all, and maybe when all this was over, her world would fall back into place instead of falling apart.

Jordan had been deliberately ignoring Rick's call since she had seen him in the hospital. Maggie, her secretary, eyes always lit up when she heard Rick's voice. "Why won't you talk to him?" He's handsome, rich, single, and has a great personality. He's hard for any woman to resist. He could take good care of you. You should spend more time with him."

"Maggie, I'm not interested."

"If John wasn't here, you would be."

"Maggie, what does that mean?"

Maggie turned her attention back to her desk. "You know."

Jordan chuckled as she walked back to her office.

The next morning, Maggie handed Jordan the phone then quickly scooted out of Jordan's office.

"Good morning, pretty lady. I'm having a barbecue tonight. Please don't disappoint me. Say you'll come." She cringed when she heard Rick's voice. She knew she couldn't hide the lawsuit from him any longer.

"Rick, I'm really not up to a party."

"You have to come. I won't take no for an answer. See you at six." He hung up before she had a chance to say no.

She drove slow approaching Rick's house, she had the urge to drive right on by, which didn't make sense. Why did she come anyway? She and Rick had shared nice lunches and had lots of pleasant conversations, and he had loaned her money. They had a lot in common being business owners, even though he hadn't had her business problems. He hadn't been pushy or persistent. He had flirted from a distance. He stayed away from anything indicating a long-term relationship. She had made it clear to him she wasn't willing to accept anything romantic. He had tested her by stealing a kiss to see if he had any territory. He had offered sympathy and acceptance with her situation and understood how and why she had trusted Scott. It was the first time she felt like someone understood, really understood, how she was struggling.

Rick was standing at the front gate when she arrived. "I was starting to wonder if you were going to come or not and whether I should've made the call." Then his smile curved upward to let her know he was teasing.

She felt self-conscious in her tan Bermuda shorts and loose-fitting flowered shirt next to his white slacks and crisp navy-blue shirt, although he wore no socks with his loafers. His clothes fit in a way that screamed tailored and not from a rack. He didn't look like he was dressed for a barbecue. He always dressed like he was going to a business meeting.

"You're shaking."

"It's cold. I forgot my sweater."

He laughed. "It's not that cold. Come here."

"No. I'm leaving."

He positioned himself between the car door and her before she could open it. He drew her firmly against him, wrapped his arms around her, and held her.

"Let me go. She wrestled to get free. "I don't belong here."

He held her tighter. "Yes, you do. Something is going on, more than what you're letting on. You've become so distant and I want to know why."

She was holding herself rigid as a slab of marble. Her hands gripped his shoulders, her fingers clenching and unclenching. She was sobbing now. He gently cradled and rocked her while hot, desperate tears flooded from her eyes and soaked his shirt. Her body violently shook like a firestorm had whipped through her. He didn't tell her to stop. even when the sobs shook her so violently it seemed her bones might snap. He didn't offer promises of comfort or solutions. He stroked her hair and cradled her while she wept out the pain. When she had cried herself dry, her head felt swollen and her throat was sore. Weak and wearied, she lay exhausted against his chest and in his arms.

"I think after all this you need to tell me why you're so upset."

She stepped away from him. "You haven't heard? I'm a business failure. My floor plan company is suing me for being out of trust with a $270,000 bad cashier's check. They served me with a one-million-dollar lawsuit. I have an attorney, and he's been to court several times. Nothing has been decided. I could go to jail."

"I don't think you're going to jail." He chuckled. Then wrapped his arms around her again. "I had no idea you were under this much pressure. I don't know that I could handle what you're handling."

"I'm too mentally drained to fight all this." Her voice became strong and with determination, she continued. "I can't stand the thought of not trying or losing."

"Fighting and losing—both those experiences teach valuable lessons. You're a smart woman no matter what happens, don't ever forget that."

"I didn't handle it well tonight. Without thinking it all caught up to me. I'm not the smart, amazing businesswoman you think I am."

He put his index finger across her lips before she could say anything else.

"Yes, you are. You're doing everything right. Hang in there, something good will come from all this. You can talk to me anytime. I know you. You will succeed."

She waved him away from the car. He opened her door. She slid behind the wheel. He took the keys from her hand and reached in front of her to start the engine.

"We'll talk later. Good night, sweetie."

She drove away watching him in her rear-view mirror until he was out of sight.

Chapter 59

Cal

In ten years, John had never been late for work without calling. Monday morning, he didn't answer his house phone, nor his cell, and he hadn't called Randy.

Jordan's bones ached. She knew deep down something was wrong.

At 4:30 p.m., John sauntered into her office. His tired eyes showed he hadn't slept. He sat down in his chair and stared at the river. She waited in silence for him to speak.

"Cal, my son from my second marriage, showed up on my doorstep Saturday night. He was stoned on something. I couldn't make any sense out of what he was trying to tell me."

Jordan blinked twice, trying to keep her eyes from widening. "Take your time. I'll listen when you're ready to talk."

John cleared his throat. "He's been asking for years to come and live with me. Lisa wouldn't allow it. Lisa and I had an agreement before we married—no children and no animals. We had a son and two dogs. You know I have a son and daughter from my first marriage, which ended when I was twenty-two. My first wife and I were too young, and neither one of us was ready to give up anything for the other one. I have no idea where those children are. They were in Tampa the last I knew. Cal is sixteen. His mother works for L'Oréal as a cosmetologist consultant to department stores in Miami. She's on the glamour queen circuit and never wanted to be a wife when I met Lisa. Lisa was suited to me. She scuba-dived with me, went to the racetrack when I raced cars on weekends, and we enjoyed our nightlife. Cal is one of the reasons why Lisa and I divorced. She never wanted Cal around."

Jordan rubbed her forehead. "You can't take care of a sixteen-year-old by yourself. You leave home before seven-thirty every morning and return home between seven and eight o'clock at night. I'm sorry. I don't know what to tell you."

John was at work early the next morning. He looked like he was only going through the motions. He was quiet most of the day. He talked when he was spoken to and gave short answers. She knew exactly what emotions were stirring inside him. It wasn't the same as her lawsuit, but both their worlds had been turned upside down.

"John, let's go to lunch. I know there's nothing I can say that will help your situation. We both need a break from being here." At lunch, John pushed his food around on his plate. She reached across the table and held his hand. "My heart hurts to see you hurting."

He kept staring at his plate. "I keep thinking things would have been different if Lisa would've let Cal come and live with us years ago."

"John, you don't know that. The divorce could've happened if Cal had come. You can't blame yourself."

"Carol's willing to move in with me."

Jordan was stunned. "Who's Carol?"

"Last year when I went to Ft. Lauderdale to renew my mechanic's license, I met her in the hotel lobby. She's a nurse. She contacted me six months ago and said she had moved to Sanford, on Lake Monroe across from the dealership. She is working at Florida Hospital in Orange City."

Jordan pushed her plate away. She was almost in shock. She couldn't believe John hadn't said anything about Carol. She thought there were no secrets between them.

She called for the check. "John things will work out. We need to get back to work."

Jordan sat in her office going over what she thought she knew when John went to mechanic's school. She knew John had stayed at

Jib's house when he was in Ft. Lauderdale. Jib and John were in class together. She didn't know the three of them had hung out together after class for drinks and dinners. Jordan's opinion of Carol was that she wanted a man and she was sure to meet one hanging out in the hotel lobby after mechanic classes.

Her mind raced with questions. How did John really feel about Carol? Was he going to let her live with him so Cal could move in? Was Carol doing this hoping for a marriage proposal? Mostly, Jordan wondered why she hadn't picked up on any of this? Was John as happy as he seemed, or was it a front? How was this going to change her bond with him?

At the end of the day, Jordan asked John to come into her office. "Tell me where our relationship stands. Is Carol moving in with you?"

John stared out at the river. "Jordan, I've replayed our situation over and over in my mind, and I have viewed it from every angle. I've watched you with people and how you run your business. I love you. I'm a mechanic, and I know no matter what we feel for each other it would never work."

"John, you're my anchor and partner. How can you say that?"

"Over the years I've been in your world. I'm not comfortable meeting with bankers, profitable businessmen, and lawyers. Carol loves me. She can help me with Cal. I don't love her as much as I love you. I need her, and she needs me."

Jordan never expected to hear these words from John.

Chapter 60

Connor's Death

After a month, Jordan had pushed the John and Carol situation out of her head. Her full concentration was back on her business. She heard the air brakes whoosh on the big rig out in the parking lot. The boat she had ordered for her friend, Connor, had arrived. Connor had been her neighbor for twenty-three years. She had been his sounding board through two divorces, been to his two daughters' weddings, and bought him another cocker spaniel after Peaches died. When Connor bought his first cabin cruiser, she bought his bow rider. It was her first boat. Their families had spent many weekends together at Silver Glen springs or just cruising up and down the river. She, Matt, and Connor went fishing a lot of afternoons at the end of her teaching day.

She didn't know who was more excited, her or Connor for him to get the boat of his dreams.

John lifted the boat off the transfer truck with the forklift to the hydraulic trailer. The cleaning crew was already headed to the service bay before Jordan had the delivery papers signed. By the time she had reached the service area, all the shrink-wrap had been stripped, and John and Randy were starting on the outdrives.

"John, I would like to call Connor. I know I ask this all the time, but when will the boat be ready?"

He pointed to everyone working on the boat. "We'll be done with it in the morning. Don't be so pushy." Then he winked.

Jordan hurried to the phone. "Connor, your boat is here. You can pick it up tomorrow." There was silence on the other end.

"Conner, did you hear me?"

"Jordan sorry. I guess reality hit me that I'm actually going to own a brand new boat after all these years. Can I come now to see it?"

An hour later, she met Connor outside the service bay.

Connor looked at the boat with a grin from ear to ear. "Wow, she's a beauty. You have no idea how excited I am. I have owned boats my whole life. This is my first new one."

John walked up behind Connor and clapped him on the back. "Wait until you see her detailed. When the guys take a break, I'll have them pull the boat out so you can go through it. Our insurance doesn't cover anyone in the service area except employees."

Forty-five minutes later, John found a stopping point and pulled the boat out of the service bay to allow Connor to board.

Connor spent an hour running his hand over all the surfaces in the cabin, sitting behind the helm, and fondling all the controls. Jordan climbed on the captain's bench beside him. "If you want your boat tomorrow, you're going to have to let John and Randy finish."

Slowly, he climbed down the ladder, still looking at every inch of the boat. "I'll see you in the morning around ten." His whole face was one big smile.

The next morning at eleven, there was no sign of Connor. "John, this is not like Conner. I expected him to be here when I got here this morning."

She called Connor's house. "Hello?" said a sobbing woman.

She recognized the voice. "Julia, what's wrong?"

In between her sobs she finally answered, "Connor's dead. He was so excited about his new boat he couldn't sleep last night. The doctor said with his previous heart conditions, his heart couldn't take all the adrenaline. He died this morning at five."

Jordan was speechless. She put her hand on her chest to slow her breathing.

After work, she went to Julia's house. Half the town was there giving their condolences and supporting Julia. Jordan loved Connor like a brother. She needed to be alone. No one would notice if she disappeared into the garden.

It was as hard for her to let go of Connor, as it was for Julia. In fact, she had known Connor longer than Julia had. At the funeral, one of Connor's best friends asked Jordan about Connor's boat.

"It's for sale. I gave the deposit back to Julia."

The following week, Connor's friend came to look at the boat. While he was there, he also had questions about other boats that were for sale, including Jordan's personal boat. After a couple of hours, John delivered Connor's boat to his friend.

Jordan sat on the back seat of the *Charisma* for the last time waiting for the prospective buyer to sea trial her boat. She hadn't taken time to take her boat out more than a couple of times since she opened St. Johns River Yachts. After Connor's death, she needed to make life's unexpected turns easy for Matt. As much as she hated to, she knew it was time to put *Charisma* up for sale.

The buyer was a night construction worker, and his wife worked days. He came to sea trial the boat with his two-year-old son. On the way back to the dock, he asked if he could drive the boat. His son was sitting in his lap. He turned to Jordan. "This is the boat I've been wanting for years. Can I dock it?"

He had proved to her he could handle the boat on the sea trial. She agreed.

John was standing on the dock. Jordan tossed him the mooring lines. The buyer was slowly entering the slip when the child pushed the throttle forward, ramming the bow into the sea wall. Jordan was thrown against the passenger seat. The buyer quickly thrust the throttle into reverse, tossing Jordan to the back of the boat against the aft seat.

John tossed the mooring lines back into the boat and jumped away from the dock.

Jordan took over the helm and docked the boat. Her shoulder was bruised but not broken.

The buyer pulled out his wallet. "Jordan, I am sorry. I'll pay for the damages."

"My fiberglass man will repair the bow, and I'll add the cost to the bill of sale."

After the buyer left. John grabbed Jordan's arm. He pursed his lips. "Why did you let him dock the boat the first time he drove it? You know better."

Jordan pulled away from John. "He didn't have any problems handling the boat. I never thought about the child grabbing the throttle. Why are you so irritable all the time?"

John turned and walked away in silence.

Chapter 61

John's Heart Attack

The next morning Jordan was at the hospital at 6:30 a.m. She hadn't talked to John since he walked off the dock yesterday afternoon. She wasn't leaving his bedside until he woke up. At 7:45 a.m. he slightly opened his eyes.

"John, do you know where you are?"

His voice was deep and groggy. "Hospital. What happened? I don't remember much of anything, and I really didn't want to know until now. I remember the pain being unbearable, like blunt nails stabbing into my chest. People were touching me, and unfamiliar faces were staring at me. Bright white lights burned my eyes. Someone kept saying stay with me, John. I remember it hurt to breathe and my chest felt like someone was sitting on it. Then I heard sirens, voices shouting, and machines beeping."

"You were at home having dinner, grabbed your chest, and fell to the floor. The cardiologist put two stents in your right ventricle and two in your left. You are very lucky that you don't have any heart damage."

He closed his eyes. "I remember, I kept drifting from darkness to light. My eyes felt heavy. I tried to open them, but it took too much effort. I was cold and green-suited people were hovering over me."

A nurse with blond hair piled on top of her head and a weary-looking doctor with gray hair walked into John's room. Jordan released John's hand and moved away from his bed.

John squinted. "Are you my doctor?"

The doctor placed his stethoscope on John's chest. "Yes, and you're lucky to be here. You had a severe attack, but you have no permanent heart damage."

"I'm tired. I just want to sleep."

The doctor turned to Jordan. "He's fine. It's going to take a while for him to recover. I'm going to keep him here for a few days."

Carol spent her days sitting with him, and Jordan stayed with him at night.

The third morning after John's surgery, Jordan opened her eyes when Carol entered his room. "Good morning, Carol." She stood and stretched. "He had a pretty good night. I'll see you tonight." She couldn't bring herself to say much more, her emotions were too raw. She hadn't accepted John and Carol being together.

On the way to work, Jordan's insides were in turmoil. Her thoughts kept drifting and wandering back to what she would do if something happened to John, then tears clouded her vision.

After dinner, Jordan walked into John's room. Lisa, his ex-wife, was leaving with their ten-year-old son. Lisa hugged Jordan. "I'm glad you're here. He's been asking for you. He drifts in and out of sleep. He needs you. This attack wasn't like anything he had years ago."

Jordan smiled and hugged her back. "He's going to be fine."

Lisa nodded and closed the door behind her.

John shifted to his left side. "Can I hold your hand?" She placed her right hand in his. She looked at his sun-tanned arm and traced the outline of his muscle with her left fingers. She held her head down and squeezed her eyes shut, struggling to stay in control. She refused to let herself become emotional in front of him—that wouldn't help either one of them. She was emotionally involved with him, and the truth was she had known it for a long time. She didn't know why their timing was always off. She didn't want him to be with Carol, but now wasn't the time to broach the subject.

The week after John's heart attack, the doctor released him with orders—no work for another week, walk a mile a day, and no coffee.

The minute Jordan pulled out of the hospital parking lot, John said. "We are going to the dealership."

Jordan almost slammed on the brakes. She pulled off the road. "John, no!"

"I'm not going to stay home. I will go stark raving crazy."

She bit her bottom lip. "We can go to work, but you are going to supervise. No tools in your hands, and no climbing in and out of boats."

Jordan made sure he followed her rules. The third week after the heart attack, the doctor gave John a full release.

St. Johns River Yachts had consumed Jordan's life. She worked seven days a week. Sunday afternoons were quiet and she used that time to catch up on her paperwork.

One Sunday afternoon, an elderly widow came in inquiring about a pontoon boat. Jordan wasn't surprised, she was selling two pontoon boats a week to older women which kept John and Randy busy giving boating lessons.

Jordan watched an alligator crawl out of the river and move across the parking lot. The gator stopped to rest under the woman's car. Jordan kept the woman occupied opening compartments under the seats and showing her the controls on the dash panel. She made sure she kept the woman's back to the gator. Jordan didn't know how she would react if she knew there was a five-foot alligator under her car.

The lady stood and stared at the boat. "If I decide to buy the boat, can I keep it here at Marina 415?"

"Yes, if you decide to purchase the boat, I know Sam has a slip." Jordan smiled and pointed to the marina office.

Jordan debated on the best way to tell her about the alligator. She decided there was no best way. She would tell her and then deal with the lady's reactions afterward.

Jordan smiled. "I think I better tell you that a gator just crawled under your car to get out of the sun. If you give me your keys, I'll move your car around to the service bay."

The lady wasn't disturbed. She handed Jordan her keys. Jordan quickly jumped behind the steering wheel and moved the car around to the service area. She led the lady through the service bay to her car.

The lady laughed. "This is a first for me. I've never had a gator under my car before."

Jordan pointed towards the river. "They occasionally come out of the water and get in the shade around the boats. They stay an hour or two and then go back into the water."

The woman put three fingers up to her lips. "Um, I'm going to buy the boat so I can tell my friends about the gator. She smiled. "You were very calm. I had no idea the gator was there. You're a strong young lady."

After the lady signed the bill of sale. Jordan walked her to the door. "My mechanic will put the boat in the slip tomorrow. You need to go over to the marina office now and sign for your boat slip."

Jordan sat and thought if the woman knew what all she had been through, and what she was going through now, strong was a weak description.

Late the next afternoon, Jordan was fueling the woman's boat when two boats made a sharp right turn towards the fuel dock to avoid the cavorting dolphins in the middle of the river.

The man being towed yelled to Jordan. "Is your mechanic still on duty?"

She radioed John to come to the fuel dock. The man smiled good-naturedly, telling John what happened before his engine died.

John ran his hand through his hair. "What you've described is going to take a few days to fix. Let me get my toolbox just to make sure the problem is what I think it is."

The boater's friend hollered from the second boat. "Since your wife is coming to pick you up, I'll see you later."

A pinprick in Jordan's arm made her jump. She slapped her arm and her warm blood splattered. Mosquitoes were buzzing all around them. The boater went to his boat and offered her a mini spray bottle of insect repellant.

Jordan continued to swat the air. "I'm fine. Really. Thanks."

"They can be bad and pesky." He smiled and offered her the spray again.

John returned and confirmed his diagnosis. She was still swatting the mosquitoes and now John was too. She hugged her arms tightly over her ruffled short sleeves.

The boater pointed to Jordan. "She's stubborn."

John laughed. "You don't know the half of it."

Jordan gave in and grabbed the bug spray from the man's hand and sprayed all three of them.

The man laughed. "She's got a sense of humor too."

John smiled. "I'll give you more details about your engine problem tomorrow and give you an estimate. You can sign the work order then."

The man's ride came. John paddled the boat to an empty slip and secured it for the night.

Jordan gave John a smirk. "So, you think I'm stubborn."

"I don't think, I know." They walked back towards the service bay. John laughed and put his arm around her shoulders.

Chapter 62

Another New Judge

Another eight months had passed since Jordan had heard from Ryan, her attorney in Daytona Beach. "Jordan, how are you today? I wanted to call and give you an update on the judge."

"I'm fine. What's going on?"

"Our judge has been transferred to child service cases."

"Ryan, we've been through two judges, and nothing is changing except judges." Her tone was low and somber and laced with disappointment.

"I've tried to get FPS to drop the lawsuit without any success. We have no choice but to see a new judge, and I'll tell this one too that you're defending the lawsuit."

Each time she had a conversation with Ryan, she felt like she was adrift in a rowboat without a paddle. Her emotions swept in and out rapidly and randomly waiting for the next wave to push her to shore or capsize her. She had to talk to herself constantly just to keep breathing.

She walked out on the dock, telling herself to take a breath. *Look around, Jordan none of this is here by accident, and neither are you. You made this choice and you'll get through this. You have gone from being a successful businesswoman to a business failure to almost losing John. She asked herself. Is this what a mid-life crisis is like?*

She returned to her office. She'd been determined to be successful. She knew she had made mistakes, and she was proud of what she had built. She slammed her hand down on her desk, her inner strength surged, no one was going to stop her. She wasn't giving up, and she hadn't lost yet. She was still counting on an eleventh-hour miracle.

Twilight was casting low shadows across the canal as John tied his boat to the dock. He poked his head in her office "Would you like to go fishing for a little bit? I think you need some downtime."

She shook her head yes. "Sure, we haven't fished in years. It would be like ole times." She skipped ahead of John down the dock, turned around laughing waving her arms in the air. "I bet I catch the first fish."

She threw her line across the canal as John was backing his boat out of the slip. A fish jumped into the air from under some lily pads. Her hook caught the bass's mouth in mid-air. She landed the two-pound bass in the boat.

John glared at her. "What are you doing?"

"Fishing. You said we were going fishing."

He yelled. "Well, not like this."

He pulled the boat back in the slip and left her sitting in the passenger seat. She hadn't expected to catch a fish, and she didn't anticipate the outcome from him for her catching one.

She laughed to herself as she watched the moon-light cast finger spears through the palm fronds across the slow-moving water. John returned to check on her. She was relaxed and felt at ease.

With a smirk on her face, she said, "I didn't mean to out-fish you."

"Yeah, right." Then he laughed.

He climbed into the boat. They watched the last bit of the day's light drift into the night. He leaned over and gave her a soft, familiar kiss on her cheek, making her wish more than ever that they could be together, but she knew deep down that was never going to happen. The wind shifted, making the air smell clean and fresh. The river could always bring her peace.

The next morning, Randy ribbed her about catching the fish before John left the dock.

She laughed. "I learned my lesson. I won't put my line in the water again until he catches the first fish."

It took John weeks to live down the so-called fishing trip.

Chapter 63

Floor Plan Services' New Attorney

Jordan hadn't had any contact with her attorney in eleven months. She walked into his office expecting the worst. "Hello, Ryan. How are you today? I don't know why you wanted to see me here. This must be bad news?" All her words ran together in one sentence.

"I'm fine, thank you. I thought we needed a face-to-face meeting. We have a new judge."

"What did he say about the other judge reducing the million dollars?"

"It was never ruled on, so it's like it never happened. I don't know what this new judge will do. He's free to do anything he wants."

"Does this mean, we have to start over from the beginning?"

"There are several other developments I need to tell you about, which is why I wanted you to come in. FPS has a new attorney on the case. I don't know what happened to the attorney we were dealing with, but I have talked to the new one. I wanted to make sure he was familiar with our case. I tried to convince him to get FPS to drop the lawsuit. I told him the case was getting too expensive, and there was a good possibility that FPS was going to lose. I tried to use a scare tactic to make him think that he wasn't going to win. He agreed with the expense and how long the case has dragged on, but he didn't agree that they would lose. He did say he would see what he could do. The other issue is with the judge. He told both of us that all the paperwork on the case had been misplaced. We have to refile all the papers from the beginning to the current date."

Jordan folded her arms tight against her body. "Do I have to do depositions again?"

"No. That will be included in the refiled papers."

She wrinkled her forehead. "What happens next?"

"I'm not going to do anything until I hear back from the FPS's attorney. It does bide us more time. I'll let you know as soon as I hear something."

On her way home, she thought about how she had been on a yoyo string for the past four years. The first judge had a heart attack without making any kind of a decision. The second judge had told the floor plan attorney to get the million-dollar suit reduced, then was transferred to child services before a decision was made. Now the third judge said all the paperwork had been lost and FPS had a new attorney, who didn't know anything about the lawsuit. She was tired of being in limbo, and she wanted a decision. No matter what the results. She was worn out and ready to move on with her life. The future she had imagined when her business was at its peak wasn't the future now. The excitement that brought her into the dealership had vanished along with her dreams. How much longer was this going to go on? She remembered Ryan saying, "Anything can happen, and it's not always bad. It's never over until the judge bangs his gavel."

The IRS agent who had done her overtime audit rang her door-bell around 5:00 p.m.

"Hi, Mr. Wilson. What are you doing here?"

"You can call me Larry. I went by the dealership and they said you were home."

She cracked a slight smile. "I had a meeting in Daytona Beach today."

He shuffled his feet and then backed away from the door. "I wanted you to hear this from me. You're under another audit for payroll taxes. Will you be in your office tomorrow?"

She squinted her eyes. "Yes. Why are they auditing me again? Has someone else turned me in?"

"No, but you're not flying below the radar, and they know about your out-of-trust lawsuit. The IRS has called the audit. Don't worry, I'll take care of you."

The next morning, a new agent was waiting for her when she unlocked the ship's store door. He was middle-aged with dark-rimmed glasses and had a deep wrinkled frown. The kind people have when they never smile.

She invited him into her office and placed the ledger on her conference table. "Here are my payroll reports. I'm sure I don't owe anything. If you need anything you can ask John. He'll help you. I'll be back later."

She made the call from her car. "Larry, I thought you were going to protect me. Why aren't you here?"

"I was removed from your case. I told the other agent to do what he could for you."

She saw the IRS agent before he left her office. She tried to wrangle information from him.

He wouldn't answer any of her questions, except to say, "You'll be hearing from the IRS office."

She didn't wait to hear from IRS. She called Larry asking him to meet with her. The next morning, she was in the IRS office in Daytona Beach with Larry and the regional office supervisor.

The supervisor glanced at her over his glasses that rested halfway down his nose. "You've missed paying your payroll taxes in some months. I don't think it was intentional, but you owe $6,000 in back taxes."

"How can that be? How far back did you audit?"

"We went back five years."

She moved forward in her seat. "There must be a statute of limitations on how far you can go back."

He rocked back in his chair. "No, as long as a business is still active, we can go back to the start date."

"I'm sorry, I really thought I had kept up with the taxes."

After two hours with Larry pushing her cause, the supervisor settled for a payment of $1,500. She was surprised IRS would settle for less. She felt a little relief. Maybe things were going to turn around.

Chapter 64

Rick and John

The next morning, after her meeting in the IRS office, she didn't need John pouting like a child. "What's wrong, with you? You've been in a bad mood for over a month."

"It's Rick. He's always hanging around you since he moved his boat into the marina."

"John, Rick helped me when my banker wouldn't. Scott was the reason all this started in the first place. Rick was being nice. I was his real estate agent for years. We've been friends for a long time."

John held his head down and shuffled his feet. "I know I couldn't do for you financially what he did, and I know nothing romantic is going on."

"John, are you feeling guilty because you couldn't help me money-wise? I couldn't do what I've done without you."

He walked towards her. "No. I don't feel guilty. I just don't want him around all the time. He tries to horn in on all your time. He did loan you money when you needed it, but he also tried to buy you a diesel truck. He tries to take you to lunch at least twice a week. To me, this means he's after more than friendship."

"You're jealous. You're acting like if you can't be with me you don't want anyone else to be either, but you and Carol are together. I learned a long time ago you can't have your cake and eat it too. You need to do some soul searching."

Jordan had accepted Rick's lunch offer today. She realized that is what had made John so irritable. Her heart ached every time she saw the disappointed look on John's face when Rick came to the dealership. Even though she and John weren't going to be together in an intimate way, she had to change things with Rick.

She smiled at Rick across the table. "You've done so much for me, and I appreciate you rescuing me out of part of my financial jam, but there's a big difference between business and personal. There can't be and won't be anything between us other than friendship. Your eyes dance when you look at me. Everyone sees it, and questions are being asked about us. We've had talks about this before, but for some reason, you're not accepting our relationship. There is no romance, and there's not going to be any emotional involvement. Too much is going on in my life to have another conflict. You want more, and I can't give more."

His smile vanished. "This is not what I expected."

"I know, and believe me, I am grateful for everything you've done, but what you want in our relationship can't happen. You helped me in a business matter, and that is all that happened. I will repay the $10,000 in May when I get my federal income tax refund."

He reached for her hand. She pulled it away. "Is there anything or something I can say or do to change your mind?"

She shook her head. "I'm sorry, but the answer is no."

Rick sat and stared at the wall behind her for a moment then without saying a word, he handed the waiter a handful of cash and walked out of the restaurant.

John was sitting in her office when she returned.

"What's going on with you and Rick?"

"Nothing is going on. You should know that by now."

She felt her defenses go up. After her lunch with Rick, she didn't need this conversation with John. She wanted to say, "What business is it of yours? You're with Carol!" But that would only make their conversation turn into a fight or a silent stand-off, and she wasn't going through that again.

"If nothing's going on, then why do you keep going to lunch with him?"

"As a friend, he did come to my rescue. I don't want to hurt his feelings. I had lunch with a friend."

"All the guys are talking, and Sam is asking why you're spending so much time with him."

With irritation in her voice, she snapped, "I'm an adult. It's none of anyone's business."

"Don't get huffy. Just end it if nothing's going on."

She raised her voice. "Get off your jealous chair."

He stood and slammed his chair against the desk and retreated to the service bay.

She felt there wasn't even a place for a friendship with Rick without making John mad.

After a couple of weeks, Jordan was still upset with how she had ended things with Rick. She wanted to be friends, and she knew he wanted more. Maybe there couldn't be a friendship. She missed their business talks. She felt like he understood what she was going through. The little flirts and the attention had been fun, but John was jealous and she wasn't going to upset John. Rick had helped her all she was going to allow. He had been her sounding board in business, and he had given her some knowledgeable and comforting advice, but she didn't like his pursuit of her when he knew there was nothing more between them than business. She knew Rick wanted a long-lasting relationship with her, but whatever had happened in the yesterdays or what he thought had happened was gone.

He was divorced and looking for companionship.

She wasn't.

Chapter 65

St. Thomas, US Virgin Islands

For many years, people had promised to buy a boat after the boat shows, but Jordan usually never heard from them again. Lloyd was the exception. He'd had eyed a 32-footer at the Miami Boat Show, asked a lot of questions, and told Jordan he was going to buy one as soon as he could get his finances organized.

"Jordan, I'm ready for my boat to be delivered to St. Thomas."

"Lloyd, I must say your call is a surprise. I sold the 32-footer, but I can order you one. Do you want the same specs that were on the one in Miami?"

"Yes, just like it. Even the same color."

"I'll order it today and call you when it's ready to be shipped. You'll need to wire the money to my account. When I get the delivery amount finalized you can wire the balance. I promise I'll get the cheapest delivery."

She called two boat delivery services, one was a float-on float-off boarding and the other was for a freighter delivery. The float on and float off was a transport tanker that lowered the body of the tanker into the water. The boats were driven onto the deck of the tanker. When the boats were secure, the body of the tanker was raised, the water drained out. The body was locked back into position. When the boats were ready to be unloaded, the tanker sank the body again, and the boats were driven off. The tanker's cargo area looked like a flatbed freighter when traveling. The freighter delivery boat had to be shrink-wrapped and loaded on a wooden boat cradle. A transport truck would take the boat to the freighter, where a crane would place the boat and cradle on the deck of the freighter. After all her evaluations, the float on and float off tanker was the cheapest way for her to ship the boat to St. Thomas.

She ordered the boat from the factory with all the buyer's amenities and had the boat shipped to Jib's marina, which was on the water, in Ft. Lauderdale. John stayed with Jib while he rigged the boat to be customer-ready. John drove the boat to the Port of Everglades loading dock. John knew the dockmaster, and with John's captain's license, the dockmaster allowed John to drive the boat onto the tanker. After all the delivery papers were signed, the boat was set to be in St. Thomas in six days.

Years earlier, Jordan had worked in St. Thomas for five months. She knew the island and most of their business customs. She called Lloyd giving him all the shipping information and the costs. After the bank notified her that Lloyd's money had been deposited, she overnighted the MSO for him to register the boat and get a mooring permit from the Department of Planning and Natural Resources in St. Thomas.

The next day, she called her friend in St. Thomas. "Irene, this is Jordan. How are you?"

"My goodness, Jordan, what a surprise. I'm fine. How are you?"

"Good, thank you. I'm calling to see if my mechanic and I can stay with you for a few days. I'm delivering a boat to St. Thomas."

Irene chuckled. "Sure thing. I'm not going anywhere. Just let me know."

Jordan and John arrived in St. Thomas the day before the tanker was scheduled to dock. It was the last week of June, and unfortunately, a tropical depression was developing in the Caribbean and it could possibly reach hurricane force.

Living in Florida, she and John had been through many hurricanes, but this was different. They were on an island cut off from the mainland. She didn't know how fast the islands could get power restored or roads cleared if a hurricane did hit. The next morning, St. Thomas was in the path of a category 4 hurricane named Dean.

Jordan called Lloyd. "John and I are on the island. Do you know where you're going to moor the boat if the hurricane hits?"

"No. I've never owned a boat when there was a hurricane and have never been on St. Thomas during one either."

She and John met Lloyd at the Sunset Grill on Nazareth Bay to discuss the situation. During lunch Lloyd said. "I'm going to moor the boat at Fish Hook Marina but they won't let any boat over 24 feet be moored there during a hurricane."

John nodded. "Your marina owner is right. Your boat needs to be anchored in the water somewhere. Do you know where the local's moor during a storm?"

Lloyd had no idea. She and John took over, calling marinas asking where they could anchor the boat in protected waters. She was told Hurricane Hole was a storm refuge in Coral Bay over on St. John. The National Park had installed a state-of-the-art storm mooring system for ninety-six boats. During a storm, boats were tied to a one-inch chain fastened to the sea floor by heavy-duty sand screws. Permits were given to boat owners who lived in the Virgin Islands for 50 percent of the storm season or longer. Lloyd qualified to apply for a permit, and once issued, the boat mooring was renewable each year.

Jordan walked to the car. "Lloyd, you need to go get a permit from the Department of Planning and Natural Resources. John and I are going to check around for mooring places. We'll meet back at your marina."

Lloyd returned with a long face. "All permits have been issued, but they told me Benner Bay and Mandahl Pond on St. Thomas are good places to moor."

When Lloyd checked out those areas, they were full too.

She looked at both John and Lloyd. "We're too late in the season to apply for permits and too late receiving notice of the storm."

Lloyd and John called all over the island without any luck. Each time they were told no, they asked if anyone knew a mooring place.

John saw the worried lines deepen on Jordan's face. "Don't worry. I was told Mangrove Lagoon is the last place to fill up in a storm, but there are no mooring facilities. Lloyd and I will go check it out while you go to Red Hook Marina ship's store and buy four anchors, 800 feet of rode lines, six shackles, and seizing wire. We'll meet you back there."

The dockmaster called Jordan to let her know the tanker was docking. John and Lloyd picked Jordan up at Red Hook. They arrived at the commercial dock in time to see the last customs officer leave the ship. John and Lloyd drove the boat to Red Hook Marina. Jordan stopped at Home Depot to pick up one more anchor before meeting them back at the marina. The three of them moved the boat to Mangrove Lagoon.

Mangrove trees grow in saltwater. Their multiple complex root system allows the roots to grow above the ground and deep in the water. The roots in the water form knots under the sand by wrapping their roots around themselves. They are strong and make for a good mooring for medium to small size boats.

The priority at this point was to secure the boat to the best of their ability. They set the anchors, tied the boat to the roots, and screwed the hatches down.

John turned to Jordan and Lloyd. "We've done all we can do to protect the boat. It has plenty of room to rock and not hit anything. All we can do now is wait."

People were in runabout boats were ferrying people back to town. The three of them caught a ride back to Red Hook, where Jordan had left the rental car and Lloyd had parked his car.

The wind was blowing over ninety miles per hour now. Lloyd insisted that she and John stay with him. She gave Lloyd a brief hug. "John and I are settled in at Irene's. We need to stay with her, she's alone. We'll see you after the storm. Good luck."

The wind blew for six hours at a steady 145 miles per hour, the strongest winds recorded on the island in years. The heavy rains resulted in flood warnings, suggesting people vacate from low-lying areas.

Irene's concrete block house was built for hurricanes. Its open ceiling beams and open roof eaves kept the barometric pressure from building up, which would collapse a wood roof. The three of them stayed in the bathtub with a mattress close by to protect them from flying glass in case the bathroom window was blown out. The house lost power around midnight. The storm surge was ten feet high and came from both sides of the island, flooding all the lower streets and valleys. Jordan peeked out the front window. "Irene, your street looks like a river."

When daylight came, the entire hillside looked like it had been beaten with machetes. Snapped and bent trees covered the street as far as they could see. With the loss of trees, they could see the rock bluff high atop the waters of a majestic, tumbling waterfall. Water was still running down the mountain like a small river, carrying debris with it. The storm had left Irene's mountain barren, but Irene's house wasn't damaged.

John left to scout the damage from Irene's house to the main road. "We need to clear the switchback road to the main road. I know we are halfway down the mountain, but we will be one of the last roads cleared with us being the only house here."

John found a chain saw in Irene's garage. Irene and Jordan followed John with shovels. At the end of the day, they had cleared the switchback halfway down to the street. They were bone tired. It had taken longer than they anticipated to cut away the downed trees. They would clear the rest of the trees to the street in the morning.

Due to the cistern overflowing, Irene boiled all the drinking water until the water receded.

Jordan looked at Irene's gas stove. "At least we can cook." Then she turned to John. "Do you think we can get to the boat?"

He looked down the mountain. "I doubt it. I'll know more when I can get to the main street."

The sun rose bright and the sky was clear, which lifted all their spirits. They started clearing the trees, and by lunchtime, Irene's road was cleared to the street. The work trucks hadn't made it up the mountain yet to clear the main street. There was no way they could drive anywhere and no way to contact Lloyd.

John put on his tennis shoes. "I'm going to walk to Red Hook. People there can give me an idea of how the island has fared." He returned to Irene's just before dark. "People were in a state of shock walking around in a daze at Red Hook. There have been some deaths.

I asked people about Lloyd, but no one had seen him, and no one knew anything about the boats in Mangrove Lagoon."

Jordan stood up and peered out the window. "How long before we can get to the boat, or how can we get to the boat?"

"I don't know." Jordan saw the concern in John's eyes.

The airport was closed until the trees could be cleared from the runway. Jordan felt trapped and cut off from the world. There was no way to get off the island and no communication.

The third morning, during breakfast, they heard trucks on the main street. They drove to the bottom of the hill to find one lane open, they continued to Red Hook.

John smiled. "There are more people here today than yesterday and more are still coming." He yelled to a man sitting in his boat. "I'll pay you to take us to Mangrove Lagoon."

Lloyd was at the boat when they arrived. John and Lloyd took inventory of the boat and found a few tree branch scratches on the side of the hull. The boat had stayed tied and not taken on any water.

Jordan moved close to Lloyd. "How is your house?"

"I didn't have any damage. Lots of downed trees. The main thing is we're all safe. I haven't been over to the marina where I'm going to dock the boat. We need to go check it out before we move the boat from here. The man that brought me out here owns a boat over there. He said he would be glad to take us to the marina."

Red Hook Marina had survived with minor damage considering the wind force. A few boats had washed ashore next to the marina, some were lying on their sides on top of the dock. The docks were in good condition except for the ones where the boats had broken loose and taken part of the dock with them.

The marina manager was in his boat tied up at the first dock. "Lloyd, there's no power on the docks, but you can bring your boat over." He pointed to the far side of the marina. "Your slip wasn't damaged."

Jordan stayed at the marina while John and Lloyd moved the boat. After the boat was safely moored, John made sure Lloyd was satisfied with everything on the boat.

John shook Lloyd's hand. "Jordan and I are going to try to go home. Good-bye, and if you need anything, call me."

The airport was open for one flight in and out a day. After they boarded the plane, Jordan looked across the tarmac and out at the harbor and said with a smirk. "I need to put a dealership here. How can anyone live on these islands without a boat?"

John held her hand. "I do know how much you love the islands and the island life."

"I do when there aren't any hurricanes. I never want to go through this again. If anyone wants a boat delivered to an island, it's not going to be during hurricane season."

John squeezed her hand as the plane lifted upward.

Chapter 66

State and Federal Laws

After a week in St. Thomas, Jordan thumbed through her mail. She opened a letter from the Volusia County Marine Dealers Association. The National Marine Manufacturers Association (NMMA) was conducting a meeting in Daytona Beach for all boat dealers and marinas in Central Florida. NMMA wanted to encourage the boat dealers to help fight a 25 mile per hour speed limit that the animal activists were trying to place on all Florida waterways that were inhabited by manatees. NMMA was asking for at least one person from each business in the boating industry to attend the state-wide meeting at the capitol in Tallahassee.

The animal activists claimed the boaters were killing the manatees. They had already lost the fight with the Florida Legislature and now they had the Florida Department of Natural Resources (DNR) behind them to fight their cause. The DNR spokesperson said, "The manatee population is dwindling due to boat props killing the manatees."

This brought all the state park rangers to their feet. The director over the park rangers showed a chart. "The figures they gave are incorrect. We are the ones who track the manatee population, and their population has increased over the last several years."

The floor opened for discussion. The boat dealers, boat manufacturers, and marine engine manufacturers all stated that putting a 25 mile per hour speed limit on the waterways would stifle the boating industry. Boats 24 feet and up plane at 30 miles per hour, with a 25 mile per hour limit, these boats would cause big wakes, and the result would cause tremendous riverbank erosion. After hours of discussion, the meeting adjourned.

DNR quietly issued a 25-mile-per-hour speed limit proposal to the Florida Legislature the day before Thanksgiving. The boating industry lobbyists protested to the legislature saying the DNR left little time and opportunity for public protests. The legislature denied the proposal, stating the DNR had to hold statewide public hearings. The NMMA filed a formal rule challenge in Tallahassee. The rumors were if the NMMA could persuade the Florida Legislature not to vote for a speed limit, the DNR would back down. Meetings were held throughout Florida with the engine manufacturers, boat dealers, and marinas to garner proof that the information given to the legislature was incorrect.

The Florida boating industry spokesperson reported, "I have proof from outside sources that shows how lost revenues would impact the entire state. This law would cause a spiraling decline in people not using their boats and cause a negative impact on boat sales. It's a known fact if a boater uses his boat, he is going to incur some type of repair cost, therefore dealerships and marinas would lose the repair revenue as well as boat sales."

The lobbyists and the marine industry lost. The Florida Legislature passed the 25-mile-per-hour speed limit on all manatee-inhabited rivers.

One marine engine manufacturer installed baskets around the propellers to protect the manatees. The baskets caused the propellers not to work proficiently by reducing RPMs that caused engine shutdowns. After six months of inefficient performance, the manufacturer discarded the baskets.

Most of the boaters did stop using their boats, and the ones who continued to run their boats at 25-miles-per-hour caused the riverbank to erode. The Central Florida drought had caused the St. Johns River to flow backward. The low river flowed from north to south. Small boats with outboards were the only boats that could use the river. In time, the riverbanks resembled an aftermath of a tornado with its eroded banks and fallen trees lying in the river.

At the same time, the speed limit law was passed, Florida added an additional gas tax to fuel pumps on the waterways, and Congress passed a luxury tax on automobiles and boats. Boats over $100,000 and higher had to pay a 10 percent luxury tax, and the tax couldn't be financed. These three major impacts on the boating industry caused boat sales to decrease dramatically, including sales and service at Jordan's dealership. The marine industry was fighting the gas pump tax for a repeal in hopes that people would start using their boats again, which would keep Jordan's service department employed. NMMA industry was fighting Congress to repeal the luxury tax.

Regulations seemed to be sliding out of control, and the government was allowing it to happen. Recession, inflation, and fuel prices were the death of many boat dealerships. Hundreds of dealers had already closed their businesses.

Jordan knew this was a very volatile industry. She tried to financially secure herself against this kind of market. When her dealership was thriving, she had created a buffer with her annual profits for her down periods. She never expected state and federal laws would affect her business.

Her life had been fun and exciting. Now it was troubled, but it was still her life, and she wasn't going to let anyone, or anything upset what she had worked so hard to gain, including the Floor Plan Services lawsuit. She was struggling to make payroll each week and her rent was due at the first of the month.

Her landlord, Sam, was unaware of all her troubles. He knew her customer base had dwindled, but he hadn't asked her about her finances. No matter what, her first obligation was to her employees. She'd never been in a position before where someone's family and livelihood depended on her. She juggled figures, toyed with them, stroked them, and decided red wasn't such a bad color. She still had a little money held in reserve but not enough to keep carrying her current load. She sat in her office many days, staring at the river. She knew she had to play safe and to do that she had to cut her overhead. Her stomach felt like it had been used as a punching bag. If she was going to survive, she had to pull in her reigns and restructure her personnel. Saving some of them was better than saving none. She saved John, Randy, and Will and kept one salesman.

Her big boat sales had dropped 71 percent. Boats under $100,000 had dropped 27 percent. The luxury tax fee applied to her 33-footers and up, the interest rates were at 23 percent, the 25-mile per hour speed limit on the river, and the newly imposed gas tax hit the boating industry and her all at one time. It wasn't unusual for her to have back-to-back days without any customers. John still had some boats in the service bay, but that wasn't enough to offset her $25,000 overhead.

Her remembrances of yesterday only dredged up the pain of today. She never dreamed in her high-flying days there would ever be a downturn like this. She had to keep reminding herself, she was a strong fighter and she would survive.

She hit a dead end when she asked the bank for a fifty-thousand-dollar loan to give her a financial cushion for two months. The bank said all businesses were in trouble, and with the high-interest rate, they weren't making any loans.

Chapter 67

Money Scam

An investor group had placed an ad in the Orlando Sentential advertising business loans up to a million dollars. The gentleman she talked to in Ft. Lauderdale asked her some preliminary questions, then told her she qualified for a meeting.

John held both her hands in his before she left. "Just a word of advice. Be careful about letting them know too much of your business."

The address she had for the meeting was in a high-rise professional office building in downtown Ft. Lauderdale. The small office on the tenth floor had a tiny desk and two straight-back wooden chairs. She expected to meet before a committee, or a couple of people, not just with one man.

"Hi, Jordan. I'm Mr. Steen."

He was dressed professionally in a black suit, white shirt, and a black and red and white striped tie.

She handed him the completed application. He kept his eyes on the paper. "I need a five-hundred-dollar processing fee."

The feeling of spiders crawling over her skin was not the feeling she expected to have in the meeting.

She sat back in the chair and crossed her legs. "You didn't tell me there was a fee. I can give you a check, but you'll have to wait until I can transfer funds into this account."

He kept looking at the application. "That's fine."

The more he talked, the edgier she became. Something about him and their conversation didn't feel right. Her tingling feeling cried scam. He hadn't said anything to give her that impression although she could feel it in her bones. She considered herself to be a good judge of people, but now she didn't trust him or herself.

He glanced over his glasses at her. "Is something wrong?"

"No." *Did he know her thoughts?* "Everything's fine."

"You keep watching the door." He scowled, and his mouth quirked upward in a way that said he knew she was thinking about bolting.

In all her business negotiations, this one didn't feel right.

She signed the papers and gave him the check and emphasized again, she would call him when she transferred the money.

As she was backing out of her parking space, she saw him pull out in front of her. A strange feeling shook her body. She followed him and watched him pull through the drive-in window at the bank. She thought he had lied to her. She wondered how many people had given him five hundred dollars today.

On the way home, she tried to justify him going to the bank. Maybe he had met other clients earlier that morning and he was depositing their checks, but she still had a feeling she had been scammed. She thought she had found an escape from her money problems, but instead, she felt like she was in a small boat in a storm holding on for dear life and a big wave was about to capsize her.

She called John. "The meeting felt all wrong. I don't have a good feeling about him."

"If it doesn't feel right, don't do it."

When John suggested what she was thinking and feeling, she called Mr. Steen. "This is Jordan. I called to let you know I've changed my mind. Please tear up my check."

"The bank said your check wasn't good."

Her heart sank, but her fight came back quickly. Her voice was strong. "I told you to hold the check until I could transfer funds."

She didn't know why, but she gave him a check on an old bank account where she kept a hundred-dollar balance. At that moment, she was glad she had listened to her feelings.

Two weeks after her meeting in Ft. Lauderdale, the news media was informing people of scammers. His name and picture appeared with him being arrested for fraudulent scams on television.

She remembered her mother's words. If it doesn't feel right, it's not right.

Chapter 68

John's Wedding

Jordan had been in her office buried under paperwork all morning. She hadn't felt the hot September sun until she climbed into an engine hatch to talk to John. He wiped the sweat from his brow with his forearm. "What are you doing? Checking up on me?"

"Yes, you and the boat." She laughed. "It's not all about you, you know."

But it was. She had kept a sharp eye on him ever since his heart attack. He cast a slight grin her way. "I know you've been watching me."

A little before noon Jordan walked back into the service bay. "How about lunch? I'm starving."

John shoved the papers from one place to another on his work desk. He rearranged some parts on the "waiting to order shelves," then finally dug the phone out from under a stack of work orders.

"How about we order pizza?"

"Pizza?" She wiggled her nose.

He moved closer to her. "I'd like to spend some time with you and not talk about business."

"Sure. Pizza's fine."

He pushed a button and winked. "Speed dial."

"Hi, it's John at St. Johns Yachts. I'm good. How about you? I want a large, fully loaded pizza delivered."

He tossed the phone back on the desk. "It won't take long. I need to go wash up. I'll meet you back in your office."

John seemed to be happier now that Rick wasn't hanging around. Whatever John thought had happened between her and Rick, he seemed to have accepted it.

She hadn't had lunch with John in her office in years—the new building, the growing business, the financial downturn, the new laws, and her lawsuit—had changed a lot of how things used to be.

Mike stuck his head in her office. "Pizza's here."

John grabbed his wallet from his back pocket.

Lunch was pleasant. No work talk. A casual conversation about where she started, when he came to work for her, the calamities along the way, friends they had made, and the joys they had shared, without any mention of the sad times.

"Jordan, I don't mean to taunt you. I think I get greedy when I spend time with you. I see what life could be and has never been for either of us."

"John, you have watched over me, kept me safe, and protected me. Sometimes you were like a brother, but most of all you're my best friend. I thought maybe, just maybe we would be together, but the cards didn't fall into place and the stars didn't line up. We weren't meant to be."

He frowned. "Do you really believe that?"

She hesitated for a long time. "I didn't until Carol showed up."

John shuffled his pizza around on his plate. "I wanted to be more than a friend. I fell in love with you. I don't know when it happened, but I became aware of it after my divorce." He paused and looked at the river then back at her. "I've asked Carol to marry me. It's a convenience marriage based on need."

Her jawed dropped.

He ran his hands through his hair. "Say something."

"I'm shocked. I knew the two of you were living together, but I didn't think you would get married. I thought when Cal moved out, she would too."

She closed the pizza box and was silent for several minutes, "John, I love you. I thought maybe, just maybe we could be together.

I wished we had met at a different time in our lives. We can't change the past."

John still didn't say a word. He gathered up the empty pizza box and left her office.

Thirty minutes later, he returned. "How come you didn't tell me your feelings? I never thought I ever had a chance with you. Don't you know how much I love you and how much I want to be with you?"

"I thought with our conversations you knew. I don't know what else to say. I know you told me living with Carol was for convenience. I didn't think that you would marry her."

John kept his distance from her the rest of the week. Her heart was broken. She knew John wouldn't go back on his promise to Carol.

John and Carol married in December. No guests were invited to the outdoor ceremony in the DeLeon Springs State Park. Jib was his best man again, and Carol's sister was her maid of honor. They spent the weekend at a hotel in Daytona Beach. Jordan thought the quiet ceremony and weekend honeymoon was strange but he, Carol, and Cal had lived together for over a year.

Jordan pictured how their wedding would have been if it had been her and John—lots of guests and a long honeymoon.

Chapter 69

Lawsuit Dropped

A year had passed without a word from Ryan. Jordan had left two messages for him to return her call. Ten minutes later after her second call, Ryan called.

"What can I do for you, Jordan?"

"What's going on with the lawsuit?"

"I haven't heard anything." Ryan cleared his throat. "Let a sleeping dog lie."

Two weeks later, Ryan called Jordan. "Did you know that FPS was bought by another floor plan company?"

"No. How do you know that?"

"I read it in *Mergers and Acquisitions* newsletter. I contacted their legal department to find out about your lawsuit. The managing partner of the acquired company had no idea there was a lawsuit pending. I gave him all the details for the past five years. I'm waiting on an answer from him."

"Ryan, what does all this mean? Am I going to be sued by the new company now?

"I don't know, but I'm going to stay on top of this. I'll let you know as soon as I hear something."

"Thanks."

She watched the river's gentle flow. She didn't know what her insides were telling her. Should she be happy, mad, or upset?

The last afternoon Friday in May, Ryan arrived at Jordan's dealership. She was sitting on the forklift holding a 32-foot boat waiting for John and Randy to position blocks for her to set the boat on. Ryan walked over to the forklift and stood with a big grin.

Jordan screeched when Ryan yelled, "Jordan!"

"You startled me! I didn't hear you walk up over the forklift noise. What are you doing here?"

"I have great news that I couldn't tell you on the phone."

John took her place on the forklift. Ryan put his hand on Jordan's shoulder. "I heard back from the attorney that acquired FPS." Jordan sat next to Ryan at her conference table. He continued. "They couldn't find any paperwork on the lawsuit. They sent me a motion on behalf of FPS releasing you and St. Johns River Yachts, Inc. of any wrongdoing. They are dismissing Jordan Harris from any lawsuits on behalf of FPS for $1,000. I couldn't tell you this over the phone."

Tears flooded her eyes. "You're telling me for a $1,000 the lawsuit goes away?"

His smile covered his face. "Yes."

"Do I have to go to court?"

"No, the courts are not involved anymore."

Her eyes stung, her vision was blurred, and a lump formed in her throat. She could barely speak. "Yes. A thousand times. Yes!" Her second yes was almost a scream. "What do I need to do?"

He squeezed her hand. "Nothing. It's over. There's no record of a lawsuit. It's like it never happened."

She sat quietly for a few moments processing Ryan's words. "My life was a living hell for five years, and now it's over as if nothing ever happened? How can people do this to someone and then walk away?"

"It's viewed not as people or a person, but a corporation without emotions."

Uncontrollable joyful tears flowed like floodgates. She had climbed from the grave to see the world in a whole new light. She was free to move on with her life without any obstructions.

When Ryan left, John came into her office. He saw her tear-stained face through her smile. All she could say was, "It's over."

He didn't move. "You mean the lawsuit is over?"

She yelled. "Yes!"

He laughed. "A celebration is in order. Is there something you want to do to mark this moment?"

"Hold me."

He couldn't hold her without giving her a long passionate kiss. She felt her skin heat from within. She looked into his eyes, her gaze steady and unyielding. He pulled her closer to him. Her head rested on his chest. This was her comfort place. He always held her in any crises, good or bad. After several minutes, she backed away and saw his tear-streaked face and the hard lines in his face had lightened. He looked like he was experiencing the same hanging weight being lifted from his body too. This was her eleventh-hour miracle, and she was sharing it with John.

After the weight of the lawsuit had lifted. Jordan sat and mulled over how it had ever occurred. She had worked with Scott for twelve years. The first six years all the business dealings with him had been above board and straight. Two weeks before Scott stopped payment on the cashier's check, Scott's brother-in-law, a retired attorney from New York, started working for him. She didn't trust him the first time she met him. Now that she was thinking more clearly, she thought Scott's brother-in-law was behind the whole scheme, but there was no way to prove her suspicions. Scott must have been in financial trouble—that was the only way she believed he would have ever betrayed her.

Chapter 70

New Floor Plan

In Jordan's excitement of the lawsuit being dropped, she had forgotten Scott had documented the 36-foot boat.

Ryan answered on the first ring and after they exchanged pleasantries, she asked. "Ryan, can I undocument the boat?"

"Yes, and if you need any help let me know."

Later that afternoon, she called Ryan again. "I'm sorry, but you're going to have to help me straighten out the mess that Scott caused with documenting the boat. Only an American citizen is permitted to document a boat. I have a Letter of Deletion from the coast guard, but with the buyer being from the Middle East and not a U.S. citizen, the boat couldn't have been documented to him. I don't know how Scott documented it. He must have used a fake name as the buyer."

"I'll take care of it."

When Jordan returned from lunch the next day, Ryan was waiting in her office.

She was apprehensive and in a low voice asked. "Why are you here? Is it good or bad news?"

He chuckled. "It's good. I got the manufacturer to issue another statement of origin stating the boat was sold to St. Johns River Yachts, Inc., and the floor plan company signed a Satisfaction Letter for FPS stating the boat had no liens or mortgages against it. The coast guard issued an Evidence of Deletion form. Here is all your

305

paperwork. The documentation office undocumented the boat. The 36-foot boat now belongs back to the manufacturer."

"Thank you. I hope this is the end."

Ryan laughed. "It is, and we all survived. Jordan, you did well. I love your strength, determination, and stamina. I've had lots of clients that would've given up. I don't know any person that could have done what you did."

This was Jordan's best July ever. Sam, the owner of the marina, threw a Fourth of July party just for her to celebrate the end of the lawsuit. All of Sam's family, Jordan's family, John's family, all her other employees were as excited as Jordan. Most of them didn't know what she had been through, but they enjoyed the barbecue.

The second week in July, a twinge of excitement flowed through Jordan's veins as she entered the Oshkosh Hotel. She knew the meeting wasn't going to be like it had been when the economy was at its peak. Nevertheless, she was glad to be back among her peers. There had been no reason for her to be at the dealer meetings the last five years without a floor plan. The manufacturer had scaled back on the extravaganzas of the previous dealer meetings to a two-and-a-half-day meeting instead of four. Half the dealers were there that had been there in the previous years.

Tom, the manufacturer's president, introduced the owner of the floor plan company that had bought Floor Plan Services. Jordan was appalled when he introduced Brandt to the dealers.

Brandt announced. "Any of you that were Floor Plan service clients are automatically approved. I do need for you to fill an application for our records."

After the general meeting, Jordan felt a hand on her shoulder. She turned to see Brandt. "Jordan, can I meet with you?"

She tried to control her shock. She gave Brandt a half-smile. "Sure, can you give me ten minutes?"

She ran to her room, washed her face, and took several breaths before she met Brandt in the meeting room. He reached out his hand. She shook it. "Jordan, I want you to know I didn't agree with the FPS lawsuit. I had to do my job. It was nothing personal."

She smiled. "I know it was business but to me it was personal. My attorney helped me to understand business and personal."

"We know it was Scott but we couldn't find him. I'm sorry you had to be the scapegoat, but you were out of trust. I want you to know you are approved with my company and there are no strings attached."

Her body relaxed.

Tom walked into the room at the end of their conversation. "Jordan, I want you to know the 36-foot boat is on your floor plan with Brandt.

She turned to Brandt. "Thank you. I promise nothing like this is going to happen again."

"Tom, thank you for trusting me. It was all Scott's fault."

Tom shook her hand. "You're one of our largest dealers. I've told you this before, if there's anything I can do for you, please let me know. It's going to be a great year working with you again. Can I give you a hug?"

She smiled. "All hugs are welcome."

"You deserve more than a hug. Have a safe trip."

On her flight home, she smiled most of the way. The thought that she would never be able to go to another dealer meeting had vanished.

She arrived at her dealership shortly after lunch. Before she could put her briefcase and purse in her office, she heard someone yell. "Where have you been! Your car hasn't been at the marina and your phone goes directly to voice mail!"

"Well, hello, to you too, Rick."

He frowned. "I'm sorry. You had me worried."

"I take it you didn't talk to John. I was at the annual dealer's meeting in Wisconsin. I had my phone on airplane mode."

"I heard about the lawsuit being dropped. I can't imagine how you must feel."

Her eyes danced. "The best way to describe it is I feel alive again."

"Jordan, I don't want to take you to lunch. Can I take you to dinner? I know what you said, but I want to celebrate with you."

"Yes, I will go to dinner with you. How about Thursday at six o'clock? You pick the place and I'll meet you there."

"Now you've made me feel alive again."

Jordan sat at her desk with thoughts of John and her life, and how the dealership had taken her on an emotional roller-coaster ride. How five years of gut-wrenching emotions were erased in one statement.

She was free. She moved around in zero gravity until she opened the letter from The National Bank, instantly she was back under the weight of the earth again.

She blurted out when Ryan answered the phone. "I didn't sign a note with Scott for $15,000!"

"Scott hasn't done you any favors."

She was still yelling. "He's disappeared, but he keeps popping up like a ghost. Will he ever go away?"

"Send me the paperwork, and I'll see what I can do."

She was strong, and now she had her second wind. She wasn't and wouldn't show any sign of weakness.

Rick was pacing back and forth in front of the restaurant door when she arrived. She knew he was expecting them to reconnect, but that wasn't going to happen. He hugged her but before he could kiss her, she turned her cheek to his lips. She had already told him he wasn't going to be in her life, and she hadn't changed her mind.

He asked the waiter to bring two crystal wine glasses and a bottle of her favorite German Riesling.

"A toast to my lady, for her strength, and perseverance for not canceling tonight."

She gave him a slight smile. "Did you think I was going to cancel?"

"Well, it did cross my mind that you might."

She sat straight-up in her chair. "Rick, thank you for all the kind words and help. Not only financially but your perspective on business ideas. Before you get the wrong idea about dinner, this is a business dinner."

She reached into her purse and handed him an eleven-thousand-dollar check.

She winked. "I told you this wasn't a gift. Here's your ten, plus interest."

He squinted his eyes and frowned.

Before he could answer, she continued, "There's more. I opened a letter this morning from an attorney with The National Bank in Stuart. Scott or someone forged my name on a $15,000 note as a co-signer with Scott. Now that Scott has filed bankruptcy, the bank is looking to me for payment. Ryan is working on it, but I don't know that I can beat this one."

He touched her hand. "Here, you keep this check."

She pushed his hand away. "No. I need to pay this debt first."

She saw the sympathy in his eyes. "You are the Rock of Gibraltar."

He sighed. "Are we ready to order, or can you eat after all this?"

Smiling she answered. "Yes, let's eat."

Two hours later, when they walked out of the restaurant, he grabbed her hand and intertwined his fingers with hers. "Let's walk down the dock."

They stared out at the water a few minutes before walking to the end of the dock. "What are you going to do about the fifteen thousand?"

She turned and faced him. "I'm almost back on my feet financially. I'm going to talk to my banker tomorrow."

"You know you don't have to do that. I'll give you the money."

She looked him in the eye. "No, I don't want to be indebted to anyone. The bank is a corporation with no emotional ties, and what I've learned from the school of hard knocks, I don't want any emotional ties in business anymore."

The moon rose over the water in slow motion. They watched a boat idle toward its slip. Rick scooped her up and wrapped her around him, making one silhouette in the last shadows of the day. Neither one of them said anything. She felt secure and held on tight. She took the embrace as a final goodbye. This was the last emotional tie she would have with him.

She held the banknote in her hand that The National Bank's attorney had produced. "Ryan, I never signed this note. Someone could have taken my signature off a check I gave to Scott."

In a matter-of-fact voice, he said. "Jordan, it does look like your signature."

"I agree, but I didn't know Scott had ever taken a loan out with the bank."

Ryan made the appointment for her to meet with a handwriting specialist. The test results showed it was her signature.

Jordan's voice cracked. "I swear, Ryan, I didn't sign the note. Someone forged my name. How did they determine it was my signature?"

"The handwriting machine takes the pressure and slant of the letters used by the instrument point. It's then compared to your signature."

"Can I get another opinion?"

"There aren't many handwriting specialists in the state. This is the only one we use in this area."

"Is this the same specialists that did a test with Scott years ago?"

He tapped his pen on the desk. "Yes."

She slightly raised her voice. "It doesn't seem fair to use the same person."

"The courts look at him as an independent expert witness in handwriting analysis. The test isn't one-hundred percent accurate, but the courts stand by the results. I'm sorry, but there's no way to fight this one. We need facts we can prove. I believe you, but I'm the only one that would."

"Ryan, I don't have $15,000. How long do I have before I have to pay them?"

"I'll see how long I can stall for you."

All the nerves in her body tingled. She knew she was in a no-win situation this time.

Chapter 71

Lake Okeechobee

The Tampa Boat Show had been a big success for Jordan. She sold a 46-foot boat to Russell Stone. Russell had insisted on her transporting the boat by water to West Palm Beach.

"Russell, have you ever made this trip before?"

"No, I want to do it with this boat and with you along to make sure I don't and won't have any problems."

She never envisioned selling a boat in Tampa that had to be sailed to West Palm Beach. She didn't want to make the trip, but this sale was too big not to conform to the buyer's request.

She sighed. "I will move the boat by water through Lake Okeechobee. I won't go down to Key West and back up to West Palm Beach."

She called John. "You're not going to believe this. We're going from Tampa to West Palm Beach by water. I can't talk the buyer into letting me transport it over land. I'll lose the sale if I don't do what he asks. I'm not going to make the trip with him alone. You're going to have to come to Tampa."

Russell conferred with John. "By the time we get across Lake Okeechobee, I'll be comfortable handling the boat, and if there are any mechanical problems, they should be resolved by the time we get to West Palm Beach."

John said. "Russell, I'll take the boat through the locks at Port St. Lucie. You'll have to sail the boat south to West Palm Beach."

Russell smiled. "I'm having my friend in West Palm Beach install all the electronics after I get the boat home."

"No way." John stared him down. "There's no way I'm going to take any boat across Lake Okeechobee without electronics. It's too risky with the lake full of rocks. The channel markers are few and far apart, and the lake is only deep in the channel."

Jordan moved her boats out of the Tampa show and back to Lemon Bluff while John installed the electronics and gave Russell advice on what he would need to stock the boat for the trip.

John was on the boat when Jordan returned to Tampa. He took her by the hand and pulled her into the cabin. "Jordan, what do you know about Russell? Something isn't right. He doesn't know much about boats or boating. Did you ask him what other boats he had owned?"

She shook her head. "No. He said he hadn't owned a yacht before. We'll keep an eye on him. I tried my best to get out of this trip, but he was adamant about me moving the boat with him and he didn't object when I told him you were coming with us."

Jordan contacted the National Oceanic and Atmospheric Administration (NOAA) for charts from Tampa Bay to Port St. Lucie through Lake Okeechobee. Along with the charts, they sent her additional information on Lake Okeechobee. She learned the lake is 152 miles across from the west side of Florida at the Caloosahatchee River across to the Atlantic Intercoastal Waterway. It would be an eight-to-ten-hour crossing depending on the weather, the time it took to go through the five locks, and the twenty-six bridges to go under from the start of the Caloosahatchee River to the Atlantic Intercoastal Waterway. The locks raise the boat from sea level to the level of the lake. Once across the lake, they lower the boat down to sea level on the opposite side. High water levels in the lake require all locks to be open to discharge the water to keep the lake below flood levels. During the period of high-level discharge, the turbulent water affects how the boat handles going through the locks. Normal water levels were the ideal time to travel. The ideal water levels are eight feet from the waterway in Stuart, through the lake to Ft. Myers, ten feet from Ft. Myers to Punta Rassa, and twelve feet to the Gulf of Mexico. The water levels in Lake Okeechobee can vary dramatically from season to season, month to month, and sometimes day to day. Rainfall in South Florida is the driving force behind the fluctuations. The Okeechobee Waterway is not a sea level canal from the Gulf of Mexico to the Atlantic Ocean. The US Army Corps of Engineers operates and maintains the waterway and sets restrictions if needed. The lock operations are restricted to ten hours a day. Water level readings are taken daily, and there can be lock restrictions if the water is too low. The Corps keeps the channel clear, but outside the channel, a boat could have outdrives, props, and hull damage.

Jordan stepped outside the cabin as the dawn's rays showed on the horizon. She watched it quickly climb to cast a yellow glow across the water. Russell rose and started organizing his things for the trip. It was almost noon before he finished fussing over every inch of the boat. Jordan had called the Corps of Engineers and found there no restrictions on Lake Okeechobee for the day.

John motored gently away from the dock into Tampa Bay. She always loved how invigorating the salt air smelled, which was one thing she missed on the St. Johns River. Dolphins played in the boat's wake, and jumped through the sun-splashed water, breaching their bodies in sleek graceful arcs. Everything about them radiated pure joy as their sprays of water glistened against the sun. It was a perfect day to start a trip.

A large tanker crossed behind them in Tampa Bay, pulling into the commercial docks and two other tankers pulled out to start their voyage. The bay was alive with the oil tankers, sailboats, and fishermen moving around in the moderate chop of the three-foot waves.

John pointed the bow southeast towards Ft. Myers. Jordan sat on the back cushions and watched the Tampa skyline grow smaller. They had been underway twenty minutes when the sky turned from dark gray to black. Again, the marine forecast was wrong about reporting clear skies.

John gripped the steering wheel. "Everyone, sit down and hold on. These high winds are going to toss and roll us."

Forty-five minutes later, the winds blew the black clouds away, and the sky turned to a light gray. The choppy waters turned into six-foot rolling waves. Jordan turned her face to the west, letting the wind blow her hair away from her face.

The engine's sound turned from a quiet hum to a strain trying to overcome the resistance of the waves. Pushing the boat up to climb each large roll of water and then purred in relief as the boat flowed down on the backside of each wave. An hour later, the summer storm had moved east. The farther south toward Ft. Myers they went, the calmer the water became.

Jordan noticed Russell had become quiet and subdued. She whispered to John, "Something is going on with him. I can't put my finger on it."

Russell, Jordan, and John sailed their way from Tampa Bay to Punta Rassa, where they entered the Caloosahatchee River to make their way to the entrance of Lake Okeechobee before the locks closed at sunset. If they could run at twenty knots, it would take a full eight hours of daylight to cross the lake taking Route #1, which was the Cross Lake route.

John discussed the route with Jordan and Russell, "We'd have to spend the night in Clewiston if we're going to take the Cross Lake route. There isn't enough daylight to run across if we don't. If we take the Rim Route, we could travel until late afternoon and dock at a marina."

Jordan sighed. "We were so late leaving Tampa it's going to take us two days no matter what route we take. I'm for spending the night here in a marina and taking the Cross Lake Route tomorrow."

John mulled it over. "Taking the Cross Lake route is a long boring trip with nothing to see but water. If we take Route # 2, the Rim Route, and running as far as we can now, we'll be in Stuart early enough tomorrow to drive back to Lemon Bluff."

He saw the expression on her face and knew they should take the Cross Lake route. When they entered the Caloosahatchee River, it was covered with green algae blooms.

Russell reached over the side. "What's all this?"

Jordan gave him a lesson in algae. "The algae makes anoxic water and causes massive fish kills and red tide. The algae comes from the fertilizer runoff from all the sugar cane fields and farmland along the river and around Lake Okeechobee."

She put a towel over her nose and mouth to cut the stench.

John turned to Jordan. "I hope the algae hasn't blocked the W P Franklin Lock. It's 400 feet long and 56 feet wide. We should be through it in thirty minutes. If the green light is on, we won't have to wait."

They entered the lock. Once inside the lock chamber, the gates closed behind them. Jordan grabbed a line from the side wall and tied it to the bow. Russell clumsily put the fenders out on both sides of the boat and tied off the stern line. She and John had to tell Russell every move to make. It was as if he'd never been on a boat before.

When John had the boat positioned, the Lock Master opened the front gates and the water rushed in like one big wave. They were moored far enough back from the opening gates that by the time the rushing water reached them, the waves were a ripple. The water filled the lock and raised the boat. The Lock Master opened the front gates, Jordan untied the bow line and Russell untied the stern. John navigated the boat through the open gates. The first lock was smooth sailing. It was easy with them being the only boat in the lock.

The farther east they went the heavier the algae mass grew. The river was completely covered at Alva and Fort Denaud, and LaBelle wasn't any better. John was quiet and concentrating on maneuvering the boat through the heavy green slime.

John looked over at Jordan. "I wonder how heavy the algae is going to be at the Ortona Lock near Coffee Mill Hammock. It seems to be getting thicker. Maybe by the time we get to the last lock in Moore Haven the algae will be lighter before we enter Lake Okeechobee."

Jordan still had her face covered. She didn't reply to John's comment.

The Ortona and Moore Haven Locks was 250 feet long and 50 feet wide. The algae was thin, and twenty minutes later they were through the lock.

John turned to Jordan. "The routes split at Clewiston. You need to decide which route we're going to travel."

She looked at her phone. "The forecast is calling for thunderstorms starting late this afternoon and throughout the night. Let's see if we can get through the Moor Haven Lock."

The sky was dark when they entered the lock.

Jordan put her hand on the small of John's back. "We were lucky to get through the Moore Haven Lock before the lightning started, or the lock master would have secured the locks and not opened them again until thirty minutes after the last flash."

John stared up at the storm. "Well, the weather made the decision for us. We'll go as far as we can this afternoon."

The rain began falling heavier and heavier, and in the distance, the lightning shot straight streaks from the sky to the water. They had to go through a sixth lock to make dockage in Clewiston at Roland and Mary Martin's Marina.

Jordan was getting her credit card out of her wallet when a huge gust of wind shifted, blowing her wallet from her hand. Her credit cards and paper business cards flew over the wet deck. She quickly grabbed as many of the papers and credit cards as she could, but the wind was faster. Her cards and papers were floating on the water. She watched helplessly as the plastic cards begin to sink. John grabbed her arm, not hard but enough to stop her from going over the side for the items in the water even though she had no plans to jump.

His grip held her where she was. His hand shifted to her shoulder. She turned and stared at him for a second then moved to the back of the boat, very aware of his touch. She knew her feelings for him were still there.

She sat on the long bench seat at the back of the boat going through her wallet trying to figure out what cards or items were floating in the lake or lying on the bottom. Fortunately, all her credit cards were accounted for. She surmised the missing cards were her ATM and AAA cards. The rest were paper receipts, which were now resting among the algae. She made a mental note to herself to contact her bank and AAA to replace the plastic cards.

Chapter 72

The Crossing

Mary and Martin's restaurant was known for its great food. After a long day on the water, the tiki bar's music gave them a pleasant, relaxed evening. The rain had stopped, and the air was cool. A bright colorful rainbow arched across the sky, showing all its colors before dark.

Jordan sat on the back of the boat watching the sun descend behind the horizon. She rubbed her eyes, gazed into the darkness, and became lost in her memories of being on the water. There wasn't a better feeling to her than being on a boat at the end of a day.

John walked out of the cabin and dropped down beside her. "Now that we are here, and the weather forecast is good for tomorrow, there's no reason we can't take the straight Cross Lake route."

She smiled, knowing he had given into her.

The orange-and-yellow morning sun rose to start a beautiful day. The light blue ripples on the lake meant a smooth crossing. Thirty minutes after they had left the dock, the generator sputtered, then stopped. John cut the engines.

On the way to the engine hatch, John turned to Jordan. "Let me know immediately if the boat starts to drift out of the channel. We don't need rocks damaging the props or putting a hole in the hull." He reached for her hand and gave it a slight tug. "Don't get out of the channel."

Jordan knew over the years, that large limestone rocks had formed on the bottom of the lake, and every boater that traveled the lake had been warned about the rocks.

John returned to the helm. "I can't find anything mechanically wrong. I think the algae must have clogged the intake valve to the generator. I don't want to get in the water with the red tide to make sure that's the problem. The boat will have to be lifted. No matter what the problem is."

Jordan looked at the chart. "We'd have to turn around and go to Port LaBelle Marina on the Rim Route. That's the only marina I saw in the information that had equipment large enough to lift this boat. We would lose a day if we went back."

John turned to Russell. "We don't need the generator to run across the lake. I can have the boat pulled after we cross."

Russell agreed to John fixing the generator after the crossing.

Halfway across the lake, the wind became still. Blind mosquitoes ascended on them like locusts. The boat looked like one big brown mass of moving wings. Blind mosquitoes don't bite, but they are annoying, and the three of them couldn't fight off that many mosquitoes.

John put the engines in neutral and turned to Russell. "Go to the lower helm and take the controls."

Russell turned the wipers on. Instantly, the windshield looked like brown gravy had been poured over it.

John yelled down to him, "Make a hard turn to port!"

Russell panicked, thrusting the throttles forward. The boat sped past a channel marker and stopped abruptly on a pile of rocks. John went sailing into the flybridge cushions. Jordan was on her way down from the flybridge to the cabin. She went flying off the ladder into the cushions on the back of the boat.

John screamed at Russell. "What did you do! I told you to go left!"

"I didn't know which way port was. This is my first boat."

Jordan and John froze. It never occurred to either one of them that a buyer for his first boat would buy a 46-footer. All the previous things that Russell had done and said now made sense.

318

John screamed, "Why!—but caught himself and lowered his voice—"didn't you tell us this back in Tampa?"

"I didn't want anyone to know. I thought by the time we got to West Palm Beach I would know everything."

John's face turned red, and the veins in his neck protruded. Jordan saw it took every inch of John's willpower to stay in control. Jordan understood his anger. He had a reason to be mad. She quickly made her way into the head. She felt that was the safest place until John settled down.

She heard the splash and knew John was overboard. She peered over the gunnel but could only see her reflection.

"I'm afraid to ask," she said when John surfaced.

John ran his hands through his hair keeping the water out of his eyes. "Could've been worse. No holes in the hull. The starboard prop is bent. We'll have to go the rest of the way on one engine."

John had climbed back into the boat when an open fishing boat pulled next to them. "Hi! anything I can do?"

John explained the hull situation and the prop. "I think the boat can be pulled backward to release it off the boulder."

John and the fisherman tied the lines to the boats. John looked up to see three racing boats fly past. The 46-footer tilted and rocked. Jordan tried to get to the stairs to hold on but another race boat blew past, blowing his horn and waving. The 46-footer creaked and rocked. She reached for a wrung on the ladder but not in time before the big wave lifted the boat, tipped it, then set it hard on the water and on part of the rock. She fell sideways, landing on her hip on the deck. The boat rocked in the other direction then sat evenly on the water. The boat had been jolted free. The helping boat freed his lines. The hull rocked, and the last scraping sound quieted.

John rushed to help her up. "Are you hurt?"

She rubbed her right hip. "My thigh hurts, but I think I'm all right."

He touched her thigh. She winched. "It's not broken but it's going to be sore."

John jumped overboard to recheck the hull. When he surfaced this time, he announced to everyone, "No holes, just scrapes."

She offered to pay the helping captain, but he refused. It was good he had already secured his lines to their boat before the racers passed. The lines had kept the boat from pounding on the rock.

Jordan had turned up the stereo to drown the grating sounds of the rocks scraping the hull. She went up to the flybridge and turned the radio off before John said anything. She could tell by the expression on his face he was still upset with Russell and not in the mood for music.

The Lock Master at Port Mayaca Lock, which is 400 feet long and 56 feet wide, had let several boats enter the lock with them. He had Jordan tie their 46-footer next to a 38-foot trawler. He had a 50-foot boat tie behind the trawler and a 30-foot boat tie behind the 50-footer.

The husband and wife on the trawler were traveling alone. When the front gates opened, the woman tried to untie the bow line from the cleat. She struggled and struggled with the line but couldn't get it untied.

The Lock Master yelled, "Leave the line and go to the back of the boat!"

The water receded and the bow line became taunt. There was no way she was going to be able to untie the line now.

The Lock Master yelled again. "Leave the line! Leave the line now!"

She didn't move. The weight of the boat on the line pulled the cleat from the boat along with part of the fiberglass attached hitting her in the middle of her forehead. Blood poured and splattered in all directions. The Lock Master climbed down the ladder into the boat. He touched her and shook his head. "She's dead."

Her husband stiffened and stood frozen in place. "No, no, she's just knocked out."

The Lock Master moved the other boats out of the lock quickly. He closed the lock until the emergency authorities gave the clearance to open again.

After the lock, John docked the boat at River Forest Yachting Center in Indiantown. The travel lift driver lifted the boat into the slings and told John the boat could stay in the lift until the generator was fixed. Twenty minutes later, John had the intake valve cleaned and the generator running. Russell bought a reconditioned prop at John's request, and John told him he could have the bent prop reconditioned in West Palm Beach.

Two hours later, they were through the St. Lucie Canal Lock.

Jordan pointed to the water. "Look at all the alligators in the canal."

John chuckled. "I know I'm trying to maneuver around them."

Jordan was squealing now. "Hundreds of them are sunning themselves on the bank."

John couldn't help but laugh. She was like a kid seeing gators for the first time. They passed under the Florida Turnpike and the I-95 bridges.

Jordan couldn't take her eyes off the water. "The water's a rust color. I thought we were going to escape the red tide. I didn't expect the algae to move across the lake and into the Atlantic Intercoastal Waterway."

John frowned. "Once it forms it's hard to control. It moves with the currents and tides."

Twilight was creeping in when they docked at Pirate's Cove Marina. Russell's friend was waiting for him. In the morning, Russell and his friend would head south to West Palm Beach.

Russell shook John's hand and gave Jordan a quick light hug. "I learned a lot about the boat and boating. I couldn't be happier. John, you're the best captain and mechanic. I know as much about the boat now as you do."

John held his cool, smiled, and said in a matter-of-fact tone. "You don't."

She could tell from John's tone he was still miffed.

Jordan rented a car for the two-hour trip home.

John placed his hand on hers. "Are you all right? That was an awful sight back at the lock. I don't know why the woman wouldn't let go of the line."

"I'm fine. I feel for the husband. He didn't accept the fact she was dead. There was nothing any of us could do." She sighed. "It was a long trip, but no matter what happens I always feel at home on the water. After Nick's death, I thought about living on a boat, but I realized I would have to rely on a mechanic all the time."

"You could now. You know no matter what I'll always be there for you."

He let the serious moment sit for a second, then laughed. "I never knew when I started working for you that I would be delivering boats all over the south."

"I never thought I would deliver any boats. I was just going to sell them."

They both laughed.

Chapter 73

Rebirth

Jordan was back at the dealership, ready to take on the world again. Her business wasn't where it was before everything had fallen apart. She would work hard to make it as close to its pinnacle as it was when she was on top. The government had changed the luxury tax law to where the tax could be financed along with the boat loan. Boaters were still trying to repeal the speed limit law, and the fuel tax on the water had been lifted by the state. Jordan saw more boaters venturing back onto the water.

She knew long hours were in her forecast again. Thinking outside the box was going to be her salvation. She may never recover the money she lost during the recession, her attorney fees from the lawsuit, and the money she had to pay for Scott's banknote, but maybe she could recoup most of it.

She called her reps and ordered two more houseboats, five pontoon boats, and four bass boats. The oldest boat manufacturer had picked up most of their boats, including the two big boats at the Daytona Beach marina when she lost her floor plan with FPS. She called the factory to find out if they would allow her to keep the boats they hadn't picked up, which consisted of three runabouts and one 24-foot cabin cruiser. They agreed since she had a new floor plan company. She ordered two 26-footers from Tom in Wisconsin.

When she talked to Tom, he wanted to send her as many boats as she would take. "Tom, you know how I love your boats. I need to start back slowly. I don't want a big floor plan each month. I know with the economy struggling you're not requiring a million-dollar floor plan minimum now. I want to sell some less expensive boats."

Tuesday morning, she sat in the bank lobby and planned all the reasons why Walter should make her a loan. Walter called her into his office, but before she finished her sales pitch to explain why she wanted a loan. Walter held up his hand to halt her.

"I have one question. How long do you want the $10,000 for?"

She smiled. "Six months or less."

"You've proved yourself in the business world. You weathered and endured more than any of us ever thought you could, or for that matter, even any of us could. Let's make the loan for four months with a renewal clause."

She stood and they shook hands. "Great. Thanks, Walter."

She left the bank feeling her inner strength surge. She had weathered a storm that she thought would have drowned her.

John and Randy were whistling and finishing the last-minute boat tests, and the cleaning crew was polishing the last of the stainless-steel bow rails. She had all the papers in order, waiting for the three buyers to arrive.

Her boat sales were beginning to increase. Her energy was back, and she had spruced up her ship's store. She was making a mental note about how to change the appearance of her showroom when a familiar voice interrupted her thoughts.

"Do you have time for me?"

She turned and saw her pontoon boat rep. She gave him a big smile and a hug. "Sure, Paul, come on back to my office."

Paul leaned the chair on its two back legs. "I have a dealer on the other side of the state that wants to open a dealership on the St. Johns River. Are you interested in selling?"

Her eyes narrowed, and her brow wrinkled. "I don't know. Selling never crossed my mind. Who wants to buy a dealership in this economy? You know, I do remember years back, you telling me I should sell. You said the economy was going to fall and now was the time. I was flying on top then. I should have listened to you."

He shook his head. "You survived. I know it was tough. Here is his name and number. Think about it and call him if you want. I didn't tell him anything about your operation here."

She smiled. "I miss our fishing days. We all tried to survive and let our pleasures go by the wayside. Things are on an even keel now. Come when you have time and we will take an afternoon and fish." She gave him a hug. "Thanks for stopping by. I'll think about it."

She clipped the name and number on her calendar two weeks forward. The view from her desk of the lazy river flowing was her comfort. She shivered, felt cold, then hot. Thoughts and strange emotions invaded her mind and body. When the lawsuit was hanging over her, selling was never an option. Was it an option now? How long would it take her to recoup her losses if she didn't sell?

Jordan had sold three boats. John was busy going over a buyer's boat before the buyer trailered it away to his marina. Randy had delivered the second boat to the dock behind the buyer's house, and Jordan had finished the last of the paperwork waiting for the third buyer.

It had been a busy day. Jordan locked the doors and turned to John. "What do you think about changing the showroom." She laughed. "Give it a facelift." She propped her arm on the parts counter. "Paul came by earlier. He told a marina owner over on the west coast that I might want to sell. I never thought about selling the business, what do you think? After fifteen years here, this is my life."

He shrugged his shoulders. "The business is yours. You can do anything you want."

"But you are a part of it with me. This should be our decision. What would you do?"

He looked at the floor. "I won't stay with a new owner. I can always find a job."

The next week, she set a meeting with the potential buyers. After meeting them, she wasn't sure they had the money to purchase her business. Borrowing money from an institution to operate a boat dealership was difficult. They would have to prove they didn't need the money to get the loan.

She met with Alan, her attorney, about her obligations to Sam and the lease.

"I put a clause in your lease that you didn't have to have Sam's approval to sell. The new buyers can take over the lease."

"I'm surprised Sam agreed to that."

"I told you I was going to take care of you."

Several weeks later, the buyers asked her to hold a mortgage on the sale. That wasn't going to happen. She didn't know them or their business ethics or management experience. A deal like that could be another disaster that could put her into another lawsuit. Maybe they thought with all her previous problems she would do whatever they asked. She didn't have to sell. On the other hand, if they had the money and they gave her the asking price, the offer would be a gift horse.

After several more meetings with the potential buyers, she told them her business wasn't for sale. She didn't feel like a business failure anymore. If she sold the business, she was going to walk away with money in hand, no obligations, and no regrets.

Chapter 74

Meeting Scott

Jordan loved her curve of the river, with its ancient oaks bowing low over its banks, giving it a feeling of never having been traveled. Blue herons and white egrets stalked their prey in the shallows as the bullfrogs croaked and the gators bellowed their evening calls. She had forgotten so many things when all her senses were dulled, and she was just existing. Now she was aware of the river's ever-changing moods, the clanging sounds of the channel markers, and the wildlife's existence. Not long ago, she had reached up to touch bottom. Now she was swimming with her head above water. Her dying dreams had come back to life. The demands of the river had become manageable again.

By September, she had put most of the loan from the bank into advertising. Her buying market needed to know she was back in full swing. She put the remainder into the Ft. Lauderdale and Miami boat shows.

Tom put three boats in the Ft. Lauderdale show. If they didn't sell, he would move the boats to her dealership and give her free floor plan and freight. She hadn't been to the Ft. Lauderdale show in six years. The show was much smaller this year than in previous years when the economy was raging. People didn't seem to be exuberant anymore. It was more of a solemn, quiet crowd.

She emerged from behind a boat, she gasped and retreated to watch without being seen, to make sure her eyes weren't deceiving her. A strange tingle slid down her back, and she felt nauseated. It had been seven years since she had seen Scott.

She reminded herself he was a snake that had bitten her. She stepped from behind the boat, and their eyes locked. She could feel the heat rising from her toes to her head. Without warning, her anger swelled. She put her hands on her hips. "Someone in your business or you forged my signature. I had to pay your $15,000 bank loan." Her inside steam was searching for a release point. "Scott, how could you do that to me and the cashier's check!"

He backed away and said to the people with him, "I don't know who this person is and have no idea what she's yelling about. She must have me confused with someone else."

She followed him through the convention hall. He managed to stay in the middle of the crowds, maneuvering farther away from her. Suddenly, he halted and turned. "Whoever you are you need to back away before I call security for stalking me."

She stopped. Her temper had calmed. A few people had stopped to glance at her, some were staring, and others ignored her. She slowly walked back to her booth, still wondering how he could have done this to her. Something had happened to him. She refused to believe he threw her to the wolves on his own. Where was his conscience?

Monday morning, she called Ryan, "I saw Scott on Saturday at the Ft. Lauderdale Boat Show. He acted like he didn't know who I was or anything about the bank loan or the cashier's check. Did you ever file a criminal suit against him for kiting?"

"No, the sheriff never found him to serve the papers."

"Now that I have seen him, do you think they can find him? I know he's around the Ft. Lauderdale area somewhere."

"I'll see what I can do. With his reaction to you and what he's done, he could've changed his name."

She watched the peaceful flow of the river. In all her turmoil, her river was her comfort.

Chapter 75

Marina 415 Sold

In February, after the Miami Boat Show, Jordan paid the $10,000 back to the bank and squirreled money away for a buffer. John and Randy were handling the service and parts departments. Her cleaning crew was working part-time, and she still had the retired manufacture's salesman working for her. Her insurance had been reduced dramatically with fewer employees, and she had stripped her boat and marine store inventory to a minimum. This was how she was going to survive.

Sam walked into her office Friday morning and slammed her door. She saw the fire in his eyes. "We need to talk."

"What's wrong? Did I do something to make you mad?"

"Why didn't you tell me you had a buyer?"

"Because I don't." He backed away from the front of her desk and sat in the chair across from her with a puzzled look.

Jordan pointed her index finger at him. "I see the river gossip got to you. I had some people that wanted to buy the dealership. I talked to them on several occasions and found out they didn't have the money."

He scratched his head. "I should've come to you when I heard the news instead of stewing over it until I made myself mad. I did call my attorney brother. He reminded me the lease stated that you didn't need my permission to sell."

"You know I wouldn't go that far without talking to you."

He smiled and placed his arms across his chest. "I do know."

He walked out a lot calmer than he walked in. He called for Duke, his dog, and they both left.

A month after their conversation, Sam asked her to lunch. "We need to have a meeting."

"You sound serious. Sure. What about?"

"I'll tell you at lunch. Be at my house at 11:30."

She had met Sam once before at his house when he didn't want to take a chance on anyone hearing his conversation. She wondered what was going on now.

Sam and his wife met her at the door. Greetings and pleasantries were exchanged, then his wife disappeared to another part of the house, leaving the two of them with a smorgasbord of lunch meats, slices of bread, and cheeses.

She took a sip of iced tea. "Sam, what's going on that we're meeting here?"

He cleared his throat. "I just wanted to make sure this would be a private conversation, and I didn't want to have to worry about big ears or interruptions." He took in a deep breath. "There are three men in Miami that own several marinas in the state. They have approached me to buy mine, and they want to buy your dealership along with it. They are also buying the marina across the river."

She couldn't have been more surprised. "What's the time frame?"

"They haven't said. We are in the beginning stages. It'll be one sale with two contracts. The question is, are you interested?"

Her eyes widened. "Yes, if the price is right."

"I'm sure it will be. They know they're going to pay top dollar."

She agreed with Sam. This was definitely the right place for lunch. This news could never get around town until the deal was done.

That night after dinner, Jordan called Matt in Orlando. "I need to talk to you."

"Mom, is something wrong?"

"No. Sam is thinking about selling the marina. He has an offer from some buyers in Miami. They also want to buy my dealership."

"Is that what you want to do?"

"I'm not sure. Matt, you know how I love the boats and being on the river."

"Have you thought about what you would do if you sold it? You love to travel. You could go to all the places you always talked about. You could get your golf game back and snow ski in the winter. You wouldn't be bored. You could move to Orlando and see us anytime you wanted. Your grandson would love that. Plus, you've proven you can be successful in a male-dominated world, and if you were trying to see how strong you could be, you've proved that too. What more do you need or want? Sam was a good landlord. You don't know anything about the new owners. If they agree to buy the marina, you don't know what kind of landlord they would be."

Over the next few days, she thought about her conversation with Matt. She put a sale price on the dealership and put a business plan together, giving full disclosures and backup ledgers to support her price. She met with Alan to draw up her part of the sales contract.

Up until the last day, her emotions ran high. She couldn't keep back the tears while John inventoried the service department. She and Randy inventoried the parts department and ship's store.

Six months after her lunch with Sam, and after many meetings with the buyers, final agreements were made between all the parties for the sale and purchase of Marina 415 and St. Johns River Yachts, Inc.

Before she finalized her part of the sale, Randy followed her to the Chevy dealership. George glanced at the odometer. He couldn't believe his eyes when he read 99,999 miles.

She shrugged her shoulders and smiled. "You told me to turn it in before the odometer hit 100,000."

He touched her shoulder and laughed. "This is so you."

On the way back to the dealership. Randy told her he was staying with the new owners.

She sat at her desk for the last time watching the river's flow and thought about the past fifteen years. Between the reorganization of her business and the sale, she had recouped all her losses. Things she'd thought that were world-turning and earth-shattering probably weren't as bad as they seemed at that time. Life was a process of storms and rebuilding, of fires and regrowth, of loss and gain. One of the paradoxes of life was that she couldn't have everything. She could have part of one thing and not another. There were trade-offs, even when she thought she was making the best decisions at the time.

She never dreamed the dealership would be so profitable and then drop to where she almost lost everything. She had learned that dealing with people, she couldn't be in control of every situation. She had walked out of a battle unscathed. She was stronger than she had ever been, and no matter what happened in the future, she knew she could take charge.

It was a beautiful, warm September day, but a sad one. She had all her personal items packed from her office, and the time had come to say good-bye to John. She had let go of her father. Death had taken him. How was she going to let go of someone so dear to her that hadn't died? She would never have been able to do what she did with her dealership if John hadn't walked into her life, and now, she and John both would have to adjust to an emotional separation. In some ways and some things, they would let go of each other, but they would always remain together, in their loyalty, gratitude, friendship, and love.

John stood by his truck watching her. She ran towards him, he caught her, lifted her off the ground, and spun her around before he set her back down on her feet. She held him tightly, not releasing him. His eyes were filled with tears when he looked down at her, then he buried his face in her hair. She wanted to tell him one last time how much she loved him but she held her silence. A thousand words passed between them without a sound, along with a million feelings and countless memories. He slowly released her. She turned away from him and placed her hand on her car door's handle. She stood still and waited until she heard the hum of his engine. Through her tears, she watched him turn left out of the marina and out of her life. She gazed at the flow of the demanding river one more time before she turned right onto Highway 415.

C heryl Corriveau is a native Floridan. As an only child, her parents instilled in her that the word can't didn't exist. She has always been an entrepreneur. After her day of teaching high school students, she coached the girls' basketball B, and tennis teams. She also taught evening real estate licensing classes. She spent her summer months at CBS Network as their pilot television program coordinator. After twenty years, she retired from the public-school system to embark on her next job as the education director of a large real estate franchise corporation. Cheryl has owned and operated several businesses—a real estate corporation, an aerial photography business, a commercial interior design business. She traveled the Southeastern United States after she acquired an interior design contract with a national corporation. After her second retirement, she became an event coordinator supervisor at the Orange County Convention Center.

Her love for boats led her to become the sole proprietor of a boat dealership on the St. Johns River. Her real-life experiences in the boating business inspired her to write the fiction novel *The Demanding River*.

She has been featured in *Outstanding Young Women in America* and received the Marine Woman of the Year Award by *Boating Industry* magazine. She holds a Master Judge certificate with the Florida Federation of Flower Show Judges.

She has become an avid golfer and has won several club championships. She lives in the Florida panhandle on the Gulf of Mexico. Her love for boats still exists, and she feels there's not a better place to be than on the water or the golf course.

CPSIA information can be obtained
at www.ICGtesting.com
Printed in the USA
LVHW041513120922
728171LV00002B/168

9 781646 546800